WODEN'S SPEAR

BOOK 1 OF THE FIRST KINGDOM SERIES

DONOVAN COOK

Boldwood

First published in Great Britain in 2025 by Boldwood Books Ltd.

Copyright © Donovan Cook, 2025

Cover Design by Head Design Ltd.

Cover Images: iStock

Map designed by CoverKitchen

The moral right of Donovan Cook to be identified as the author of this work has been asserted in accordance with the Copyright, Designs and Patents Act 1988.

Every effort has been made to obtain the necessary permissions with reference to copyright material, both illustrative and quoted. We apologise for any omissions in this respect and will be pleased to make the appropriate acknowledgements in any future edition.

A CIP catalogue record for this book is available from the British Library.

Paperback ISBN 978-1-83656-327-3

Large Print ISBN 978-1-83656-326-6

Hardback ISBN 978-1-83656-325-9

Ebook ISBN 978-1-83656-328-0

Kindle ISBN 978-1-83656-329-7

Audio CD ISBN 978-1-83656-320-4

MP3 CD ISBN 978-1-83656-321-1

Digital audio download ISBN 978-1-83656-322-8

This book is printed on certified sustainable paper. Boldwood Books is dedicated to putting sustainability at the heart of our business. For more information please visit https://www.boldwoodbooks.com/about-us/sustainability/

Boldwood Books Ltd, 23 Bowerdean Street, London, SW6 3TN

www.boldwoodbooks.com

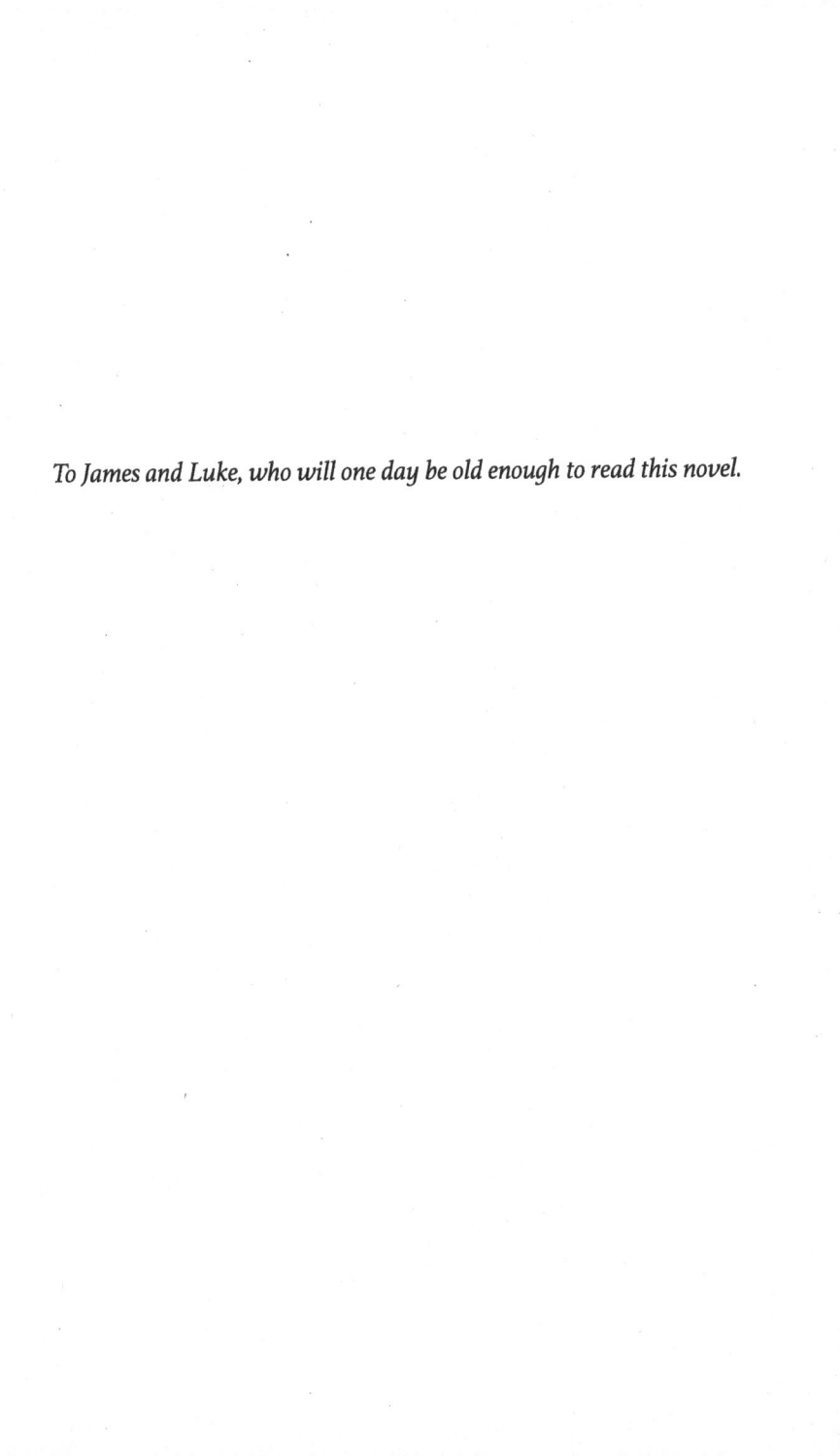

To James and Luke, who will one day be old enough to read this novel.

BRITAIN
(449AD)

‒‒‒‒‒ Roman road

WALL OF ANTONINE

SELGOVAE

NOVANTAE   HADRIAN'S WALL

Shrine to
Brigantia

Corstopitum

MONAPIA
(Isle of Man)

BRIGANTES   PARISI

OCEANUS
GERMANICUS
(NORTH SEA)

OCEANUS
HIBERNICUS
(IRISH SEA)

Cair
Hebrauc

MONA
(Isle of
Anglesey)

Cair Ligion

Cair Urnahc

CORNOVII

ORDOVICES

Cair
Loit-Coit

CORIELTAUVI   ICENI

CATUVELLAUNI

DOBUNNI

TRINOVANTES

DEMETAE

SILURES

Cair Lion

ATREBATES   Cair
Lundein

RUYM
ISLAND

CANTIACI

DAMNONII

DUROTRIGES

Cair
Segeint

BELGAE   REGNIS

VECTIS
(Isle of Whight)

LITUS SAXONICUM

OCEANUS BRITANICUS
(ENGLISH CHANNEL)

CHARACTERS

Saxons
Octa – son of Frithowald and Berthild
Witta – chief warlord of the Saxon people
Frithowald – warlord and Octa's father
Berthild – wife of Frithowald and Octa's mother
Odalric – Frithowald's friend and warrior
Reinald – leader of the Saxon foederati posted by Hadrian's wall

Jutes
Hengist – brother of Horsa and leader of the Jutes
Horsa – brother of Hengist and leader of the Jutes
Eadric – warrior who fights for Hengist and Horsa

Britons
King Vortigern – high king of Britannia
Vortimer – son of King Vortigern
Brigid – lover of King Vortigern
Badulf – brother of Brigid and warrior of King Vortigern

Ceretic – King Vortigern's interpreter
King Gwyrangon – king of the Cantiaci

1

AD 449, OLD SAXONY

The flames of the hearth fire danced as smoke drifted towards the thatched roof of the mead hall, collecting in a thick cloud before seeping through the straw and escaping into the night sky. Logs crackled and sparked as embers jumped out of the flames to land on the large stones which surrounded the hearth fire. Two slaves, their faces glistening with sweat, huffed as they turned two boar carcasses over the flames, the smell of the roasting meat making those in the hall salivate in anticipation.

The timber walls of the mead hall trembled as Saxon warriors sang songs of old battles while stamping their feet and banging their cups on the tables that lined the walls. Women laughed as they gossiped and pointed at drunken men while hounds crawled under the tables in search of scraps dropped by drunken eaters. Slaves moved around the hall, like bees hopping from flower to flower, as they refilled cups and handed out food, while children ran around the hall, playing out mock battles to the amusement of the adults as the early summer sun sat low in the sky outside the hall and the birds returned to their favoured trees to roost.

Octa's mouth watered as the smell of the roasted boar reached his nostrils and his stomach rumbled like an angry wolf. With his glassy eyes, he stared at the boars and licked his lips as he waited for the slaves to bring him a cut of meat. Octa was tall and had broad shoulders, like most of the men in the hall, and had seen almost eighteen winters. His long hair was worn loose and his beard had been trimmed, not that he usually wore it long, but he had wanted to look his best for the feast. On his fingers, he wore rings of gold and silver, with thick golden bracelets around his wrists.

'Drink!' Uhtric, Octa's cousin and younger by a season, shouted, and the group sitting around them at the high table cheered before they emptied their cups. Octa wiped his mouth clean with the back of his hand and laughed as one man, the same age as him, vomited over his leather shoes. 'Bastard can't hold his mead!' Uhtric said, laughing as he smacked the table.

Octa laughed as he pushed the man over so he landed in his own vomit, which only made the others cheer even more. The man stayed where he was, too drunk to get back to his seat, and soon their laughter was interrupted by loud snores.

Octa and his cousin, along with their friends, had been drinking for most of the day and by the time the feast to celebrate the coming battle had started, Octa's head was already spinning. But he was the son of a warlord, and not just any warlord. He was the son of Frithowald, the cousin of Witta, who was the mightiest warlord of the Saxon people.

Octa lifted his cup and puffed out his chest. 'Tomorrow, we face the bastard Thuringians who have been trying to steal our lands. We will greet them with Saxon spears and feed the ravens of Woden!' Octa emptied his cup as his friends cheered and stamped their feet before they drank from their own cups. He winked at Heilwig, the daughter of one of Witta's warriors, and she blushed before her mother pulled her away and her father glared at him. Octa didn't care. He was too drunk and too full of himself to even think that the warrior might try to hurt him.

'Silence!' Octa's father roared, his hard voice hushing the mead hall of Witta. Octa looked towards his father, and for a moment feared that he had angered the man he barely knew. But his father was not paying any attention to him as he sat down again.

Witta, the man the other warlords had voted as chief warlord, stood and stared at Octa before he turned his attention to the rest of the hall. 'My friends!' He paused until he had the attention of everyone in the mead hall, which didn't take long. Witta was a barrel-chested man with a thick neck and eyes that promised nothing but violence. His trunk-like arms were covered in scars from the many battles he had fought, while they said his back contained not a single one. Witta was one of the greatest warriors of the Saxon people and the most powerful of the warlords.

Octa remembered hearing stories of how Witta fought giants and trolls. Of how he slew dragons in far lands and took their treasures for himself. That was how he had built his famous mead hall and filled his benches with more warriors than any of the other warlords. That was also the reason the other warlords had voted for Witta to be the chief warlord when the Thuringians, a tribe from the south-east, started pushing into Saxon lands. The Thuringians and the Saxons had raided each other's lands for many generations and had fought battles against each other, but the Thuringians had always stayed in their lands. That was until a new threat came from the east and, since then, they had heard of many tribes pushing westwards to escape this threat.

'We live in troubled times. For as long as we can remember,

we have lived in these lands, with the Romans to the south, the Franks to the west and the Angles to the north. We lived in some sort of peace. We raided alongside the Franks and we traded with the Angles. The gods blessed us and we prospered.' The warriors cheered and called out to the gods. 'But the gods are angry and so we suffer. They are angry because tribes come from the east, chased here by creatures they say are half-horse and half-man and for too long we have done nothing about it.' Many of those in the hall rubbed the metal of their seax knives to ward off the evil of the horse-people from the east. Octa had heard of them. They all had heard of the Huns. A people so frightening that even the mighty Roman Empire cowered from them. 'And now we must defend our lands from those tribes. The gods demand it!' Again, the warriors cheered. Witta waited for the mead hall to calm down and then indicated for his son to stand.

Uhtric swayed slightly, but he straightened his back and puffed out his chest. Octa's cousin looked very much like the son of the richest warlord should. He was handsome and, like his father, had a broad chest and thick arms. He wore a fine tunic, made especially for him by his mother for this feast, and wore a thick golden chain around his neck.

'We have learnt of a large raiding party who think they can attack our people and steal from them. Tomorrow my son, Uhtric, will lead some of our army to the east and send those bastards back to where they came from!' Witta's voice thundered the last words and the mead hall shook as the warriors cheered and bumped their fists against the tables. Hounds howled at the noise and Octa shivered with excitement. Like Uhtric, this was to be his first battle, and he was determined to make the gods and his father proud. He looked at his father, who was lean and broad shouldered, and had a scar over his left eye. Frithowald had fought for the Romans in his youth, as had many of the Saxon men of his generation, and he had been very good at it. Unlike Witta though, Frithowald was not as wealthy and his army not as big. But he was Witta's cousin and the two men loved each other. Frithowald and Witta often fought together against their enemies and Octa knew it was his father who had convinced many of the other warlords to make Witta the chief. The Saxon people did not have a king, not like the other tribes around them. Warlords ruled over their clans and they would often meet to discuss laws and dispense justice. But when the Saxon people faced a great threat, they would vote for a chief warlord, one who ruled them like a king until the threat had passed. And many of the warlords did not like Witta for that role. Octa had heard the whispers, but he kept them from Uhtric. Some warlords thought Witta was too greedy and that he would refuse to give up the mantle once the crisis was quelled. But Octa knew that many of them were only jealous of his father's cousin because he was more powerful than them all. In fact, combined with Frithowald's army, Witta's army was larger than those of most of the warlords together.

'My cousin.' Frithowald stood and faced Witta. Frithowald was taller than Witta by half a head, but Witta still seemed to tower over him. 'Before our friends and the gods, I will ask a favour of you.'

Witta smiled. 'What favour is that?' Octa sensed they had already discussed this favour, but like those around him, he raised an eyebrow.

'You know my youngest, Octa. He was raised in your hall and you fed and clothed him. You taught him to fight with spear and shield. Octa and your son are more like brothers than Octa is to his own.' Octa frowned as he wondered what his father was doing. Everyone knew Octa was raised by Witta. He was the youngest son and Witta wanted him to stay in his hall so that he could guarantee the loyalty of Frithowald. But Frithowald had been too eager to give him up. He already had three other sons and five daughters to feed, so one less mouth in his hall had suited him. The gods, though, had deemed that Octa would be Frithowald's only remaining son. His brothers had all fallen in battles against other tribes, and his older sisters had been married off. One of them to Uhtric, so that the two cousins had an even closer family bond. The three younger sisters were still children and it would be many winters before they were old enough to be married off.

'Octa is a fine man and skilled with the spear.' Witta looked at Octa, whose heart raced at the compliments. The spear was the weapon of Woden, the chief god worshipped by the Saxon people and the Angles to the north and the other tribes in the region, and so the spear was the principal weapon of the Saxons. Although, many of the experienced warriors had swords and axes as well. A sign of their status as swords were expensive and the only way most of them got one was to kill another for it. Uhtric clapped Octa on the back and his friends all cheered, but then fell silent as Octa's father spoke.

'Then I ask that you allow my son to be one of Uhtric's shield bearers in the battle tomorrow.'

Everyone in the hall gasped, and even Octa gaped at his father. The shield bearer was a role reserved only for the best of the warriors because their role was to protect the warlord. Often by giving their own lives. Octa looked at his mother, who was sitting beside Frithowald and smiling at him. She had always told him he was fated to be a great warrior. Like her father had been.

'Octa,' Witta called. 'Do you think you have what it takes to be a shield bearer? To protect my son from the spears that mean to take his life?' The mead hall fell silent as all eyes fell on Octa. His heart fluttered when he looked at his father and saw the fire in his eyes. Frithowald meant for Octa to raise his standing with Witta. That way, the gods would bless Octa and his path forward would be easier. But Octa had never thought his father would ask for him to be Uhtric's shield bearer. Octa did not really know his father that well. They only saw each other during feasts or when Frithowald came to march off to battle with Witta. And since Octa had become a man, he had stayed in Witta's hall. All his friends were here, and he needed to prove himself in battle before he could return to his father's hall. His mother would visit more often, and since his father had two more wives, Frithowald never seemed to care, so Octa had a much stronger bond with her. He looked at his mother again, who nodded. Her eyes, like Frithowald's, were filled with fire.

Octa glanced at Witta's shield bearers, two grizzled old warriors with arms and faces covered in scars, and saw how they glared at him. Instead of feeling embarrassed, Octa was annoyed by them. Why could he not be a shield bearer? He might never have fought a battle before, but Witta, the greatest of the Saxon warriors, had taught him how to fight with all weapons. He had even bested Uhtric as many times as Uhtric had bested him in sparring sessions. Octa was as good a warrior as everyone else in Witta's mead hall and he was certain that he would make a name for himself when they fought those who wanted to steal their lands, so he squared his shoulders and returned the glares of the older warriors. 'I do, Lord Witta.' Octa raised his cup. 'I swear to the gods we hold sacred, to Woden, Tiw and Thunor, that I will stand by Uhtric's side and protect him, even if I must give my life to do so. My shield will never drop and my spear will never waver. I will kill all those who try to harm Uhtric, and I will feed their corpses to the ravens.'

Witta watched him for what felt like a long time, as did everyone else in the hall as the flames continued to dance in the hearth fire. Then Witta smiled. 'Then so be it. Octa will be one of Uhtric's shield bearers when they fight the Thuringian bastards.' Witta turned to Frithowald, and the two of them gripped forearms as those in the hall cheered. Apart from Witta's shield bearers, who scowled at Octa. Octa ignored them as his friends clapped him on the back and Uhtric filled his cup.

'To my shield bearer!' Uhtric roared, and they emptied their cups. Octa felt his head spin and wasn't sure if it was because of the mead or the occasion as the slaves brought cuts of meats around the tables for the people to eat. At the back of the mead hall, Octa saw an old man sitting by himself, his broad-brimmed hat on the table in front of him. He was astonished to realise that the old man only had one eye, and that it was fixed on Octa. But Octa then forgot about the old man as he stuck a chunk of meat in his mouth and glanced at Heilwig, who barely took her eyes off him. The gods had blessed him and tomorrow Octa would make a name for himself in the battle against the invaders. Just like his father had done, but tonight, he would make Heilwig his woman and there was nothing her father could do about it.

2

A boot to the ribs woke Octa the following morning. His eyes snapped open, and he was about to curse the bastard who kicked him when he saw his father standing over him.

'Father.' The word struggled to come out of his dry mouth, and he looked around for some mead to wet his throat but couldn't find any. Frithowald did not respond. Instead, his eyes lingered on the woman still sleeping beside Octa. Octa glanced at Heilwig, who, like him, was wearing nothing under the furs they were under. He looked around him, trying to find his trousers, and saw that most of the warriors were already up and preparing for the battle. Uhtric winked at him when he saw Octa looking his way and Octa scowled, wondering why he hadn't woken him.

'You better hope her father doesn't find her here. He is a proud man and will cut your head off,' Frithowald said, but there was no anger in his voice.

Octa rubbed the sleep from his eyes and smiled as he remembered sleeping with Heilwig after the feast. She had been more eager than he had anticipated and, judging from the scowls on the faces of some of the warriors, louder too. 'Fridomar can try if he wants. The bastard is too old to lift his spear.'

Frithowald grunted. 'That might be, but he is still good with a sword. Now come, we must talk.'

Octa nodded and climbed out from under the furs. Heilwig opened her eyes and when she saw where she was and who stood over them, her face turned red and she hid under the furs. 'Where's my dress?' she whispered to Octa, who only shrugged.

'How in Friga's name should I know? I don't even know where my pants are.' For a moment, Octa wondered if Uhtric and the others had hidden their clothes, but then his father handed him his trousers and tunic.

Octa nodded his thanks and got dressed as his father said to Heilwig, 'Get home, girl. Before your father finds you here.' Heilwig poked her head out from under the furs and wrapped them around her before she got to her feet and scurried out of the mead hall, her cheeks bright red as the other warriors whistled at her. 'Fucking a man's daughter is one thing, son. But did you have to do it in the mead hall? Her reputation, and her father's, will be ruined because you thought only with your cock.'

Octa grinned at his father. 'It doesn't matter what others think. Now they know she is my woman.'

'You plan to wed her?' his father asked with a raised eyebrow.

Octa shrugged. 'Perhaps.' Octa knew his father would prefer that he marry someone with a higher standing, but it was normal for their people to have more than one wife.

Frithowald grunted, before he said, 'Today you march to your first battle.' Octa stood straight and faced his father, even as his head spun from drinking too much the night before. 'You will be Uhtric's shield bearer and you should look like one.' Octa frowned and then spotted his father's slave behind him with a bundle in his hands. Frithowald signalled for the man to step forward and he placed the bundle on a nearby table. 'I'll not need this today, so you wear it. It has kept me safe in many battles.'

Octa's eyes widened as he stared at his father's chain-mail vest. 'F... Father, are you sure?' Very few warriors had chain-mail vests. They were expensive and hard to maintain. Those who did usually took them from those they killed. It was a sign of their skill as a warrior, and Octa was certain that many warriors would resent him for wearing one when he was still an untested warrior. But he didn't care about that as he ran his fingers over the many links that had been meticulously riveted together. It must have taken the blacksmith many moons to make this vest.

'You are my last remaining son. My heir. I do not want to lose you like I lost your brothers. I am too old to make more sons, and your sisters have only given me granddaughters so far.'

Octa raised an eyebrow at his father, who had only seen forty winters, but kept quiet about that. 'I will wear it with pride, Father.'

Frithowald nodded and his face turned serious. 'Good. Remember, Octa. Keep your shield up and protect Uhtric. It took much to convince Witta to let you stand as his son's shield bearer, so do not let me down.'

'I won't, Father. I will make you and Mother proud.'

Frithowald stared at Octa for a few heartbeats and then nodded. 'Gods be with you, my son.'

Octa barely heard the words as he stared at his father's chain-mail vest, just as he didn't notice his father leaving and Uhtric approaching him.

'That's a fine gift,' Uhtric said, and when Octa looked up, he saw that his cousin was also wearing a chain-mail vest. But his was made especially for him, and Octa knew that none of the other warriors would be disgruntled about Uhtric wearing it. 'We will look like gods when we face the Thuringians.'

Octa returned Uhtric's smile and lifted the chain-mail vest from the table. He grunted at its weight, which only made Uhtric laugh before he helped Octa put it on. Octa rolled his shoulders and did his best to adjust the chain-mail vest, but no matter what he tried, it still sat uncomfortably. It was too large for him as his father was broader in the shoulder, and Octa prayed it would not hinder him during the battle.

'How do they fight in these things?' he asked, and Uhtric shrugged.

'Father said you get used to it.' A horn blew from outside the hall before Octa could respond, and they both stared at the open door. 'We leave soon,' Uhtric said with a broad grin on his face.

Octa's hand went to his stomach as it clenched and he told himself that it was because he had drunk too much. 'I need a piss,' he said when Uhtric frowned at him.

Uhtric laughed and clapped him on the shoulder. 'Then go piss before you wet your trousers and meet me outside.' Uhtric left Octa, who rolled his shoulders again as he tried to get used to the weight of his father's chain-mail vest.

Octa went to the armoury, which was beside the mead hall, and was about to grab a spear when a hand gripped his arm.

Sigifrid, one of Witta's shield bearers, curled his lip at Octa. 'I have fought more battles than there are hairs in your beard. It should be me standing by Uhtric's side, not a boy like you.'

Octa smiled at Sigifrid, even though his heart was racing in his chest. Sigifrid was one of Witta's most experienced men and had even helped teach Octa how to fight. 'Perhaps Witta feels you are too old.'

Sigifrid glared at him, and then that glare turned into a smile. 'Perhaps. Or perhaps your father overestimates your skill. He has never seen you fight, has he?' The older warrior leaned closer. 'You better pray to Tiw you do well, boy, because if anything happens to Uhtric, then it is not just Witta's wrath you'd have to deal with.'

'It is our enemy that needs to pray, not me,' Octa said, but he still did what Sigifrid said and prayed to Tiw and Woden, asking both gods to guide him. The horn blew outside again and the warrior smiled at him as he handed him a spear.

'You better go, Octa, son of Frithowald. They are waiting for you.'

Octa grabbed a shield and rushed out of the armoury. Outside, there was an excited murmur as the people of Witta's village mingled with the warriors who were about to march off to battle. Young boys gaped at the warriors in their armour and Octa remembered how he had once stared at the warriors the same way. It seemed that even the gods were excited as the sun shone brightly in the sky and not a cloud could be seen. Octa caught sight of Heilwig, now dressed, and was about to wink at her when he saw her father standing beside her, his face dark as he glared at Octa. But Octa knew the old warrior wouldn't do a thing to him, even if he wanted to. Witta treated Octa like he was his own son, which meant very few of the people in the village would do anything against him.

Uhtric stood beside his father, and Frithowald and his mother stood beside them. They both smiled when they saw Octa wearing his chain-mail vest, but Octa saw how Witta raised an eyebrow. He also heard how many of the other warriors grumbled as only experienced warriors should wear chain-mail vests, not untested ones. But he ignored them as he took his place beside Uhtric. On the other side of the warlord's son stood Landric, the second shield bearer. He glanced at Octa and shook his head, but Octa paid him no attention. Despite the uneasiness he felt in the pit of his stomach, he knew this was the day he would make a name for himself. This was the day he would show them all who he really was.

Witta took a few steps forward. 'Today is a proud day for me. It is the day my son will lead my men to battle those bastard Thuringians who think they can steal our lands. Today my son will become a man!' The people of Witta's clan cheered as Uhtric puffed out his chest and mounted his horse.

'Men of Witta! Let's go to war!' He punched his spear into the air, and the people cheered even more. They all knew this wasn't going to be a large battle. The Thuringian raiding party had no more than fifty men, if that, and Witta had made sure to send just as many warriors with his son, most of them young warriors like Octa about to fight their first battle, but there were also experienced warriors amongst them. The real reason for this was for Uhtric to get a taste for leading men into battle, and for Octa to learn to fight by his side. Just as his father fought beside Witta.

Octa was about to mount his horse when Witta grabbed his arm and dark eyes bore into him. 'Your father is one of the best warriors I know,' he said and Octa nodded, not sure what to say to that. 'I pray to the gods that his blood runs in your veins because if you don't bring my son back alive, then your blood will run in my hall.'

Octa paled as Witta smiled and walked away. His father gripped his shoulder. 'Pay no mind to him. Just remember, Octa. Keep your shield up and your eyes open.' Frithowald took his sword belt from his waist and tied it around Octa's.

'Father?' Octa's eyes widened. 'Are you certain?' He looked at his mother, who smiled at him, her eyes filled with pride as she nodded at him.

'Aye, you are my son and I will have you be able to protect yourself.'

Octa looked at his father, unsure of what to say. He did not know his father as well as he wanted to and had always thought of him as a hard man.

'You are destined for great things, my son,' his mother said as she put a hand on his cheek. 'And that journey starts today.'

Octa smiled at his mother as he mounted his horse and followed Uhtric as he led his father's army out of the village gates. Out of the corner of his eye, he saw the same old man he had seen in the mead hall the night before and he frowned at the way the one-eyed man smiled at him as a raven crowed from the trees.

* * *

Octa swallowed hard as a sweat bead ran down the side of his face, desperate to keep the bile from reaching the back of his throat. He wanted to believe it was because he had drunk too much at the feast they had the night before as he stared at the approaching army, led by a large man whose horse looked small under him. Cheers and war songs drifted over the breeze, only making the trepidation he felt worse, while others cried out to the gods.

'This is it, cousin. Today we kill these bastards and make our fathers proud.' Uhtric slapped Octa on the shoulder, which nearly made him vomit. Octa tried to smile, but was sure it came as more of a grimace. The unease he had felt before had only grown as they rode to the place of battle not far from Witta's village. Octa had tried to find the courage he had felt the night before, when he had made the oath to Witta, but couldn't, no matter how hard he tried.

Uhtric did not have his father's full army behind him. He did not even have his best warriors. But that was because this wasn't a battle worthy of the gods. Their enemy was a large raiding party of Thuringians, and Uhtric was sent by his father to kill them and to send a message back to their king. And that message was that this land belonged to the Saxons. Witta and Frithowald, along with the other warlords, had stayed behind in Witta's mead hall to plan for the real battle, which was sure to come after this skirmish. But even though this was only a skirmish, Octa could not stop the fingers of fear gripping his spine.

Like Uhtric, Octa had never fought a battle before. The only blood he had ever seen at the end of his spear belonged to the animals he had hunted. Unlike Uhtric, who behaved like the son of a warlord should, and the fifty warriors behind them, their songs and war cries making his head hurt, Octa was terrified. Uhtric stood tall, his dark hair blowing in the wind as he puffed out his chest and grinned at his enemies. Octa guessed his cousin did not feel the same fear as he did. Like Octa, Uhtric wore a chain-mail vest, but his had gold rings along the edges, and he had a fine sword in his hand. He glanced at the shield in his hand and remembered the oath he had made to Witta at the feast. In front of the gods of the Saxons – Tiw, Woden and Thunor – he had sworn that he would stand by Uhtric's side as his shield bearer and that he would die if he needed to protect his cousin. Octa had stood tall when he had made the oath, his father beaming at him, and Octa was sure the gods were watching him.

On Uhtric's other side stood Landric, a man who had fought more battles than Octa had seen winters. He glanced at Octa and said, 'If you need to empty your bowels, then do it now, Octa. Once the battle starts, the only thing that should be in your head is keeping Uhtric alive.' Behind them, their horses were led away so they wouldn't be spooked by the battle. The Thuringians had spotted them and instead of turning and running like Octa was hoping they would, they dismounted their horses and formed a battle line. Their leader stood in front of them, undoubtedly scowling as he stared at the Saxons in front of him.

Uhtric laughed. 'Don't worry about Octa. He will not let me down.'

Octa took a deep breath as he gripped his spear and shield to hide his fear and whispered a prayer to Thunor, asking the hammer-wielding god to protect him and to give him the strength he needed. The courage he had felt the night before when Witta's mead flowed through his veins and his stomach filled with boar was gone and in its place was only a fear he had never known before. He did not see Uhtric give the signal and his heart jumped when the horn to announce the attack blew near him.

'For Tiw! For Woden! For my father!' Uhtric shouted, his voice barely carrying over the noise of the fifty warriors behind him, and charged at the enemy. Octa thought he was about to piss himself, or perhaps he had, because his trousers felt wet as he ran to keep up with Uhtric. The shield in his hands felt heavier than it had a few moments ago and Octa worried he might faint as he struggled to breathe under the weight of his father's chain-mail vest. As the enemy came closer, Octa just had enough time to notice the scar on the cheek of the leader of the Thuringian raiding party.

A thunderous crash, like a mountain being ripped apart, tore through Octa and, before he could stop himself, he vomited.

Luckily, Uhtric was too focused on the enemy in front of them, his eyes wild with anticipation, to notice and Octa's cheeks burnt with shame, even as he tried to keep the shield and spear up. Landric glanced at Octa and shook his head before he lifted his shield and blocked the blow aimed at Uhtric. He stabbed forward with his spear, skewering the Thuringian who had tried to kill Uhtric and all Octa could do was watch.

Uhtric, oblivious to the attack, stabbed forward with his sword, laughing as it struck the shield of his opponent, while Octa cowered behind the shield he was supposed to protect Uhtric with.

'Octa! Lift your shield!' Landric roared at him, and Octa nodded as he fought the urge to run. He caught the glimpse of an axe and instinctively raised his shield, more to protect himself than Uhtric, and felt his heart thud as the axe struck his shield. Something warm and sticky splashed across his face, making him scream out in shock and when Octa glanced to his left, he saw Otgar, one of his friends, gaping at him, his throat cut. Octa tasted the blood in his mouth and vomited again, as the man he had shared mead the previous night with died.

Uhtric was not aware of anything around him as he struck at his opponent again. This time his sword came back with blood on it and as he turned to Octa to gloat, roaring with delight, the Thuringian leader stepped into the place of the warrior Uhtric had just killed and swung his large two-handed axe at Uhtric's head. Octa screamed as he forced himself to lift the shield and cried out as the shock of the blow rattled his arms and numbed his fingers. With wide eyes, he watched as the shield fell from his hands while the large warrior pulled his arm back to attack again.

Octa knew this was his moment to make a name for himself. The moment his mother had told him about. All he had to do was thrust his spear forward and stab the leader of the Thuringians in the stomach before he could kill Uhtric. Then he would be the hero and others would sing songs about him. But instead, Octa froze as a spear streaked past the large warrior and caught Uhtric in the shoulder. Uhtric staggered backwards from the blow, but Octa's relief at seeing that the links of his chain-mail vest held was short-lived when another spear sliced Uhtric's cheek open.

Uhtric's eyes were wide when he saw that Octa no longer had his shield in his hands, but before he could say anything, they both heard the large warrior roaring and turned to see the axe coming for Uhtric's head. Everything seemed to slow down for Octa as he looked past Uhtric, praying to the gods that Landric had seen the threat, and felt numb when he saw the man on his knees with a spear in his side and his eyes vacant. At that moment, Uhtric must have known what was about to happen because he shook his head at Octa and muttered something that Octa could not hear over the blood pumping in his ears. Octa glanced at the large axe coming for Uhtric, his cousin and closest friend. The man he had grown up with and shared mead with. The man whose life he was supposed to be protecting.

Octa, no longer able to control his fear, dropped his spear and fled before the large warrior's axe split Uhtric's skull open.

3

Octa ran. He ran until he could no longer hear the sounds of the battle behind him, and then he ran further. As he ran, all he could see was Uhtric's face just before the axe came down. His eyes pleading with Octa to help him, to save him. Tears streamed down Octa's cheeks as his lungs burnt, but still he kept running. He kept running until his legs gave way and he fell to the ground. The hilt of his father's sword dug into his stomach and as he tried to get back to his feet, the chain-mail vest his father had given him weighed him down.

Octa wrapped his arms around himself and cried because of the death of his cousin. A death caused by his cowardice. He was supposed to make a name for himself, to make his parents proud. Just like he was supposed to protect his cousin. But instead, he had run from a battle. Octa curled into a ball as he sobbed and cursed himself.

A while later, Octa opened his eyes, and for a moment thought he was still in Witta's mead hall. But as his eyes focused on what was in front of him, he frowned at the grass and the blue sky above his head. He was about to rub his face when he saw his hand was red with blood and remembered what had happened.

'Uhtric, forgive me,' he said as fresh tears wet his cheeks, but he knew there was no point. Uhtric was dead because of him. Octa sat there for a while longer and when he could cry no more, he forced himself to his feet. His shoulder ached, and he did not know if it was because of the battle or from the fall. He stared at the dried blood on his hands, and before he could stop himself, he dropped to his knees and retched. There was no food left in his stomach to vomit out. That had all come out during the battle.

Wiping the bile from his mouth with the back of his hand, Octa stared at the darkening sky and watched as the clouds drifted past and birds flew overhead. He wanted to blame the gods. He wanted to curse Tiw and Woden. And Thunor. But he knew it was not their fault. He was the one who had failed his cousin. And not just his cousin, but his father and clan as well. His hand went to the hilt of his father's sword as he remembered how proud Frithowald had looked that morning when he had given him the sword. Octa had wanted so much to be the brave warrior his father and Witta were, but in the heat of the battle, his courage had deserted him and he had left his friends behind to die. Images of the battle flashed through his mind again. Snarled faces and men calling to the gods. Spears and swords flashing in the sunlight, and blood spraying through the air. And the large Thuringian warrior, his axe held above his head as he prepared to kill Uhtric.

'Forgive me, Uhtric,' Octa said again as he closed his eyes, hoping that it would stop what had happened next from coming to him. But it didn't and Octa curled on the ground again and a fresh wave of tears came. He stayed like that as the sun set and the moon rose. And as the stars shimmered in the night sky, he closed his eyes and fell asleep.

Octa woke the next morning, his head pounding and his mouth dry. His stomach rumbled, and he remembered he had not eaten or drunk anything since the day before. Octa looked around him as he tried to work out where he was, but all he saw were hills and forests in the distance. He guessed he must still have been in the lands of the Saxon people as he struggled to his feet, feeling weak from the lack of food. Octa had never gone half a day without eating and he felt like he might faint. He glanced at the sun, trying to work out which direction he needed to head, but then a thought struck him and almost dropped him to his knees.

Where do I go?

He looked west, in the direction of Witta's hall, and knew he couldn't go back there. Fleeing a battle was one of the worst crimes a Saxon could commit. They were a proud, warlike people. That was why they had so many war gods. And Octa had fled. He dropped to the ground again, his legs unable to hold him as he remembered the oath he had sworn in Witta's hall when the warlord's mead ran through his veins and then he shivered when Witta's words the next morning came to him. *If you don't bring my son back alive, then your blood will run in my hall.*

Octa thought of his father and his mother and knew he couldn't go to them either. He had brought shame to both of them and was certain they would not help him. His mother was from a line of famous Saxon warriors and would not tolerate cowardice. His father was Witta's closest ally and would never go against him. Even if he wanted to, he couldn't help Octa. Although Octa doubted his father would want to. To shelter a coward made you guilty of the same crime and his father had too much to lose to do that. Octa was on his own. The life of luxury he had known was gone. No more days drinking the finest mead with his friends or sleeping with any woman he wanted. No more Heilwig, either. She would never go to him. Not after what he had done. And no more Uhtric. His friend and cousin, killed because of him.

Octa stayed where he was as the sun moved through the sky and birds flew over his head. After a while, he frowned as he realised he didn't know who had won the battle. Had the Saxons fled, like he had, after the death of Uhtric, or had the Thuringians been beaten and sent back to their lands? Did it really matter? His temples throbbed with all the questions, and Octa decided he needed to know what had happened. He needed to do something.

Octa picked himself off the ground and walked towards where the battle had been fought. His stomach growled again and Octa tried to calm it by putting his hand on it. He almost flinched at the feel of the cold metal links of his father's chain-mail vest and felt ashamed that he was still wearing it. But Octa could not get himself to take it off. He did not have the strength to lift the heavy vest over his head, so he kept it on and forced himself to walk to where he had shamed his father and fore-fathers.

He walked for half a day before he reached the battlefield. Along the way, he came across a stream and drank thirstily from it before he washed his face and hands clean of the blood that covered him from the battle. But the blood was still under his nails, a constant reminder of his shame.

As the sun was past its midpoint, Octa stood at the edge of the battleground, his legs trembling and his heart racing as he stared at the dead bodies that littered the ground. He wanted to turn and run away as the image of Uhtric dying came to him, but Octa knew he couldn't. He needed to find out what had happened. Taking a deep breath, he forced himself to walk amongst the dead and wished he was one of them, instead of what he was at that moment. A nobody and a coward.

Most of the dead were Saxons, which told Octa the Thuringians had won this battle and had driven Witta's men off so they couldn't collect the dead. He wondered if it was his fault and decided it must have been. His mind replayed the battle as his feet took him to the spot where he had shamed himself. His vision blurred from the tears as he stared at the body of Landric, still with the spear in his side. And then there was Otgar, one of Octa's close friends, his eyes still open in shock. Octa's stomach clenched as his eyes fell on Otgar's open throat and he remembered how his friend's blood had sprayed over him.

'Forgive me, my friend,' Octa said, but could not get himself to kneel and close Otgar's eyes. He looked around and frowned when he failed to see Uhtric's body. A shiver ran down his spine as he considered what that meant. Either the Thuringians had taken his body with them to parade around like a trophy, or the surviving Saxons had taken his body back to his father. Octa prayed it was the latter. His cousin deserved a proper funeral, but he was certain the Thuringians had taken Uhtric's body with them. Even if they didn't know who he was, the way he was dressed had made it obvious that Uhtric was someone important.

Octa stood where he was, surrounded by the dead of his people, and wondered what he was going to do. Again, he thought about going to his father, but then dismissed the idea. He had already disgraced Frithowald by running from the battle. Not even his mother could help him. All Octa could do was pray that they believed he was dead as well. But Octa was on his own. The gods had abandoned him and he was no longer a Saxon. Because Saxons did not run from the battle. Not knowing what else to do and not wanting to stand there any longer, Octa turned and walked away from the battleground and away from his people.

He followed the sun, not really sure of where else to go, as his head hung low and his stomach rumbled. Octa still wore the chain-mail vest of his father and he still had his sword around his waist. He had wondered if he could use them to go somewhere else and make a name for himself, perhaps even regain his honour, but he dismissed the idea before it even finished in his mind. He had run from a minor battle against Thuringian raiders. How was he going to fight battles and make a name for himself? Octa wondered why the gods had made him a coward. He was a skilled warrior. He knew how to fight with spear, axe and sword, but he did not have the courage he needed to stand and face his enemy. To protect his cousin and bring honour to his family.

Octa did not know how long he had been walking for when he came across a bush of berries. His stomach roared like a wild beast as soon as his eyes landed on the dark blue berries that grew on the small tree near the path he was walking on and he ran towards the bush, grabbing its branches as he ate the berries off them. He did not stop to wonder if these berries were poisonous. Part of him even prayed they were as he gorged himself until his stomach was full and he sat there panting. But there were no agonising stomach cramps or blood-filled vomiting.

Octa licked his blue fingers clean and wiped his mouth with the back of his hand, before he lay down next to the bush and stared at the darkening sky. As the stars came out, he wondered where he could go. He knew he had to leave the lands of the Saxons. Witta would want his head and was sure to send men after him. And if they found him, he would be tortured before

Witta hanged him. They wouldn't even sacrifice him to Woden or Tiw because neither god would want a coward sacrificed in their names. Only the brave had that honour. His stomach filled with the berries, Octa's eyes closed and he drifted into a deep sleep, interrupted only by the nightmares of Uhtric being killed and him running away.

* * *

'My son is dead?' Witta stared at the injured warrior in front of him, his mind unable to make sense of the man's words. Word had reached him that they had lost the fight against the Thuringians, but Witta forgot about all that as he glanced over the warrior's shoulders as more injured warriors came into his hall. Some had minor injuries, but a few had to be helped by others. One warrior clutched his stomach and, from the dark blood that seeped through his fingers, Witta knew the man would be dead in a few days. All that he understood, but the man's words still made no sense to him as he scanned the injured warriors for Uhtric, his oldest son. 'My son is dead?' He repeated the question as he felt his limbs go numb. He jumped to his feet, his heart pounding in his chest as he stormed towards the injured warriors, determined to find his son amongst them. Uhtric could not be dead. The gods would not do that to him. Witta had been faithful to the gods. He had made his sacrifices and had honoured them. But as he searched amongst the injured for Uhtric, there was no sign of him. None of the injured men were his son.

Walaric, Witta's youngest son and Uhtric's younger brother, followed him, his hand gripping Witta's tunic as he wailed. The sound only irritated Witta even more as he turned to the warrior that had brought him the news, his face red and fists clenched.

'Where is my son?'

Walaric's mother grabbed him and took him away from Witta before he lashed out.

The warrior looked uncertain of what to say or do as he lowered his head. 'Forgive me, my lord. Uhtric—'

'Where is Landric?' Witta grabbed the warrior by his chainmail vest. Landric would not lie to him. Landric would have made sure that Uhtric had survived, Witta was certain of that, but there was no sign of the man he had sent to keep his son safe. 'Where is he?'

The warrior paled. 'Dead, my lord. Killed in the battle.'

'Dead? How? What happened? We should have won!'

The warrior stammered for a heartbeat. 'They overwhelmed us, my lord. And when Uhtric died, the younger warriors panicked and the Thuringians took advantage of that. They slaughtered most of us.'

Witta gaped at the warrior as his words sunk in. If Landric was dead, then Uhtric... Witta couldn't even finish the thought as he dropped to his knees, not caring about what the warrior had just told him. Of how the Thuringians had killed most of the men he had sent to fight them. 'My son!' His face was red as the tears ran down his cheeks. Witta struggled to breathe as his tears choked him up. He did not think about the fact that they had lost the battle or what that meant for him. 'My son!' His body shuddered as he cried.

'Witta?' Frithowald walked towards him and put a hand on his shoulder, but Witta did not respond. He couldn't because he still didn't understand. How could Uhtric be dead? His son was a skilled warrior. Witta's best men had trained him. 'Where is his body?' Frithowald asked, and the warrior looked away.

'The Thuringians took it with them, my lord. There were too

many of them and we couldn't stop them. We had to leave the rest of our dead out there as well.'

'And what of my son?' Frithowald asked the warrior, who glanced away from Witta's cousin. Witta looked up and scanned the warriors, but saw no sign of Octa either. Octa, whom he had raised as if he was his own son.

'He...' The warrior hesitated.

'Where is my son?' Frithowald asked again.

The warrior took a deep breath, but before he could say anything, Waldhar, one of Witta's most experienced men and one of the few survivors, stood in front of Frithowald. His nostrils flared even as they were caked with dried blood.

'Your son ran.'

'What?' Frithowald said, and Witta could hear the shock in his voice. Even in his grief, Witta looked up at Waldhar, a warrior he had trusted to keep Uhtric safe. Just like Frithowald, he could not believe that Octa would run from a battle. Like Uhtric, he was skilled, and he was brave. Witta's men had taught him to fight. He would never dishonour Witta like that.

Waldhar glared at Frithowald. 'Octa dropped his spear and shield in the middle of the battle and he turned and fled with his tail between his legs.' Waldhar looked at Witta, his face softening. 'Forgive me, Witta. Your son died because of Oc—'

Frithowald punched Waldhar in the face before he could even finish Octa's name. Waldhar staggered backwards and Frithowald kicked him to the floor. 'Do not lie! The gods know my son will never run from a battle!'

Waldhar tried to get to his feet, only for Frithowald to punch him to the floor again. So he lay where he was and wiped the blood from his mouth as he glared at Frithowald. 'As Tiw is my witness, I do not lie. Octa froze just as a large Thuringian faced him and Uhtric. And when the Thuringian lifted his axe, Octa turned and ran. Your son is a coward.'

Frithowald roared and launched himself at Waldhar, who could not raise his arms fast enough to protect himself as Frithowald kicked him in the head. Witta watched, stunned, as his mind struggled to make sense of what he had just been told. He looked at Frithowald, his cousin who was stomping on Waldhar's head before the other warriors could drag him away, his mouth frothing as he screamed at the fallen warrior.

'You lie! You bastard!'

Witta struggled to his feet and rubbed his head as he tried to clear the fog in his mind. 'Octa ran?'

Waldhar, his face bloodied and bruised, nodded at him. 'I wish it wasn't so, Witta. I liked the boy as much as I liked your son. But he proved to be nothing but a coward and he caused your son's death.'

Witta's anger slowly took over his grief as he looked at his cousin, the man who had asked for his son to be Uhtric's shield bearer. At first, Witta had thought it was a good idea. He had believed Octa was strong. For a moment, he heard a whisper in his mind. Was this part of Frithowald's plan? Did he want Uhtric to die? As the thoughts came to him, he noticed an old man with a broad-brimmed hat sitting in the corner of his mead hall, but Witta then forgot about him as he glared at his cousin.

'My son did not run. He is no coward,' Frithowald said, but even Witta could hear the doubt in his voice. Witta glanced at the other surrounding warriors. They all turned away from him, so he pointed at one of them: a young man he knew to be a friend of Uhtric and Octa.

'Does Waldhar speak the truth?'

The young man nodded, even as he avoided looking at Witta

and Frithowald. Witta glared at Frithowald, who shook his head as his face paled.

'Octa would not—'

'Octa did,' Witta said, his voice strained because of his grief and anger. 'Your son ran and my son died because of it.'

'Witta—'

'Get out of my hall and out of my village. Get out of my sight.' Witta clenched his fists as he struggled to control himself. 'I will grieve for my son and collect our dead warriors. And then I will decide what to do with you.'

Frithowald opened his mouth to speak, but then seemed to think better of it as he turned and walked out of the mead hall, his warriors behind him. Witta turned to the others in the hall.

'From this moment onwards, Octa's life is forfeited. He is a coward and will be known as Octa the Coward. If he is seen, it is your duty to the gods to cut him down and to bring me his head. As the gods are my witnesses, Octa the Coward will pay for the death of my son!'

* * *

Octa woke the next morning, his stomach rumbling and his mouth dry again. But even as he stared at the berries on the branches above him, he lost the will to eat them as Uhtric's face came to his mind. Octa turned away from the berries and wrapped his arms around himself as he tried to get the images of the battle out of his mind.

As he lay there, a twig snapped near him and Octa turned, his hand going to the hilt of his father's sword as he expected to see one of Witta's men, but then his face paled when he saw the creature standing there, its beady eyes fixed on him. Octa let go of the sword and slowly got to his feet. Someone had once told him to play dead when you came across a bear, but Octa did not have the courage to see if that would work. He slowly backed away from the berry tree while the bear's eyes stayed on him.

'Forgive me, friend. I did not know this was your tree,' he said, his voice trembling with fear.

As if in response, the bear roared at him and Octa turned and ran. He did not look over his shoulder to see if the bear was chasing him, even as he cursed the chain-mail vest for slowing him down. As he ran, he closed his eyes, certain that the bear would catch him at any moment. He had heard stories of how the large animals could outrun even the fastest of the Saxon warriors. Octa tripped over a stone that stuck out from the earth and his heart skipped a beat as he hit the ground. He kept his eyes closed, not wanting to see the beast take the first bite, but when nothing happened after many heartbeats, Octa opened one eye and saw no bear near him. Opening both eyes, he sat up and wondered where the bear was and was relieved to see that it preferred the berries over him.

'Thank you, Thunor,' he prayed to the thunder god as he sat there and watched the bear eat. But then he wondered why the gods were protecting him. Surely he deserved to die because of what he had done. He got to his feet and wiped the dirt from his father's chain-mail vest and walked away before the bear changed its mind.

Octa spent the next few days wandering aimlessly and foraging for food wherever he could. He tried fashioning a fishing spear out of a branch with his seax knife, but could not catch any fish from any of the streams he came across and soon gave up on that idea. Instead, he lived on berries and other fruit he found, but his eyes were always peeled for any more bears or wolves that he knew roamed the lands, as well as the warriors he knew were hunting them. He had almost stumbled into a group of warriors on one day, but again the gods had been with him and they had missed him as he hid in the undergrowth.

Octa was exhausted, though, and hungry. The chain-mail vest weighed down on his shoulders, but he did not have enough strength to pull it off. He struggled to sleep at night because of the nightmares and his empty stomach, and had even prayed that the bear would find him and kill him. Octa was not made for living like this. He was the son of a warlord and had been raised in a mead hall filled with food and mead. The only time he ever hunted was for sport and not for food, and there were always others there to help him. He had tried to use his fishing spear to catch a rabbit he had spotted, but the animal vanished before he could even get close enough to kill it. Starving and exhausted, Octa knew he would die if he kept going like this. He stared at the moon as it sat in the cloudless sky, judging him for his cowardice, and Octa knew he had no choice. Octa had to go home. He had to face what he had done.

4

Octa closed his eyes and for a few heartbeats enjoyed the calming sounds of the forest, the rustling leaves and singing birds at odds with the turmoil inside him as he hid amongst the trees near his father's village. He had walked for many days to get here, avoiding towns and those hunting for him, but couldn't get himself to take the final few steps. His fear ate away at him, as did the doubt in his mind. Was he doing the right thing? The question had plagued him for many days, but Octa did not know what else to do or where else to go, even if he knew his father would most likely hand him over to Witta. Perhaps a part of him hoped that his mother would somehow help him. She was a woman of high standing and many respected her. All Octa knew for certain was that he did not have the skill to survive out in the wild like outlaws and wolves and there were only so many berries he could eat before he hated the stuff.

Octa watched as the people from his father's village went about their daily routines. Slaves walked to the nearby river to fetch water or to wash the clothing of their masters. Children ran around and played their games. The girls with little dolls made of straw and boys chasing each other with sticks as they pretended to be brave Saxon warriors. Something Octa had always wanted to be. Men worked in the fields, while even at this distance, he could hear the ringing sounds of weapons being forged by the smithy. His hand went to the hilt of his father's sword and then recoiled as if the sword had burnt his hand. Octa was not worthy of the blade.

His heart raced when he spotted his mother walking around the village with his father's other wives. He knew they did this every day so that they could be seen by his father's people and offer aid where it was needed. He wanted to call out to her, but knew he couldn't. His father's other wives resented him because their sons had died and he still lived. He wondered if they had laughed with joy when they heard of what he had done, but dismissed the idea from his mind as he tried to work out his next move. Octa might have been born in this village, but he had spent little time there and didn't know the people very well. He thought of Odalric, one of his father's oldest friends and best warriors. The man had always been kind to him, even when they went to Witta's hall, but he doubted that Odalric would help him. Odalric was a brave warrior and would not accept cowardice.

Octa stayed where he was, watching the villagers until the sun set and the villagers went to their homes. He took a deep breath and, ignoring the hunger pains in his stomach, summoned whatever courage he had, before he pushed himself away from the tree he was hiding behind and walked towards his father's hall. His stomach ached because he had eaten nothing since the day before, which made it hard for him to stand straight. Octa had thought about going to the river to drink water, but was afraid of being spotted.

He kept his head low and took a route he remembered from

when he was a small boy. One he had often used to sneak out of his father's hall unseen, so that he could run around the forest with the other children. His father had scolded him for it many times, but Octa had never feared the wolves and bears they had told him about. Or the trolls that liked to eat children. But he never thought he would use the path to sneak into his father's hall.

Holding his breath, he snuck around the wall that surrounded the village until he came to a gap which was covered by bushes and was glad that his father had never thought to have the hole fixed. Octa made it to his father's mead hall without being seen and leaned against the wall, his heart racing faster than it had ever done before. He worried that his trembling legs would refuse to take him the final few steps into the hall. And then another thought struck him. What would he say to his father? Would his father even listen to him?

Octa tried to ignore the questions in his mind as he snuck around the hall and into the back door that the slaves used to come and go unseen.

Octa held his breath again as he placed one foot in front of the next, something which felt harder than it should have been, and after what felt like a long time he reached the back end of his father's hall. The hall was just like he remembered it from his last visit four winters ago. The large hearth fire in the centre of the hall burnt strong, its shimmering light reflecting off the axes, spears and shields which hung on the walls of the hall. Torches fluttered on the wooden pillars which supported the thatch roof and the benches which lined the walls were half full of Frithowald's warriors. Octa cursed his rotten luck. He had hoped the hall would be empty and guessed that he would have to wait for the warriors to leave before he could approach his father. He was about to sneak out of the hall again when he heard his mother's voice.

'I refuse to believe it! Octa would never do such a thing!'

Octa froze and knew for certain that news of his cowardice had reached his parents. He knew he should leave, but he needed to hear his father's response. He lowered himself to the floor and crept as close as he could get without leaving the shadows. As a boy, he had often hidden in this corner of the hall and listened to his father talking to his visitors and warriors. That was how he had learnt of the death of his oldest brother. It was also how he had learnt he would be sent away to live with Witta.

'Berthild, why would they lie about that?' Frithowald said and Octa wished he could see his father's face. Were his eyes filled with tears or were his brows creased? Frithowald's voice sounded tired, but it did not tell Octa how his father felt.

'But Octa would not run from a battle!' Berthild shouted. 'And he would not let his cousin die like that. My son is no coward!'

'Don't you think I want to believe that also?' Octa saw a cup fly across the hall and many of the warriors looked away from Frithowald. 'By Woden, I was the one who convinced Witta to let Octa be Uhtric's shield bearer! He was supposed to bring us honour, not shame us!'

Octa felt the thud in his chest as if his father's words had kicked him. He clutched his chest as he struggled to breathe and felt the tears running down his cheeks.

'No! That wasn't Octa!' his mother said. Octa saw her standing in front of his father, her face creased with anger and hands clenched by her sides. 'The gods know Octa would never do that!'

'Forgive me, Lady Berthild,' Odalric said, his head lowered. 'I love the boy as if he was my own son, but many of the survivors say the same thing. That Octa ran and Uhtric died because of it.'

Octa's mother dropped to the floor and wrapped her arms around her as she cried. 'No. No. Not my son. Not Octa.' She looked at Frithowald. 'You have to find him. You have to find Octa.'

'Berthild, there's nothing I can do for the boy. I need to make sure that Witta doesn't think that I am behind the death of his son.'

'But why would Witta think that?'

'Because I asked him to make Octa Uhtric's shield bearer, remember?'

'Why, in Tiw's name, did I let you convince me it was a good idea?' Berthild stared at Frithowald with wide eyes. 'It was his first battle.'

'To bring us more honour! Witta is the most powerful warlord of our people!'

'What will Witta do to us?' one of Frithowald's other wives asked. Octa did not realise they were also in the hall.

Octa heard his father sigh and pictured him slumped in his chair. 'He has a larger army than I have. I can't fight him if he decides I am to blame.' There was silence in the hall as everyone waited for Frithowald to continue. The flames in the hearth fire danced away as if they heard a song no one else did, and cast strange shadows across the walls of the hall. Octa resisted the urge to creep closer. He wanted to see his father's face, but more than that, he wanted to hug his mother. He wanted her to protect him from what he was certain was going to come. 'I must do whatever I can to protect my people from Witta's wrath.'

'But what about Octa?' Berthild asked. 'What about your son?'

Again, there was a long silence and when Frithowald spoke again, Octa felt like he had been stabbed by an unseen blade.

'My sons are dead. All of them.'

Octa wanted to run. He wanted to sneak out of the hall and run as far as he could, but he couldn't get his body to obey him. His limbs refused to move, as if his father's words were true. As if he really was dead. And perhaps he was. Perhaps he was a spirit roaming the lands on a quest to redeem himself. But he had not seen his body on the battleground, so he knew that was not true. He crawled deeper into the shadows and waited as the hearth fire died out and everyone went to sleep. His mother had sat on the floor and had cried for a long time and it had angered Octa that none of his father's other wives had comforted her. She had comforted them when their sons had died, and yet they had left her on her own, no doubt gloating. Those warriors who had their own homes had left, while the others had made themselves comfortable on the floor and gone to sleep. All the while, his father had stayed in his seat, not moving once until he went to his bedchamber. Octa's mother had followed, her head hung low and her soft cries reaching his ears. It was like she was mourning his death, which only made it worse because he was there and they didn't know it. But Octa now knew his father would not help him. He had brought shame on his bloodline of proud warriors and no words could make his father see past that. As far as Frithowald was concerned, Octa was dead.

Octa stayed in the shadows, his mind in turmoil, long after his father had left, and when he was certain everyone was sleeping he undid the sword belt and struggled out of the chain-mail vest of his father. Holding his breath, Octa snuck to his father's seat, being careful not to wake any of the sleeping warriors or the hounds. One of them lifted its head and a soft growl escaped from its throat, but then it turned towards the door of the mead hall and the growling stopped. Octa glanced at the door, wondering what the hound had seen, but then forgot about it as he stared at his father's seat. A seat he had always hoped to make his own. With a quick glance around him, Octa placed his father's chain-mail vest and his sword on the seat. He was not worthy of such fine armour and weapons, and he did not want to disgrace his father further by wearing them. For a moment, he wondered what his father would think when he found his chain-mail vest and sword in his hall. The warriors sleeping might be in trouble, but Octa did not care about them. Just like they no longer cared about him.

'Forgive me, Father,' he whispered before he turned and snuck out of the hall again. He had thought about grabbing some of the food left on the tables, but did not want to risk waking any of the sleeping warriors.

Once outside, Octa stared at the stars and wondered why the gods had done this to him. Had he angered them somehow? Octa could not think of what he could have done to anger the gods, so decided that they were just cruel. Woden was known as being mischievous and playing with people's lives just to amuse himself. And perhaps that was what this was. Woden amusing himself at his expense. If Octa hadn't been so afraid of the gods, he would have cursed the raven god, but instead he turned and walked away from the hall he had been born in.

'Octa?' His mother's voice froze him to the spot, and Octa was almost too afraid to turn around. 'Octa, is that you?'

Octa took a shuddering breath and nodded. 'It is me, Mother.'

His mother grabbed his shoulder and spun him around. Octa flinched as if she was about to stab him. And for a moment, he wished she would, so that he would not have to live with the shame of what he had done. But instead, his mother embraced him, her tears wetting his dirty tunic.

'My son. Is it really true? Did you run from the battle?' Octa noticed that his mother was in her nightdress with her hair loose and a cloak around her shoulders. She must have not been able to sleep and had decided to go for a walk, something she had told him she liked to do some nights.

Octa shuddered as his tears soaked into his mother's hair. He dropped to his knees and wrapped his arms around her. 'Forgive me, Mother. But I was afraid. I tried to stand my ground, but I was too afraid. I'm a coward.'

His mother went rigid and, for a moment, he worried she would shun him, not that he could blame her. But then she lifted his head with her hands and stared into his eyes. 'You are my son. You are no coward.'

'But I ran and Uhtric...'

'I also grieve for Uhtric, my son, but you should never have been made to be his shield bearer. Your father was a fool for thinking it was a good idea, and I was a greater fool for listening to him. Even the sharpest blade can break.'

'But Uhtric still died because of me.' Fresh tears ran down his cheeks and Octa struggled to stay on his feet.

'No.' His mother shook her head. 'He died because that was his wyrd. You cannot punish yourself for that. You mustn't let that bring you down.'

Octa stared at his mother, but couldn't see what was in her eyes because of the night sky. 'I don't know what to do.'

'You need to run, Octa.'

'Run?' Octa frowned at his mother.

'You are not safe here. Not on Saxon lands. Witta has sent

men to find you, and your father will send his own men after you to save his own skin.'

Octa's breath caught in his throat and it took him a few heartbeats before he could speak again. 'Where will I go?'

'Go north, to the lands of the Angles. And then keep going until you reach the lands of the Jutes. I will pray to the gods that will be far enough and that Witta will never find you.'

'But we will never see each other again.'

His mother nodded. 'But at least I'll know that you are alive.'

Octa tightened his grip around his mother. 'But, Mother, I can't. I barely survived the last few days.'

'But you did survive. And you came here. That shows you are not a coward. But you need to go now, before the sun rises.' Berthild pulled Octa to his feet. 'Go, my son. Go north and earn your reputation. Perhaps then the gods will see fit for you to come home.'

Octa's heart raced in his chest as he struggled to make sense of what his mother was telling him. 'But how can I earn a reputation when I am too afraid to stand in a shield wall?'

Berthild put a hand on Octa's cheek and he pressed his face into it, feeling some comfort from her touch. 'The gods will show you the way, Octa. And don't forget, you were named after your grandfather, who was a brave warrior and a great warlord. No matter what others say, his blood runs in your veins.'

Octa nodded, strengthened by his mother's words. 'I will make you proud, Mother.'

His mother stared at him for a few heartbeats, as if she was searching his soul for the truth. 'You better.' She took the spear pendant from her neck and placed it in Octa's hands. 'So that Woden watches over you and keeps you safe.'

Octa wrapped his fingers around the spear pendant, something that most of the Saxon women wore either around their neck or around their waists, as his mother reached up and kissed him on the cheek.

'Now, go, my son. Go before your father's men realise you are here.'

Octa nodded and took a few steps backwards before he turned and ran away from his family.

5

Octa had lost track of how many days he had walked before he reached the land of the Jutes. He was weak, exhausted and starving, but he had forced himself to put one foot in front of the next as the summer sun burnt his skin, all the while wondering if his mother had told his father that she had spoken to him. He doubted it, because then she would have to tell Frithowald where Octa had gone and so far there had been no sign of anyone hunting him. And Octa had spent the entire time looking over his shoulder to make sure. He had also avoided many of the farmsteads and villages while he was still in the Saxon lands, afraid that he might be recognised. Octa didn't know how far word of his cowardice had spread, but was certain that Witta would send men all over the Saxon lands to tell people of how he had fled from the battle.

He had found plenty of streams where he could drink water and had tried his hand at fishing again, but as before, he had been unsuccessful. But luckily for him, it was summer still and there was plenty of food growing from the trees and bushes, although Octa made certain never to fall asleep near them. He did not want to be woken up by another bear.

When Octa had reached the lands of the Angles, he risked going into small villages where he had stolen food from markets or fields, anything he could get his hands on without being caught, or otherwise had paid for food with the jewellery he still had on him, which was the rings on his fingers. A few days into the lands of the Angles, he had come across a farmstead and was about to steal some freshly baked bread when an old woman had caught him. At first, she had beaten him with her broom, but then she had invited him into her home and fed him some broth with the bread he had tried to steal. The woman's hospitality had confused Octa, but all she had said was that the gods taught them to be kind to travellers. Her husband, a man old enough to have been his grandfather, had grumbled, but they had let him sleep by their hearth fire. Not that he had slept much as he had worried they would slit his throat and steal what little he had. And the nightmare of Uhtric's death that haunted his nights did not help either. After a morning meal of porridge and sweet cakes, he had left the old folks and continued north, but not before giving them the last of the golden rings he wore on his fingers.

Octa had since wondered if they had thought he was one of the gods. Woden was known to disguise himself and to wander the lands, often asking to spend the night sleeping by people's hearth fires. Those who agreed were rewarded, but those who refused usually found that their livestock suddenly died and their crops failed. That was why the people of not just the Saxon lands, but the Angles and the Jutes, even the Franks, always treated travellers with kindness. Just in case it was really Woden, or one of the other gods.

Octa stood a distance away from the large village by the east coast of what he believed was the land of the Jutes and scruti-nised the villagers as they went about their days. The village was busy and, even from where he stood, he could make out many ships by the wharves. Warriors seemed to be everywhere, but Octa doubted he had to worry about them. Witta's men would not have come this far north, he was certain of that. He did not know exactly where he was any more, but he was tired of wandering the wilderness and having to scavenge food wher-ever he could. Only a few days ago, he had chased a fox away from the carcass of a cow and had eaten whatever meat was left on the bones without even thinking of cooking it. He had been that hungry, that it had tasted like one of the best meals he had ever had. The vomiting and shitting that came after were not great and had left him feeling even weaker than before, but once he could, he had got back to his feet and kept going, his mother's words still in his head. Octa gripped the spear pendant she had given him and wondered what his father's face must have looked like when he discovered his chain-mail vest and sword on his seat. Octa almost smiled as he imagined his father's eyes almost popping out of his skull in shock, but then he pushed the thoughts from his mind and stumbled towards the village. His stomach rumbled and his head swam, but Octa kept going.

Many of the villagers glanced at him as he walked past them. Mothers grabbed their children and men glared at him, but Octa did not blame them. He was dirty, he stank and he was certain he had lost a lot of weight because his ripped clothing felt too large for him. Octa had never been to the lands of the Jutes before and was surprised at how similar to the Saxons they looked. As did the Angles. Most people had light-coloured hair and blue eyes, but there were some with darker hair and eyes. The men were all tall and broad shoul-dered and most looked like they had fought many battles. Octa knew that the Jutes and the Angles believed in the same gods as the Saxons and that proving themselves in battle was as important to them as it was to the Saxons. So he was determined to avoid anyone that looked like a warrior, which was difficult as even some of the women looked like they could kill him.

Octa passed a tavern and his stomach growled as the smell of food reached his nostrils. Somewhere nearby, a boy laughed at him before his father cuffed him. The man glared at Octa, as if he was to blame for that, and dragged his son away.

'Even the mighty bear would be startled by the sound of your stomach,' an old voice said from behind Octa and, when he turned around, he saw an old man wearing a broad-brimmed hat and with only one eye smiling at him. Octa frowned, certain he had seen the man before, and then gaped when he remembered it had been in Witta's hall. Panic gripped him and his eyes darted around the streets of the village as he expected Witta's men to rush out and grab him. The old man laughed and said, 'Calm yourself, young man. I mean you no harm.'

Octa stared at the old man, who was shorter than him. Apart from the broad-brimmed hat, he had a tattered old cloak over his shoulders, even though it was warm. His beard was long, almost reaching the bottom of his belly, while one sharp eye watched him from under bushy eyebrows.

'I... I saw you in...' Octa was too afraid to say where he had seen the old man. He was still worried that Witta had found him and knew he could not outrun Witta's warriors.

The old man stroked his long beard. 'It's possible. I travel as far as my feet will take me and visit many lands.'

Octa took a step back, wanting to distance himself from the old man. 'I... I saw you before...' He couldn't get the words out as his eyes darted at the people walking past them, trying to see if any of them posed a threat, but most people looked the other way or grimaced at him.

'Aye, before. Not the way you thought it would turn out, but wyrd often does that to you.'

'Wyrd?' Octa raised an eyebrow at the old man. 'Why is this my wyrd?'

'Are you hungry? I'm hungry.' The old man looked around him as if he didn't know there was a tavern behind. And when he saw it, he beamed. 'Let's go. I'll get you something to eat.'

Octa's stomach growled again, but he didn't trust the old man. He couldn't explain why, but something about the old man made his muscles twitch. 'Why?'

'Because I'm hungry, and I know you are hungry. The entire village knows after hearing your stomach.' The old man walked towards the tavern without looking to see if Octa was following.

Octa stood his ground and was tempted to walk away, but in the end his stomach won and he followed the old man into the tavern. The old man ordered two broths and three ales as he sat on an empty bench.

'What do you want from me?' Octa said as he sat down across the bench from the old man.

The old man eyed the spear pendant that Octa wore around his neck. 'It's what you want from me, Octa, son of Frithowald.'

Octa's eyes widened. 'How do you know my name?' His heart raced and he had the sudden urge to flee, but the limbs refused to obey him. Especially when a woman put two large bowls of broth and three cups of ale down on the table. Octa stared at the ale and the old man smiled.

'Drink up. You need it.'

Without hesitation, Octa grabbed one cup and emptied it in one breath. He closed his eyes and savoured the taste of the ale, the first he had drunk since the feast before the battle. And when he opened his eyes, the old man pushed the second cup towards him while he took the third for himself. But Octa ignored the second cup and wolfed down the broth, not caring that it was too hot for his mouth. He felt the heat reach his stomach and spread throughout his body, and before he could stop himself, he groaned.

'Aye, they make good broth here. And the best ale in the northern lands.'

Octa nodded as he took the second cup and drank from it. 'How do you know my name?' he asked again, and the old man smiled.

'I told you. I travel to many places. See and hear a lot of things.'

Octa looked away. 'So you know of my shame?'

The old man nodded. 'And I know of your redemption.'

Octa's brows creased. 'My redemption? What are you talking about, old man?'

The old man did not respond for a while as he ate his broth. Octa watched, growing more frustrated with each spoon the old man put into his mouth, but then the old man smiled. 'Worthy of the gods, don't you think?'

Octa raised an eyebrow as he glanced around the tavern. It looked just like any mead hall he had ever seen. There was a hearth fire in the middle of the hall with a large pot sitting on the flames. A woman, her face glistening with sweat, stirred the pot and filled bowls, while at the rear of the hall, where the warlord would usually have his seat, a man stood behind a table and collected payments for the food and drink. Large barrels filled with ale stood behind the man, and every now and again, he would dip a cup into a barrel before handing it to someone. Like his father's and Witta's mead halls, shields and weapons hung from the walls, as well as banners which Octa did not recognise. 'I doubt the gods would come in here. They have better places to go to.'

'You really believe so?' the old man asked, with a hint of a smile in his beard.

Octa shrugged and leaned forward. 'What do you know of my redemption?'

'Your redemption?' The old man frowned and then smiled as Octa's face creased. 'What do you know of Gungnir?'

'Gungnir?' Octa frowned. 'Woden's spear?'

'Aye, the very one.'

Again, Octa shrugged. 'What everyone knows. That it was made for Woden by the dwarfs. That with it, Woden has never lost a battle.'

The old man stroked his beard as he stared at Octa. Octa felt like he was being judged and wanted to get away from the old man and his strange words. But the old man had provided him with food and ale, which meant Octa couldn't just get up and leave. 'Do you know it was stolen?'

'Stolen?' Octa raised an eyebrow. 'What do you mean, stolen? And who would steal Woden's spear?'

'Who is not important. Not yet, anyway. But, aye, Woden's spear was stolen, and he needs it back.'

Octa felt his head itch and wondered if he had got lice from sleeping rough. He scratched his head as he thought about the old man's words. 'Then why can't he get it back himself? He is Woden after all.'

The old man laughed. 'Aye, if it was only so simple. Just turn into a falcon and fly to the spear.' For the first time since they entered the tavern, the old man looked annoyed, which only confused Octa even more. 'Woden can't get his spear, because he is being prevented from doing so.'

'Woden? Being prevented from getting his own spear?' Octa

was beginning to think that the old man had lost his wits, and he wondered why he was still sitting here and talking to him. He should just thank the old man for the broth and ale and leave the tavern. But even as he thought about it, Octa couldn't get himself to stand up and walk away. Octa had nowhere else to go and, besides, something about the old man's words intrigued him.

'There is magic that even the gods fear and the one who took the spear is using that magic to ensure that Woden can't get to it.'

'What magic?' Octa felt the hairs on his arms standing on end. He couldn't understand what magic Woden could be afraid of. Woden was one of the most powerful of the gods. He was also cunning and could outwit anyone.

'That is not important,' the old man said. 'What is, is that I know where the spear is.'

Octa's heart raced, and he leaned forward. 'Where?'

'Britannia.'

'Britannia?' Octa had heard of the island to the west, but he knew very little about it. 'Why is Woden's spear in Britannia?'

The old man's face darkened for a moment, but then he took a deep breath and relaxed. 'Because he who stole the spear from Woden gave it to the Romans and they took it to Britannia.'

'And Woden can't go to Britannia to get his spear?'

The old man shook his head and drank from his ale. Octa followed his example and finished his cup. 'I told you. Old magic is being used against Woden, which means he can't get his spear himself.'

Octa stared at the old man, still trying to understand why he was telling him all of this. 'Why are you telling me this?'

The old man smiled. 'Tell me, Octa, son of Frithowald. What would you do to redeem yourself? To wash this stain off your name, and not just your name, but your father's and your forefathers'? To atone for the death of your cousin?'

Octa frowned when he realised where the old man was going with this. 'You want me to go to Britannia to get the spear?'

'No,' the old man said. 'Woden wants you to go to Britannia and get the spear.'

'Why me?'

'Because Woden has seen the courage you possess and believes that you can succeed where no one else has,' the old man said, his smile parting his grey beard.

'Courage? What courage does Woden see in me? I ran from a battle and my cousin died because of it.' Even saying it made his guilt eat away at him and Octa looked away from the old man. 'If what you say is true, then Woden would be better served by finding a real warrior. Not a coward like me.'

The old man watched him for many heartbeats and then smiled when Octa noticed it. 'Bring Woden his spear and he will make sure that everyone would know that you are no coward. He will make you the first king of the Saxons. You will be more powerful than your father and Witta.'

6

You will be more powerful than your father and Witta.

The words rung in Octa's head as he tried to sleep that night. Over and over until he gave up and sat up and stared at the moon, which glowed in the cloudless sky. Full moon was a few days away, which meant that the nights weren't as dark. Not that that made Octa feel more comfortable about sleeping outside, but he had nothing left to trade for a room in the tavern, so he was forced to sleep out in the open again.

After he had finished his broth and ale, Octa had thanked the old man for his kindness and had left, determined to forget the tale the old man had told him. He doubted anyone could steal Woden's spear. Woden was too powerful. Even amongst the gods, it was only Tiw who could match Woden. Perhaps that was why the two gods were so different. Tiw stood for honour and law, whereas Woden was all chaos and trickery. But the Saxons worshipped both gods in equal measure. Tiw to give them the courage and guidance to stand proud in battle and Woden to give them the cunning to defeat their enemies.

Even if someone had stolen Woden's spear, Octa was not the right person to go to Britannia to retrieve it. He did not have the courage of Tiw. Neither did he have Woden's cunning. And besides, he did not even know how to get to Britannia. He had no ship or men to row it, and he didn't know anyone with one. But even as he tried to dismiss the idea, the words of the old man kept coming to him.

You will be more powerful than your father and Witta.

The problem for Octa, though, was that he did not want to be more powerful than his father. He wanted his father's respect and love. He wanted his father to look at him like he had his brothers, and the way he had looked at Octa the morning before the battle. Octa wanted his father to acknowledge him as his son and heir. He also wanted to make his mother proud. To repay the faith she had in him.

As the night wore on, Octa kept thinking about the spear and about how it could restore his honour, perhaps even wash the shame away for abandoning his cousin in the heat of a battle. And by the time the sun rose, Octa knew he had to find the spear of Woden. He wasn't sure if the tale the old man had told him was true, but if there was even a slight chance it was, Octa had to take it. He had to find the spear. Then he would take it to his father and show him he was not a coward. That he was worthy of his ancestors. And with Woden's spear, his father could replace Witta as the most powerful of the warlords and Octa would be his heir. Although Octa was not sure if his father would want to do that. Frithowald had always seemed happy to let Witta take all the glory, something Octa never understood.

Octa washed his face in a bucket of water, ignoring the scowls of the slaves, and made his way to the tavern where he had last seen the old man, praying that he would still be there.

A scream made Octa turn and his eyes widened when he saw a boy no older than seven winters on the ground, while a horse reared above him. People screamed as the horse, its eyes wild, stamped down and narrowly missed the boy and Octa's heart skipped a beat when nobody rushed to help the boy as the horse reared again. The boy shrieked and before Octa realised what was happening, he rushed towards the boy and the horse. He did not know what he was doing. All he knew was that he could not let that boy be trampled on by the horse. Octa shoved people out of the way and before the horse could come down again, Octa stood in front of it, his arms spread out wide and screaming. The horse turned and narrowly avoided Octa. It seemed to glare at him for a moment before it shook its head and ran away, leaving Octa, his limbs trembling, and the villagers baffled by its actions. Octa's heart was pounding away, and he had forgotten all about the boy as he watched the horse disappear.

'My son!' someone shouted, and Octa turned and saw the boy was still on the ground, his face pale as he stared at Octa. 'My son!' A warrior, about thirty winters old, rushed to the boy and scooped him up before embracing him. 'Boy, are you hurt?' the warrior asked after he put the boy down and checked him over.

The boy shook his head. 'The man saved me. He scared the horse away.'

The warrior looked at Octa and raised an eyebrow at him. Octa understood why. He was dirty, his once fine tunic ripped, covered in mud and sweat stained. His boots, once so beautiful, had holes in the bottom and the insides were stained with blood from his feet, which were not used to walking the distances he had forced on them. His hair and beard were matted with dirt and had bugs crawling all over them. He looked the complete opposite of the warrior, whose chain-mail vest almost blinded him, as did the many rings the man wore on his fingers. Rings like the ones Octa used to have, but had to trade for food. The warrior's hair and beard were the same colour as Octa's, but were combed and decorated with small golden finger rings. He stood taller than Octa, his shoulders almost as broad as Witta's and his arms just as thick. The man was not just a warrior, Octa realised as the man stared at him. He saw the man's fine leather boots, the arm rings on his wrists and the large golden buckle, almost as big as his hand, on the man's belt. He was a warlord.

'You saved my son,' the man said, and gripped Octa by his shoulders before embracing him. 'I am in your debt, stranger. Tell me, what is your name?'

Octa swallowed back his nervousness. 'Octa, son of...' He stopped himself before he said his father's name and looked away.

The warrior frowned for a heartbeat before he smiled. 'This is my son, Oisc. And I am Hengist, son of Wihtgils.' The warrior frowned at Octa. 'I've not seen you around here before. Where do you travel from, Octa, son of no one?'

Octa tried to use the saliva in his mouth to wet his tongue. 'I am from the land of the Angles,' he lied, not wanting to tell Hengist he was a Saxon.

Again, Hengist raised an eyebrow at him. 'You are an Angle.'

Octa nodded and was almost certain Hengist didn't believe him. Not that it mattered. By nightfall, he would be gone from this village. Perhaps further north, he could find a way to get to Britannia. But first he needed to find the old man to find out where in Britannia the spear was.

'Well, Octa the Angle. I could use a man of your bravery in my and my brother's fleet. You should join us.'

'I'm not br—' Octa started and then stopped himself, before

he shook his head. He glanced at Hengist's son, who was frowning at him.

'He is strange,' Oisc said, and Hengist smiled.

'Aye, but he saved your life. So you mustn't be rude.'

'No, forgive me,' Octa said. 'It has been a strange morning.'

Hengist beamed at him. 'That it has. Only the gods know where that horse came from. I will find the farmer it belonged to and flog the bastard.'

'How did you know what to do?' Oisc asked, his nose crinkling as he stared at Octa.

Octa hesitated for a moment. 'Horses are important to my people and I was raised with them. Learnt how to ride as soon as I could walk.'

'Important to the Angles?' Hengist asked with a raised eyebrow, and Octa hesitated again before he nodded. Hengist smiled before he fished some hack silver out of his pouch and gave it to Octa. 'Woden blessed us today that you were here then. Get yourself cleaned up and some new clothes. Some food as well, my new friend. Friga knows you look like you need it. And if you change your mind, then come find me in our camp outside the village.'

Octa was about to turn down Hengist's gift, but then his stomach rumbled and he took the hack silver. Hengist nodded at him before he and his son walked away, leaving Octa standing to stare at their backs. He stood there for a while as the villagers got back to their chores and the children back to their games. His stomach growled again and Octa remembered the broth he had at the tavern the day before. He prayed that the old man would be there as he walked towards it, but his heart sank when there was no sign of him.

'Don't bother looking for the old bastard,' the woman who

had brought them their food and drinks the previous day said. 'He never stays for more than one day. Just long enough to send some poor fool to his death.'

Octa frowned at the woman. 'What do you mean?'

'The old man you were with yesterday. You are not the first he has told that story to. So be smart like most of the others and forget about it.'

Octa's heart raced as he only half listened to what the woman was saying. 'You've heard him tell the story to others?'

The woman looked at him as if he had lost his wits. And perhaps he had, but everything that had happened so far that day made him believe Woden wanted him to find the spear. For a moment, he wondered if it was a good idea to betray the war god, but then he dismissed that thought. Surely Woden would understand why he needed the spear. 'Too many times,' the woman said, and carried on clearing the benches.

Octa followed her and asked, 'So you know where the spear is?'

The woman stopped and raised an eyebrow at him. 'You really think you will find it? That old man has been coming here for as long as I can remember and has fooled many with his tale of Woden and his lost spear.'

'And did any of those men find the spear?' Octa asked, dreading that he was too late, but the woman only shrugged.

'Never seen any of those men again, so most likely they are dead.' The woman picked up some empty cups from one bench and added them to the others in her hands. 'Be smart. If you can fight, take Hengist's offer and make a coin for yourself. If not, then move on and live your life.'

'So nobody found the spear?' Octa asked, ignoring the woman's words.

'Look. That old bastard probably fought on that island for the Romans and he lost something important to him. And now he sends others to get it, because he can't go himself. That tale he told you is nothing but an old man's lonely imagination. He just wants to feel important.'

Don't we all, Octa thought, but didn't say. 'It doesn't matter. I have nothing left in my life. Even if the tale is false, I lose nothing by believing it is true. Please, all I need to know is where in Britannia the spear is.'

The woman looked at him and sighed. 'Friga knows you men are all fools. If I remember, he told the others that the spear is in a cave, north of the island. Near a wall built by the Romans.'

Octa rubbed his head. 'A wall built by the Romans? They must have built many walls.'

The woman shrugged. 'That's all I ever heard him say. There is a cave with a shrine to a god of the island near this wall and the spear is in there. Be smart and forget about it.' The woman walked away, leaving Octa scratching his head.

A cave near a wall built by the Romans. A shrine belonging to a god. It was not much to go on, but it was a start and Octa was determined to find the spear and give it to his father.

The woman returned to fill the cups of some of the other people and then sighed. 'The gods know you are a fool for believing the old bastard, but if you really are determined to do it, then you should ask Hengist to join his fleet.'

'Hengist? Why?'

'Because the rumours are he is going to Britannia.'

Octa's eyes widened, and he looked over his shoulder at the spot where he had spoken to Hengist. Was Woden behind that encounter? Did he want Octa to find his spear? Octa realised the woman was still standing there, staring at him, and he thanked her for the information.

'Don't thank me. I don't want your death on my mind.' The woman walked away, leaving Octa to ponder what the chances were that he would meet the man who could take him to the spear so quickly.

Octa bought himself some broth and an ale from the tavern keeper and, after finishing both, found a bathhouse where he cleaned himself up and bought a new tunic and boots. The boots weren't as comfortable as the pair he had before and the tunic itched as if it was covered in lice, but Octa was glad to have clean clothes on his back and shoes that had soles on them.

The following morning, Octa made his way to the camp Hengist had told him about and was surprised to see how large it was. He gaped at the many tents and more warriors than he could count as his head turned this way and that. Witta didn't even have that many warriors, even with his father's warriors combined. Not watching where he was going, Octa bumped into a large warrior, who turned and glared at him.

'Watch where you're going!' The warrior grabbed Octa by his tunic and almost lifted him off his feet. 'Unless you want me to drown you.'

Octa paled at the warrior, but then noticed how similar he looked to Hengist, only younger. He shook his head at the man as the nearby warriors laughed at him and worried that he had made a mistake in coming here. He was no warrior, not like the surrounding men. Most of them wore thick leather jerkins, but some had chain-mail vests on and a few even had swords around their waists.

'Octa!' Hengist greeted him as he appeared from behind the warrior still holding on to him. 'Horsa, put him down. This is the man that saved Oisc from that horse.'

'Him?' Horsa raised an eyebrow. 'Nearly shat himself when he bumped into me.'

Hengist laughed. 'You have that effect on most. Now put him down.' The warrior did that and Octa took deep breaths to calm his nerves as Hengist smiled at him. 'What brings you here? Have you changed your mind?'

'Changed his mind about what?' Horsa asked.

'About joining our fleet.'

'Never.' Horsa glared at Octa. 'He has no steel in him. You can see it in his eyes.'

Octa looked away, worried that others saw the same, but Hengist gripped his shoulder.

'He is brave. He saved my son, so I know what I'm talking about. So, you want to join our fleet?' Octa nodded, unable to look Hengist in the eyes, but that didn't seem to bother the Jute. 'Good—'

'What do you mean, good?' Horsa interrupted his brother. 'By Tiw, the bastard doesn't have any armour or weapons! What is he going to fight with?'

Hengist nodded as he frowned at Octa. 'Aye. You are right.' He looked around and then smiled when he spotted an older warrior. 'Eadric! Come here.'

'What are you doing, brother?'

Hengist ignored his brother and continued to grip Octa by the shoulder as the older warrior approached them. 'This is Octa the Angle. He needs armour and weapons.'

Eadric glanced at Octa. His lips curled in disgust as he took in Octa's thin frame and gaunt cheeks. 'Why? He won't last more than a few heartbeats in a shield wall.'

'Then you will make sure he does,' Hengist said. 'Octa is a brave man. He saved my son.' Eadric shrugged as Hengist said,

'Find him some armour and a spear, and somewhere to sleep. You will be in charge of his training.'

Eadric grunted. 'Fine, but the gods know that there is little I can do if he can't fight.' The older warrior looked at Octa. 'Follow me.'

'Thank you,' Octa said to Hengist, and followed Eadric before Horsa could object. But as he walked away, he could hear the man arguing with his brother.

7

The spear trembled in Octa's hand as images of the battle flashed in his mind and he felt the knot in the back of his throat as he thought of Uhtric. Even though he had set out to make a name for himself, Octa had never thought about holding a weapon again. His palms were sweating and, no matter how hard he tried, he could not stop the spear from trembling and neither could he get Uhtric's face out of his mind.

'Have you ever fought in a battle before?' Eadric scowled at him.

Octa's eyes widened at the question. 'No,' he lied, because to tell the truth would only get him killed.

Eadric watched him for a few heartbeats and then nodded. Octa got the sense that the older warrior didn't believe him, but he decided he would stick to that lie. He'd rather have them think he had never faced another in battle than think of him as a coward. Even if that was what he was. 'Let's see what you can do.'

Octa's legs trembled at the thought of sparring against Eadric, but he tightened his grip on the spear and faced Eadric.

'Show me your battle stance.'

Octa obeyed and stood the way he had been taught, his left foot forward and his shield held in front of him. He pulled his spear arm back and rested the spear on the rim of his shield. It was the most basic stance and the first thing that Saxon boys learnt when they started their training before their balls dropped.

'Good. So that you know at least,' Eadric said as he scrutinised Octa's stance. He took a few steps towards Octa, and then rushed at him. Before Octa could react, Eadric shoulder barged into his shield and forced him back a few steps. Octa resisted the urge to drop the shield and gritted his teeth as he tried to push back, but Eadric was too strong for him. And then his heart skipped when Eadric hooked his foot behind his leg and tripped him up. As soon as Octa's back hit the ground, Eadric ripped the spear from his hand and stabbed it at him. Octa lifted his shield with both hands, more out of instinct than anything else, and cried out as the spear struck the wood. Eadric pulled the spear back and stabbed again, but this time Octa rolled out of the way and jumped to his feet. His heart raced in his chest and all he wanted to do was run away, but he knew he couldn't. Only because he had nowhere to go. Eadric stabbed the spear at his face and Octa ducked under it. He spotted an opening where, if he had been brave enough, he could have struck Eadric in the side with the rim of his shield. Eadric saw the same and held his stance. 'Why didn't you strike? You would have had me there.'

'I... I...' Octa tried to think of an excuse, but he couldn't. He didn't know why he didn't strike. Just like he didn't know why he hadn't tried to save Uhtric. The large axe-wielding warrior came to his mind, the way he was just before Octa ran. Octa had a chance to kill him and to save Uhtric. All he had to do was stab the warrior in the stomach with his spear. Then Uhtric would still be alive and they would be drinking mead in Witta's hall. But instead he had run. Just like he wanted to run now.

Eadric straightened up and lowered the spear. 'Fighting in the shield wall is one of the most terrifying things most of us will ever do. But it is not a place for everyone.' He tilted his head as he scowled at Octa. 'You better find your steel because if Hengist and Horsa see you freeze in battle, they will kill you themselves. Don't be fooled by Hengist's friendly nature. The man is as ruthless as they come and unfortunately for you, he likes you because you saved his son. And that means he expects you to show the same bravery when you fight in the shield wall.'

Octa nodded and took his spear back from Eadric, determined to do better.

This went on for many days, and slowly Octa became more comfortable holding a spear and shield in his hands again, although he doubted he would ever feel as confident as he had before the battle. Eadric had even warmed up to him and, one night, they were sitting by the same fire and eating their meal of beef stew.

Octa dipped his bread into his stew before he chewed on it, his eyes on the older Jute. The stew was not as good as what he was used to, but it filled his stomach and helped build the muscle he had lost. And that was another thing he had struggled with. Octa was used to living in luxury. A large hall with plenty of food and mead. Women at his command and soft furs to sleep in. He missed those days, but knew that this was part of his punishment. The gods had taken his comfort away from him, but at least there was hope of redemption, which made sleeping on hard ground more bearable.

'How did Hengist and Horsa become warlords?' Octa had never heard of the brothers before, but guessed they must have been successful if they had managed to raise an army such as the one around him.

Eadric shrugged. 'They fought hard and fought clever. It helped that their father was a cousin to the king, but the brothers would deny that.'

'You've fought for them for a long time?'

Eadric nodded. 'For the last five or so winters. I had my own crew once. My own ship. But the brothers defeated me in battle and gave me a choice. Join them or die.' Eadric smiled. 'Wasn't ready to die yet, so I joined them. Not once have I looked back. Despite that defeat, the gods were good to me and so were the brothers. Raid after raid, they became richer and their reputation grew. So much so that some say even the king of Jutland feels threatened by them. That is why the brothers are leaving. They don't want to fight the king.'

'Where did they raid?'

'Everywhere their ships would take them. No land is safe from Hengist and Horsa. No kingdom has men smart enough to defeat them.'

Octa nodded as he listened to Eadric's words. He was struck by how much the older warrior respected them. He had never heard anyone speak of Witta like that. Witta was feared more than respected by his own men and Octa had heard many stories of how he had beaten his own men when he was displeased with them. And it was not just his warriors, but the other warlords as well. They never trusted Witta or liked him. The thought brought Uhtric's face to his mind and Octa asked the real question he had wanted to to distract himself from his guilt. 'Are we really going to Britannia?'

Eadric stopped chewing and glanced at him. 'Who told you that?'

Octa shrugged, trying to do his best to seem uninterested,

even though he was desperate to know. Just like he was desperate to see the old man again. Octa had been here for many days, but there had been no sight of him. 'It's being whispered around the camp.'

Eadric chewed for a bit more and then said, 'Perhaps.'

Octa's heart raced at that and his hands would have gone to the spear pendant his mother had given him if they didn't have food in them. 'When do we leave?'

Again, Eadric stopped chewing and glanced at him. 'Why?'

'Why?' Octa frowned.

'Aye.' Eadric lowered his bowl. 'Why are you so eager to know?'

Octa felt his hands trembling and worried that he had pushed too far. 'I'm curious. That's all.'

Eadric grunted and carried on eating. Just when Octa thought he would say nothing, the older Jute said, 'They're waiting for the summer solstice, when the seas are calmer and the journey will be easier.'

Octa had to hide his smile behind his loaf of bread because he knew the summer solstice would arrive soon. He glanced at Eadric, who had gone back to his meal, and thought about asking him about the Roman wall the woman in the tavern had mentioned, but decided not to.

When the summer solstice arrived, the mood in the camp and the village affected even Octa. His dark mood was gone and even his nightmares were chased away. The brothers threw a feast to celebrate the summer solstice and to ask for the gods' blessing as they prepared to leave. By this time, everyone knew the destination, but Octa still had not been able to ask Eadric if he knew anything about the Roman wall.

During the feast, the warriors ate and drank. They sang songs, told poems and danced as the sun climbed high in the sky and the day seemed like it would never end. Octa tried to enjoy the feast, but all he could think about was the last feast he had been to. As he drank his ale, he remembered how he and Uhtric had drunk Witta's mead and had boasted about the glory they would get. Octa gripped the spear pendant around his neck and prayed to the gods that he would not fail in this quest.

The feast went on until the moon finally arrived, but by that time most of the men were passed out and even the brothers had gone back to their tents, both with a number of women hanging on their arms. Octa was still sitting where he had been all night, staring at the bonfire as it slowly died out until he eventually fell asleep.

The next day, Octa learnt something about himself. He hated the sea. Or more specifically, he hated sailing.

'Don't worry about it, lad,' Eadric said, and all Octa could do was smile at him on the first day as he leaned over the side and emptied his stomach into the sea.

And many days later, Octa still struggled. At least, though, the others had stopped laughing at him. They hugged the coast of the mainland as rowing across the open water would have been too dangerous, or at least that was what Eadric told Octa. Along the way, they stopped in the lands of the Franks once to top up their provisions, but the rest of the time they avoided going ashore.

'The Romans are fighting to maintain what little control they have left there,' Hengist said when Octa asked why. 'And we want to avoid the Romans if we can. Much is happening on the continent, which makes it difficult to know who to trust.'

'That is why many are on the move,' Eadric added. 'Some people push south, into the lands of the Romans, while others have crossed the seas in search of a new home.'

'So there are already Jutes on Britannia?' Octa asked between bouts of vomiting.

'Not just Jutes. Saxons, Angles, Frisians. Even Franks. That is how we know the Britons are having problems with the Picts,' Hengist said.

'Still not sure about this one,' Horsa said to his brother, ignoring the conversation as he scowled at Octa. 'A man who can't deal with the waves won't be worth much on the battleground. Everyone knows that.' Octa's cheeks burnt red with shame because of the truth of Horsa's words. But Octa was not planning on doing any fighting. As soon as they reached Britannia, he would slip away and search for this important cave by a wall the Romans had built. First, though, he had to find out where this cave and wall were.

Hengist laughed at his brother's words. 'Octa is a brave man. He showed courage while the others did nothing.'

Horsa, still scowling at Octa, grunted. 'How do you know he didn't bring that wild horse with him and set the whole thing up? You never found out who it belonged to.'

Hengist raised an eyebrow and then looked at Octa, who was sitting by the side of the ship so he could just lean over the side when he needed to vomit. 'Octa, did you bring that horse into the village?'

Octa saw how many of the others frowned at him and shook his head. 'Where would I get a horse from? That beast surprised me as much as it did everyone else.'

Hengist smiled and clapped his brother on the back. 'See, Octa did not bring the horse. Don't you concern yourself with him, brother. We have more important things to concern ourselves with.'

Horsa grunted again before he said, 'Fine. But Tiw knows I do not trust a man who can't stomach being at sea.'

Octa felt his stomach heave again and leaned over the side of the ship to empty his guts, but nothing came out other than bile, just like the last few times. Octa prayed they would reach Britannia soon, because he didn't know how much more of this he could endure.

'Ignore Horsa,' Eadric said when Octa gave up trying to vomit and dropped on the deck beside the warrior. 'He is the more serious of the two brothers and always finds a reason to complain about something or someone. I doubt the bastard is ever happy unless he has something to complain about.'

Octa glanced at Horsa, who reminded him of Witta. 'They seem a strange pair.'

'Aye, but they know what they are about and have never had an unsuccessful raid. The gods know I pity the kings of Britannia.' Eadric smiled as he pulled on his oar.

'Kings?' Octa frowned. 'How many kings do they have in Britannia?'

Eadric shrugged. 'The gods know they have more than they need, but it seems that every bastard with ten men and two cows declares himself a king and then he spends the rest of his life fighting others who also want to be king.'

Octa frowned again as he fought another wave of nausea. 'Why are the Romans not helping them? Britannia is still part of the empire, is it not?'

'Most of the Roman armies have left Britannia to fight the empire's enemies to the east and the north, especially the Huns who came from the east. Those vicious bastards drive other tribes into the Roman lands and the Romans need their armies to defend those lands,' Hengist said, coming over to join Octa and Eadric. 'Britannia hasn't been part of the empire for many winters now, but there are many on the island who still think of themselves as Romans and try to live as the Romans did. Unfortunately, being part of the empire for as long as they have, they have grown weak and now that the Roman armies aren't there to protect them, the Picts have been attacking them. By Woden, even we do. Horsa and I have led many raids against Britons, as do the Saxons and the Franks.' He went silent for a while as he watched the waves and Octa wondered if he knew who he really was, but then dismissed the idea. 'As Eadric said. Since the Romans left, the Britons went back to the ways of their ancestors and many declared themselves kings, even though they barely have enough warriors to defend the two cows they have.'

Octa looked at the other two ships in Hengist and Horsa's fleet. 'But why only take three ships?'

'Because that's all we have,' Horsa said from the rear of the ship. 'And besides, the gods know we won't need more than the warriors we have to defeat the enemies of the Britons.'

'You only have three ships?' Octa asked, frowning again. He had seen many more ships and warriors in the village before they had left and he glanced at Hengist, who smiled at him, certain that there was more going on than what they were telling him. Not that he was telling them the truth, either. He prayed to Woden that he found the spear quickly, before whatever Hengist and Horsa were planning came to be.

They rowed for many more days, hugging the coast of the continent, until they saw white cliffs across the seas. That was when Hengist gave the order and the ships changed course and headed for the cliffs. Octa had thought that the journey so far had been bad, but this crossing was the worst experience of his life. Worse even than the battle he had fled from. Octa prayed to Thunor to protect him and keep him safe as gigantic waves washed over the sides of Hengist's ships, drenching the men with sea water. But the warriors on the ships did not seem bothered by this as they continued to row towards the island.

'You're lucky. The seas are calm today,' Eadric said, the smile on his face showing that he was amused by Octa's discomfort.

Octa wondered what it was like when the seas weren't calm and the thought made his stomach clench. He wanted to lean over the side to vomit, but then a wave washed over and threw him back onto the deck. The warriors on the ship laughed as he spat sea water out of his mouth.

'Come, grab an oar and row. Keeping your body busy will make your mind forget about the waves,' Eadric said and helped Octa to the rowing bench. Octa was doubtful, but he grabbed the oar and rowed, just like Eadric had shown him before. The trick seemed to work as he was too focused on the man in front of him and trying to match his rhythm to notice how the ship rolled with the waves.

'Why didn't you tell me about this before?' Octa asked, and Eadric laughed.

'It's our suffering that makes us strong and you needed to suffer a bit more.'

Octa scowled at the older warrior, but then focused on rowing as he felt the queasiness return to his stomach. But he soon forgot about that as they reached the island of Britannia. Octa craned his neck as he looked at the tall white cliffs, and he wasn't the only one to do so, as many of the new warriors did the same. Hengist gave the order and, as they kept rowing along the coast of Britannia, Octa stared at the many small fishing boats he saw in the seas near the coast. Many of those fishermen had stopped what they were doing and seemed to stare at the three warships that had come from across the seas. Octa couldn't help but wonder what those men were thinking as they stared at Hengist and Horsa's ships. Did they see invaders or men come to protect them from their enemies? Their expressions showed the apprehension they must have felt, although a group of boys ran along the beaches as if they were chasing the ships. They shouted things out in their tongue and one boy grabbed his crotch and shook a fist at the Jutes, which only made them laugh. This carried on until one warrior took a small throwing spear and launched it at the boys. Octa watched it arch through the air and land just in front of the boy, who screamed and ran away, his friends close on his heels.

'Good throw,' another warrior said.

'What do you mean good throw?' the warrior who threw the spear said. 'I missed the little bastard.' The other warriors laughed and Octa felt his hands tremble as he wondered what kind of men he had joined.

A short while later, they came to a small island and Horsa looked up at the sky. 'The sun's setting.'

Hengist followed his brother's gaze. 'Aye.' He scrutinised the island and nodded. 'We'll stop here for the night. Tomorrow we continue inland and find the king of these lands.'

Octa looked at the island they were rowing towards and saw the thin trails of smoke which showed the island was inhabited. He was about to pray that the people on the small island left them alone when he felt Horsa's eyes on him. He still did not feel comfortable with the man's gaze on him and wanted to grip the spear pendant around his neck. He wondered how he would find someone to lead him to this Roman wall and to find the shrine. But first, he'd have to find a way to get away from the brothers and their men.

8

The three ships moored on the beach by the island and the Jutes all disembarked and began preparing their camp for the night. Octa gaped at the efficiency of the warriors as they carried war chests off the ships and unpacked their tents, while others went to nearby trees and started chopping off branches for the fire. Tents were put up without an order being given and by the time the sun was sitting low on the horizon, the camp was ready and the Jutes were eating their evening meal.

Octa eyed the warriors who had been on watch and knew that soon it would be his turn. He had been with Hengist and Horsa's army for weeks, and almost half of the summer was gone, but he still didn't feel like he was part of the army. Although that was more because he rarely spoke to anyone other than Eadric and occasionally Hengist, rather than the others not accepting him. Octa wasn't planning on staying with Hengist and Horsa for longer than he needed to. As soon as he found Woden's spear, then he would leave and return home to give it to his father. Hopefully then he would be redeemed and perhaps even be forgiven.

He ate his salted meat and washed it down with some ale as he turned his attention to the surrounding landscape and wondered how far they were from the Roman wall he needed to find. Octa wondered how he was going to find the right wall, because there must have been many built by the Romans. His father had told him once that the Romans could build homes worthy of the gods, some so grand that it seemed that giants must have built them. He had always wanted to see these buildings and hoped he would get a chance while he was in Britannia. But first he had to find the wall with a shrine to a god of this island and Octa did not know where to start. He prayed that he might find someone who could take him to this shrine by the Roman wall. Octa cursed himself for not paying more attention to the old man that day he had told Octa about the spear. The old man might have told him exactly where to find the spear.

The night passed peacefully. Octa stood watch for most of the night, his role as he was one of the few new recruits, and was glad when he was relieved. Although he knew he wouldn't be able to get any sleep. The sun was rising, and he knew he'd be exhausted all day, but he couldn't complain. Not any more. He was no longer the son of a warlord and had to do what was needed so that others would not suspect who he really was. But before Octa got to his tent, he heard men screaming and a horn blowing.

'We're under attack!' someone shouted, and another blew a horn. It didn't take long for the Jutes to come rushing out of their tents, spears and shields ready even if few wore any armour.

Horsa came out of his tent. His sword in his hand. 'Protect the ships!'

Octa turned to the sound of the attack and in the dim morning light he saw men dressed in dark tunics rushing towards their camp, many of them wielding spears, but some with axes and pitchforks. His legs felt weak and the shield in his hands felt too heavy for him to hold as the Britons reached the camp and the fighting began. Octa watched as Hengist blocked a spear thrust from one Briton with his shield and stabbed another in the chest with his own spear. The other Jutes were just as effective as they cut down any Briton within reach of their spears. It was hard to believe that many of them had just been woken by the attack. Horsa twisted out of the way of a spear and punched the Briton with the rim of his shield as more Jutes joined the fight.

'Octa, beside you!' Eadric shouted, and Octa turned in time to see a Briton stab a pitchfork at him. Panic gripped him and Octa couldn't move as the pitchfork came towards his head. In his mind, he saw the axe that had killed his cousin come down on his head and Octa knew he would die before he ever got to find Woden's missing spear. But then a loud thud broke him from his trance and he saw Eadric standing in front of him, his face a grimace as he blocked the pitchfork with his shield before he turned it and stabbed the Briton in the guts with his spear. The Briton's eyes bulged as he dropped his weapon and grabbed the spear in his stomach, but then Eadric punched him in the face with the rim of his shield and the man dropped to the ground, his breathing so faint that Octa was certain he was dead.

'I... I...' Octa tried to say when Eadric glared at him.

'Keep your shield up and your eyes open!' he said, the same words Octa's father had said to him the morning of that battle. Octa felt his breath get knocked out of him by the memory of his father, his eyes filled with pride as he handed his sword and chain-mail vest to him. And then the words he had heard his father say in his hall a few days later came to him and Octa had to use whatever strength he had not to cry. *My sons are dead. All of them.*

The attack was over soon after as the remaining Britons fled, leaving fewer than a handful of the Jutes dead and many of the tents in flames. Octa saw one of the warriors who had joined Hengist and Horsa a few days after he had amongst the dead. A young Angle who had wanted to earn enough to marry the woman he loved. Octa wondered if she would ever find out that her lover was dead, or would she instead believe he had left her? He thought of his mother and her words to him. Would she ever find out if he died on this island?

Hengist called for his men to stop and they obeyed instantly. If Octa hadn't been gripped by his fear, then he would have been impressed as the Jutes all took a step back, but kept their shields and spears ready as they protected what was left of the camp. Instead, Octa stayed rooted to the spot and stared at the Briton who had almost killed him and could hear Woden laughing at him in the cries of the injured. He looked at his crotch, almost expecting to see his trousers wet, but was surprised when they were still dry. The shield weighed as heavy as an ox and all Octa wanted to do was drop it and run away, but never got the chance as Eadric grabbed him by his tunic.

'What in Tiw's name was that?'

Octa's eyes widened, and he saw Hengist staring at them. 'I—'

'Never mind,' Eadric interrupted him before he leaned closer. 'Hengist thinks you are brave because you rescued his son, but that was not what I just saw.' He glanced at Hengist, who was still staring at them. 'Do not disappoint Hengist, or Horsa. Your end will not be pretty, that I can promise you.' Eadric let go of Octa and walked away, leaving Octa to again stare at the Briton who had almost killed him. He knew then that if he was going to find Woden's spear, he would need to find a courage he did not possess.

'Bastards!' Horsa said as he glared at the dead Britons. 'You bastards!' He paced around the camp, his face red as he took in the damage from the attack. Many of the tents were burning and some of the warriors were injured by the attack that had caught them by surprise.

'At least the ships weren't damaged,' Hengist said as he stood near Octa. 'They must have thought we were raiders.'

Octa avoided Eadric's gaze, but he still felt the older warrior glaring at him as the Jutes picked through the remains of the camp to see what could be salvaged. Octa did not want to fight. He had not come to Britannia to fight. But as he stared at the Britons who had attacked them, he realised that he might not be able to avoid fighting.

'What do we do now?' Eadric asked Hengist, who was glaring at the dead Britons.

Horsa ordered men to deal with the injured and the dead as Hengist checked the edge of his sword. The Britons were thrown into the sea, even those who were still alive, while the few Jutes who had died were taken to one side so they could be buried with their weapons. Octa knew that was not the way they buried the dead. Like the Saxons, the Jutes preferred to cremate their dead, but he guessed they didn't want the funeral pyres to draw more attention to them.

'We find where these bastards came from and make sure they don't attack us again.' He looked around the camp and then at his brother. 'And we leave soon before they come back with more men.'

9

CAIR URNAHC, ROYAL HALL OF KING VORTIGERN

Brigid held her breath as she snuck into the hall of King Vortigern, the high king of Britannia. The stone walls, built by the Romans many generations ago, had many passages only she knew about and she had often used them to listen to King Vortigern and his councillors from the shadows. But even as she found a place to hide where no one would spot her, she couldn't help but think of the recurring dream she had been having recently. A white horse approaching a wolf amongst a pack of wolves. Their noses touching as the other wolves watch on before they run off into a land filled with fire and death. Brigid sensed the dream was important, a message from the old gods of Britannia, but even as she turned her attention to those in the hall, she still couldn't understand what it meant. She had been born with a mark on her chest, just below her collarbone. A mark that almost looked like the head of a spear. Most had thought nothing of it, but her mother had sensed that the old gods of Britannia had chosen Brigid as their messenger. The initial dreams had started when her first monthly blood came and Brigid had been terrified of them. That was when her mother had sent her away to live with an old healing woman who could teach her the ways of the old gods and how to read the dreams. That was the last time Brigid saw her mother, who had been killed by a drunken Christian priest. Now all the family she had left was her brother, who was one of King Vortigern's warriors.

King Vortigern sat on his raised seat in his hall as the other kings of Britannia argued amongst themselves, his face dark and his fingers drumming away on his knee. The argument was the same as it was at the last council of the kings, what to do about the Picts from the north raiding their kingdoms. And as before, the kings would not come to an agreement.

The king of kings was grey and had lost much of his strength. He dressed the way that most Britons dressed. A mix between traditional clothing and clothing that the Romans had brought with them. The crown on his head was a simple gold band with a large gem in the centre of it. As was the large cross he wore around his neck, although Brigid knew that King Vortigern did not really believe in the Christian god. But many of his people did and so he had to pretend that he did so as well, just as Brigid was forced to. Christians weren't accepting of other gods. Brigid remembered when she was a child and her grandfather still lived. He had told her that the Romans had once believed in other gods, but then they abandoned those gods in favour of the Christian god. Brigid often wondered if that was why their empire was crumbling and why they had left Britannia. She prayed to Brigantia, the mother goddess, she would live long enough to see the collapse of the Roman Empire because she wanted to piss on the ashes of the empire that had left them to fend for themselves like an unwanted child.

King Vortigern was the king of the Cornovii but had recently become the high king of Britannia. Something he had worked hard for for many years, gathering the support of some kings and buying it from others. But Brigid knew that there were many who still did not agree with him holding the position as she watched them from the shadows of the hall. They believed the role belonged to another. A king more sympathetic to the Christian god the Romans had brought to Britannia and left behind when they abandoned the island.

Brigid was King Vortigern's lover, one of many, but she was the one he listened to more than his wife. Her grandfather was a Saxon who had come over with the Romans and had stayed behind when his employment was done. He had married a British woman and fathered her mother. Because of that, she and her brother, Badulf, were taller than most. That was what had attracted the king of kings to Brigid and she had made sure to use that to her advantage. Brigid had seen twenty winters and most said she should have had a husband with children by now, but she cared little for that. There was only one thing she cared about. Something she had once believed King Vortigern could help her with. She wondered if he still could as she toyed with the bead necklace she wore while the kings of Britannia argued amongst themselves. It was no surprise the Picts raided them with impunity. Killing innocent people and burning their farms while these kings drank wine from golden cups and did nothing but argue as they waited for others to fight their battles for them.

The situation in Britannia was not great. Many wondered if the Christian god had abandoned them with the Romans, especially when the raids had started. And it wasn't just giant men from across the seas, men the Romans had once paid to protect this part of their empire, but it was also the Picts from the north. King Vortigern rubbed his temples as the other kings ignored what he had said and Brigid wondered why these men worked so hard to make it easier for others to attack them. She knew, though, there were those who did not support him in this hall, which had once been a forum of a Roman city.

She glanced up at the thatch roof. A storm had destroyed the tile roof the Romans had built and no one in Vortigern's kingdom had the skill to replace it. It wasn't just their armies the Romans had taken with them. The skills needed to cut stone from a mountain and use it to build large temples and homes were gone, as was the knowledge of how to move water across vast distances. The roads they had built were damaged by weather and farmers stealing the stones to build walls, and no one knew how to replace them. But the people of Britannia were resourceful. When the Romans left and took all their knowledge with them, those who remained behind went back to the old ways. So when tile roofs collapsed, they replaced them with the roofs their forefathers had built. Wood and thatch. That was what the Britons knew and understood. And that was what they used to repair damaged walls and homes. Just like Brigid prayed the old gods would replace the Christian god.

'We should send another letter,' one king said, and Brigid saw how King Vortigern sighed.

'We already sent a letter to the Romans. Many years ago and there was no response,' another said. An old king who had lived as long as King Vortigern had. Almost fifty years.

King Vortigern had told her that there were still some legions left in Britannia, although they had so few men that she doubted they could be called legions. Just remnants of a once mighty army left to defend the north of the island against the Picts. Yet those tribes still killed people and burnt their farms.

'We should send another letter,' the king said again. 'Perhaps they never received the first one.'

King Vortigern sighed again and stood up from his chair.

'We can send as many letters as we want. We can send priests and messengers. The Romans won't come. We are no longer important to them. Not while they fight for their very survival.'

The other kings gaped as he walked past them to the door of his hall. Brigid noticed how he tensed his shoulders as if he expected one of them to stick a knife in his back and shook her head. He was the high king. He was supposed to show strength and if she saw him tense, then the other kings would have done as well.

'So what must we do then, King Vortigern?' another king said, his voice filled with scorn. He was one of the many that still believed they were part of the Roman Empire, even though they had not received any new Roman coins in Brigid's lifetime, nor had she seen the empire bring her fabled army to these shores.

'We must fend for ourselves. Like our ancestors did before the Romans came,' King Vortigern said.

'The Romans defeated our ancestors,' the same man said.

King Vortigern nodded. 'They did. But it took them many generations to do so.' He tuned to face the other kings. 'Our people were once mighty warriors who almost drove the Romans back across the seas. We all heard of how Caratacus fought them for many winters and how Boudicca almost broke them and sent them running. But now.' He looked at the king who had just spoken. 'We are nothing but sheep waiting for the wolves to take us.'

'And we all heard how they were defeated by the Romans. And now the Romans took all of our fighting men with them when they left. How are we supposed to fight these wolves?'

King Vortigern shrugged, and Brigid scowled at him from the shadows. 'We need to become the wolves.' The others laughed, and a few shook their heads at him, but before anyone could say anything, the door to the hall opened and a guard walked in. The kings all fell silent and glared at the warrior who interrupted them, but Brigid was more focused on the young man behind the warrior, who looked like he was about to faint.

'What is the meaning of this?' one of the kings asked, and King Vortigern scowled at the man who believed he could talk to one of Vortigern's warriors like that.

The warrior looked at King Vortigern. 'My king, this man brings news from Ceint.'

'Ceint? My kingdom?' King Gwyrangon of the Cantiaci, and one of the few who supported King Vortigern, said, his eyes wide. 'What news?'

The warrior cleared his throat. 'Pirates, from across the seas.' Brigid saw the panic on the faces of all the kings. It had been many winters since the last time they had to deal with pirates from across the seas. Warriors from the lands of her grandfather. Tall and broad-shouldered men who were raised on the battlefield and who worshipped gods as old as the gods she worshipped.

'Saxons, my lord,' the young man said, even as he struggled to stand on his feet. 'They landed on the island of Ruym. We attacked them, hoping to send them back.'

'And did you?' Vortigern asked.

The young man's cheeks turned red as he looked away from Vortigern's gaze. 'They were too strong for us, my king. And after that, they attacked my village and captured everyone.'

'What do they want?' King Gwyrangon asked.

'To kill everyone and take everything,' one of the other kings said, and many agreed with him. Some kings even dropped to their knees and prayed to the Christian god. Brigid curled her lip in disgust at these weak men.

'How many pirates were there?' King Vortigern asked.

The boy frowned. 'It is hard to say, but we saw three ships.'

'Three ships?' King Gwyrangon asked and looked at the others. 'Most likely gone by now.'

Brigid decided that she had heard enough and was about to sneak out of the hall when someone grabbed her arm. Her hand went to the small knife hidden in her dress and when she turned and saw King Vortigern's son, Vortimer, glaring at her, she let go of the knife.

'Women are not allowed in the hall when the kings meet to discuss important matters.' His eyes bore into her, and she knew he wanted to frighten her. But she only smiled at him.

'And what important matter do they discuss, Vortimer? Which way to run when our enemies come?'

'Watch your words, bitch.' Vortimer leaned closer, again trying to frighten her. 'One day I'll be king and then the fact that you are sleeping with my father won't protect you any more.'

Brigid smiled at Vortimer, even though her heart was racing in her chest. Vortimer hated her because he had wanted her. He had chased her for a long time when they were younger, but then his father had noticed her, as she stood out because of her grandfather's Saxon blood, and made her one of his lovers. At first, Brigid had wanted to refuse, but then she saw how weak-minded King Vortigern was and how she could use that to her advantage. Yet Vortimer had blamed her for that instead of his father. 'You're only angry because your father is still more man than you can ever be.'

Vortimer raised his hand to strike her, but he must have seen something in her eyes because he let go of her and said, 'Don't let me catch you in here again.' Vortimer stormed off, leaving Brigid smiling at him.

Later that day, Brigid found King Vortigern alone in his hall, his face dark as he stared at nothing. She filled a cup with wine as she watched him, knowing that she would need to be careful with her words. Brigid had spent the day wondering what the arrival of the Saxons meant and if that had anything to do with the dreams the mother goddess, Brigantia, had been sending her.

'What troubles you, my king?'

King Vortigern looked up as she handed him the wine and smiled at her. 'I'm sure you already know.'

Brigid returned his smile. 'The news of the raiders?'

King Vortigern nodded. 'As if I don't have enough to worry about. The Picts raiding from the north. The other kings conspiring behind my back and now pirates from across the seas arrive as well.' King Vortigern drank from the cup. 'Why are the gods punishing us?' King Vortigern knew about Brigid's connection to the old gods, which was the only reason he listened to her advice.

'The gods are punishing us because we stopped listening to them. Tell me, my king. How do farmers protect their sheep from the wolves?'

King Vortigern frowned at her. 'They use dogs to chase the wolves away.'

'Exactly.' Brigid smiled. 'They use dogs.'

'But what does that have to do with anything?'

'To protect ourselves from the wolves that threaten us, we need to get dogs large enough to chase them away. Or larger wolves when the dogs are too frightened.'

'What are you saying?'

Brigid almost sighed at how blind the king was. 'You could use the Saxons to protect yourself and your kingdom. There will be peace again and your position as high king will be strengthened.'

King Vortigern shook his head. 'The other kings will never agree to that.'

Brigid grimaced with annoyance before she calmed herself and smiled at King Vortigern. 'But are you not the king of kings?'

King Vortigern frowned as he nodded at her.

'And does the king of kings need the permission of the other kings to do what he wants?'

King Vortigern's face hardened. 'You are right. I can employ them, like the Romans used to. Your grandfather was a Saxon warrior who fought for the Romans, was he not?'

Brigid nodded. 'He was.'

King Vortigern stood up from his seat and walked around the hall, rubbing his beard as he thought. 'Then we need to find out where these Saxons are.' He looked at Brigid who was sitting in his seat and watching him. 'Your brother speaks the Saxon tongue, does he not?'

Brigid nodded, not feeling the need to say anything.

'Good, I'll send him tomorrow to find these Saxons and to bring them here.'

Brigid smiled as her hand went to the beads she wore around her neck, a gift from the old woman who had trained her. With the Saxons' help, she would chase the Christian god from Britannia and the old gods of Britannia would rule again.

10

Octa watched as a group of Britons on horseback arrived from over the hills and onto the beach. There weren't many of them, but the Jutes still prepared for battle. For all they knew, there was a large army behind the small group of riders. Octa glanced at the clouds in the sky, which had darkened since the morning, and hoped that it would not rain. Octa did not like the rain. After the attack on their camp, Horsa had led a group of warriors to find the village that had attacked them. Octa was glad that he did not have to go with them. Instead, he had to help dig the graves for the few Jutes that had died during the attack. The task had been gruelling and by the end his muscled arms were numb, but Octa still preferred doing that than having to fight another battle. The Jutes were buried in their armour with their weapons around them so they could use them in the afterlife and Hengist had given each man a pouch filled with hack silver. The remaining warriors sang songs and Hengist had called out to Woden to lead the men safely to the afterlife.

During the entire funeral, Octa had thought of Uhtric. Octa still didn't know whether his body had been taken back to his father or if the Thuringians had taken it. He doubted he would ever know and, while Hengist prayed for his men, Octa prayed to Woden, asking the war god to watch over his dead cousin's spirit, wherever it was.

When Horsa returned the following day, Octa had expected to hear them talk of how they had slaughtered all the people in the village, but instead only those who had attacked them had been killed and the rest were left alive as Horsa decided they were not a threat any more. The elders of the village had even agreed to provide the Jutes with food so that they wouldn't attack them again. Octa had been surprised by this. He had believed that Hengist was the smart one, but he guessed that he had underestimated Horsa, something he reminded himself not to do again.

That had been many days ago and, since then, the villagers and the Jutes had found some sort of peace, even though they struggled to communicate with each other. Some of the men had even taken women for themselves, and it seemed that every day there were more Britons in the Jutes' camp. Octa had focused on his training with Eadric. The attack had made him realise that he had been naïve to think he could get the spear without having to fight for it. He remembered that the old man had told him that another god had taken Woden's spear from him and Octa was certain that this god would do what they could to stop Octa. The training had helped grow the muscles on his body, but they did not stop the nightmares from coming to him every night. A constant reminder of how he had let his cousin die. All Octa could do was pray that his fear would not control him the next time he needed to fight.

'The kings of Britannia?' Hengist asked, his voice bringing Octa back to the present. 'Thought there would be more of them.'

'How many kings do they have?' Octa asked.

Hengist shrugged. 'How many fleas does a dog have?'

'More than it needs,' Horsa said as he glared at the Britons.

'Aye, more than it needs,' Hengist agreed with a smile. 'Now come, let's get ready to meet these kings. Octa, join us.'

'Why?' Horsa and Octa almost asked at the same time.

Hengist looked at his brother. 'Because he saved my son and I trust him.'

Horsa glared at Octa and, when Hengist was out of earshot, he leaned closer and said, 'I don't know what spell you have over my brother, but I don't trust you. If you betray us, then I swear by Woden, I'll cut your balls off and shove them down your throat. And after that, I'll drown you in your own piss.'

Octa felt the blood leave his face and his hands trembled at the thought of dying that way. He nodded at Horsa, unable to speak, and then stayed where he was as Horsa walked back to his tent, while shouting orders at his men. The tide was out and the water was low enough for the men to just walk across, but Octa had been told that the mud could swallow a man whole if he stepped in the wrong place. That was another reason he would have preferred to stay in the camp. But Hengist wanted him nearby and Octa doubted he could refuse the warlord.

'He likes you,' Eadric said before he, too, returned to the camp. Octa could hear Eadric's laughter on the breeze and turned his attention back to the Britons as they stood on the beach. Even though there weren't many more than a handful of them, Octa could not stop the feeling of fear in the pit of his stomach. A short while later, Eadric returned from the camp. 'Here.' Eadric handed him his spear and shield. 'There shouldn't be a battle, but if there is, then stay close to me.'

Octa took the spear and shield from Eadric, too afraid to argue, and nodded as Hengist and Horsa returned, both men dressed in their finest war gear. They wore their chain-mail vests, which shone brightly despite the dull daylight, and had thick golden bands around their necks and wrists and golden rings on most of their fingers. Both brothers also had swords on their waists, but neither carried any spears or shields. That was what the group of warriors behind them were for. Octa glanced at Eadric and noticed that he, too, was wearing his chain-mail vest. Octa felt out of place with his old leather jerkin, but Hengist wanted him to go with them, so he knew he had no choice.

'Let's meet our new friends.' Hengist walked towards the waiting Britons, seemingly knowing where to walk so the beach wouldn't take them, while his brother and a group of their best warriors followed. Octa, gripping the shield and spear Eadric had given him, followed and did his best to hide his fear. He guessed he wasn't succeeding when Eadric glanced at him and shook his head.

'Stay calm, lad.'

Octa nodded and looked ahead at the Britons, trying to ignore the memories the shield was giving him as he studied them. Their armour was different from those worn by the Jutes and the Saxons. The Britons wore leather plate armour, which, unlike the chain-mail vest, was made of small metal plates sown onto a thick padded tunic. Octa had seen one in Witta's hall and knew the Romans liked to wear them as well. Their helmets had cheek plates to protect their faces and a neck guard, something the Saxon helmets did not have. Even the shields they carried looked like Roman shields. Unlike the Saxon shields, which were round and covered in leather and had a metal boss which the Saxon warriors gripped, the Britons' shields were more egg-shaped. Like the Jutes, the Britons carried spears and swords, although their swords seemed shorter than the ones the Jutes liked to use.

One of the Britons stepped forward and Octa noticed that, even on a horse, he was taller than the rest. The warrior stayed on his horse as he scrutinised Hengist and Horsa before he looked over the rest of the Jutes. After a short while, he said, 'Greetings. My name is Badulf, and I was sent by King Vortigern, the king of kings, to invite you to his hall.'

The Jutes all glanced at each other as the warrior spoke their tongue and Octa saw how Hengist smiled. 'Your name, it's Saxon.'

The warrior nodded. 'It was my grandfather's, who was a Saxon.'

'And that is why you speak our language?' Horsa asked, and the warrior nodded.

'My grandfather taught it to his daughter, who taught it to me.'

'And you fight for the British king?'

'I serve King Vortigern.'

The brothers glanced at each other and, after a while, Hengist said, 'Where is the hall of this King Vortigern?'

'King Vortigern's hall is in Cair Urnahc, which is about six days' ride from here.'

Hengist glanced at Horsa before he nodded. 'I need horses for twenty men, as well as for myself and my brother, and your word that the rest of my fleet will not be attacked. We come as friends, not as enemies.'

The warrior nodded and spoke in the British tongue to one warrior behind him, who glared at the Jutes before he said something in return.

Badulf scowled and then said, 'He wants to know why you attacked the people of Ruym Island if you come as friends.'

Horsa hawked and spat. 'They attacked us first. We only defended ourselves.'

'We were told you slaughtered the entire village.'

Horsa shook his head. 'Only those who attacked us. As Tiw is my witness, the village is untouched.' He looked at the warrior behind Badulf. 'Your man can go see for himself if he doesn't believe me.'

Badulf translated Horsa's words and Octa saw how the Briton glanced over their heads at the Jutes' camp before he responded.

Badulf nodded and turned to the Jutes. 'He swears that your men and ships will not be attacked as long as they remain on the island. And we will arrange horses for your men.' The warrior turned his horse and said, 'Be ready to leave tomorrow at sunrise.'

'We'll be ready,' Horsa said, and they watched as the Britons turned and rode away, apart from the one Badulf had spoken to. He stayed behind for a few heartbeats and glared at them before he too followed the others.

'The king of kings wants to see us,' Hengist mused as he stroked his beard.

'Could be interesting,' Horsa said, and Hengist nodded.

'Aye, brother. It could be.'

'Do we really trust them not to attack our camp?' Eadric asked, and the brothers scowled at him.

'No, I don't think we can,' Hengist said.

'So what do we do?'

'We take the ships to the other side of the island,' Horsa said. 'The camp will be easy enough to defend if there is treachery. The Britons can only attack during low tide and have to cross this beach to do so. Our archers and spears will cut them down before they can even get close.'

Hengist glanced at his brother and smiled. 'Then we shall do that.' He looked at another of the Jutes, another warrior who seemed to be close to the brothers, like Eadric. 'As soon as we leave, move the ships as Horsa suggested. If you can, build a fence around the camp and make sure the men stay vigilant and do not attack the locals. Remember, we are here as friends.' The warrior smiled as he nodded, and Octa sensed he knew something that Octa didn't as Hengist turned to Eadric. 'Select twenty men to come with us to this Cair Urnahc. Make sure they are well armed.'

Eadric nodded and turned to Octa. 'Octa, what are you waiting for?'

Octa realised they were all heading back to the camp. Hengist and Horsa were walking close together, the brothers locked in a deep conversation while the warriors distanced themselves so they couldn't overhear what was being said. He couldn't help but wonder what the brothers were up to, but then glanced over his shoulder as he remembered his own quest. He needed to find someone who could take him to the wall, or to tell him where it was. His only hope was to sneak away after Hengist and Horsa left to meet the British king. Octa was certain that many of the other warriors wouldn't notice if he was gone. But he would need to wait for the tide to come in because Octa doubted he would be able to find a path across this beach on his own. Swimming seemed like a safer option.

'Make sure your spear is sharp, because you are coming with us,' Eadric said as soon as the thought came to him. Octa dropped his head and wondered if whoever had taken the spear was making sure that he would never get to it.

The following day, Badulf, the Saxon Briton, arrived as the sun rose with enough horses for everyone. Hengist and Horsa, along with their twenty Jutes were already on the beach, something which seemed to surprise the Britons.

'Good day,' Hengist greeted them, the smile on his face showing that he enjoyed surprising the Britons.

Badulf greeted them, his face as hard as it was the day before, before he instructed his men to give the horses to the Jutes. A light-coloured mare ignored the warriors around her as she walked towards Octa and stood in front of him, which made the others laugh.

'Octa has a new wife,' one man joked as Octa stroked the mare's nose. He had always loved horses, as most Saxons did, and had been raised around them. But even he was surprised by the horse's actions.

Hengist clapped Octa on the shoulder. 'She does seem to like you.'

Octa could only nod as the other warriors laughed. He walked along the horse, inspecting her and, satisfied she was in good condition, he mounted her. The horse whinnied and Octa stroked her as he leaned forward and whispered in her ear. 'I don't know if you can understand me, but you take care of me and I'll take care of you. Deal?' The horse shook her head, but Octa sensed she agreed with him. 'Does she have a name?'

Badulf only looked at him and Octa frowned at the look on his face, but he understood the scowl on Horsa's face. Horsa had complained when Octa had joined him that morning, and that had only made Hengist laugh. Octa wondered then if Hengist wasn't keeping him around just to annoy his brother, but Eadric had told him to be ready, and so he was.

He stroked the horse's forehead. 'Horses should have names. I'll call you Warda.' The horse raised her head as if nodding. Octa was glad that she liked her name, which meant guardian –

Octa was certain he would need one. Around him, the others frowned at the way he was with the horse.

'You understand horses?' Badulf asked, and Octa nodded.

'They are important to our people. We learn to ride before we learn to fight.'

'You are a Saxon?'

'I...' Octa almost agreed, but then remembered what he had told Hengist. 'No, I'm an Angle. Similar to the Saxon, but different.'

Badulf grunted at him and Octa resisted the urge to look at Hengist, whose eyes he could feel on him.

They rode for six days, just as Badulf had said they would, along a road made of stone which Badulf told them was built by the Romans that had once ruled the island. Octa marvelled at them as the horses' hooves clattered on the stone blocks which were laid out so neatly. It seemed impossible for men to have built such things and he wondered if this road could lead him to the wall he needed to find. Warda surprised Octa during the six days, as she seemed to sense what he wanted as if they had been together for many winters, which made Octa feel like he had given her the right name.

The journey was tense as neither the Jutes nor the Britons trusted each other. They made camps at night, and the Britons always kept their distance from the Jutes, but the Jutes were happy about that because Octa sensed they weren't interested in mingling with the Britons either. Octa had been amazed by the fertile lands they travelled across. Fields, green with fresh crops, were everywhere, and they came across more farmsteads than he could count. It was very different from the lands he had come from, where most men had to rely on their skill with sword and spear rather than a pitchfork or a hoe. He sensed that Hengist and Horsa felt the same as they stared at the rolling hills and rich forests. But the fort of the British king took their breath away more than the countryside ever could.

Cair Urnahc was surrounded by large mound walls with a wooden palisade. A large ditch, too wide to jump over on horseback, surrounded the fort and the only way to cross the ditch was by the wooden bridge that spanned it. Badulf blew on a horn as they approached the gates, which were opened as they crossed the bridge, and once inside the walls, Octa felt like his eyes were going to fall out of his skull. Inside the earth mound walls were more homes than he could count. The smoke that came from the thatch roofs made it hard to breathe and Octa wasn't the only one who coughed because of it. But the Britons didn't stop there as they led the Jutes through the town to what could only be described as a fortress built for the gods. Octa couldn't help but gape at the stone walls that stood before him. And he was not the only one, as many of the Jutes did the same. Only the brothers and Eadric looked unimpressed. Horsa yawned as he gazed at the walls, while Hengist seemed more interested in the towers which stood on the corners. It was a fort inside a fort and Octa couldn't understand why they would do that.

'This used to be a Roman fort and when they left, King Vortigern's father made it his fort,' Badulf explained, as if he read Octa's mind. 'And over time, the town grew and the late king built the earth wall to protect his people from raids. It's probably the strongest fort in all of Britannia.'

'Probably?' Hengist asked.

Badulf shrugged. 'I haven't seen the entire island, so I can't say for certain.' He led the Jutes through the gates of the stone walls and Octa was surprised to see buildings made of stone.

'The Romans built this?' he asked, and Badulf nodded.

'There are many forts like this around Britannia. A reminder that we were once part of something greater.'

'A reminder that you were the slaves of someone more powerful,' Horsa said, and ignored the glare Badulf gave him. 'We Jutes never bend our knees to anyone. We never run from battle and we were never cowed by the Romans.' Octa's heart raced as images of Uhtric flashed in his mind.

'We also never faced the Romans,' Hengist said with a smile, but his brother only shrugged.

'Aye, but we would have beaten them back if we did.'

Octa kept his thoughts to himself as the Jutes laughed. The Saxons had never fought against the Romans, either. They had never needed to because the Saxon people and the Roman Empire had come to an agreement. The Saxons got to keep their independence as long as they provided warriors for the Roman Empire. That was how many Saxon warriors, even Octa's father, fought for the Romans across their vast empire.

Hengist looked at the large stone building Badulf led them to and, as they dismounted, Octa stared at the other stone buildings built around the enormous building in the centre. The paths seemed too straight and all the buildings seemed too tidy. There was too much order, and Octa doubted the Saxon gods would have approved. They preferred things to be natural, to have feeling and chaos. All that was missing as Octa watched the Britons going about their daily business, all of them doing their best not to stare at the twenty Jutish warriors. Octa couldn't help but wonder why these Britons got to live behind the stone walls while others were forced to live outside. He guessed it was because those behind the stone walls were more important than those outside of it. It was the same in the lands of his people. Those with status and wealth had better homes, slaves and more horses than they needed. They had the best farming lands and never went hungry. Those with no status had to struggle to grow food on land that refused to yield and often had to rely on the goodwill of others to survive the cold winters.

Octa glanced at the large stone building and noticed that, unlike the other buildings, it had a thatch roof. He wanted to ask about that, but then he saw a woman walk towards Badulf and the two of them embraced. At first he thought they were husband and wife, but then realised they looked very similar to each other. He frowned as Badulf said something to the woman and they both looked at him. Something about the woman's gaze unsettled him and Octa had to resist the urge to grip the spear pendant.

'Looks like it's not just the horses here that like you,' Eadric said as he clapped Octa on the back. 'Now come, let's go find somewhere where we can find some ale.'

'We're not going into the hall?'

Eadric shook his head. 'We don't need to know what Hengist and Horsa say to this king. All we need to do is fight who they tell us to.'

Octa nodded, disappointed that he couldn't go inside the hall. He wanted to see what this king looked like, but as he followed Eadric and the other Jutes, he felt the woman staring at him. For reasons he did not know, he had the urge to pray to Thunor and to ask for his protection.

11

'Greetings to our friends from across the seas. I am King Vortigern of the Cornovii and I am the king of kings of Britannia. Behind me stand the other kings of Britannia.' Brigid, her mind still troubled by what Badulf had told her, snuck back into the hall just as King Vortigern introduced himself and Ceretic, his official interpreter and a man who reminded her of the venomous adders her father used to kill, translated the words. She winced at his bad pronunciation and wondered why they had not allowed her brother to do it. But Ceretic was a man who was too proud for his own good and he would never let a mere warrior interpret for the king on occasions like this. She turned her attention to the Saxon warriors, although her brother had told her they called themselves Jutes. Brigid didn't know what that meant, but guessed they were a different tribe to the Saxons.

One of the Saxons, or Jutes as they called themselves, stepped forward and said, 'I am Hengist and this is my brother, Horsa, and behind me are brave warriors from Jutland. We have travelled far to offer our swords and spears to the great king of kings of Britannia.' Brigid knew that King Vortigern would be pleased by being called a great king. Like Ceretic, he was too proud, and she was certain that would be his downfall one day. All she had to do was make sure she got what she wanted before that. Brigid looked at the men from across the sea again, who stood taller than the kings and the warriors of Britannia. Their faces were hard and spoke of men used to violence, and even under the chain-mail vests they wore she could see their warrior builds. They looked like she had imagined her grandfather had in his youth. Even the handful of warriors that stood behind the two brothers looked like they could kill everyone in this hall.

Brigid frowned when she didn't see the young warrior Badulf had pointed out, the one chosen by one of the horses. Not a white horse, like in her dreams, but a light-coloured one. Brigid had told Badulf about her dream before and was surprised when he had told her what he had seen. She had been even more surprised when Badulf had told her that the young warrior gave the horse a name. Horses were intelligent animals and could sense a person's heart. That was one of the reasons the gods often used them as messengers. But Brigid could only wonder what part the young warrior had to play. All she knew was that she and her brother had to be careful. Her dreams had not yet told her what Brigantia's plan was, and even though she didn't know if the young warrior needed to be feared, she had still warned Badulf to be wary of him.

King Gwyrangon of the Cantiaci stepped forward, his face red as he shook a fist at the Jutes. 'They killed my people. They should be made to pay for that!'

The Jutes almost seemed bored as King Vortigern scowled at the king of the Cantiaci, but Brigid noticed how the sharp eyes of the one who called himself Hengist scrutinised the kings as they spoke. 'Your people attacked them and they defended themselves. Your man said so himself, did he not?'

King Gwyrangon nodded, but he did not give up on his argument. 'We still don't need their help. The Roman Empire will send her armies to help us. Just like she did in the past.' Even Brigid shook her head at that. The Romans had abandoned them even before she was born.

King Vortigern sighed. 'The Romans are too busy fighting those who invade their lands. We've all heard the stories that come from the continent.' King Vortigern walked around his hall, and Brigid almost admired him as he stood tall in front of the other kings. 'My brothers. The Almighty knows it is hard for me to say this, but it is time we accept that the Roman Empire has forgotten about us.' A few of the kings jeered at this, which made the Saxons frown, and King Vortigern shake his head. 'It is time we look to ourselves to defend our lands from our enemies to the north.'

'And how do you suggest we do that?' the king of the Corieltauvi asked as he glared at the Saxons. 'By employing these barbarians?' Along with the Brigantes in the north, the Corieltauvi despised King Vortigern the most and would often object to anything he said.

King Vortigern shrugged and, again, Brigid was impressed by how calm he seemed. 'Why not? The Romans employed them as foederati. There are still Saxon foederati all over Britannia, so why should we not do the same? We can pay them to protect our lands from the Picts and also to train our warriors so we can rebuild our armies. And that way, we don't need to rely on the Saxons for longer than we need to.'

Brigid had to admit that King Vortigern had thought this

through better than she had anticipated after she had planted the idea in his head. Perhaps she had underestimated the old king. Her eyes went back to Hengist and again she saw how he scrutinised those in the room. The shiver that ran down her spine told Brigid that he was a dangerous man and that she needed to watch him closely.

Without waiting for a response from the other kings, King Vortigern turned to the Saxons. 'We do not deny that we live in difficult times. My fellow kings still have faith that the Lord and the Romans will come to our aid. But out of curiosity, what do you want in return for your services?'

'We do not ask for much. Food and clothing for my men. Perhaps even a small patch of land that we might call our own.'

The kings of Britannia cried out when Hengist's words were translated, but then King Vortigern raised his hand and silenced them. 'And what will we get in return for this?'

Hengist looked around the hall and some of the kings seemed to cower under his hard gaze. 'I swear by our gods that your enemies will flee when they hear our battle horns and our battle cries. They will cower under the rocks they came from when they see the sharp blades of our spears and swords. By Woden and Tiw, we will free your lands from those who wish you harm, and we will bring peace and prosperity back to the island of Britannia.'

King Vortigern stroked his beard as he pretended to think about it, but Brigid knew he had already made his mind up. 'Your words intrigue me. If you swear in the name of our Lord that you will not attack our people, then I believe we can accept your offer.' Some of the other kings, and King Vortigern's son, Vortimer, shook their heads at this and Brigid could only pray that this didn't rip the island apart.

Hengist smiled at the man that looked like he was his

brother before he turned to King Vortigern. 'I swear on your god, as well as Tiw, our god of war and honour, that we will not attack your people unless they attack us first.'

King Vortigern beamed while the other kings looked less pleased. 'The Lord knows I am grateful to hear that. Now come, we should celebrate the arrival of our friends from across the seas.'

* * *

'They call it a church,' Eadric said when they stopped in front of a small building that had a strange-looking cross on its high roof. 'It's where the Christians worship their god.'

Octa frowned. He had heard of the Christians before and their strange ways. 'Why do they need a building to worship their god?'

Eadric shrugged. 'We have shrines to our gods.'

'Aye, but our shrines are in the open. In forest clearings or in fields. Why do they need to build homes for their god?'

'Perhaps he stays here when he visits?' one of the other warriors suggested. They had been in Vortigern's fort for a few days, and the Jutes had been allowed to walk around while Hengist and Horsa negotiated with King Vortigern. King Vortigern had provided one of his halls for the Jutes to stay in, which was larger than Witta's mead hall, and twenty Jutes fit in there comfortably, although they all had to sleep on the floor.

The townspeople kept their distance from the Jutes, who towered above them, although the children seemed to be braver than the adults as a group of them kept following Octa and the others wherever they went. One warrior had pulled a face at them, which had sent the children fleeing with piercing screams, but they had soon returned.

'You really think he comes to visit?' Eadric asked the warrior, who shrugged.

'Our gods do. We've all heard the stories of Woden wandering the lands.'

Eadric waved a hand at the man. 'Those are just stories.'

'Don't know,' the warrior said as he scratched his beard.

'Don't know? How many times has Woden come to you? I know I've never met him.'

Octa thought about the old man that had told him about the spear as Eadric and the other warrior argued and wondered if that could have been Woden. He had known who Octa was and what he had done, but then Octa dismissed the idea. He doubted that the man would have been Woden, because if he had been, then he would have gone to Hengist and Horsa and asked them to get his spear back.

They carried on walking, the Jutes still arguing with each other while Octa's mind went to the spear. He needed to find it and soon, but he still did not know how. He hoped to ask the locals about this wall, but since they had arrived, Eadric had never left his side.

'How long do we have to stay in this place for?' one of the warriors asked.

'Until Hengist and Horsa make a deal with King Vortigern,' Eadric responded. 'And don't ask me when that is because I don't know.'

'What does King Vortigern want us to do?' Octa asked, and noticed how Eadric raised an eyebrow at him saying 'us'.

'From what I have heard, tribes from the north have been attacking them ever since the Romans left and the Britons can't fight them off. King Vortigern wants us to defend his kingdom and those of the other kings if needed.'

'And what do we get for doing that?'

'That is what Hengist and Horsa are working on,' Eadric said, and then stopped and looked around as if to make sure that no one was listening. 'But I wouldn't be concerned about that. It feels to me that the brothers are up to something.'

'Like what?' Octa asked before he could stop himself.

Eadric frowned at him. 'I don't know.' He turned and walked on as the others glanced at Octa. He sensed that they still didn't trust him, but then he forgot about that as he spotted Badulf standing by himself near the market. Unlike the last time Octa had seen him, Badulf wasn't wearing his armour. Octa glanced at the Jutes who weren't paying any attention to him as they were still arguing amongst each other and he decided it was his best chance to find out about the Roman wall.

Octa glanced over his shoulder as he made his way to the Briton to make sure the others hadn't noticed what he was doing. But then Octa froze as the woman Badulf had spoken to before appeared. Octa stared at her, until he realised Badulf was frowning at him.

'The Saxon who is good with horses,' Badulf said with no warmth in his voice, and Octa wanted to correct him, but decided it didn't matter as he continued to stare at the woman. She looked a few winters older than him and, like Badulf, was a bit taller than the other Britons. But it was her eyes that caught his attention. Something about them spoke of a wisdom far greater than he could understand, and it made his hands tremble. The woman said something to Badulf, who laughed before he said to Octa, 'She doesn't think that you can speak.'

Octa cleared his throat and tried again. 'My name is Octa.'

'Greetings, Octa. This is my sister, Brigid.'

Brigid smiled at Octa, who smiled back as he tried to find his composure. Octa then turned his attention back to Badulf. 'I have been told that there is a great wall built by the Romans a long time ago.'

Badulf frowned for a moment and Octa worried that the woman in the tavern had lied to him, but Brigid responded in Saxon.

'You must be talking about the wall built by Emperor Hadrian.'

'Ah yes, I forgot about that wall,' Badulf said.

Octa gaped at Brigid, surprised that she too spoke his language, even though he should have guessed she could if she was Badulf's sister. And knowing that she could understand what he was saying made it harder for him to speak.

After standing in silence for a few heartbeats, Badulf asked, 'What do you want to know about this wall?'

Octa shook his head to clear his mind. 'Forgive me. Where is this wall? I'd like to see it.'

Badulf frowned. 'This wall is far to the north. In the lands of the Brigantes. The Emperor Hadrian had it built to defend the Roman lands against the Picts.'

'The same people that threaten us yet again,' Brigid added, and Badulf nodded, as she gave Octa a glance he did not understand.

'Yes, they hate us because we sided with the Roman Empire.'

Octa nodded, but he wasn't really listening. His heart raced at the fact that the wall was real, but he was disappointed that it was far away. He should have guessed, though, that this wouldn't be easy. He scratched his head and looked north. 'How long will it take to get to the wall?' He wanted to ask if there was a shrine to a British god, but he didn't want to push his luck.

Badulf was about to answer, but then he looked at something behind Octa. Octa turned and saw Eadric standing there, his face red as he glared at Octa.

'What is this about a wall to the north?' he asked, and Octa fought to keep his legs steady under him.

'Forgive us, but we must be going,' Badulf said, and pulled his sister by her arm. Before they disappeared into the crowd, she glanced at Octa over his shoulder and, for a moment, he forgot where he was.

'Why are you so interested in a wall?' Eadric asked when Octa did not respond to his first question.

Octa cleared his throat as he tried to think of an excuse. 'No reason. I was told about a great wall built by the Romans and hoped to see it, that's all.'

Eadric stared at him for a long moment, his face unreadable, before he nodded. 'Well, you could have asked me about it. I know of this wall, but I doubt you'll see it. It's in the north and from what I've just heard, we won't be going there.'

'What do you mean?' Octa frowned.

'You'll have to wait like everyone to find out. Hengist wants us all to go to the hall we're staying in.'

'Why?' Octa asked, and regretted it as Eadric's face turned red again.

'If you're not too busy, why don't you join us so you can find out?'

Octa nodded and resisted the urge to glance over his shoulder to see if he could spot Badulf and his sister. But he noticed Eadric look in that direction as they walked back to the hall.

The other warriors were already there by the time Octa and Eadric reached the hall and they had to push their way through to get to the front, where Hengist and Horsa were talking to each other. Both men had smiles on their faces, which made Octa guess they had got what they wanted from King Vortigern.

Hengist looked up and raised his eyebrow as if he had just

noticed the warriors in the hall. His smile grew larger, and he took a step forward before clearing his throat.

'Our loyal men. Warriors of many battles and slayers of many. Feeders of ravens and wolves. You have followed us to this island in hopes of wealth and glory. Some of you have left family behind, knowing that you may never see them again. But you still followed us, trusting that fate and the gods would be on our side.'

The warriors were silent as Hengist spoke. Octa found it unsettling as he could hear the men behind him breathe between Hengist's words and somewhere he thought he could hear a man scratch his beard. But they were all rapt by Hengist's words and even Octa had to admit that he was curious about what the warlord had to say.

'My brother and I have spent many days talking to King Vortigern. A man who believes that he is smarter than us and that he has the upper hand. For a moment, we will let him think that, but King Vortigern has agreed to our first demand. Food and clothing will be provided for you all and we know it is not gold or silver—'

'Or land,' Horsa interrupted, and Hengist nodded.

'Or land, but we get to stay on the island they call Ruym which we will return to soon and rejoin the rest of our men. But we need to be patient. Just like Woden hanged himself on the great tree for many days and nights, believing that he would be rewarded for his sacrifice, so must we be patient and believe that we will get our rewards.'

'So we go back to the island and wait?' one warrior asked, and Hengist laughed.

'Wait? Who said anything about waiting?' Hengist stared at his men. 'We do what we do best and we show King Vortigern and the other kings of this island why they need us. We will

12

They did not have to wait long to fight. A few days after Hengist's speech to the Jutes, just before they were due to depart for the island where the rest of the Jutes were, news reached them that a small force of Picts had marched south and were raiding King Vortigern's kingdom. Hengist and Horsa decided that the twenty warriors they had with them would be enough to deal with the Picts, but King Vortigern insisted on sending six of his warriors as well, led by Badulf. The warriors cheered when they heard this news and the next day they left King Vortigern's fort and marched north-east to meet the Picts.

Octa's hand trembled as he stared at the campfire, knowing that the following day, he would have to fight another battle. Just the thought of it made his stomach clench, but he was forced to put a brave face on as he sat with the brothers and Eadric, as well as Badulf, who had been invited to share a meal with them. Badulf had been useful to the Jutes as they hunted the Picts, passing by many burning farmsteads with survivors telling them of the slaughter. At every farmstead, the Briton would ask for any news of the raiders and soon they were on the tracks of the fight their enemies and drive them back to the caves they come from. And with each victory and each raid we repel, the more King Vortigern will be in our debt.' He paused again and Octa was certain that all the men were holding their breath as they listened to their leader. Even Eadric's eyes were wide as he paid attention to Hengist. 'And when the time is right, we demand that the debt be repaid.'

Picts who were rampaging their way through King Vortigern's homelands, steadily moving south as they went.

As the wood the flames were feasting on cracked and popped, Horsa looked up, his gaze on Octa for a few uncomfortable heartbeats, before he turned his attention to the Briton. 'Tell me, Badulf. These lands, they belong to King Vortigern?'

Badulf looked up from his meal, his eyebrows raised for a moment before he nodded. 'That is correct.'

'But he is also the king of all of Britannia?'

Badulf frowned for a while. 'Not quite. He is the king of kings, but each king still rules their kingdom. King Vortigern has no say on how they should do that, but when there is a threat to our island, the other kings send their armies to join his and he leads them against our enemies.' To Octa, this sounded like what they had back in the lands of the Saxons, but he kept those thoughts to himself as he remembered Uhtric again. But then that memory was replaced by one of his mother telling him to make a name for himself. Octa sent a silent prayer to the gods as he hoped this coming battle would be the start of that.

'Who rules his kingdom while he does this?' Hengist asked.

'His sons. The oldest, Vortimer, stays with him in Cair Urnahc, but his other sons rule different parts of his kingdom while he is away.'

Octa wondered about the way he said the name of King Vortigern's son, but then decided it had nothing to do with him as he stared at the flames again.

'He must trust his sons,' Eadric said, and Badulf frowned at him.

'They are loyal to their father.'

Hengist glanced at Eadric, and then he asked, 'Whose lands are to the north of here?'

Badulf scratched his bearded cheek. 'The Brigantes.'

'And the Picts would have to march through their lands to get to King Vortigern's kingdom?'

Badulf raised an eyebrow and then nodded. 'They do.' Octa wasn't the only one staring at Hengist as he wondered what the man was getting at. But Badulf understood as he said, 'King Vortigern is not a popular high king and there are many who are not as loyal as they should be.'

'I suppose there are many who believe that they should be high king themselves?' Hengist asked.

Badulf surprised them all by shaking his head. 'Many don't want to be high king. It might bring a lot of power, but many don't have the stomach for it. Only King Vortigern is strong enough to hold the position.'

'Then why do they allow the Picts to march through their lands to attack King Vortigern's lands?' Horsa asked.

Badulf stared at the flames as they danced in the breeze for a while before he responded. 'There are those who don't believe that he should be high king. They believe another should hold the position and that King Vortigern stole it from him. They want to punish King Vortigern, so they let the Picts cross their lands to attack the lands of the Cornovii.'

'Who is this other king?' Octa asked, surprising everyone around the fire. But he couldn't help it. The situation Badulf was describing reminded him a lot of the situation back home. Few had wanted Witta to be the chief warlord, but none of them would go against him. Tiw told them to be honourable, and that's what the Saxons were.

'A man called Ambrosius.'

'Sounds like a Roman name,' Hengist said before he spat into the fire. The flame sizzled, but stayed strong.

'Because it is. His father was a Roman general, and many

believed that if he was high king, then the Romans would have responded to the request for help.'

'The Romans are too busy fighting their own wars to help anyone else right now,' Horsa said, and Hengist nodded.

'Where is this Ambrosius now?' Hengist asked, and Octa caught the glance he gave to his brother in the flickering light of the flames. Did he see this other king as a threat? Octa wondered.

Badulf shrugged. 'Somewhere in the west.'

Hengist nodded and then smiled. 'Well, if what you say is true, then it shows that King Vortigern is the right person to be high king. He saw an opportunity and took it. In our lands, only the strongest survive. The weak' – he glanced at Octa, who frowned as he wondered if there was any meaning in that – 'die.'

'That is what I believe, which is why I follow King Vortigern.'

'And I'm sure you do him proud,' Horsa said before he stood up. 'Now we must sleep. If Woden is with us, then tomorrow we meet these Picts and kill the bastards. Every single one of them.'

'Aye, perhaps we will even visit these other kings and remind them of who their high king is,' Hengist added as he, too, stood up. Eadric glanced at Octa before he got up and went to his tent.

Octa waited until they were all out of earshot before he moved closer to Badulf. 'This wall you told me about. How far is it from here?'

Badulf frowned at him. 'Emperor Hadrian's wall? Many days walk to the north. And not one that I suggest you do on your own. A Jute on his own will not live long in the north of our island.'

'I'm not a Jute,' Octa said faster than he should have, and cursed himself. 'Do you know of a shrine to a god of your people near this wall?'

Again Badulf frowned and hesitated before he responded, 'This I do not know. I was raised a Christian and was told nothing of the old gods of our people.' He got to his feet and walked away before Octa could ask him anything else and again Octa cursed himself. He had pushed the Briton too hard, but he had no choice.

Octa had hoped to sneak off during the night when the men slept and make his way to the wall. Perhaps he still could. All he had to do was reach it and then he could travel along it until he found this shrine. But then he felt the fingers of his fear grip his spine as he thought about what Badulf had said. Octa might not have been a Jute, but he was still an outsider, which meant the journey would be very dangerous. For a moment he wished that the old man had never told him about the spear, but what had passed had passed and there was nothing he could do now but move forward. That was what Witta had told them once. And move forward was what Octa was going to do. He would wait until everyone was asleep and then he would sneak away and find Woden's spear.

Octa was kicked awake the following morning and when he opened his eyes and saw the morning sun, he cursed.

'What is your problem?' Eadric, who had kicked him awake, asked.

'I slept on a stone,' Octa lied, and struggled to hide his irritation at himself for falling asleep and missing his chance to slip away.

Eadric stared at him for a few heartbeats before he grunted. 'Well, forget about that. We leave soon, so get ready. By Woden's grace, we meet these Picts today and see why the Britons are so scared of them.'

Octa nodded, but he did not feel the older warrior's excitement. He hid his trembling hands from Eadric as he looked around him to see the twenty warriors of Hengist and Horsa, as well as the six British warriors walking around the camp. A few already had their armour on, but many were still struggling into their leather jerkins, which they wore over thick woollen tunics. Those with swords tied the sword belts around their waists and made sure the swords were secure while others checked their spears and shields. The scene reminded Octa of the morning before the battle against the Thuringians, and his stomach clenched at the memory of Uhtric smiling at him. They were supposed to make their names that day. But Uhtric was dead because of him and every day Octa prayed that the spear of Woden would redeem him from his actions. As Octa watched the warriors prepare, he wondered if he could slip away during the confusion of the battle. Surely no one would be paying any attention to him while they were fighting the Picts and Octa doubted he would be in the front of the battle. More likely, they would put him at the back so that he was out of the way. All he had to do was survive long enough for the right moment.

'There he is. The man who saved my son. Octa the Brave,' Hengist said as he approached. He already wore his chain-mail vest, so Octa frowned at the helmet he had in his hands. 'The man who saved my son will not fight by my side without a helmet to protect his head.'

'B... by your side?' Octa asked, and knew the gods were laughing at him. It almost felt like someone didn't want him to find Gungnir. Perhaps whoever had taken Woden's spear.

'Aye. Today you will show the others the bravery that I saw the day you saved my son and you will earn your place as one of my warriors.'

Octa struggled to stop his hands from trembling as he took the helmet from Hengist, who smiled and clapped him on the shoulder. 'Thank you,' Octa said, and cursed himself again for falling asleep as he stared at the helmet. It was a simple helmet with a low crest and cheek plates, nothing like the helmet his father or Witta had, with the elaborate faceplates and gold bands that rimmed the helmet and were decorated with images of the gods.

Eadric gripped his shoulder and stared at him. 'Stay close to me and remember what I told you. Keep your shield up and when you see your chance, take it. You either kill them or they kill you. And if anything happens to Hengist, then I'll kill you.' Satisfied that Octa understood his words, Eadric nodded and walked away as Octa struggled to breathe.

He would take his chance if he got it: not to kill a Pict, but to run. To run far from here and forget about Woden's spear and his redemption.

A horn startled Octa from his thoughts and he saw that many of the warriors were already on the horses that King Vortigern had given them. Octa hesitated for a heartbeat, but then went to his horse and mounted it with practised ease. He saw how Horsa raised an eyebrow at him and wondered why, when Eadric said, 'Your spear, Octa. How are you going to fight without it?'

'Octa the Brave doesn't need a spear. He will fight the Picts with his bare hands!' Hengist said, and the warriors laughed as Octa's cheeks burnt. He nodded as one warrior handed him his spear and prayed that Thunor would send a lightning bolt to end his life.

Octa gripped the spear tightly as they marched towards the last known location of the Picts. Horsa had sent scouts ahead to find them and Octa spent the entire morning praying that the scout would not find them and that they would continue to march north. That way, at least he would be closer to the wall and would have another night to sneak away. But his hopes were dashed when one of the scouts came racing towards them. He pulled his horse to a stop in front of Hengist and Horsa, and although Octa could not hear his words, he knew what the man was saying.

'We found the Picts.' The scout pointed in the direction he had just come from, and from the smiles on the faces of Hengist and Horsa, Octa guessed they weren't far away.

'Looks like we'll be fighting soon,' Eadric said from beside Octa, whose stomach clenched at the prospect.

'At last,' one of the other warriors said. 'Woden knows I'm tired of doing nothing.' The other warriors grunted their agreements, and Octa sensed Eadric's eyes on him.

'I bet Octa the Brave can't wait to get stuck into the enemy.'

Octa's heart raced as he felt the other warriors staring at him. 'Aye,' was all he said, and then he pretended to look at something in the distance just to avoid the gazes of those around him.

Hengist turned his horse around. 'The bastard Picts are just over that hill! They have set up camp. The bastards don't expect anyone to attack them!'

'We'll show them the error of their ways!' Horsa said, and the men cheered. They did not seem to care that the Picts might hear them as Hengist spurred his horse towards the hill and the others followed. Horsa turned to Badulf. 'Your men will stand at the rear. They can join in once the killing starts.' Badulf nodded and told the Britons what Horsa had said. Octa saw a few pale faces amongst the Britons and, for a moment, he was tempted to turn Warda around and run the other way, but he knew he wouldn't get far. He glanced at Badulf and frowned at the way the Briton was staring at him before he followed the others.

By the time Octa reached the hill, Hengist and Horsa had already dismounted their horses and were staring at the Picts, who were jumping to their feet, surprised by the sudden arrival of an army. The Picts grabbed their weapons and shields as one warrior stood in the centre of their camp and barked orders.

Hengist stepped forward, spear and shield in his hands, and spread his arms out wide. 'I am Hengist, son of Wihtgils! My brother and I have come to send you to the hall of the slain. By Tiw and Woden, I swear that your days of raiding these lands have come to an end!'

Badulf translated his words and when he was done, one of the Picts stepped forward and shouted something back. Badulf glanced at Hengist and seemed reluctant to repeat what the Picts had said.

'What did he say?' Horsa asked.

'He said you should go fuck your mother.'

Badulf averted his gaze from them as if he expected the Jutes to lash out, but even to Octa's surprise, Hengist said, 'That's rude of him.' He looked at his brother with a grin on his face. 'Shall we go teach them some manners?'

Horsa smiled back, a wolf grin that meant only one thing. 'I thought you'd never ask.' He glanced around him and saw that all the Jutes were ready. Even Octa had got off his horse and stood just behind Eadric, hoping to hide from the battle behind the older warrior. Horsa's eyes lingered on him for a few heart-beats before he took the horn that was attached to his belt and, after taking a deep breath, he blew into it.

13

The Jutes formed a loose shield wall. They stood side by side in two rows, their shields in front of them, but not overlapping, and their spears ready. Fifteen Jutes stood in the first row, while the rest with Octa and the Britons stood in the second row, their spears held over their heads, ready to stab at the Picts as they fought those in the first row.

Hengist and Horsa stood in the centre of the line, both brothers looking like Tiw as their armour glinted in the sunlight. Their faces were covered by the faceplates of their helmets, as were the warriors that stood around them. Eadric was there as well, with Octa standing behind him and, as he glanced around the Jutes, all of them grinning in anticipation of the battle, he felt like his bowels might empty. Octa fought hard to stop the shield from trembling in his hands, but he could not. All he saw in his head was the large Thuringian that killed Uhtric. His hair was soaked with sweat and not just because of the helmet and the heat. Octa was terrified. His head spun and no matter how many deep breaths he took, it felt like he might pass out at any moment.

The Picts had rushed from their camp and formed a line of their own. Their leader, a large man wearing a chain-mail vest, waved his spear in the air as he shouted something into the sky.

'He's calling to his gods. He's telling them how they will slaughter you and take your heads back to their village to be placed on their altar,' Badulf said.

'Thought they were Christian,' Horsa said, and Octa saw him tilt his head.

He couldn't see Badulf but sensed him shrug. 'The Romans never made it to their lands, so they kept their old gods.'

Hengist laughed. 'Well, Woden knows they'll need their gods because they've never fought the Jutes.' He lifted his spear into the air and roared, 'For Tiw! For Woden!'

The Jutes echoed his calls, but Octa could not open his mouth to do the same, as he feared he might vomit. His heart lurched when the Jutes charged and he was forced to go with them. He glanced over his shoulder at the horses, which were guarded by a couple of Britons, and wondered if he could reach them without being spotted by the Jutes.

The Picts gave out their own war cry and charged up the hill. They outnumbered the Jutes and the Britons, but that did not seem to bother the men from the continent as they called out to the gods. Octa even heard cries of joy and knew he could never be like these men. He wanted to glance over his shoulder at the horses again, but then the Jutes and the Picts crashed into each other. The noise was deafening and Octa almost pissed himself as Eadric was pushed back into him. But the older warrior roared and punched out with his shield, forcing the Pict back. The Jute beside him stabbed the Pict through the neck with his spear, and then left the weapon there as he pulled out his hand axe and killed another Pict.

All Octa wanted to do was hide behind his shield as the

battle raged in front of him. He cried out when a spear streaked past Eadric and struck his shield. His legs felt weak and Octa had to fight the urge to drop to his knees. He looked up and saw Hengist skewer a Pict with his spear, before he punched the dying man away with his shield and pulled the spear out. Horsa swung his spear as if it was a large sword and its tip sliced a Pict's face open. The man dropped to the ground, and another Jute rushed forward and stabbed him with his spear. But then that Jute was killed by the Pictish leader, who punched him in the side of his head and stabbed him with his spear.

Men screamed and called out to the gods as blood sprayed through the air and men fought for their lives. The Picts cried out in their own language and all Octa wanted to do was run. When he could no longer control his fear, he turned and was about to run when somebody grabbed him by his leather jerkin and threw him towards the Picts. Octa's heart felt like it stopped beating when he suddenly found himself amongst the enemy, all of them grinning at him, before one of them rushed forward and stabbed at Octa with the long knife in his hand. Somehow, Octa deflected the blade with his shield before a spear pierced the man's neck. But Octa had no time to watch him die or avoid the blood that squirted out of his neck as the spear was pulled out. A shriek behind him made him turn around, and the movement meant the spear that was aimed at his back missed its mark, but he still felt it cut along his leather jerkin. Octa punched out with his shield, just like he had seen Horsa do, and almost dropped it when it struck the man's skull. Even over the sounds of battle, he heard the man's skull crack, but before he could think about the bile which rose from his stomach, someone pushed him to the ground.

Octa cried out and prayed to Thunor to protect him as he landed on his back and looked up to see the grinning face of a fat Pict with a large club in his hands. Again, he saw the large Thuringian in his mind, and worse still, he saw Uhtric's face moments before he died. The disappointment in his eyes cut Octa to his core because he could have saved him. All he had to do was stab with his spear. *All he had to do was stab with his spear.* Octa closed his eyes and did exactly that. Not because he wanted to live. But because he knew that if he died, then he would go to the afterlife where Uhtric was waiting for him. And Octa was not ready to face his cousin yet. Not until he had redeemed himself. He felt the spear strike the fat Pict, felt the resistance as if something was stopping the point of the spear and then that something gave way and the spear moved freely. The Pict grunted and somehow Octa heard that through all the noise of the battle being fought around him. Octa opened his eyes and saw the bulging eyes of the fat Pict, his club still held above his head. Both of them looked down at the spear which had entered the Pict under his ribs and had torn through his lungs. The fat Pict spat out a mouthful of blood before he collapsed, almost falling on top of Octa.

Octa forgot about the battle, his body frozen, as he stared at the dead Pict. The first man he had ever killed. Empty eyes stared back at him, even as the look of shock still sat on the Pict's face. Then his eyes went to where his spear had pierced the man's body and all he could do was turn around and empty his guts. He didn't know how long he lay there for. He was certain he never heard the horn, which called the battle to a halt, or even noticed the remaining Picts fleeing the battleground. Octa only knew it was over and that he still lived when one warrior grabbed his shoulder.

'It's Octa. He still lives.'

'By Woden! Are you sure?' Eadric asked.

'Well, he is breathing and is covered in his own vomit, so I'm sure.' The warrior pulled Octa to his feet, something he wished the man hadn't done when he bent over and vomited again.

Octa wiped his mouth with the back of his hand and straightened up to see Hengist and Horsa facing him. Both men were covered in blood and had their swords in their hands. Their faces were clean, apart from the rings of dirt around their eyes, but what struck Octa the most was the looks on their faces. They weren't smiling, as he thought they would be after their victory. Instead, they seemed disappointed.

Octa frowned at them. 'What?'

'It would have been better if you died,' Hengist said before he stepped forward and struck Octa on the side of his head with the flat of his sword. Before Octa understood what was happening, his world went black, and he dropped to the ground.

When Octa woke again, he frowned at the stars in the sky and the sounds of men celebrating. He wanted to rub his head, which was aching from where Hengist had struck him, and for a moment he couldn't understand why he couldn't move his hand. But then he realised his hands had been tied behind his back.

'Finally, you are awake, you dumb bastard,' Eadric hissed at him. Octa turned his head and was shocked to see the older warrior sitting near him, and sharpening a knife in his hands.

'What is going on?' Octa asked.

'What is going on?' Eadric barked a laugh as Octa looked around him. He saw the camp the Jutes had made and the large fire in the middle of the ring of tents. In the light of the flames, he saw the silhouettes of the Jutes as they drank and danced. He also saw a group of men approaching them and even if he couldn't see their faces, he knew who they were. 'I know the truth about you, Octa. I know what you really are,' Eadric said. His eyes, filled with anger, bore into Octa. 'I didn't believe it at first because I liked you. Hengist liked you. But then...' Eadric looked away as if he could not say the words.

'What?' Octa frowned, certain he knew what Eadric was going to say, but before Eadric could respond, Horsa stopped in front of Octa and slapped him across the face. Sparks flew in Octa's vision and he kept his eyes closed for a moment until the blinding pain went away.

'What were you planning?' Horsa asked him when he opened his eyes. Octa struggled to make sense of the hatred he saw in Horsa's eyes.

'What do you mean?'

Horsa slapped him again, and again, Octa had to keep his eyes closed until the pain lessened. 'You and the Briton. I saw you whispering in his ear. What are you planning?'

Hengist stepped forward and put a hand on Horsa's shoulder before Octa could respond. He leaned down and stared at Octa for a while, but Octa saw nothing in his face to give him an idea of what was going on.

'Octa the Brave. Octa the Angle,' Hengist said. 'Octa the Saxon.' Octa's eyes widened, which only made Hengist smile. 'I've met enough Angles to know that you are not one. Just like I know a Saxon when I see one. At first, I didn't mind that you lied to me. I figured you had your reasons and because you saved my son's life, I left it at that. I even let you join our force. But now Eadric tells me he keeps seeing you talking to the Briton. Whispering things in his ears. Horsa believes you mean to kill us, or betray us.'

'I told you I don't like him. You can see it in his eyes. He's a coward.' Horsa glared at Octa, who thought the warlord was going to strike him again.

Hengist stayed silent as he stared at Octa, who was trying to make sense of things. 'Bring Badulf. Let's ask the man himself.'

Eadric nodded as he stood up and walked towards the Britons, who were sitting by their own fire.

When they returned, Horsa pulled the seax knife from his belt and grabbed Badulf, whose eyes widened in shock as Horsa pressed the knife against his throat. Before the Britons could react, the Jutes jumped to their feet and surrounded them, but Badulf raised his hand to tell them not to do anything as he glared at Horsa.

'What are you and the Saxon planning?'

Badulf's eyebrows creased as he glanced at Octa. 'We're not planning anything.'

'I don't believe you,' Horsa said, adding more pressure to the knife against Badulf's throat. 'Why does he keep talking to you when he thinks no one is looking?'

'I already told you. We are not planning anything. He keeps asking me about Hadrian's wall!' Badulf said, his face pleading for them to believe him.

'Is this true?' Hengist asked Octa.

Octa glanced at Badulf and for a moment he thought about lying, but then he saw no reason to do that. He was going to die anyway, so he might as well tell them the truth. 'It is. I'm not conspiring against you or Horsa. I only wanted to know about a wall built by the Romans.'

'Why?' Horsa asked as he leaned over Hengist.

Octa hesitated, not sure if he wanted to tell them that part.

'If you tell us why you really wanted to come to Britannia, then I'll let you live,' Hengist said. 'You saved my son, so I owe you that much. But if you lie to us, then I won't stop my brother from killing you.'

'He already tried to kill me,' Octa said as he remembered that somebody had thrown him amongst the enemy.

'Because you tried to run.' Horsa glared at him. 'I saw you turn your back to the enemy, so I grabbed you and threw you amongst them. Let them deal with a coward like you.' Octa looked away, his shame burning his cheeks. 'I thought you Saxons are supposed to be brave warriors?' Horsa said with a sneer on his face.

'Saxons are,' Octa said. 'But not me.' He no longer saw the need to hide what he was, just like he no longer saw the need not to tell them why he was really in Britannia. Perhaps they would find Woden's Spear and then Woden would reward them. He had been a fool to believe that all he had to do was walk to this wall and take the spear. He should have known there would be dangers to face and battles to fight. Nothing involving the gods was ever easy. Witta had told them that many times. Octa sighed and looked at the brothers. 'I came for Gungnir.'

'Woden's spear?' Hengist frowned at Octa, who nodded.

'I think you struck him too hard,' Horsa said to his brother, but even in the dim light of the night, Octa saw something in Eadric's eyes that he didn't understand.

'You believed the old fool?' Eadric asked. Hengist and Horsa raised their eyebrows at him and Eadric explained. 'That old bastard that is always pestering us back in Wodenberg. For many winters he's been telling people this damned tale of Woden's spear which he claims has gone missing.' Eadric looked at Octa again. 'But most are smart enough to know that he is just an old man that had lost his wits.'

Octa looked away again, not wanting to tell them why he believed the old man. He glimpsed Badulf, scowling at them as he listened to their conversation. Octa had almost forgotten about the Briton.

'The old man with the large hat?' Hengist asked, and Eadric nodded. Hengist looked at Octa, his brows furrowed. 'What did he tell you?'

'Hengist, you don't really believe him?' Eadric asked, but Hengist held a hand up to silence him.

'Tell me what he told you,' Hengist said to Octa.

Octa took a deep breath and told them what the old man had said to him about Woden's spear being stolen from him and how it was hidden on this island. Hengist and Horsa shared a look, which Octa missed as he looked at the ground, expecting them to ridicule him.

'Told you. The old man has lost his wits. He's been coming around for more winters than I can remember telling people that story.' Eadric waved his arms in the air, but Hengist did not seem to agree with him.

'Did he tell you where this spear is?'

Octa shook his head. 'I didn't believe him at first, but then I changed my mind. I went back to the tavern the following day to find him and to ask him for more information. That was when I saved your son.'

'So how do you know it is by this wall?' Horsa asked.

'The tavern keeper's wife told me. She had heard him tell the story to others.'

'That wall crosses the island. From east to west,' Eadric said. He turned to Badulf. 'Tell them, Briton.'

Badulf nodded. 'He speaks the truth. It was built from coast to coast. It will take you many years to find this spear.'

Hengist and Horsa stared at Octa, who didn't like the look in Horsa's eyes. 'The woman told me it was kept in a shrine to a British god near the wall built by the Romans. His magic prevented Woden from taking the spear himself.'

Badulf frowned at him and Octa felt that the Briton knew something about this, but he kept those thoughts to himself as Horsa turned to Badulf.

'You know of this shrine?' Horsa asked Badulf, who shook his head.

'I already told Octa. I don't know of any shrine. I was raised a Christian.'

'Could you find this shrine? Ask the people who live near the wall?' Hengist asked Badulf, and this time Octa frowned.

'You believe him?' Eadric asked Hengist, who again glanced at his brother. The two smiled at each other and, again, Octa sensed there was more happening here than he knew about.

'If this story is true, just think of what we could do with the spear of Woden.' He looked at Badulf and repeated the question.

Badulf gaped at Hengist for a moment before he responded, 'Why would I do that? My orders were to help you find the Picts and I've done that.'

'Because if you don't' – Horsa smiled at him – 'then we'll convince King Vortigern to give your sister to us. Just think of how much fun our men will have with her.'

Badulf glared at Octa, who had to look away from the hatred he saw in the Briton's eyes.

Hengist put his hand on Horsa's chest and took a step towards Badulf. 'There'll be no need for that. If what Octa says is true and the spear of our war god, a god your grandfather believed in, is really on this island, then we can use it to drive the Picts into the seas and your people can live in peace. Just like you did when the Romans were here. We can use it to secure King Vortigern's position and your sons will never need live in fear of being attacked by the Picts or the other kings of this island.'

Badulf scowled at Hengist. 'And what happens afterwards? When the Picts are gone?'

Hengist glanced at his brother, who smiled at him. 'We take the spear and return to our homeland. Maybe use it to make ourselves kings.'

'Horsa?' Eadric frowned. 'You don't really believe him?'

Horsa shrugged. 'Like my brother says. We could do much with the spear of Woden. You will take ten men with you and find this spear. And when you do, bring it back to me and my brother.'

Eadric gaped at them. 'Me?'

Horsa nodded. 'I trust you more than everyone apart from my brother. Find the spear for us and you will get your own ship again.'

Eadric scowled at Octa as he seemed to think about it. And then he sighed. 'And what about him?'

'Kill him.'

Octa's eyes widened, but then Hengist put a hand on his brother's shoulders. 'No, Horsa. I told Octa he would live if he told us the truth. We need to keep him alive until we can make sure he has.' He looked at Eadric. 'Take him with you, but make sure he comes back alive.' Hengist turned to Badulf. 'You can take your men with you, if that makes you feel more comfortable.'

Badulf's mouth twitched at the implication, but then he nodded. 'I'll need to send two back to tell King Vortigern about the battle against the Picts.'

Hengist nodded. 'Good. And have them tell your king that we will be returning to the rest of our men on this Ruym Island. Our ships will patrol your shores as we agreed and we'll kill any Pictish raiding band we find.'

Badulf nodded and, with one last glance at Octa, he went to his men.

Hengist turned to Eadric. 'Do what my brother asked and you can be your own man again.'

Eadric sighed. 'Fine. We'll leave at first light.'

14

'How much further do we need to go?' Eadric asked as he huddled under his cloak, as if that was going to protect him from the rain. It had been two days since they left the camp and it had rained for both of them. The other Jutes looked just as miserable as Eadric as they hunched over their horses and with their cloaks wrapped around them. Octa, shivering as he had no cloak and drenched to his core, rode in the centre of the Jutes, with one man always holding Warda's reins.

Badulf shrugged as he rode ahead of the Jutes, his three companions with him. The Britons seemed as miserable as the rest of them, something which Octa found strange because they were born on this island, so they should have been used to the rain. 'I don't know. A few more days, perhaps more.'

They were travelling north, towards a Roman road Badulf had told them would take them all the way to the wall and avoided the towns and villages they saw as Eadric did not want to draw too much attention to themselves. Something which was hard not to do because even Octa knew that a force of sixteen warriors always drew attention.

'A few more days, perhaps more,' Eadric repeated, his irritation clear in his voice. 'I thought you knew where this wall is?'

Badulf glanced over his shoulder at the Jutes. 'It's in the north. That's all I know. That's all everyone knows.'

'But where in the north?' Alard, one of the other Jutes, asked. Octa barely knew the man, but was aware that he had once sailed with Eadric, before he submitted to the brothers. Most of the ten men that Eadric had picked had once called Eadric lord.

'How in God's name would I know that? I've never been there. All I know is that it is in the north.'

'Even I know it's in the north,' Eadric said. 'So what do we need you for then?'

Badulf pulled on his reins, the horse whining at the sudden movement, so he could face Eadric. 'You asked me to lead you.' His face turned red and Octa almost admired him for not showing fear to the larger Jutes. 'And unless you learn to speak my language, you'll never find this spear without me.'

Eadric glared at Badulf and then shrugged. 'We'll stop at the next village we come across. We are running out of food and you can then find out how many more days before we get to the wall.'

Badulf stared at Eadric for a few heartbeats and Octa thought he was going to refuse, but then the Briton nodded and carried on along the track.

Thunder rolled in the dark skies and Eadric tightened his cloak around him before he glanced at Octa, who looked away.

'Why would Woden's spear be in Britannia?' one of the Jutes asked. Rembert, his name was: another who had fought for Eadric before.

'So that Woden can't get it back,' Octa said before he could stop himself.

Rembert raised an eyebrow at him. 'But how? Woden is one of the most powerful of our gods.'

'Enough of this. The spear is not real!' Eadric said. 'If anyone talks about it, then I'll cut your tongue out.'

The warriors glanced at each other behind Eadric's back, but they remained silent as they rode on. Thunder continued to follow them, but the rain lessened as they carried on north towards the wall the Romans had built. Octa tried to picture a wall large enough to span from coast to coast, but he couldn't. Even with the large stone buildings he had already seen, he could not believe that any men could have built anything like that.

That night they were forced to sleep along the road, something none of them were happy about because the ground was wet from the rain, which had stopped at least. But there had been no sun to dry the ground and Octa groaned as he lay down and felt his cold tunic stick to him.

'Stop your complaining,' Eadric said as he wrapped his cloak around him. 'It's your fault we are here.'

Octa stared at the older warrior as the Jutes got a fire going. There would be no meat for them to chew on, though, as they had finished that the day before. All that was left was wet bread, which the men ate with a grimace on their faces.

Octa's mind went to the battle against the Picts as he chewed on the wet bread. His hands trembled as he remembered the fear he felt when he thought he was about to die and wondered if Uhtric had felt the same fear before the Thuringian killed him. He fought to stop the tears from flowing down his cheeks, not wanting the Jutes to see him cry as he wondered if Uhtric would ever forgive him in the afterlife. His hands went to the spear pendant his mother had given him and he thought of her words. That Uhtric's death was not his fault. That it was his wyrd to die that day. But if that was true, then what was his wyrd? To die in Britannia, despite what his mother believed of him. Octa found it hard to see how he would ever be a great warrior like his legendary grandfather, or his father. Not while his fear still controlled him.

He felt eyes on him and looked up to see Badulf scowling at him as he sat with the other three Britons, all of them with their cloaks wrapped around their shoulders. Octa turned away from the Briton before he tried to sleep. But every time he closed his eyes, Uhtric's blood-covered face came to him. Just as it had done every night since the fight against the Thuringians.

The next morning, they woke to dark clouds, and the men grumbled as they shook the stiffness out of their bones and went to their horses.

'Does it always rain so much?' Alard asked.

'It does,' Badulf said as he stroked his horse. 'But you get used to it.'

'Woden knows I'll never get used to this rain.' Eadric pulled himself onto his horse and adjusted his cloak.

'Then I pray you go back to your lands soon so you don't have to find out,' Badulf said, and frowned when Eadric smiled at him.

'It'll be a long time before I return to those lands. If I ever do.' He turned his attention to Octa, who was rubbing his arms to warm himself up. 'Stop wasting time.'

Octa glared at Eadric as he walked to Warda and rubbed her muzzle. The horse whinnied at him as it lowered its head and Octa pressed his forehead against her wet fur.

'What is it with you Saxons and horses?' Eadric asked as they all stared at him. Octa had greeted the horse the same way each morning and as the days went on, he felt like the bond between them was getting stronger.

'Horses are important to us.'

Eadric raised an eyebrow at him and shrugged before he turned his horse towards the road. 'How far to the nearest village?' he asked Badulf.

Badulf sighed. 'I don't know.'

Eadric grumbled at Badulf before he nudged his horse forward. The Jutes laughed and followed him as Badulf glared at the back of Eadric and muttered something in his native tongue to the other Britons, who all smiled.

They rode for half a day until they reached a town which looked like it might have been a small Roman fort in the past. One part of the wall had collapsed and had been rebuilt using timber, and there were many houses which had been built outside the walls as thin trails of smoke drifted to the sky from the houses and cows grazed in the nearby fields.

Badulf hesitated as he looked at the town. 'I don't think we should go there.'

Eadric raised an eyebrow at the Briton. 'Why not?'

'That town was a Roman fort, which means now it belongs to someone important.'

'And what does that have to do with us?' Eadric asked.

'Because news of your arrival and that King Vortigern has hired you would have spread all over Britannia by now. Twelve large Saxons will raise eyebrows—'

One of the Britons interrupted Badulf, who scowled as he nodded.

'What did he say?' Eadric asked.

'He says we are in the lands of the Corieltauvi. The large hill we crested the day before was when we entered their lands.'

'The who?' Eadric raised an eyebrow again as Octa looked at the town.

'The Corieltauvi. They control the lands to the east of King

Vortigern's lands.' Badulf scanned around him and the other three Britons did the same, all of them looking uncomfortable.

'Is that a problem?' Eadric asked, his hand on the hilt of his sword.

'The Corieltauvi dislike King Vortigern and don't agree with him being the high king. They also objected to King Vortigern employing you Saxons.'

'We're Jutes, not Saxons,' Eadric said, and then looked at the town again. 'We need food and we need to know where to go.' He glanced at Badulf and the Britons. 'And I don't trust you enough to let you go on your own.' He scowled as he thought about it. 'The Britons, Octa and I will go. Along with you two.' He pointed at Alard and Rembert. 'The rest of you, stay out of sight and keep your eyes open.' They all nodded as Octa frowned at Eadric.

'Why me?' He had hoped to stay outside the town with the others. That way he might escape them, because he doubted they knew horses as well as he did.

'Because the gods know I don't trust you enough to let you out of my sight. So you are coming with us.' Eadric dismounted from his horse. 'We leave the horses behind and go on foot. We'll draw less attention to ourselves.'

They all dismounted and Octa patted Warda on the neck before he followed the others towards the town. The two other warriors walked behind him and Octa tensed as he felt their eyes on him, while the Britons with Eadric led the way.

'Tell me, Octa,' Eadric said from the front as they entered the town. Octa almost didn't hear him, as he was distracted by everything around him. The small wooden houses built close to each other, some even with two floors, and the straight tracks that ran between the houses towards the centre of the town. The people, many of them with dirty faces and ragged clothing, stared at them, their eyes filled with a mix of fear and curiosity. 'What were you going to do when you found the spear?'

'I thought you said the spear isn't real.' Octa glanced at the older warrior.

'It's not. It's just a story that you were dumb enough to believe.'

'Then why does it matter what I was planning?'

Eadric shrugged. 'I'm curious. You risked much to join Hengist and Horsa's army, all so you can come here and find a spear. And all because of a story an old man told you.'

Octa didn't like the ring of truth in Eadric's words. But he had his reasons for believing the old man's story and Eadric did not need to know that. Octa had nothing left to lose and a promise to his mother to fulfil. That was why he chose to believe the old man's tale. 'I had no plan. I just wanted to find the spear and return it to Woden.'

Eadric laughed. 'You sound like a weak-minded child who still believes the stories his mother told him. The spear is not real.'

'How can you be so certain?'

Eadric shrugged again as they walked past a group of children who had stopped their game to gape at the tall warriors. 'Because I know it isn't.'

Octa glanced at the older warrior. 'I believe it is.'

'That is because you are a fool, as well as a coward. And this fantasy will only get you killed,' he said as Octa sucked in air and rubbed his neck. Eadric was right. He was a fool, and he was a coward. And that was why he needed to find the spear.

15

'We're being watched,' one of the Jutes said while they waited for Badulf and his companions to buy food from the market. Octa glanced over his shoulder and saw two Britons watching them from a distance. One of them said something to the other, who nodded before he disappeared.

'Of course we are being watched. We are bigger than everyone here,' Eadric said, but frowned as he looked at the man watching them. 'Perhaps the Briton was right.' He turned to one of his men. 'Fetch the Britons. We need to leave.' The warrior nodded and did what Eadric asked of him before Eadric turned to Octa. 'If you try anything, then I'll stab you and leave you dying in this town.'

Octa could only nod as the Britons returned, carrying a sack of food they had purchased.

'What is the matter?' Badulf asked when he noticed the concern on their faces.

'Warriors are watching us. We need to leave,' Eadric said, his eyes still fixed on the remaining British warrior who was staring at them.

'I told you this was a bad idea.' Badulf followed Eadric's gaze.

Eadric grunted and grabbed the sack of food from Badulf and handed it to one of the Jutes. 'Come, let's go before his friend gets back with more warriors.'

'What does it matter?' Rembert asked. 'The Britons are weak. We can take them.' Badulf bristled at that, but the warrior ignored him.

'We are not here to fight. Let's go.' Eadric turned and walked back to the gate they had entered the town from. Everyone followed him, glancing over their shoulders to see the British warrior trailing them. Eadric and Alard walked in the front, using their size to push people out of the way, while Rembert walked behind Octa and the Britons. The townspeople parted before Eadric, the glare on his face and his size making sure that no one would dare to challenge them.

Octa leaned closer to Badulf and asked, 'Did you find out how far the wall is from here?'

Badulf raised an eyebrow at him, but after a moment he nodded. 'Another two days to a city called Cair Hebrauc and then about three days along the Roman road. But no one knows anything about any shrine.'

Octa's heart dropped at that. He had hoped that Badulf could find the location of that as well.

'Stop whispering to each other.' Rembert glared at them, his eyes filled with mistrust.

Octa glanced over his shoulder at the Jute and for a moment he wondered if he could catch the man by surprise. But then the warrior smiled at him and his hand went to the knife on his belt.

'Try it, Saxon. Like Eadric said, you'll be left bleeding to death in this town and will never know if the spear is real or not.'

Octa clenched his fists as he glared at the Jute and faced the front again. He wanted to believe that he could take Rembert in a fight, but even he knew he never could. Octa had barely survived the fight against the Picts whereas Rembert was a seasoned warrior.

They made it out of the town without any problems, but every time they looked over their shoulders, the British warrior was still following them. And worse still was that more warriors had joined him. Outside the town walls, Eadric said, 'Stay calm. If we run now, they will think we are up to something.'

'But we are, aren't we?' Alard asked.

'Aye, but they don't need to think that.'

Octa thought about running away as Alard laughed at Eadric's response, but knew he wouldn't get far. Running had never been something he was good at. Even as a child in Witta's village, he was slower than everyone else. And besides, if he ran now, then Eadric would get to the spear before him and Octa would never know if it was real. So he pushed those thoughts out of his mind and kept pace with the others around him as another thought came to him. All he needed to do was play along, not cause any problems for Eadric and, along the route, he could perhaps think of a way to get the spear before the others could. He prayed to Woden, asking the war god to help him.

'They're not following us any more,' Rembert said, and they all looked back towards the town to see the British warriors standing by the gate and watching them.

'Doesn't mean we should hang around. Let's get back to the horses and leave this kingdom. The sooner we reach this wall, the sooner we can get back and tell Hengist there was no spear.'

'But why don't we just go back now?'

'Aye, tell Hengist we reached the wall and found no shrine or spear.'

Eadric scowled as he seemed to think about it, but then he shook his head. 'Hengist and Horsa are not dumb. If we go back now, they'll know we never reached the wall.'

'But how?' Alard asked.

'Because they would have asked someone how long it would take us to reach the wall. Never underestimate the brothers.' Eadric glared at Octa. 'Come, let's get going.'

They all nodded and followed Eadric back to the other men.

'We need to go,' Eadric said as he walked to his horse and mounted up.

The warriors frowned and Rembert explained, 'We were followed by people who looked like they didn't want us around.'

Octa stroked his horse's snout and mounted her. She snorted under him and Octa could sense her frustration and knew she felt the tension between him and the Jutes. He stroked her neck as the others got on their horses, wanting to tell her that everything would be fine, but Octa somehow felt that might not be the case.

Eadric gave the order and they travelled as fast as they could to put as much distance between them and the town. After a while, Eadric called Badulf to him.

'How far are we from the wall?'

Badulf told Eadric the same he had told Octa. 'It's a two-day ride to a city in the north, the capital of the Brigantes. From there we follow the Roman road for another three days then we should reach the wall.'

Eadric chewed on his lip as he glanced at the setting sun. 'Is there another way north to the wall?'

Badulf frowned. 'You think they will chase us?'

Eadric shrugged. 'I don't know, but if I were them, I'd talk to everyone you talked to. Find out what you were saying. If they learn we are heading to the wall, then they might try to block our path.'

Badulf scratched the back of his neck and looked at the other Britons. 'We could head east for a day and that might throw them off our scent, but that would take us deeper into Corieltauvi land. And add more time to our journey.'

Eadric nodded and turned to his men. 'We go east for a short while and then turn north again. It's only five more days until we reach the wall so, gods willing, we can get there without those bastards catching us.' Eadric glanced at Octa and the Jute beside him. 'And keep a close eye on him.'

The man nodded as Octa looked away from Eadric, wondering why the gods were punishing him like this. Had they not done enough already by giving him hope only to take it away? Now they had to torture him by watching as others took the spear of Woden for themselves.

They travelled east until the sunset, and then Eadric made them turn north again. Under the moonlight, they found a track used by herders and followed that, making sure to avoid any settlement they could see in the dark.

'I don't like this,' Alard complained. 'I feel like I am being watched.'

'There is no one here,' Eadric said, but Octa had to agree with the warrior. He felt the shiver run up his spine as he sensed something watching him.

'Aye, that's what worries me. There's no one here and I still feel like I am being watched.'

'You bastard, now I feel like something is watching me,' one of the other warriors said, and the others agreed with them.

'My mother used to tell me stories of the old spirits of these lands,' Badulf said, and Octa thought he could hear a smile in the man's voice. As if he was enjoying the fear the Jutes felt.

Although Octa saw how even the Britons kept glancing around them as they held on to the small crosses around their necks.

'What spirits? I thought you Christians didn't believe in those things,' Alard said.

'There are spirits even us Christians still fear. That's why even we don't venture out in the dark.'

Eadric stopped his horse and turned around so he could face them. The horse complained at the sudden movement as Eadric glared at them. 'We spent many nights sleeping out in the open! None of you complained then.'

'Aye, because everyone knows that the flames of the campfire keep the spirits away,' one warrior said, and Eadric grunted.

'Well, we're not making a fire. We need to keep moving.'

'And what if a spirit grabs me from my horse?'

'I knew of a man that happened to. He rode out in the middle of the night and was never seen again,' Badulf said, and again Octa thought he could hear a smile in the man's voice.

'Briton, you are not helping,' Eadric said, and turned to his men. 'You are Jutes. You are warriors of Woden and Tiw. Now behave like it!' He turned his horse around and kept going without waiting for the rest of them. Octa thought he saw him rub the hilt of his sword in the darkness and wondered if Eadric wasn't afraid as well. If he was, though, he was hiding it very well. The other warriors glanced at each other and then followed Eadric, but all of them had a hand on their weapons. Not that that would help. They all knew that their weapons couldn't kill the spirits.

As they travelled along the thin path, Octa guided Warda closer to Badulf.

'Is it true about the man?'

Badulf shrugged. 'That's what I heard.' They spoke in low voices, but the Jutes seemed more concerned about the spirits of the land than what Badulf and Octa were doing. 'You don't have spirits in your homeland?'

Octa nodded, even if he wasn't sure that Badulf could see him. 'We do. When I was a boy, my cousin...' Octa paused as he remembered Uhtric and how he had failed him. He coughed to clear his throat of the tears and continued. 'My cousin and I would sneak out in the middle of the night to see if we could catch a spirit.'

'Why?'

Octa shrugged. 'An old lady told us that if we caught one, then its magic would come to us, but I think she probably just hoped the spirits would take us away.'

Badulf smiled. 'When we were children, my mother would tell us stories of the old gods and spirits that ruled these lands before the Romans brought the Christian god. She would tell us that the gods were angry that the people turned their backs on them and that one day they would get their revenge. Perhaps that was why the Romans abandoned us and left us to fend for ourselves.'

Octa thought about that and remembered what the old man had told him about Woden's spear.

'Your people still follow the old gods?'

Octa nodded. 'We do. The Romans never made us part of their empire, but they paid our warriors to fight for them. So their god never found us. Not that it would have mattered, though. Tiw and Woden are too strong for the Christian god to replace.'

Badulf smiled. 'I'm sure my people believed the same at first.' He looked at Octa. 'What is so special about this spear?'

Octa glanced around him, but the other Jutes weren't paying any attention to him. Although he noticed Eadric had his head tilted their way. 'It belongs to Woden, one of our war gods.'

'One of your war gods?'

Octa smiled. 'My people and the Jutes love to fight. So we have many war gods, but each has a different role.'

Badulf nodded. 'You'll have to tell me about it one day. I'd like to hear about the gods of my grandfather.'

'Your mother never told you?'

Badulf shook his head. 'She knew little about them. So the spear?'

'It was made for Woden by the dwarfs who live under the mountains in a land far to the north.'

Badulf nodded again. 'And why do you want it?'

Octa glanced at Eadric and noticed how he slowed his horse down to listen to his response. 'I have my reasons.'

16

'They're gaining on us,' one of the Jutes screamed as the wind rushed past Octa's ears. He glanced over his shoulder to see the large force of Britons were gaining on them.

'Bastards! How did they find us?' Eadric said, his words almost plucked away as they pushed their horses to go faster. It was a good question. They had travelled through the night and had avoided any settlement they had come across. When the sun rose, Eadric had them stop so the horses could rest and they could eat their morning meal of grainy bread and old cheese. The men had been too tired to talk, so the meal was spent in silence.

They had stuck to the track they had found, keeping their distance from villages and the Roman road, but the sun had barely climbed when they had heard the horn behind them. They had all turned in shock as a large group of Britons on horseback chased after them. Eadric had not taken any chances and had ordered them to flee as he kicked his horse in the ribs. Octa doubted Eadric knew where they were heading, all the older warrior seemed to care about was getting away from the

Corieltauvi warriors. Even Badulf and the other Britons were pale-faced as they urged their horses to keep up with the Jutes. And just when it seemed that they were getting away from their pursuers, they crested a hill and found another band of Corieltauvi warriors waiting for them.

'Bastards!' Eadric roared as he reined his horse in, and Octa couldn't tell if that was aimed at the warriors blocking their path or the gods, because to Octa it felt like the gods had abandoned them.

'What do we do?' Rembert asked as the remaining Jutes and the Britons all reined in and stared at the wall of warriors in front of them. Octa guessed there were fewer men than what they had, but then there were the warriors who had been chasing them. Those warriors had stopped behind them, but they remained on their horses and kept their distance. Something Eadric also noticed.

'They're not attacking us, which means they want to talk.' He turned to Badulf. 'Can we trust them?'

Badulf shrugged. 'I wouldn't. Like I said, they don't like King Vortigern or the Cornovii.'

Eadric grunted as Rembert said, 'I think we should fight. We charge at them and catch them by surprise. Break through before the bastards behind us can react.' The other Jutes all nodded and Octa prayed that Eadric would not agree to it, but from the scowl on his face, it seemed like he was considering it.

'The one in the centre is the Corieltauvi prince,' Badulf said. 'You kill him and you risk war between the Cornovii and the Corieltauvi. That is not the reason King Vortigern wanted you to fight for him.'

Eadric glanced at the Briton, his jaw muscles tense under his beard. 'We'll talk first, but be ready to fight.' The Jutes all grunted as they dismounted their horses and waited for the

Corieltauvi to approach. Like the Saxons, the Jutes didn't like to fight on horseback.

Badulf gritted his teeth and dismounted his horse as Eadric and the other nine Jutes formed a shield wall. The other Britons looked unsure and Badulf spoke to them. Their frowns told Octa they were not pleased by what was happening, but they were outnumbered so they did the same as the Jutes.

The prince of the Corieltauvi, recognisable because of the large plumage on his helmet, stopped a few paces away from them and shouted something as he pointed his short Roman sword towards them. The ones that had been chasing them were also approaching and without Eadric needing to say anything, the Jutes formed a circle with their shields.

'He wants to know who you are and why you are in his father's lands.' Badulf translated his words.

Eadric spat before he responded. 'It's none of his business. We are just passing through.'

Badulf spoke to the leader, who frowned and asked another question, which Badulf answered.

'What are you saying to him?'

Badulf glared at Eadric. 'He is the son of the king. What we are doing on his land is his business. I told him we are travelling north towards the Roman wall.'

'Why?'

The leader of the Corieltauvi said something and Badulf frowned.

'He wants to know why you want to go to the wall?'

Eadric tightened the grip of his spear and glared at the Corieltauvi prince. 'Tell him to let us go. By nightfall, we'll be out of his father's lands and he can forget about us.'

Badulf translated Eadric's words and Octa saw the smirk on

the prince's face and knew that he would not let them go, even before Badulf told them his response.

'He says that his father does not like that King Vortigern hired your kind—'

'Our kind?' Eadric asked.

'Dirty heathen bastards,' the prince said in the Saxon tongue, surprising all of them. 'You die—'

Before any more words came out of his mouth, Eadric threw his spear at the prince. The throw was poorly aimed, and the prince saw it coming, but it was enough to distract the other Corieltauvi warriors.

'Kill them!' Eadric roared as he punched the horse in front of him with the boss of his shield. The animal reared up and threw its rider as the Jutes all rushed at the Corieltauvi while Badulf cried out for them to stop. They stabbed with their spears and killed a handful of the Corieltauvi, who were too slow to react. A few of the Corieltauvi got their shields up in time, but one of those was pushed off his horse by the strength of the spear jab. Eadric rushed forward and pulled his seax knife from his belt and stabbed the Corieltauvi he had unseated, with Alard doing the same, while the prince of the Corieltauvi shouted something at the remaining British warriors, a few of them as pale as Octa as the Jutes' ferocity stunned them.

One Jute swung his spear in a wide arc at the prince and sliced his cheek open, but he was quickly killed by one of the Corieltauvi warriors as they all snapped out of their stupor and attacked the Jutes. The Corieltauvi still outnumbered them by almost two to one, but Eadric and his Jutes were warriors who had fought and won many battles, unlike the Corieltauvi who were still on their horses. Badulf and the other three Britons joined in the fight as well and Octa watched as Badulf blocked a spear aimed at his head.

'Give me a weapon!' Octa shouted at Badulf, who hesitated for a moment before he gave Octa his knife.

One of the Jutes glanced at him, his eyebrows raised by the knife in Octa's hand. Distracted, the Corieltauvi the Jute was fighting stabbed him through the neck with his sword, but Octa did not see any of that as he kept his head low, desperate to get away from the fight somehow. Octa's hand trembled as his fear coursed through him and he stood frozen as the fighting raged around him and Badulf's Britons.

Alard blocked the strike from one of the Corieltauvi and Rembert stabbed this man in the side, leaving only a handful of the Corieltauvi alive, including the prince, who was bleeding from his cheek. Seeing that he had lost, the prince called out to his remaining warriors, and they all turned and fled, but not before one of the Corieltauvi stabbed at Octa with his spear. Octa gaped at the spear in his thigh and his stomach clenched at the pain and the sight of his blood as he fell to the ground. He tried getting up, but the pain was too much for him and he cried out before dropping to the ground again. He looked back at the Jutes in time to see one of them throw a spear at the fleeing Corieltauvi, which missed. For a few heartbeats, nothing happened until one of the Jutes looked at Octa and smiled.

'Bastard got a spear in his leg.'

Eadric glanced at him, but Octa saw no sympathy in the man's eyes. Whatever bond they had before was gone as, behind the Jutes, Badulf and the three Britons stared at the Corieltauvi dead.

Eadric looked behind him, towards the Britons. 'We need to get going. Those bastards will be back with more men.'

'And what about him?' Alard said, and pointed at Octa, whose head was swimming because of the pain from the spear still in his leg.

Eadric glared at Octa before he bent down and pulled the spear out of Octa's leg. Octa screamed as the pain seared his leg. His vision blurred, and he thought he was about to pass out when Eadric tapped him on the side of the head with the butt of the spear. 'You don't get to pass out.' He turned to one of his men. 'Tie his leg up. We need to stop the bleeding.'

'Why not just kill him here?' the man asked.

Eadric hawked and spat before he responded. 'Because Hengist wants us to bring him back alive. And we all know what happens if we disobey Hengist.'

The men nodded as if they understood before Alard found a piece of cloth and tied it around Octa's leg, making sure to cause as much pain as he could.

'Stop your complaining,' Alard said when Octa cried out again.

Eadric sent the other men to fetch the horses before he turned to Badulf, who approached them. Badulf glared at Octa as Eadric said, 'They were going to kill us all, even you and your men. You said it yourself; they don't like your people or king.'

The other warriors returned with the horses, although a few of them had run away, as Badulf nodded. Warda came towards Octa and nudged his head before she shook hers and grunted.

Eadric pulled Octa to his feet and almost threw him on the horse. 'The next time, keep your eyes open and on the fight.'

Octa looked at him and wondered if all this was a punishment from the gods for running from the fight that got his cousin killed. Was Tiw angry at him for not being honourable or was Woden toying with him, making him wish he had died in that battle as well? Before they mounted their horses, one of the Jutes looked back at the dead Britons and Jutes.

'What about our men? We can't just leave them here.'

Eadric, already on his horse, looked at the dead Jutes. 'We

can't take them with us, and we don't have time to bury them. Something else we can thank Octa for.'

The Jutes all glared at him and Octa lowered his head as they all mounted, and Eadric gave the order for them to ride off. He had hoped they would go slowly, but Eadric seemed to want to get away from there as fast as possible and all Octa could do was grit his teeth at the pain in his leg as the horse moved.

They rode for a while, and when the sun started setting, Eadric stopped and asked Badulf, 'Where are we now?'

Badulf looked around him and shrugged. 'I'm not sure.'

Eadric growled at Badulf before he took a deep breath. 'Are we still in the Corieltauvi kingdom?'

Badulf's brows came together as he thought about it. He asked the other Britons and, after a short conversation, he said, 'They think we're in the lands of the Brigantes now.'

Octa, his head spinning from the pain in his leg and the loss of blood, looked at Badulf, but it seemed that Eadric had the same question as he had. 'So we are safe now?'

Badulf shook his head. 'You weren't safe the moment you left King Vortigern's kingdom. I told you. There are many who don't agree with him hiring you.'

Eadric grunted and looked around him, his brows furrowed as he scrutinised the landscape. 'We'll have to be more careful then. How long before we reach this city?'

Badulf frowned as he thought about it. Octa prayed they would hurry because he needed to sit down. His trousers were soaked with the blood from his wound, which was stinging with every movement, and was sticking to his leg. Already flies were gathering around the wound and Octa could only pray that it would not get infected.

'Another day or two north, I'd say. Then we should reach Cair Hebrauc.'

'We should avoid it,' Rembert said, and Eadric nodded. But Badulf shook his head.

'If you want to find out about this shrine, then we need to go there. There are more people there, so there's a better chance that someone might remember something about it. It's also still a busy trading centre, so no one will pay any attention to you.'

Eadric stared at Badulf as he thought about it, and then he nodded. 'Makes sense. We camp here tonight and tomorrow we head for this Cair Hebrauc.'

Octa sighed with relief, before he fell off Warda and lay on the ground as the Jutes tied their horses up and prepared the camp.

'What do we do with him?' Alard asked, and Eadric glared at Octa.

'We should leave him and hope he bleeds out,' another Jute said, but Eadric shook his head.

'No, he comes with us. I'd rather keep him close until we find this spear.'

'Then we need to treat his wound,' the man said. 'And Woden knows, I'm not doing it.' The others agreed with this warrior, and Eadric sighed.

'I'll do it,' Badulf said, surprising them all.

Eadric glared at the Briton for a while and shrugged. 'Fine, but I'm keeping an eye on you.'

As the Jutes got a fire going and Eadric set two of them on watch before he made himself comfortable, his eyes rarely left Octa and Badulf. Badulf helped Octa remove his trousers before he rained the wound with some of their drinking water.

'It'll leave a nasty scar, but it looks clean.' He prodded the wound, which only made Octa cry out and the Jutes laugh, before he pulled some linen out of the large pouch he had been carrying with him. 'Why didn't you fight?' he asked as he wrapped the linen around Octa's leg, making sure it was tight enough to cause him pain.

Octa gasped and took a deep breath before he could answer. He glanced over his shoulder at the Jutes and felt the tears sting his eyes, although he wasn't sure if it was because of the pain or his shame. 'Because I am not like them. I am not a warrior.'

Badulf scrutinised him for a while. 'Then why come here looking for a weapon you believe belongs to your god?'

'Because I hoped it would turn me into one.' Octa wasn't sure why he told Badulf all of this. Perhaps he felt that Badulf deserved an explanation.

'My sister thinks there is something special about you.'

Octa's eyes widened as Badulf said this. 'Your sister?'

Badulf nodded. 'She...' He frowned as he tried to find the right words. 'The old gods talk to her. Have done ever since she was a child.'

'And the gods told her about me?'

Badulf shook his head. 'They warned her about you.'

17

Octa forgot about the pain in his leg as he saw the walls of the place Badulf called Cair Hebrauc. He couldn't say if it was larger than the fort of King Vortigern, but it still took his breath away. Stone walls and giant towers loomed over them as they approached one of four gates that led into the old Roman fort, but Octa could see places where parts of the wall had been replaced by timber.

The Jutes, though, did not seem as impressed by the fort as Octa and he guessed they had seen many of them before. They appeared relaxed as they rode their horses through the gates of the city, but their hands were never far from their weapons. Unlike Badulf and the Britons, who were nervously glancing around themselves as if they expected another attack.

'So the king of the Brigantes lives here?' Eadric asked.

'The Brigantes don't have a king. They are ruled by a Dux.' Badulf shielded his eyes as he scanned the streets of Cair Hebrauc.

'A Dux?' Eadric asked.

'A military leader, like a warlord.'

'So why not just call him warlord?' Alard asked, and Badulf shrugged.

'Because he is called a Dux.'

The Jute stopped and glared at Badulf, who only stared at him.

'Enough,' Eadric said. He stopped his horse and looked around the busy town. 'This is a crowded place, so we should blend in. We might even find our kin here, so spread out and ask around. See if you can find any information about a shrine to this god. At sunset, we'll meet by that tavern and find somewhere we can sleep for the night.' The Jutes all nodded and spread out, ignoring the protestations of the townspeople as they pushed their horses through them.

'What about us?' Badulf asked Eadric, who was the only Jute to remain with them.

'Get your men to do the same, but you stay with me.'

Badulf scowled at Eadric, but then said something to his men and they soon disappeared amongst the crowd.

'I need to rest. My leg hurts,' Octa said, who struggled to stay upright on his horse. Badulf had replaced the linen bandage around the wound that morning, but during the ride to Cair Hebrauc, the wound had reopened and the bandage was covered in blood again.

'He needs a healer. There's only so much I can do,' Badulf said.

Eadric grunted. 'There's only so much you need to do for now.'

Badulf dismounted his horse and helped Octa off his, before finding him somewhere to sit. Octa closed his eyes and took deep breaths as he tried to fight the pain, but it was worse than anything he had ever experienced before. His entire leg felt like it was on fire and he struggled to put any weight on it.

'Come, we need to go. We don't have much daylight left.' Eadric waited for them to get back to their feet, which Octa struggled to do before he led them away.

They had little luck on the first day. None of the people Badulf spoke to knew anything about a shrine to one of the old gods by the Roman wall and by the time the sun was setting, Octa could barely stand any more.

'We should go back to the tavern,' Badulf said, and Eadric grunted as he glared at the back of the last person Badulf had asked.

'Are you sure you are asking the right questions?' Eadric raised an eyebrow at him.

Badulf shrugged. 'You can ask them next time then, if you don't trust me.'

Eadric turned his glare to the Briton. 'I don't trust you, but no one here speaks my tongue.' Eadric shook his head. 'How is it possible that no one knows anything about the gods of this island?'

'We've followed the Christ for at least three generations on Britannia, so for many, the old gods are just stories their parents told them. But few really pay attention to them.'

Eadric's mouth twitched at that and he glanced at Octa, who was leaning against the wall of the house behind him. 'Let's go back. If Woden is with us, then the others might have something for us.'

They walked back to the tavern, with Octa, his face pale and vision blurred, having to lean on Badulf for support. He wasn't sure how long they had walked to get back to the tavern, but it felt like it was days. Badulf helped him inside and found him a bench to sit on, while Eadric stood nearby and glared at him. A large man with grey hair approached them and from the scowl on his face and the apron around his waist, Octa guessed the man was the tavern owner, as he had a heated discussion with Badulf. But a few heartbeats after, Badulf placed some coins in the man's hand and, with one last glare at Octa and his bleeding leg, the man turned and walked away.

'What was that about?' Eadric asked.

'He wasn't happy with having an injured man in his tavern. He thinks we will bring trouble, and he doesn't want that, so I had to pay him double for the rooms.'

Eadric nodded and then turned when the first of the Jutes returned. Both men had wide grins on their faces and swayed as they walked towards them. 'By Tiw,' Eadric said as they dropped down on the bench next to Octa. 'You bastards were supposed to be asking around for the shrine, not go drinking.'

One of the Jutes stared at Eadric with his glassy eyes for a few heartbeats before he nodded. 'We did.' He burped before he continued. 'We went to another tavern and asked around, but they kept giving us their piss excuses for ale.'

'You still drank it, I see.'

The man shrugged as the other started snoring beside Octa. 'Aye. Had to. Ale is ale and the gods won't be pleased if we don't accept it.'

Eadric shook his head. 'Did you learn anything about the shrine?'

The Jute shook his head. 'Only that their ale is shit.'

The tavern owner returned a short while later with some cups and a jug of ale, and they drank while they waited for the rest of Eadric's men and Badulf's Britons to return. By the time it had gone dark, all but one were sitting in the tavern and drinking ale. Octa's leg ached, and he struggled to stay awake, but he was determined to keep his eyes and ears open. The last thing he wanted was to pass out and be left behind without knowing where to go.

'Where is he?' Eadric asked as a vein throbbed in his forehead.

'Perhaps he got lost?' Rembert said, and Eadric raised an eyebrow at him.

'Have you ever known him to get lost?' Rembert shook his head, and they all fell silent before Eadric said, 'Something has happened to him. I can feel it in my bones.'

'All I can feel is—' Rembert turned and vomited before he could finish his sentence and Octa's stomach clenched as the stench of his vomit reached his nostrils.

'You Jutes are disgusting,' Badulf said, which only made the other warriors laugh.

'Well, if you Britons could fight, then you wouldn't need us,' Eadric said before he got to his feet. 'I'm going to sleep. Hopefully, he will be here in the morning and then I'll beat the shit out of him.'

Octa stayed where he was as the Jutes who were still awake followed Eadric to the room Badulf had got them, and was surprised when Badulf didn't go with the Britons to their room.

'I'd rather sleep here,' he said when he saw Octa frown at him. Octa nodded and before long his eyes were too heavy for him to keep open and he fell asleep.

The next day, they walked the streets again. Eadric was angry, his fists constantly clenching and unclenching as Badulf asked the townspeople if they knew anything about a shrine by the Roman wall. The missing warrior had never returned, and it had spooked the rest of them because they were certain that something must have happened to him. Before they left, Badulf had cleaned Octa's wound again and put a clean bandage on it. The leg still hurt, but so far there was no sign of infection, which Octa was grateful for at least. But he still struggled to keep up with Eadric and Badulf as they walked the streets of Cair Hebrauc.

That wasn't all that bothered him, though. Octa couldn't explain it, but it felt like they were being followed. He had decided not to say anything to Eadric, because every time he turned around, he saw no one that looked suspicious and he didn't want Eadric to mock him.

They stopped an old man, whose eyes widened at Eadric towering over him, but when Badulf asked about the shrine, the old man's face paled and he just turned and walked away as fast as his old legs could carry him.

'What in Woden's name is that? What did you say to him?' Eadric asked Badulf.

'The same thing I asked everyone else.'

Eadric glared at Badulf. 'Well, no one else reacted that way. The old bastard knows something.'

'Yes. But something that scared him more than you.'

Eadric raised an eyebrow at this, and even Octa had to admit that was strange.

The old man wasn't the only one who reacted that way. Three other people they asked did the same and after the third person rushed off, Eadric was red in the face.

'Bastard. I should torture the information out of him.'

Badulf shook his head. 'The man is old. He'll die before you get anything useful.'

'Can we rest? My leg is aching,' Octa asked, and then regretted it as Eadric turned on him.

'No,' Eadric said.

He turned to walk away when Badulf said, 'Octa needs to rest or his leg won't heal.'

Eadric turned, his eyes blazing. 'I don't care about the coward's leg. The only reason he is alive is because the man I swore an oath to would want to kill Octa himself. And I want to see his face when he realises he came all the way to Britannia for no reason.'

Octa felt his anger ignite, something that didn't happen very often, and he glared at Eadric, who only smiled at him.

'What are you going to do, Octa? You didn't have the stomach to fight before you got a spear in the leg, so I doubt you will fight me now.'

Octa glared at Eadric for a few more heartbeats, and then he looked away, knowing that the older warrior was right. Octa didn't have the stomach to fight.

Eadric grunted. 'Let's go.'

Octa struggled to his feet and ignored Badulf's gaze as he limped after Eadric.

A while later, they were back in the tavern and Octa sensed he was the only one who was glad about that as he sat on the bench and rested his leg. The bleeding was less, which meant that the wound hadn't reopened, but it still ached from him spending most of the day on his feet. Eadric's face was dark as he nursed his cup of ale. As the day had worn on, they had found fewer and fewer people willing to talk to them and on many occasions Octa felt like they were being followed. But he knew that what was angering Eadric even more was that another of his men had not returned when he should have done.

'It feels like we are being hunted,' Rembert said, which earned him a glare from Eadric.

'We are the wolves. We do the hunting!'

'Some farmers hunt wolves to protect their flock,' Badulf said, and didn't react fast enough to dodge Eadric as the older warrior grabbed hold of his tunic.

'How do I know you are not behind my men disappearing?'

'What would I gain from that?' Badulf held Eadric's glare as the other Britons tensed, clearly not wanting to get into a fight with the Jutes.

Eadric glared at the Briton for a while, before he let go of him and sat down again. 'Tomorrow we leave. I don't think we will learn much more in this place.'

'Do we go back to the fleet?' one of the Jutes asked, and Eadric shook his head.

'We go to the wall and find this shrine ourselves. Even if it takes us the rest of the summer.'

The Jutes' shoulders dropped, and Octa wondered why Eadric was so determined to find the spear. At first, Eadric had denied its existence, but now, when even Octa felt like giving up, he was the driving force behind the hunt for it.

They left the next day. Eadric was furious as they rode out of the gates and glared at everyone as if he dared the Britons to fight him. But everyone turned away from the angry Jutes and soon the city walls were behind them.

'Are you sure that your men aren't just drunk somewhere?' Badulf asked as they rode away from Cair Hebrauc. 'You heathens are known for drinking too much.'

Eadric glared at the Briton. 'Not them. They have been with me for many winters and I know they can hold their ale. Something happened to them.'

Octa believed Eadric. He still hadn't told anyone that he believed they were being followed, but he knew he wasn't imagining it.

'But who would kill them?' Rembert asked.

Eadric scowled at the question. 'I don't know, but if I ever find out, then I'm going to skin those bastards alive.'

'You might find out sooner than you think, Eadric,' Alard said.

'Why?'

'Because we are being followed.'

Octa's heart raced in his chest as he remembered the last time they were followed. That had led to the battle against the Corieltauvi prince and Octa with a spear in his leg. But when they all turned around, they saw it was only one man on a horse who was keeping his distance from them. The man didn't seem like much of a threat as he had no armour or visible weapons, and no one said anything at first, or made it obvious that they knew about the man, but as the day went on, it became undeniable that he was following them.

'What do we do?' one of the warriors asked.

'We trap him,' Eadric said, and without another word two of the Jutes broke off when the man was out of sight and rode off to the side before they disappeared from view. Octa wanted to look over his shoulder to see if the man was still following them and see what the other two were going to do, but he knew he couldn't. Even with the fear he was feeling, he wanted to know who the man was and why he was following them.

They rode on in silence for a while longer when a horn sounded. Eadric turned his horse around, as did the other Jutes, and they rode back the way they had just come from, leaving Octa and the Britons behind.

Badulf raised an eyebrow at Octa, almost as if asking if he was going to make a run for it, but Octa only shook his head. If he made a run for it now, then he most certainly would be dead soon. And not by Eadric's blade. In his injured state, Octa was sure that some of the locals wouldn't think twice about attacking him for the horse or anything of value he might have. Or just because he was a foreigner in these lands. So Octa followed Eadric and the Jutes.

'You think he is the same man that was following us in Cair Hebrauc?' Badulf asked, and Octa's eyes widened.

'You felt that as well?'

'I did, and I'm sure Eadric did. I wonder if that man had anything to do with the two Jutes that disappeared.'

Octa wondered the same as he frowned at Badulf.

By the time they reached the others, Eadric was already off his horse and had his knife at the man's throat. The man was older than Octa, but not as old as Eadric, and at first glance, he looked like he was a farmer, which made it even more strange that he was following them. Eadric looked up and almost seemed surprised to see that Octa hadn't run away, before he turned his attention back to the man.

'Ask him why he is following us.'

Badulf asked the man, who shook his head before he responded. 'He says he wasn't.'

Eadric punched him in the face, splitting his lip open. 'Ask him again.'

Badulf again asked the man, who again shook his head and responded with the same thing.

This time Eadric pulled his knife away from the man's neck and stabbed him in the leg. The man cried out and Octa thought he could see a marking on the man's neck, although he couldn't make out what it was, as Eadric pressed his knife against the man's throat again. 'Ask him again and this time tell him that if he doesn't tell me the truth, then I will dismember him piece by piece until only his head is left.'

But before Badulf could ask, the man laughed and said something in his language. He then pushed his own head down and forced Eadric's knife into his throat.

'Bastard!' Eadric said as the man, still smiling at them, choked on his own blood. 'What did he say?'

Badulf, who had turned pale, said, 'He said Brigantia will kill us all.'

18

'You gave them land in my kingdom?' King Gwyrangon almost screamed as soon as he walked into Vortigern's hall. Brigid watched from the shadows, as she usually did when King Vortigern met with his advisers.

King Vortigern looked up from the conversation he was having with his advisers and sighed. Brigid knew he had been expecting this, but it must still have annoyed him to be addressed like that. 'Greetings, King Gwyrangon of the Cantiaci. I pray the Lord has provided you with a pleasant journey.'

'You gave those Saxon bastards land in my kingdom! And worse, the island at the mouth of the Tamesis River!' King Gwyrangon's face was red as he glared at Vortigern, who signalled for his advisers and the other people in his hall to leave. As they did, Brigid saw Vortimer glancing towards the shadows of the hall, clearly trying to see if she was there. But Brigid was smart enough not to stand in the same place again. She knew this hall better than most and knew of all the places to hide.

'They are Jutes,' King Vortigern said as he turned his attention back to the angry king of the Cantiaci.

'What?' King Gwyrangon said.

'They are Jutes. Not Saxons.'

Brigid frowned and wondered why King Vortigern had made the distinction. She had not been paying much attention to the high king recently, and she worried that that might have been a mistake. She knew he had had many meetings with the two brothers that led the foreigners, but Brigid had been too worried about the fate of her brother to keep an eye on King Vortigern.

King Gwyrangon shrugged. 'They look like the Saxon bastards the Romans had brought with them. Smell like them too.' King Gwyrangon shook his head. 'Why did you give them land in my kingdom?'

King Vortigern stroked his short beard as he stared at King Gwyrangon. 'Because they need somewhere to stay and Ruym Island is the best place for them. From there they can patrol the coast with their ships and use the rivers to get inland to repel raids from the north. And the Lord knows they deserve it.'

'Deserve it?'

'Yes. The Jutes have beaten back several Pictish war bands and have kept both our kingdoms safe. Or are you forgetting that trade has increased in Cair Lundein since they arrived?' Brigid knew this was true. Over the summer, the Jutes had sent many patrols to Ceint and Powys, the lands of the Cornovii, from Ruym Island and had defeated many Pictish war bands. There was now a sense of calm amongst the people that Brigid had never known, as they no longer feared the Picts. Many even started greeting the Saxons warmly when they came to King Vortigern's fort and British warriors often joined them on patrols.

'Then why not give them land in your kingdom?'

'Because I am the high king of Britannia, so I can give them any land I want.' King Vortigern's face turned red and Brigid wondered if it was because of his anger at being spoken to like that, or because he had not given them the island of Ruym. The Saxons, or Jutes as they called themselves, had taken the island for themselves, but King Vortigern did not have the stomach to tell them to leave the island.

'You're only the high king because me and the other kings supported you in that. Don't forget that, Vortigern.' King Gwyrangon glared at Vortigern, who clenched his jaw at the king of the Cantiaci. 'Giving them that island was a bad idea.'

'I gave them that island so they are not on the mainland and so that they can protect the river from raiders across the seas. Raiders you've been complaining about.' King Vortigern clenched his fists and Brigid hoped he didn't do anything foolish.

'And do you know what they do when raiders show up by the mouth of the river?'

King Vortigern shook his head, and Brigid frowned, wondering what King Gwyrangon was going to say. 'I presume they fight the raiders and chase them away.'

King Gwyrangon shook his head. 'The Jutes invite the raiders to join them. Already two new ships have joined them from the continent and it won't be long before more come once they hear of this.'

King Vortigern frowned at this news as Brigid wondered what this meant for her plans. Would the people from across the seas allow the old gods of Britannia to flourish like they once had, or would their gods replace them? Brigid pushed the question from her mind and wondered if King Vortigern was concerned about the deal he had made to provide the Jutes with clothing and food. 'The more there are of them, the less chance there is of them being defeated by the Picts and other raiders from across the seas.'

King Gwyrangon scowled at King Vortigern. 'Aye, and the harder it will be for anyone to oppose you with an army of Saxons behind your back.'

King Vortigern's mouth twitched as King Gwyrangon said the words and Brigid wondered how many other kings had the same thought. All of them, most likely, but it did not matter because what King Gwyrangon had said was true. Brigid knew that Hengist and Horsa had sworn to crush any of the kings who dared to stand against King Vortigern. King Vortigern smiled. 'The Jutes are here because we asked them to help us. They do not serve any one king, but all of us.'

King Gwyrangon grunted, clearly not believing his words. 'I wonder who is really serving who.'

Again, King Vortigern's mouth twitched. 'What do you mean by that?'

'Are you aware that a group of the Saxons—'

'Jutes,' King Vortigern interrupted him and, again, Brigid frowned at that.

King Gwyrangon shrugged, as if it didn't matter to him. 'A group of them travelled north. There is even word that they fought a skirmish against the Corieltauvi.'

'North?' King Vortigern frowned, as did Brigid, as she wondered why Hengist and Horsa had sent men north and why they hadn't mentioned this to the king. Her heart raced as her mind went to a story the old woman who trained her had told her many winters ago. But try as she might, Brigid could not remember what the story was or why it was important.

'Yes, north. And your half-Saxon is with them.'

'Badulf?' The frown deepened on King Vortigern's face and Brigid's heart felt like it had stopped beating. She had to cover her mouth with her hand to make sure she made no noise to give herself away and knew the fear she had felt for her brother was real. Brigid wondered if this was the reason the mother goddess was silent.

King Gwyrangon grunted and, before he turned to leave, he said, 'You better keep a close eye on the Jutes before they do something we all regret.'

King Vortigern glared at the back of the king of the Cantiaci as he left his hall while his hands balled into fists. Brigid knew he must have been trying to think of a reason why Hengist and Horsa would send men north and, more importantly, why they needed Badulf. Even Brigid couldn't understand that, and then she remembered the young warrior had asked them about the Roman wall. She knew the two were connected somehow, but couldn't work out why. All she knew for certain was that the gods feared the young warrior.

19

The warriors were tense as they rode north. After the death of the Briton from Cair Hebrauc, the Jutes had argued amongst themselves. The warriors wanted to go back to the fleet because they did not want to risk the wrath of a god from these lands. Especially a god they didn't know, but Eadric had insisted that they carried on north.

'Thunor will protect us,' he had said as he glared at the warriors.

'Just like he protected the two killed in Cair Hebrauc?' one warrior had retorted.

'We don't know that they're dead,' Alard had said, but Octa could hear from the sound of his voice that he too believed they were dead.

Those were the last words spoken before they had all mounted their horses and left the corpse of the Briton where he died.

Octa felt the fear in his chest as the man's words kept repeating in his head. Badulf had told them that Brigantia was an old goddess of these lands and was important to the Brig-antes, the people whose lands they were in now. He wondered if it was Brigantia's magic that kept Woden from finding his spear. If it was, then he knew he needed to be careful because only a powerful god would be able to stop Woden.

They pushed the horses hard as they rode north, something which did not help Octa's leg as the jolting motion of the horse sent waves of pain from his wound. So Octa was relieved when the sun started setting and Eadric called for them to stop.

'We rest here for the night, but be vigilant.' He looked at Badulf. 'If the gods are with us, then we should reach the Roman road tomorrow.'

Badulf nodded, but said nothing. Just like the others, he had not spoken since he translated the man's dying words and Octa wondered why a Christian would be so frightened by a goddess they didn't believe in, especially when he saw how Badulf's hand trembled as he dismounted his horse and helped Octa off his. The other three Britons, their faces as pale as the moon, looked like they wanted to be elsewhere as well.

Octa nodded his thanks, but Badulf turned away from him before he could see it. Shrugging to himself, Octa limped to a place where he could sit down and take the weight off his injured leg. Warda stayed where she was, watching him as if she was waiting for him to do something, but Octa was in too much pain, so he ignored her and closed his eyes for a moment.

A kick to his stomach woke him up, and Octa stared at Rembert who stood over him. 'Our friends are dying because of you, and here you lie, sleeping as if you had no care.' The Jute kicked him again before Octa could respond.

He had not meant to fall asleep. All he wanted to do was close his eyes for a few heartbeats until the pain in his leg subsided a bit.

'Enough!' Eadric said, and Rembert turned on him.

'Why?' The others stepped closer, but their faces showed they were uncertain of what to do. 'Why shouldn't we just kill the worm now and go back?'

'Aye,' one of the others agreed. 'We don't know what this goddess is capable of, and I don't want to find out. Especially not after that bastard would rather die than betray her.'

Eadric glared at the warriors. 'We don't know that he died for her. The man probably didn't have any wits left in him.'

Rembert hawked and spat. 'Well, Tiw knows I don't want to find out. I say we go back.'

Eadric took a step closer to the man, who was half a head taller than him. 'Then go back. Get on your horse and ride back to Hengist and Horsa. And then you tell them how you got frightened by a witless man and ran away.' He turned to face the other warriors. 'All of you. Run back to the fleet and tell the others how you are no better than this coward.' He pointed a finger at Octa, who wanted to be angry at that, but couldn't be because Eadric's words were true. The warriors all looked away from Eadric's glare, which only made the older warrior grunt. 'We are Jutes and we are warriors. We all swore an oath to Hengist and Horsa and they told us to find Woden's spear. And that is what we will do, unless you all want the brothers to hang us from the biggest tree.'

'Can we at least kill the Saxon? The gods know I'm fed up with having him around.'

Eadric shook his head. 'Hengist wants us to bring him back alive. So that is what we do.' The warriors all grumbled at that and Octa again wondered why Hengist wanted that. Perhaps Hengist wanted to kill Octa himself, but then why not keep him in the camp with them? Why send him with Eadric to find the spear?

Rembert kicked Octa again, before he started getting the campfire ready. 'How do we know there aren't more of those bastards around?'

'There are,' Badulf said, speaking for the first time since the man had died. The Jutes all stared at him, and even Octa raised his eyebrows as he struggled to get his breath back.

'What are you talking about?' Eadric asked.

Badulf took a deep breath. 'This island might have been introduced to the Christian god by the Romans, but we have heard stories of cults who still cling to the old gods. They meet in secret and worship the gods of our ancestors by sacrificing children and sometimes drinking their blood.'

Octa felt a shiver run down his spine as Badulf spoke, and when he glanced at the Jutes, he saw they were just as frightened as he was. Even Eadric rubbed the hilt of his sword as if he was trying to ward off the evil of Badulf's words. 'And you think that man was part of a cult?' Eadric asked.

Badulf nodded. 'He had a mark on his neck. The head of a spear. It was the same mark I've seen on others who had been executed for being part of a cult.'

Octa's heart skipped a beat as Badulf said this and if he hadn't been sitting then he would have fallen over. Brigantia had the spear, he was certain of that now. But why? Why would a god of this island have Woden's spear? And how did she get it? Octa had been too obsessed with finding the spear to really wonder about why it was in Britannia in the first place. All the old man had told him was that the spear was stolen and he had claimed that he didn't know who stole it.

'So there are more out there?' Rembert asked Badulf, his eyes scanning the open lands around them.

Badulf shrugged. 'I don't know if that man had any accomplices with him, but we are in the lands of the Brigantes and Brigantia was their chief god. So there will be more of them.'

Eadric grunted. 'Then all we need to do is capture one of the bastards and force him to tell us where this shrine is.'

'You really think any of them would do that?' Badulf asked. 'They will all rather die than betray their god. Would you not do the same for yours?'

Eadric stared at Badulf. 'My gods only ask that I fight well and die a glorious death. Not cut my own throat and die like a snake.' He turned to the warriors. 'Be vigilant and keep the fire going. That way, they can't sneak up on us.' The warriors all nodded, but Octa saw how their hands were on their weapons as they prepared the night camp.

Octa doubted that any of them slept that night. He knew he couldn't because every time he closed his eyes, he felt a presence looming over him. A dark figure with its hands inching towards his throat, but when he opened his eyes, there was no one there. On more than one occasion, one of the others would cry out, which made him wonder if they were experiencing the same thing he was. It had felt like the land itself did not want them there.

When the sun rose the following morning, they all seemed to sigh with relief that they had made it through the night. But all of them had blue rings around their eyes and seemed sluggish as they moved around. Badulf walked to Octa and handed him some stale bread.

'How is your leg?'

Octa gently touched his leg and grimaced at the pain. 'Still hurts, but I don't think it is infected.'

Badulf nodded and walked towards the other Britons without saying anything else, leaving Octa to eat the stale bread. No one spoke as they ate their morning meal. They were all still tense and Octa saw how their eyes constantly scanned the horizon as they searched for threats.

'The Roman road is not far from here,' Badulf said. 'We can take that and it will lead us to the wall, but it will also take us to one of the old Roman forts.'

'So another town?'

Badulf shrugged. 'I don't know what we will find. In the south, we heard that a few of the forts still had remnants of Roman soldiers, but which forts and how many of them are still left, I don't know.'

'Can't be many. The Romans left a long time ago,' Eadric said, and Badulf nodded. 'We'll take the road and stay out in the open.' Eadric didn't need to explain why he wanted to do that. They all understood as they prepared to leave.

Octa struggled to his feet and limped to Warda. He still couldn't put much weight on his leg, but he felt it was slowly healing. He greeted Warda, who pressed her head against his chest while he waited for someone to help him, but none of the Jutes were eager to do that. With a sigh, Octa tried to mount the horse himself, but he only hurt his leg even more. Eventually, Badulf came and helped him mount his horse.

'Thank you,' Octa said, and Badulf nodded at him before he mounted his own horse and led them towards the Roman road.

It didn't take them long to find it as it wasn't hard to miss. It was like a giant snake had died on the ground and all that was left was its grey skin. Octa looked at the large stones as the horses' hooves clattered on them, neatly placed beside each other as if they had sprung out of the ground, and marvelled at how men could have done that. Occasionally, a few stones would be missing and in many places plants had forced them-selves through the gaps in the road as nature fought to reclaim the ground. *Like a battle between men and gods*, Octa thought as he kept his eyes on the road.

As the day before, they rode in silence. Octa grimaced as they pushed the horses as fast as they could, which again sent jolts of pain up his body. But as much as he wanted to stop, he couldn't. They were close to the wall, which meant they were close to the spear. Octa still didn't know how he could escape Eadric and the Jutes, and more importantly, do that with the spear, but he knew he had to come up with a plan soon. He prayed to Woden, hoping that he would help Octa because he had come here to get his spear. But then Octa thought of something else that he had not thought of before and it sent a shiver down his spine. Perhaps Woden knew that Octa never intended to give him back his spear. Perhaps he knew Octa wanted to take it to his father and use it to redeem himself. Octa glanced at the Jutes around him as they raced towards the wall. Could all of this have been happening because Woden wanted to make sure that Octa didn't get the spear? Had Woden made a deal with these men as well?

The questions plagued him as they carried on along the Roman road towards the wall, but then Octa forgot about them when they reached the fort at the end of the road and he gaped at the sight before him.

Like Cair Hebrauc, enormous stone walls with towers on the corners greeted them, and when they pulled their horses to a stop, Octa had to crane his neck backwards to see the top of the towers. But that was not what had left Octa gaping. A gigantic wall, taller than three men and built with large stone blocks, broke off from the fort on both sides and ran as far as he could see before disappearing into the distance. He remembered Badulf had told them that the wall ran from coast to coast, but until now Octa had been too focused on finding the spear to really think about what that meant.

'Even if the spear is real, we will never find it,' one of the Jutes said, trembling as he, too, gaped at the wall. 'The wall never ends.'

'Aye. There is no way men could have built this wall,' Alard said, and Octa agreed with him.

'They say the Romans built it, but it was before my father's time,' Badulf said as he too stared at the wall with wide eyes. Octa guessed he had never seen the wall himself.

'That shrine could be anywhere along this wall,' Rembert said. 'And we don't even know if it is on this side of it.'

Octa glanced at the man, but before he could think about what the warrior had said, a horn blew from the fort. They all turned towards the gates of the fort as a group of soldiers marched out towards them. The men were tall, taller than the Britons, and carried large oval shields in front of them, while spears pointed at the Jutes. The warriors were all dressed in Roman armour and had Roman helmets on their heads. But the armour looked old and on some of the warriors Octa saw new leather straps holding the plates of the armour together. The Jutes all tensed as they watched the Roman soldiers approach.

'I thought you said the fort was abandoned,' Eadric said to Badulf, who shook his head.

'I said I don't know if it is abandoned. But if these men are Roman soldiers, then they must be old men by now.'

'Could have recruited more men from the local people,' one of the Jutes said.

'Aye, could have done,' Eadric agreed. 'Stay on your horses, but be ready.' They all nodded as they waited for the Roman soldiers to stop twenty paces away from them.

For a while, both groups stood and stared at each other

before one of the Roman soldiers, a man whose helmet looked different to the others, stepped forward.

'Tell me why a band of Jutes are approaching my fort from the south,' the soldier said in the Saxon tongue.

Octa gasped as he recognised the man's accent and so did the Jutes. 'He's a Saxon.'

'Bollocks,' Eadric grumbled under his breath, and Octa almost smiled as he saw a chance to escape the Jutes.

20

'Welcome to Corstopitum, or Coria as the locals call it,' the old Saxon warrior said as they entered the fort and Octa gaped as he saw more Saxons and Angles inside, but what disappointed him, though, was that most of them had grey hair and beards and they looked like their fighting days were long past them.

'You are the Jutes that King Vortigern has hired?' the old Saxon warrior asked. He introduced himself as Reinald and, though his smile was friendly, Octa noticed the suspicion in his eyes.

'Aye. He needs us to fight his battles for him.'

Reinald glanced at the other six Jutes. 'Thought there'd be more of you.'

'There are. Most of the army is still in the south,' Eadric responded.

Reinald nodded and glanced at Octa. He raised his eyebrow when he saw Octa's leg wound. 'You have a Saxon with you?' Eadric nodded, but said nothing as he watched Reinald. 'What happened to your leg?' Reinald asked him.

Before Octa could respond, Eadric said, 'We were attacked

by one of the tribes and Octa was injured in the fight. We've not been able to treat his wound properly.'

Reinald nodded. 'We have some men here skilled in the matters of healing. They can help with his leg.'

Octa wanted to accept, but the look in Eadric's eyes made him keep his mouth shut.

'We thank you, but we have no time. We are on an urgent quest for my lords, Hengist and Horsa.'

'A quest?' Reinald now raised an eyebrow at Eadric.

Eadric scowled at the old Saxon for a few heartbeats and then said, 'We seek a shrine to Brigantia. We were told there was one near the Roman wall.'

'A shrine to Brigantia?' Reinald scratched his grey beard. 'And here we thought you sought to make an agreement with the Picts.'

'We are here to fight the Picts, not talk to them.'

Reinald smiled as he raised his hand. 'I mean no offence, friend.'

Eadric grunted as he looked around the fort. Octa did the same and saw that it was in a good condition, almost better than the cities he had seen further south. The buildings were perfectly square and laid out in a way that all the paths around them ran straight. All the roofs were tiled and there were a few places where he saw what looked like newer stones in the walls of some of the buildings.

Octa saw about two hundred warriors in the fort and most of them were old. There were some younger warriors as well, and some of them looked like Britons, while others looked like Saxons.

'Well, we didn't expect to find Saxons here,' Eadric said.

Reinald smiled. 'Aye. We came with the Romans as feoderati

and when they left, we stayed behind. Or were left behind. But it's the same thing, really.'

'To do what?' Eadric asked.

'What we were told to do. Protect the wall.'

Eadric looked at his Jutes and smiled. 'Well, Woden knows you're not doing a good job of it. We fought a large force of Picts in the south not that long ago.'

'Woden also knows that this is a large wall and there are only so many of us. There are places where the wall has collapsed because the locals steal the stone for their buildings. We stop the raids we can, but many make it past the wall.'

'Then why bother?' Alard asked.

Reinald shrugged. 'Because it is our duty and Tiw commands we do it.'

'Even if you know the Romans have forgotten about you and won't send any reinforcements?'

Reinald shrugged again. 'It is our duty and if we must die here, then that is our wyrd.' He looked at Octa again. 'Now you tell me. Why are you so interested in this shrine?'

Eadric glanced at Octa and scowled as he searched for an answer to give. 'My lords, Hengist and Horsa, heard that she is an important god and want to ask for her blessing. If we are here to protect her lands, then we need to know she is on our side.'

Reinald nodded, but something in his face told Octa he didn't believe Eadric. 'The Britons have forgotten about the gods of these lands.' He glanced at Badulf and the other Britons with a raised eyebrow. 'They follow the Christian god now.'

'Warriors of King Vortigern, sent to guide us north,' Eadric said when he saw who Reinald was looking at. 'Do you know about this shrine?'

Reinald scratched his grey beard again and glanced at Octa's leg. 'First, let us help with your man's leg and then we will tell you where to find this shrine.'

'You know where it is?' Octa blurted out before he could stop himself.

Reinald nodded. 'We've been here a long time. There's not much about these parts we don't know about.'

Octa grimaced as he was helped off his horse and he felt the other Saxons staring at him.

'Get him to Vellocatus,' Reinald said to one of the men, who nodded and led Octa, helped by Badulf, towards a building away from the centre of the fort. 'The rest of you can take your horses to the stables. Then go the mead hall where we will provide you with some food and ale.' Octa saw the Jutes smile, even the Britons when Reinald's words were translated to them, before he and Badulf were led into a building that looked just like all the others around it.

Inside the building was dark, and it took a moment for Octa's eyes to adjust. When they did, he frowned at what he saw. There was a large bloodstained table in the centre of a large room and near this table was a smaller one filled with tools you'd expect to see in a smithy, not a place where the injured were treated. Large metal tongs and smaller ones with sharp edges. Knives of all sizes, their sharp edges glinting in the light provided by a nearby lamp, as well as many more things he did not recognise. Octa's stomach clenched as his heart raced, especially when he saw an old Briton waiting for him inside, the man's severe face showing no compassion. The Briton raised an eyebrow at Octa as Badulf helped Octa to the table.

'What happened?' the Briton, whom Octa thought must have been Vellocatus, asked in accented Saxon.

'A spear,' was all Octa said.

'A spear?' Vellocatus repeated as he removed the bandage

Badulf had wrapped around the wound. He tutted to himself as he studied the wound, prodding it here and there and causing Octa to grimace. 'You should have rested to let it heal properly. Especially if you want to walk without a limp.'

'If I could, I would,' Octa said through clenched teeth. Vellocatus raised an eyebrow and Badulf said something to him in their tongue. The frown turned to a scowl and the two Britons had a tense conversation as Vellocatus tended to the wound. Octa closed his eyes so that he didn't have to see what the old Briton was doing and wondered what Badulf had said to the man.

'You need to rest the wound and let it heal. I suggest you stay here and let your companions carry on with their journey.' Octa opened his eyes and saw Vellocatus wiping his hands clean on a dirty cloth. He looked at his leg and saw the fresh bandage wrapped around the wound, but before he could respond, Eadric walked into the building and glared at him.

'We stay here tonight. Tomorrow, we look for the shrine.'

'Shrine?' Vellocatus asked, and his eyes went to Badulf, who gently shook his head.

Eadric glared at the two Britons for a short while before he turned to Octa, his eyes glancing at the clean bandage around Octa's thigh. 'You stay here. One of my men will be outside.' Without waiting for a response from Octa, he turned and left again.

'It seems you are more a prisoner than a companion,' Vellocatus said, and all Octa could do was nod. 'You sleep. That is what your leg needs. I'll talk to Reinald. Perhaps he can get your leader to let you stay.'

'Is Reinald the leader here?' Octa asked, and Vellocatus shook his head.

'Saebald is the commander of this fort. But he is away

visiting another fort to the east. Reinald is his second in command, so for now I guess he is,' Vellocatus said, before he walked out, leaving Badulf and Octa on their own.

'What did you say to him?' Octa asked.

Badulf stared at Octa for a short while and then he said, 'I told him what we were looking for and asked if he knew anything about it.'

'Did he?'

Again, Badulf stared at Octa for a short while. 'He said that if we want to live, then we need to stay away from the shrine of Brigantia. There are those who are tasked with protecting it.'

'Like the man who followed us from Cair Hebrauc?'

Badulf shrugged. 'I don't know.'

Octa looked at his freshly bandaged leg. 'Help me escape Eadric.'

Badulf raised an eyebrow at him. 'Why would I do that?'

'Because if Hengist and Horsa get their hands on the spear, then they will turn this island into their kingdom,' Octa said, even though he didn't know if that was true. He did feel that the brothers were up to something and did not believe that they would be happy being King Vortigern's warriors. Not after what he had seen from them. They were men who led, not followed orders from others.

'You don't know that. And even if that was true, they don't have enough men to do that.' Badulf shook his head. 'And besides, what happens after I help you escape?'

Octa frowned as he still stared at his leg. 'We find the shrine and get the spear.'

Badulf laughed as he shook his head. 'You still want the spear? After everything that has happened and after being told that we will be killed if we go near there?'

Octa looked up from his leg and stared at Badulf with a

determination he didn't know he had until that moment. 'They're going to kill me, anyway. This way I might survive.'

'And then what?' Badulf asked again. 'Where do you go then? It's not like you can go back to Hengist and Horsa.'

'I go home. Back to the lands of the Saxons.'

'With the spear? You don't even know if it is real.'

'The spear is real.'

Badulf stared at him for a while. 'King Vortigern has the finger bone of some saint who was crucified by the Romans before they became Christians. The priests believe it brings him luck, but I know that at least two other kings also claim to have the same finger bone from the saint.'

'People have many fingers. They all could be right,' Octa said, not sure where Badulf was going with this.

Badulf nodded. 'That is what the priests say. But it could also just be a finger bone someone dug up and claimed to belong to the saint.'

'The spear is real,' Octa said once he understood what Badulf was saying to him.

'Why are you so sure?'

Octa looked away so that Badulf couldn't see the doubt in his eyes. 'Because it has to be.'

'Because it has to be,' Badulf repeated, and then stood up from the stool he had been sitting on. 'If I help you, then I die. You can go back to your homelands, but these are mine. Even if what you say is true, I can't help you.' He turned and walked out of the building before Octa could say anything. Not that there was anything he could say. He had expected that response, especially after everything that had happened, but he needed to try.

Octa lay back down on the table and closed his eyes as he tried to understand why Woden had done this to him. Or perhaps it wasn't Woden. Perhaps it was whichever god had taken the spear that was trying to stop Octa from getting the spear. But which god could be strong enough to oppose Woden? There was only one god he could think of. Tiw. But Tiw stood for honour and fairness. He wouldn't steal Woden's spear and give it to the Romans to hide in Britannia. Or at least, Octa didn't think that Tiw would do that.

Octa sighed as he pushed the thoughts from his mind. It didn't matter. Not any more. He had failed and he would die without redeeming himself. When he was a boy, he had been told the stories of warriors who died with honour and with bravery. They told him how these warriors went to Woden's hall of the slain. But no one ever said what happened to those who died in disgrace. The ones who fled from battles and left their friends to die. He thought of Uhtric, the first time in days, and wondered if his cousin had gone to Woden's hall. That might have been his first battle, but he fought bravely and would have lived if it had not been for Octa's cowardice. His hand went to the spear pendant around his neck, and he remembered how his mother had told him to make a name for himself. Then he could return home and be redeemed. He had tried to do that, but he had failed her just like he had Uhtric. And just like he had done his father.

A tear ran down his cheek as he remembered those he had left behind. 'Forgive me, cousin. Forgive me, Mother and Father. I have let you all down.'

* * *

Brigid looked around to make sure she was not being followed before she slipped out of the fort gates. One warrior whistled at her, but Brigid ignored the man as she worried about her brother. His absence disturbed her more than it had before, and she could not understand why.

She made her way to the small forest near the fort. The only one that had not been cut down for timber, but only because the people feared the secrets the trees held. Secrets very few really understood, and Brigid was lucky enough to be one of those few. She glanced over her shoulder to make sure that she was not being followed as she walked past the first trees of the forest and followed a path only she and others like her knew. But Brigid was not as relaxed as she usually was as she passed old oak trees. The songs of the birds did not bring the same joy as they normally would and this time she didn't keep her eyes peeled, hoping to see the fox that lived in this forest. Instead, her head hung low as she thought about the conversation she had overheard between King Vortigern and King Gwyrangon. She didn't understand why her brother had gone north with the Jutes, but she knew it was because of Octa.

Brigid had warned her brother about the tall warrior. Just like the mother had warned her about him. She walked along the hidden path until she came to a small clearing and paused. Taking a deep breath, Brigid walked into the clearing and towards the old tree that stood on the opposite side. Most who found the clearing would not think anything of it or understand why it was important. But they all, even the Christians, would not want to linger here long enough to discover its secrets. There was a dark presence that everyone felt, but only the few like Brigid understood what it really meant.

Brigid walked to the old tree and knelt in front of it. She looked up at the branches, noting they were quieter than usual. But it had been the same the last time she was here and the time before.

'Mother, I come to you again. I worry about my brother and

your silence. I know I should not have said anything to my brother about the Saxon, but I had to warn him.' She looked up at the branches again, but saw nothing to tell her the old goddess was listening to her. 'Change is coming. I can feel it around me. King Vortigern believes he can control the men from across the seas, but I fear he underestimates them. And that his arrogance will be his downfall and the ruin of our people.'

The leaves on the branches rustled as a breeze picked and swirled around Brigid. Somewhere above the trees, a hawk screamed at her. Brigid felt the shiver run down her spine and prayed that Badulf would return soon.

21

'You're awake,' the voice said when Octa opened his eyes the following morning.

For a moment, he lay there and stared at the wooden beams that supported the tiled roof of the building he was in as the scent of herbs and honey reached his nose. His nose creased as another scent reached it, stale sweat and dried blood. Octa sat up and grimaced at the pain in his leg, but he was glad it was not as painful as the day before. The night's rest had helped numb the pain, or perhaps it was whatever Vellocatus had put on it when he had treated it the day before. Octa turned to the man sitting beside him and raised an eyebrow when he saw it was Reinald.

'How is your leg?' the old Saxon asked.

'Feels better.' Octa stared at him, wondering why he was sitting there. Eadric had told him that one of his men would be outside, but then he guessed the Jute couldn't prevent Reinald from entering.

Reinald nodded. 'I don't know what is going on and I don't believe that a group of Jutes travelled all the way to the wall just to see a shrine to a goddess they know nothing about because they want her blessing. Men like Eadric and whoever his lords are don't care about things like that.'

'How do you know about men like Eadric?'

Reinald shrugged. 'We weren't always stationed here in Corstopitum. When the Romans first brought us over, we were stationed in one of their forts to the south. Our orders were to protect the coastline from raiders.' Reinald stopped and scratched his neck. 'Eadric reminds me of the type of men we used to fight. Men with no honour. So that makes me curious about why you are with them.'

'Why do you care?'

'Because I can see that you are not like them. And the way Eadric watches you makes me think you are more of a prisoner than a companion.'

Octa's heart raced in his chest as he wondered where the old Saxon was going with this conversation. Was he offering to help him? Octa remembered the conversation Badulf had with Vellocatus the day before and wondered if that was why Reinald was here. But then Octa remembered his cousin and sighed. He did not deserve to be rescued. 'I might not be like them, but I am still a man of no honour.'

Again, Reinald shrugged and for a moment he sat there, looking around the building as if he had never been inside before. 'You are not the first who seeks that shrine and I doubt you will be the last.' He smiled as Octa gaped at him. 'Aye, I know exactly why you are here and though I don't care about your motivation, I'd still warn you not to go.'

Octa opened his mouth to speak, but for a few heartbeats no words could come out. 'What do you know about the shrine?' he eventually asked.

'All I know is that all those who came looking for it died

before they could reach the shrine. There are those who protect it and its secrets.'

'Why are you telling me this?' Octa frowned at Reinald.

'I don't care about the Jutes. I spent too many winters and lost too many friends fighting those bastards and others like them. But you are not like them. I could see that even as you approached the fort. If you want, you can stay here in Corstopitum, join our ranks.'

Octa wanted to laugh at how the gods enjoyed toying with him. But instead, he shook his head. 'I can't. I have my reasons for wanting to go to the shrine. And besides, the Jutes won't let me stay behind.'

Reinald smiled, which caused Octa to frown. 'Eadric agreed you could stay, provided we never allow you to go to the south.'

Octa gasped at this news and then shook his head. 'No, Eadric would never allow that.'

'It wasn't easy to convince him, but after a few ales and songs, we came to an agreement. I'll tell him how to get to the shrine and you stay here.'

'Why did you do that?' Octa couldn't understand that. Reinald knew nothing about him. He did not know how Octa had run from a battle, and if he did, he would never have made that deal with Eadric. And that was something else he struggled to make sense of. Why would Eadric agree to that? Octa had thought that Eadric wanted to kill him, but then, when the others had suggested it, Eadric had always found reasons they shouldn't. Something else that he struggled to understand.

'My son was about your age and was eager to make a name for himself. He wanted to show me he could be as brave as the Saxons, even though his mother was a Briton. So against my better judgement, I let him lead a patrol north of the wall.' Reinald paused and Octa saw the tear run down his cheek. 'I never saw my son again. And worse than that, to this day, I still don't know what happened to him. I led patrols north to find the answers, but the gods hid them from me. I never even got a chance to bury his body.' He looked at Octa. 'I'll not let your father go through the same thing. Not if I can prevent it. So stay here and let your leg heal. Then you can go back to the homeland.'

Octa shook his head and felt his heart thud in his chest at the mention of his father. 'My father doesn't care what happens to me.' *And I made a promise to my mother that I can't break.*

'All sons feel that way, but—'

'No, you don't understand.' Octa's hands trembled as he sought the courage to tell Reinald the truth. He didn't know why he wanted to do that. Perhaps he didn't feel like he deserved Reinald's help and wanted to give him a reason to hate him. 'I ran from a battle and my cousin died because of it. I am a coward and because of that my father disowned me and if I return to the homeland, my uncle will kill me.'

But instead of the anger and disdain he expected from Reinald, the old Saxon only nodded and said, 'Then stay here. No one needs to know the truth.'

Octa shook his head. 'You don't understand! I am a coward! I deserve whatever fate the gods decide for me!'

Reinald sighed. 'And you believe the spear of Woden will change that?'

Octa gaped at the old Saxon. 'You know what is in the shrine?'

Reinald smiled a sad smile as he got to his feet. 'I told you. Many have come to find the shrine and all of them died before they could find out there is no spear. But your life is your own and if you are so eager to throw it away, then you better hurry. Your companions are preparing to leave. But I warn you again.

The forest the shrine is in is sacred and hides many dangers.' Reinald left the building before Octa could say a word and, for a moment, he just sat there and tried to work out what Reinald had hoped to achieve.

Octa pushed the thoughts from his mind as he struggled to get to his feet. He grimaced at the pain in his leg, but he found he could put some weight on it. Octa looked around the building and saw clean clothes and new shoes next to the stool Reinald had been sitting on. Perhaps the old Saxon had expected the answer Octa gave him, which only made the conversation they had even more confusing, especially when Octa found the seax knife hidden amongst the clothes. Octa struggled into the trousers and somehow managed to get the shoes on his feet. They were too large for him, but they were more comfortable than his old ones, which had been worn out. He rinsed his face with water from a bucket next to the clothes and pulled the tunic over his head before he hid the seax knife and made his way to the door.

Octa stood for a few heartbeats, his hand on the door, and thought about the conversation he had with Reinald. For a moment, it was tempting just to stay here. To forget about the spear and, gods willing, to find some peace. He could forget about what had happened and maybe even settle down. But then Uhtric's face came to his mind, as well as his mother telling him to go out and to make a name for himself so he could return home, and Octa knew he could not stay here with the other Saxons. Taking a deep breath, Octa pushed the door open and limped out into the morning sunlight.

'Bastard still lives,' one of the Jutes said, the disappointment clear in his voice as Octa walked to his horse. Eadric stared at him, but Octa did not want to look at the older warrior to see what expression he wore on his face.

He reached Warda and rubbed her neck as one of the Saxons came to help him mount. 'You should stay here,' the man whispered as Octa settled on the mare, but Octa only shook his head. 'May Thunor watch over you, Octa.' The Saxon walked away and stood next to Reinald, who stared at Octa for a short while before he turned his attention to Eadric.

'You remember the way I told you?'

Eadric nodded, his eyes also on Octa for a few heartbeats. 'Travel east along the wall for half a day and then turn southeast when we see the marker along the path. Keep going until we reach the sacred forest. After that we follow the path through the trees.'

'Aye. The cave you seek is not far from there.' He glanced at Octa again. 'Keep your eyes peeled and not just for the cave.'

Octa looked at Badulf and raised an eyebrow at the fresh bruise on his face as the Briton sat on his horse. He saw the other three Britons who had travelled with them stand by the large building in the centre of the fort, two of them with bruises on their faces as well, and wondered what he had missed during the night as Eadric bid farewell to the Saxons and called the order for his men to leave. Apart from Octa and Eadric, there were only six of them left, and they all nodded to the Saxons before they followed Eadric out of the fort. Octa looked at Reinald, and the old man nodded at him.

'I'll pray to the gods that you find what you are looking for, young Octa. And that you survive this journey.'

Octa's hand tightened on Warda's reins and, without saying a word, he turned his horse and followed the others out.

They rode in silence until they were out of sight of the fort, before Badulf said to Octa, 'You should have stayed behind. The old Saxon worked hard to get Eadric to agree to that.'

'What happened to your face?' Octa asked instead.

Badulf glanced at him before he sighed. 'The others thought we should go back to Cair Urnahc. They're afraid of what might happen if we find the shrine.'

'And you fought over that?'

Badulf shook his head. 'They insulted my sister.'

Octa raised an eyebrow at Badulf, but before he could ask why they would do that, Eadric turned around.

'You two stop your chattering.' He looked at Octa. 'I'm surprised you came with us. You had the chance to stay behind.' Octa shook his head and didn't say anything because he didn't know what to say. 'Perhaps you're not such a coward after all.'

'Or he's too dumb to understand the gods had given him a way out,' Alard said as they carried on following the wall. Octa glared at their backs, not wanting to tell them he was still working on a plan to get the spear for himself. Instead, he studied the giant wall as they rode along the path.

'How did the Romans build it?' he asked Badulf, who could only shrug.

'No one knows. It was built a long time ago, and the Romans took those secrets with them.'

Rembert waved a dismissive hand at Badulf. 'No man built this wall. It's impossible.'

'Then who built it?' Badulf asked the man.

'Giants. Who else?' The other Jutes agreed with Rembert and even Octa had to admit that made more sense because he could not understand how men could have built a wall this size with stone.

Badulf raised an eyebrow at the Jutes. 'Well, then I hope those giants aren't the ones protecting the shrine, because then you'll never find that spear.'

The smiles fell from the faces of the Jutes as their faces paled at the thought of giants protecting the shrine, but then Eadric said, 'Don't listen to the Briton. Thunor chased the giants out of our world a long time ago. And everyone knows the giants don't like the sun, so if we go to the shrine during the day, then we won't have to worry about any giants.'

Octa's hand went to the spear pendant he wore around his neck and prayed that Eadric was right because he knew he could never face a giant. Octa didn't even have the courage to face a man.

22

They travelled along the wall like Reinald had told them to in silence. The Jutes were too tense to talk as they kept their eyes peeled along the path, both for the stone marker and for any signs of trouble. Although Octa wasn't sure if they were looking for men or for giants. He hoped it was men as he thought about the conversation he had had with Reinald before, and Badulf's warnings about the shrine. His hand was gripped around the spear pendant around his neck as he, too, scanned their surroundings.

'How do we know if we find the right shrine?' one Jute asked. 'There must be many shrines out there.'

'How many shrines have you seen to the old gods of this island?' Eadric asked the man, who frowned, and Octa scratched his head at that.

'None, now that I think of it. Some Christian churches, but no shrines to the gods.' He turned to Badulf. 'Why are there no shrines to the gods?'

'There are,' Badulf said. 'There is a larger stone circle in the south, although no one is really sure what it is for any more. The

Romans killed anyone who had that knowledge. And I've heard tales of stone circles in other places.'

'So we are looking for a stone circle?' Eadric asked, and Badulf shrugged.

'I don't know what we are looking for. I was raised as a Christian, just like most in Britannia.' Octa remembered what Badulf had said about his sister and was certain the man was lying.

Eadric grunted. 'Explain why we brought you with us?'

Again, Badulf shrugged. 'That is something I ask myself every day.'

The men fell silent after that as they rode along the path. Octa had lost interest in the wall by now. It looked the same here as it did near the fort, although here and there he saw places where stones had been removed. His leg wasn't aching as much either, and he wondered what the Briton at the fort had put on it and why he hadn't asked for a jar of the stuff. He put his hand on the clean bandage and again wondered if he should have stayed behind. But then he shook his head. He needed to find the spear. He had to take it to his father, although as hard as he tried, he could not think of a way to get it. Especially not with Eadric and his six Jutes constantly watching him. Even without the wound to his leg, he would never be able to defeat one of them, let alone the seven of them. They were all experienced warriors and even though he had been trained by Witta, one of the greatest Saxon warlords, Octa was not a warrior.

Lost in his thoughts and with his gaze wandering the landscape, he spotted a large stone that seemed out of place. 'What's that?'

'What?' Eadric asked, and Octa pointed at the marker. But as soon as Eadric looked at it, one of the Jutes cried out. They all turned to him and gaped at the arrow in his chest as the warrior stared at them for a heartbeat and then he slipped off his horse.

Chaos broke loose as more arrows whizzed from the nearby trees, and Badulf kicked his horse with a scream.

Octa ducked low as more arrows flew over his head, killing another of the Jutes.

'Arrows!' Eadric roared.

'The Briton!' one of the Jutes screamed as Badulf made a break for it. Octa glanced at him and prayed that the man would make it, but then a spear flew through the air and pierced his back. Octa watched with wide eyes as Badulf fell from his horse, but before he could work out who had thrown the spear, Eadric grabbed the reins of his horse and pulled it along as they raced away from the hidden archers. The remaining Jutes all held shields over their heads and Octa saw more than a handful of arrows in them as the wind whipped past his ears.

'This way!' Eadric ordered his men and, to Octa's surprise, he wasn't leading them away from the danger, but in the direction that Reinald had told them to travel once they found the marker. He struggled to understand why Eadric was still leading them towards the shrine as arrows missed them. They raced along the path, with Octa staying low on his horse and with his eyes shut, praying to Thunor to protect him from their hidden killers, so he didn't notice that the arrows had stopped once they were away from the marker on the road.

The first he knew of it was when Eadric ordered them to stop. 'Bastards!' he roared.

Octa opened his eyes and saw they were amongst trees and frowned at that. He looked at the remaining Jutes as they broke the arrows from their shields. One of them had a cut on his arm, but it didn't seem to affect him as he turned his horse and scanned their surroundings. The trees around them were dark and the air was suffocating as if there was no life in this forest. Octa shivered when he saw what looked like human bones in the undergrowth. A reminder of those who had failed before. Even the Jutes seemed uneasy as they glanced around them.

'Could the Saxons have betrayed us?' Alard asked, and Eadric glared at Octa.

'What did he say to you in the building before you came out?'

Octa struggled to get his mouth to work as his fear still coursed through him. 'N... nothing. He only asked me to stay.'

'Maybe because he was planning this and didn't want you to die,' one of the Jutes said, and glared at Octa as if he was about to punch him off his horse.

'The gods know that doesn't matter now.' Eadric looked around him. 'They were waiting for us, but I don't think they expected us to get away from that. So that will buy us some time to find this shrine.'

'You still want to go to that cursed shrine?' Rembert asked, his eyes wide in shock.

'We just lost two more men,' another said. 'We should go back. Tell Hengist and Horsa we couldn't find it.'

'Aye, I'm not dying—' Before the man could get his words out, Eadric rushed his horse at him and punched him off of his. Octa gaped at them as the man landed on the ground, his bloody face grimacing in pain.

'You will die for what Hengist and Horsa tell you to die for!' He turned to face the other warriors. 'We are oath bound to them and the gods demand we bring them back the spear. Even if it kills us.'

The remaining four Jutes glared at Eadric and, just when Octa thought they might turn against him, they nodded.

'I thought you didn't believe in the spear?' Octa frowned at Eadric, but before the older warrior could respond, they heard a branch snap not far from them.

Eadric raised his hand, signalling for them all to be quiet. At another signal, the Jutes dismounted their horses and, for a moment, Octa was tempted to dig his heels in his and make a run for it. But then one of the Jutes pressed the point of his spear against Octa's neck and he knew he'd be dead before the horse could take her first step. Reluctantly, he dismounted and grimaced as he followed Eadric, who led them away from the horses.

They travelled as silently as they could, using hand signals to communicate with each other as they avoided the men who had ambushed them earlier on. Eadric led them with a practised ease, as they never moved in a straight line and regularly stopped to scan their surroundings. Octa struggled to keep up with them, but he wasn't given much of a choice as one of the Jutes stayed close behind him and pressed his knife against Octa's back. At one point, they found one of the men hunting them. A Briton wearing a dark cloak and with a bow in his hands. He was standing by himself, his eyes focused in the wrong direction.

Eadric signalled for them to stop. He crept towards the Briton and stabbed him in the back before the man even knew he was there. Despite his fear, Octa marvelled at how these large Jutes could move like wolves on the hunt, barely making a noise as they crept through the undergrowth of the forest, littered with fallen branches and the bones of the dead.

You shouldn't be here, a voice whispered in his head, and Octa felt a shiver run down his spine as he remembered Reinald telling him that the forest was sacred and that even the Christians avoided it. But he kept that to himself as he did his best to keep up with the Jutes.

'Look,' one Jute said, and they all stopped to see what he was pointing at. Eadric grinned and Octa's heart thudded in his chest as they stared at the cave in the middle of a clearing.

'That has to be it,' Eadric said, and Octa had to agree with him as he stared at the seven Britons who were guarding the entrance. Like the one Eadric had killed earlier on, they were all wearing dark cloaks and were armed with bows. Although Octa spotted the knives on their belts.

The Jutes all pulled their weapons from their belts. There were only five of them left, including Eadric, but Octa doubted the Britons would be able to stop them. The seven guarding the cave did not look like warriors. If anything, they looked like hunters and farmers. Men who lived off the land and not by the spear.

Go away from here, the voice came again and this time Octa was certain the Jutes heard it as well as they glanced around them.

'If you run, you die,' Eadric warned Octa, who looked at his injured leg. He couldn't run even if he wanted to, so he nodded. And besides. He was here. The spear was so close. He sent a silent prayer asking Woden to at least kill two of the Jutes because that would increase his odds of getting his hands on the spear. But Woden did not want to help Octa, because the Jutes rushed out of the undergrowth, catching the Britons by surprise and killing them all before they could even react.

They stood in front of the cave, their shields raised just in case there were still people inside, but after a few heartbeats, Eadric stepped forward and peered into the cave.

'I think it's empty.' He glanced at one of his men. 'Fetch the Saxon.' The Jute nodded and rushed back to grab Octa, but he didn't need to as Octa limped out of the clearing. The Jute raised an eyebrow at him, and Octa shrugged.

'I came all the way to find the spear. Do you really think I'm going to run away now?'

The Jute scowled at him and then nodded before he turned his back on Octa, unaware of the seax knife in Octa's hand. Octa's whole body trembled with fear, but he knew he had nothing left to lose. As soon as they found the spear, Eadric would kill him. He was certain of it, even if Eadric had been ordered to bring him back alive. They had already lost most of the men who had travelled north with them. He kept the knife hidden as he closed the distance between him and the Jute, knowing the only way he would succeed was if he caught them by surprise, and when he was close enough to reach out and touch the Jute, Octa lunged at him.

The Jute cried out as Octa buried the seax knife in his back, finding a gap in the man's armour as he had been taught to. The others, expecting another attack from the Britons, all turned and ducked behind their shields as they faced the wrong way, just as Octa hoped they would. He pulled his seax knife out of the dead Jute's back and ran as fast as his injured leg allowed him to into the cave. His only hope was to grab the spear before Eadric could and pray that it would help him kill the remaining Jutes.

Octa made it into the cave before the others realised what had happened and was surprised by the torches which lined the walls of the cave, their flames bringing light into the dark cave and what was inside it. He stood frozen to the spot as he gaped at the figure carved into the wall of the cave. Staring back at him was the stony face of a woman wearing a long dress. In her left hand, she held an orb, and in her right hand was a carving of a spear. But it was what stood in front of her, stuck in the ground, that caught Octa's breath. A spear.

Octa snapped out of his trance, aware that Eadric and the

remaining two Jutes would come after him, and limped towards the spear. His eyes were fixed on the gold-rimmed blade and the golden rings around the shaft of the spear. It looked just like he had expected Gungnir to look like, but as he reached out to take it, a sharp pain shot up his injured leg and he collapsed to the ground. Octa looked up at the angry face of Eadric, who held his sword in front of him.

'You really thought you could take the spear for yourself?'

'The spear is mine,' Octa said through gritted teeth. 'The old man told me about it, not you.'

Eadric struck his wound again with the flat side of his sword, and Octa cried out in pain. 'You are not the only one the old bastard told about the fucking spear!'

Even in his pain, Octa wondered what Eadric meant by that, but before he could ask, Alard said, 'We should just kill him.'

'We should have killed him a long time ago,' Rembert said.

But Eadric shook his head. 'If we'd killed him before, then we'd never have got our hands on the spear.'

'What do you mean?' Alard asked, and even Octa wondered about that.

Eadric stared at Octa, a sudden sadness in his eyes that Octa did not understand. 'You really think we can just take Woden's spear and leave here alive without giving something in return?'

'You mean—' Alard asked as he, too, stared at Octa.

'Aye. A life for the spear. That is one part of the story young Octa here never got. To take the spear, we need to make a sacrifice to the goddess who guards it. You really should have stayed in the fort, Octa.'

23

Octa's mind raced as Eadric's words rung in his ears, and the Jutes laughed. The old man had never told him about this. But then, the old man was not the one who had told him where to find the spear. Octa didn't know if he should curse himself or the gods. He should have known there would be something like this. Nothing that involved the gods was ever easy. All the stories he had heard about the gods told him that. There was always a price to be paid. But then Octa thought of something else and he frowned at Eadric.

'How do you know this? Did the old man tell you the story?'

Eadric's face darkened even more. 'Not me. My son.'

Octa frowned. 'Your son?'

Eadric's eyes were fixed on the spear in front of the statue. 'Aye. The old man told him the story of how Woden lost his spear and how the warrior who can bring it back will be rewarded. My boy was about your age and eager to make a name for himself. He believed he could do it, wanted me to go with him, so he told me the story the old man had told him. But I thought it was a fool's errand, so I refused to go. Begged my boy to forget about it and come raiding with me. He refused. Called me a coward and set off on his own. That was the last time I ever saw him.'

'Is that why he left?' Alard asked. 'You never told us what happened to your boy.'

Eadric clenched his fists. 'I didn't want anyone to know. All I wanted was to kill the old bastard who had used my son for his amusement.'

'Then why didn't you?' Octa asked, and Eadric raised an eyebrow at him.

'You don't see it, do you? You really don't know who the old man is?'

Octa shrugged as he tried to creep away from Eadric. 'He is just some old man.'

Eadric laughed. 'You fool. That is what I thought until I cornered him one day and was about to stick my knife in him. That old bastard is Woden!'

'Woden?' Octa frowned as he tried to remember what the old man looked like, but couldn't. 'It can't be.'

'It is.' Eadric glared at the spear in the middle of the cave, his jaw muscles tense under his beard. 'I lost everything because of that cursed thing. My son, myself and most of my warriors. I was a warlord, a man whose name many knew and then I lost it all.'

'That was why you joined Hengist and Horsa?' Rembert asked, and Eadric nodded.

'They gave me something to fight for again.' Eadric clenched his fists. 'And after we give them the spear, I'll have my own ship again. I can be the man I once was. I had planned on killing Badulf, but he's gone now.' Eadric turned to the remaining warriors. 'Grab him.'

Two Jutes grabbed Octa's arms while Rembert punched him in the face. Eadric walked to the statue and for a few heartbeats he stood there and stared at it before he took the spear. They all held their breath and glanced around the cave as if they expected something to happen. But nothing did. There was no lightning outside the cave. No monster's roar or even the cry of a raven. All Octa could hear was his own heart beating in his chest and the heavy breathing of the Jutes around him. Even Eadric frowned as his eyes darted around the cave while he held on to the spear.

'Nothing?' Alard asked, and Eadric shrugged. 'I expected more.'

'Perhaps this goddess isn't as powerful as she used to be. The Briton told us that most have forgotten about her.' He looked at the spear in his hand and all Octa could hear was the gods laughing in his ears. He had failed to get Woden's spear and now would die and his mother would never know about it.

'How do we know it is the real spear?' Alard asked, and the others nodded.

Eadric looked at the gold-rimmed blade and raised an eyebrow. 'It looks like what you'd expect a spear of the gods to look like.'

'Aye,' the warrior said. 'But many have spears that look like that. How do we know this one is real?'

Again, Eadric shrugged. 'It doesn't matter. As long as Hengist and Horsa believe it is real.' He turned to Octa. 'Time to make that sacrifice.' He took a step towards Octa and lowered the spear. 'I liked you, Octa, but just like my son, you will die because of the spear.'

Something woke inside Octa and, before he knew what he was doing, he pulled his arm free from the grip of the Jutes, who were too focused on the spear to react in time. And before Alard could react, Octa grabbed the man's knife from his belt and stabbed him in the groin. He pulled the blade out, his hand drenched in blood, as Alard's scream pierced the fog in the minds of the others, and turned to stab the other Jute. But this warrior jumped out of the way and all Octa did was cut his leg before Rembert brought his axe down on Octa's head. Octa sensed the movement and rolled out of the way, grimacing as his leg protested, and felt the axe miss him. He turned to face Rembert and was about to stab him in the exposed side, just as Eadric had taught him to do, when the older warrior rushed forward and struck Octa on the side of the head with the shaft of the spear.

Octa's head snapped to the side, and he dropped the knife before the second Jute kicked him in the stomach. Whatever Octa had felt before that had given him the courage to attack the Jutes left him and all he could do was cover his head as Eadric and the remaining Jutes stomped on him. Octa cried out in pain as boots landed on his face and chest, but as he lay there, waiting for the final blow to end his life, he thought of Uhtric and of his mother. People he loved more than anyone else and had betrayed more than anyone else. He thought of the last moment he saw his cousin, just before he turned and fled from that battle, and of the last time he saw his mother, the promise he had made to her still fresh on his lips. He had let both of them down, but at least Uhtric would get a chance to face him in the afterlife.

The stomping stopped, and the Jutes stepped away, leaving Octa a bloody mess on the ground. But just when he thought it was over, Eadric leaned over him and grabbed him by his hair. Octa screamed in pain as Eadric dragged him towards the statue of Brigantia and dropped him by her feet.

'Kill him and get it done with,' Rembert said, and Eadric shook his head.

'No, a quick death will be a blessing this coward does not deserve.'

'What about the sacrifice?' Rembert asked, and Eadric looked at Alard, who had bled out during the brief fight.

'The gods have their sacrifice. It's time for us to leave before more of the Britons arrive.'

Eadric's words felt like a stab in his chest as he realised what the older warrior had planned. 'You can't leave me here,' Octa said, and Eadric smiled at him.

'I can and I will.' He looked around the cave. 'You should have stayed in the fort. I gave you the chance to live, and you didn't take it. You wanted to come here to find Woden's spear, so it's only right that you die in here.' He turned and walked away.

'You sure that's a good idea?' Rembert asked.

'Look at him. He'll be dead by nightfall. The bastards that ambushed us will be here at some point and they will kill him when they find him.'

The Jute nodded as he thought about it and then asked, 'What do we do?'

'We go back to Hengist and Horsa and we give them the spear and I will get the ship Horsa promised me.'

'And what about us?'

Eadric looked at the remaining two warriors. 'I'll make sure the brothers reward you.'

The Jutes both glanced at each other, and then one of them shrugged before he followed Eadric out of the cave. Rembert walked towards Octa and spat in his face before he kicked him in his injured leg. But Octa was in too much pain to react at that point and just lay there as they left.

Octa stayed where he was. Even if he wanted to move, he couldn't. Not with his body wrecked by pain. So he lay there and waited to die, or for the Britons to come and kill him. His hand went to the spear pendant around his neck.

'Forgive me, Mother. I failed you, just like I failed Uhtric and Father.' He wondered if she would find out that he had died and prayed she wouldn't. He'd rather that she believed he was alive and making a name for himself and not that he had died in some cave. His mother's face came to his mind, her stern eyes almost berating him for giving up. 'I did my best, Mother. But it was not good enough.' His mother's face refused to go away, even when he squeezed his eyes shut. Then Uhtric came to him, his face creased in anger at what Octa had done. Octa groaned and shook his head as tears rolled down his cheeks.

With a cry, Octa rolled over onto his knees and gripped the statue so he could get up. He had promised his mother he would return to her, and he would not let her down. Not like he had failed Uhtric and his father. Using the statue for support, Octa struggled to his feet. He pressed his bleeding hand against the face of the statue and leaned against it as he tried to work out how he was going to get out of the cave and where he was going to go. The Saxons in the Roman fort seemed his best option. If he could get there, then he could recover from his injuries and stay with them. Reinald had told him he could.

Octa heard a flap of wings and felt a breath of wind on the back of his neck. Frowning, he looked around him and, although he couldn't see anything, he sensed he was not alone in that cave. Octa peered towards the entrance, expecting the Britons to walk in, but there was nobody there. He looked back at the statue and saw his bloody handprint on her face, but as the light from the torches inside the cave flickered, something about the stone spear in the statue's hand caught his eye.

Octa frowned as he stared at the stone spear, his mind racing as he tried to understand what he was seeing. It was hard to see

it in the dim light of the cave, but as the light of the torches flickered, it looked like the stone spear was a different colour to the
rest of the statue. His trembling hand reached out to touch it
when, again, he heard wings flap and felt something rush past
his head. Octa ducked and looked around, but again saw
nothing.

'Who's there?' he called out, but got no response. For a
moment, he stood there, his heart racing in his chest as he
scanned the cave before he turned his attention back to the
spear. Again, he reached out with a trembling hand and touched
the stone spear. To his surprise, some of the stone flaked off and
in the flickering light of the torches, he thought he saw the glint
of metal. Frowning and with his heart racing even faster, he
peeled the rest of the stone away to reveal a plain spear, unlike
the one that had stood before the statue.

Octa's mind reeled as he stared at the spear, unable to make
sense of what he was seeing. *That can't be Woden's spear*, he
thought as he continued to stare at the spear, which looked like
one every man in his homeland had. But then he noticed something on the blade of the spear, something he only saw because
of the flickering light of the torches. Octa struggled to breathe as
he saw a raven, a symbol of Woden, etched on the blade, but just
as he was about to reach out to take the spear from the statue,
there was another flap of wings above his head. Octa flinched as
wing tips brushed his head and he fell to the ground, his hand
going to his head as if he had been struck. As he lay on the
ground in front of the statue, he gaped at the white owl that was
sitting on the statue's head, peering at him like an evil spirit.
Octa's hand went to the spear pendant around his neck as his
eyes flickered towards the spear in the statue's grip.

The spear will not give you what you want. Leave this cave and forget you saw it. A woman's voice echoed around the cave, and Octa frowned at the owl.

'How do you know what I want?' Octa asked the owl, convinced it was the bird speaking to him, even if he didn't understand it.

What you want is of no concern to me. Leave this cave.

Octa shook his head and wondered if he was seeing things that weren't there. Perhaps he was already dead, and this was part of the afterlife, but then he was in too much pain to believe that. Octa grimaced as he struggled to his feet, the cut to his legs stinging enough to make him think it had opened again and the rest of his body aching from when the Jutes had beaten him. But he gritted his teeth and forced himself to stand straight.

'I need that spear.'

The spear will only bring death.

'I've lost too much just to walk away now. I won't let you stop me,' he said with a sense of conviction he didn't have before. The sight of the spear seemed to ignite something inside him and Octa swore he would fight the gods if he needed to to get his hands on that spear.

And you will lose much more if you take the spear out of this cave.

'I have nothing left to lose, so it doesn't matter.'

You have much to lose, Octa, son of Frithowald.

Octa staggered backwards as he heard his name and, again, he looked around the cave before his eyes landed on the owl on top of the statue. 'Who are you?'

The owl ruffled its feathers and then stared at him again.

Leave this cave and forget what you saw here.

'I'm not leaving here without the spear.' He clenched his fists. 'I won't let you stop me.' Octa took a step towards the statue and expected the owl to attack him, but it only stared at him.

Take that spear and you will regret it for the rest of your life. You do not know the god it belongs to.

Octa gritted his teeth again as he struggled to walk towards the spear in the statue's grip. 'The spear belonged to Woden and now it belongs to me.'

He stopped in front of it and held his breath as he wrapped his fingers around the shaft of the spear. In his mind, he saw Uhtric on the battlefield the moment before Octa had disgraced himself. He saw his mother the night she caught him by his father's hall. Both of them staring at him. Both of them telling him to do it. Octa gripped the spear and frowned when nothing happened, although he wasn't sure what would happen. He just expected that something would. Octa glanced up at the owl and shivered as its dark eyes stared at him.

You cannot trust the god whose spear this is. He is malignant and cruel. A god who only cares for his own pleasures and would sacrifice your life to amuse himself. He will not give you what you want and when he has the spear in his hands, he will bring destruction and death to this land and many others.

Octa glared at the owl and, with a final deep breath, he pulled the spear from the statue's grip. The owl screeched and flew at Octa, its sharp talons aiming for his face. Octa raised his arm to protect himself and cried out as the owl's talons cut into his flesh. With a final warning, the owl flew out of the cave.

The spear will not be your redemption, Octa, son of Frithowald. It will be your death.

24

Brigid looked up at the old tree as its leaves rustled in the gust of wind that blew through the clearing. Her hands went to her mouth as tears ran down her cheeks. She didn't know what the message was, but she knew it wasn't good. Not for her or the people of Britannia.

She had come to the tree every day since King Gwyrangon brought his news of the band of Jutes who had travelled north with her brother, but as before, the voice of the mother goddess remained silent. Brigid had thought of seeking the elder who had taught her how to control her gift, a woman far older than her own mother had been. But the woman had gone north many winters ago and Brigid did not know how to find her.

Brigid placed her hand on the bark of the tree with the face of the mother goddess carved into its trunk. 'Mother, please talk to me. Where is my brother?' She heard a flap of wings and smiled as she looked up at the branch where the bird landed above her. But instead of seeing the white owl she was used to, Brigid saw a large raven, its beady eyes sending a shiver down her spine. She froze as the raven opened its large beak and screamed at her, its cry sounding like dark laughter. Fear gripped Brigid and before she knew what she was doing, she jumped to her feet and fled the clearing, her hands covering her ears as she tried to block the raven's cries from reaching her.

She ran back to King Vortigern's hall as fast as she could, desperate to speak to the king. She had to warn him, tell him of the danger he had put them all in. Of the death and destruction he had brought to Britannia.

* * *

Octa stared at the spear, his legs trembling under him as he struggled to stand. He had hoped to feel something, a sense of Woden's power perhaps, but all he felt was the pain from the beating he had taken. He turned the spear in his hands, his eyes fixed on the spearhead and the two ravens etched into the metal on both sides. The ravens looked different from each other and Octa wondered if they represented Woden's ravens. Octa had heard of warriors carving the mark on their weapons because they believed Woden would protect them during battles and, as he stared at the marks, he wondered if that was not what he was looking at. But then he frowned as he thought about the owl. He was certain the bird had been talking to him, warning him not to trust Woden.

Octa shook his head and turned towards the opening of the cave. The sun was sitting low in the sky and soon it would be night. Octa needed to leave, but he did not know where to go. South was not an option for him, not after everything that had happened. He doubted he could return to Hengist and Horsa, even with the spear. They would kill him and take the spear for themselves. Although which brother would use it, Octa didn't know or care about. The only option he could think of was the

Saxon feoderati in the Roman fort. But what would stop them from killing him and taking the spear?

Octa stared at the spear as he felt his anger grow. With a scream, he turned and threw it at the wall of the cave. He watched as the spear struck the wall with a spark before it fell to the ground. Octa had risked everything to get the spear and, now that he had it, he wished he had never found it because he didn't know whom to trust. Especially as the words of the owl still rang in his ears. *It will be your death.*

But Octa had found the spear. He had done what no one else before him could. He had found the spear of Woden and with it he would make his name and return home to his father and mother and he would ask for their forgiveness. Octa would give the spear to his father and prove to him he was not a coward, but a Saxon warrior. The flames in the cave fluttered as if they heard his thoughts, and Octa glanced at the torches before he limped to the spear and picked it up, before he left the cave.

As soon as he was out of the cave, his head spun and Octa felt the rest of his strength leave him. He almost laughed at the thought that he had found the spear and was most likely going to die from his injuries. His leg was bleeding heavily again, as was his arm where the owl had cut him, and his body ached from the beating. Octa could barely stand and had to lean on the spear for support.

As he reached the trees at the end of the clearing, he heard a flap of wings and looked up, expecting to see the owl again. But instead, he was met by a large raven, which tilted its head as it stared at him. Octa shook his head and was about to ignore the raven when it screamed at him.

Spear, it seemed to say, and Octa gaped at the large bird. *Spear*, the cry came again.

'Did Woden send you?' Octa asked. Everyone knew Woden

had two ravens that sat on his shoulders and whispered things to him.

Spear, the raven seemed to say again.

Octa looked at the spear and remembered what the old man had promised him. That Woden would reward the warrior who brought him his spear. But what reward could be better than having the spear of Woden? The old man had said himself that Woden was weak without the spear, so how was he going to stop Octa from keeping the spear for himself? Octa looked at the raven again, this time with a sneer on his face. 'No. The spear belongs to me. I am the one who found it and I will give it to my father. That way, I will earn my redemption. You can tell Woden that he can have his spear back when I'm done with it.'

The raven stared at Octa as he swayed where he stood and, with one last cry, it flapped its large wings and took to the sky. Octa tried to follow its path, but his head spun violently and before he knew what was happening, Octa was on the ground and was staring at the darkening sky before his world turned black.

* * *

Octa felt rough hands grab him and lift him off the ground. He felt the spear being taken from his grip and, as hard as he tried, he could not tighten his fingers around the shaft. *The spear belongs to me*, he wanted to say, but the words could not come out. His mouth refused to obey him. He heard voices around him as he was placed on something hard, one of them familiar, but he could not make out the words spoken. It sounded like he was underwater and, for a moment, Octa wondered if he had died. If Woden had taken his life because he had defied the war god. Or perhaps it was Brigantia, preventing him from taking the spear back to Woden.

Octa tried to open his eyes, to see where he was and what was happening. He tried to speak, to make a sound, but his body refused to obey him. All he could do was lie on the hard surface that felt like it was moving and try to make sense of the words spoken around him. But as he did that, he felt himself slipping back into a deeper darkness that he was already in. *This must be death. I must have died,* he thought before the darkness took him. *Uhtric, forgive me.*

* * *

Witta sat in his seat in his mead hall, his fists opening and closing as he tried to control his rage. His temples throbbed from all the smoke from the hearth fire and he glared at the slave who was stoking the flames and creating all the smoke, wanting to rip her head off her shoulders. He closed his fists again, squeezing them tightly until his fingernails dug into his palms. Closing his eyes, he took deep breaths, but nothing worked. Nothing could calm him down, as the people in his mead hall seemed oblivious to his anger. His warriors, who should have been out searching for Octa the Coward, were laughing as they told stories, while nearby his four wives were sitting together and gossiping. Their voices rang in his ears and sent his heart pounding every time they laughed. Walaric, his youngest son, was sitting with them, instead of being outside with the other boys and learning how to fight. No one seemed to care that Uhtric was dead. The favourite of all his children. His oldest son and the best of them all. Dead because the son of his cousin was a coward. It might have been many moons since that battle, but to Witta it still felt as if it had only happened that morning. Unable to take it any more, he jumped to his feet and roared at everyone.

'Enough!'

Everyone in the mead hall froze as they all stared at him. Walaric started crying, and Witta glared at him.

'Why are you crying? Stop crying!' he screamed at the boy, which only made him cry even more. Witta stormed towards Walaric, only for his mother to step in front of him, her eyes fierce and showing more steel than most men.

'Don't harm my son,' she said to him as the boy cowered behind her.

'Then get him out of my hall and turn him into a man. Or he is no longer my son.'

His wife glared at him and he wondered how she could have given him a son like Uhtric only to produce a coward after that. And his other wives weren't much better. All they had given him were daughters when he needed more sons. Witta glared at his wives, who all stood up and left the hall before he turned his anger toward his warriors.

'And why are you still here? Octa is out there somewhere and the bastard Thuringians are stealing our lands. And you sit here and drink my mead and tell stories!' He grabbed a cup and threw it at his warriors, who all rushed out of the hall, leaving Witta on his own. Or so he thought, until he spotted the old man sitting in the corner of his mead hall, his broad hat on the table in front of him. 'Get out of my hall, stranger. You are not wanted here.'

The old man looked up and Witta felt like he had seen him before. 'It is not wise to throw those wanting hospitality out of your hall, Witta the Bear.'

Witta raised an eyebrow at the old man, whose one eye

glinted in the dim light of his hall. 'Go find hospitality some-where else.'

He turned to go back to his seat when the old man said, 'And where should I go? To the hall of Frithowald, your cousin? Or the other warlords conspiring against you? Or to the Thuringians who day by day push deeper into your lands while you sit here.'

Witta turned and glared at the old man. 'What do you know of what happens in these lands?'

The old man smiled. 'I travel and so I see things and hear things.'

Despite his anger, Witta was intrigued by the old man's words. 'And what do you hear and see?'

The old man lifted the cup in front of him and looked inside of it. 'My throat is dry and my tongue sticks to the top of my mouth.'

Witta clenched his fists, but then took a deep breath to calm himself before he took a jug of mead and walked over to the old man and filled his cup. 'Tell me what you know.'

The old man drank from his cup and smiled. 'This is good mead. Worthy of the gods, I think.'

'The gods can go fuck themselves,' Witta grumbled. 'They took my son from me and now the Thuringians are taking my lands as well. And the gods do nothing to help me,' he said when he saw the old man raise an eyebrow at him.

'It's not up to the gods to solve your problems for you. The Thuringians are only taking your lands because theirs are being taken from them.'

'And why should I care about that?'

The old man shrugged. 'You don't have to.' He drank more of his mead and held the cup for Witta to fill it up again. Witta stared at the old man for a few heartbeats and then refilled his cup. 'And as for your son. Perhaps he died for a reason.'

Witta's heart almost ripped out of his chest as the old man said that. Through clenched teeth, he said, 'And for what reason did my son have to die?'

The old man shrugged. 'I don't know, or perhaps I do. I don't really know any more.' He drank more of the mead. 'This mead is really good.'

Witta, unable to hold his rage any more, slapped the cup out of the old man's hand. The cup bounced against the wall, its contents spilling out as thunder rolled outside his hall. To his surprise, though, the old man only looked at him.

'A pity. That was really good mead.'

'Get out of my hall,' Witta said, struggling to stop himself from killing the old man.

The old man stared at him for a few heartbeats before he shrugged and stood up. He took his broad-brimmed hat and put it on his head, and walked towards the door of Witta's mead hall. But before he left, the old man turned and said, 'I wonder how Frithowald got his chain-mail vest and sword back.'

Witta frowned at the comment and then his eyes widened as he remembered Frithowald had given his sword and chain-mail vest to his son the morning of that battle. He stormed out of his hall, hoping to see the old man outside, but there was no sign of him. His heart racing, Witta called out to his warriors. 'Get the horses ready!'

One of his warriors frowned at him. 'Where are we going?'

'We are going to visit my cousin.'

25

Octa opened his eyes and winced at the flash of bright light beside him. He blinked a few times as he waited for his eyes to adjust and glanced at the source of the light. A torch on the wall near him. He stared at the dancing flame as he tried to make sense of what had happened, but all he could see in his mind was a large flame in a cave, a woman glaring at him as she held something in her hand. Something important. Octa turned away from the torch, away from the woman's glare, and looked at the roof above him. A roof he had seen not that long ago, but his foggy mind could not remember when or where. He groaned as he tried to sit up, desperate to find out where he was, when someone pushed him back down again. Panic gripped Octa, and he wanted to scream when a soothing voice said, 'Calm yourself, Octa. You are safe. Calm.'

Octa turned to the source of the voice and saw a wrinkled face staring at him, a familiar face with long grey hair and a grey beard. At first, he thought it was the old man from Jutland. Woden. But then he remembered he had seen that face recently.

Octa frowned as the name came to him and it took his dry mouth a few attempts to say it.

'Reinald.'

'Aye, my friend.' Reinald smiled at him. 'You are safe now.' Reinald handed him a cup and lifted Octa's head so he could drink from it.

Octa almost cried when the sweet taste of ale washed over his tongue and down his throat. It meant that he still lived. As he finished the cup, he looked around him and realised where he was. 'I'm at the fort?'

Reinald nodded. 'I had a few men follow you. When they saw you got ambushed, they raced back to find me. I led a search party and found you by the old shrine. Thought you were dead at first, but then you stirred and we brought you back here.' Reinald smiled. 'Found your horse as well, standing over your body as if she was protecting you. The beast wouldn't leave your sight and followed us back to the fort.'

'Why?' Octa frowned at the old warrior, unable to understand why the man was so intent on helping him. First by convincing Eadric to let him stay in the north, then by looking for him afterwards. But he was glad to hear that Warda was still alive and well. The mare had been given the right name after all, it seemed.

Reinald stared at the torch on the wall, like Octa had done. 'I don't really know. Something inside me told me to find you. Perhaps I wanted to make up for never finding my son.' He smiled as he shrugged it off. 'Only the gods really know what goes on in our minds.'

'Thank you,' Octa said, and Reinald smiled at him. And then Octa remembered the spear of Woden. He lifted his head to search for it, but Reinald put a calming hand on his chest.

'Your spear is safe.' Octa's eyes flickered towards the old

warrior who must have seen the suspicion in them, because he smiled again and said, 'I have no interest in that spear. Once you are ready, I will give it to you. But first you must rest and recover from your injuries.'

Octa nodded, sensing no deceit in Reinald's voice or words. 'What about the others? Eadric, Badulf?'

Reinald shrugged. 'We found a few more dead Jutes, but there was no sign of the Briton that travelled with you. I warned you the path was dangerous. You're lucky you are still alive.' Reinald watched him for a few heartbeats. 'What happened after the ambush?'

Octa frowned as he tried to remember, but his mind was still covered by a fog that seemed to block everything. 'The ambush? Badulf made a run for it, but they killed him.'

'The arrows?'

Octa shook his head. 'A spear. Someone threw a spear at him.'

'We didn't find his body, but if he stayed on his horse, then it could have taken him anywhere. What happened afterwards? In the shrine? We found another Jute inside and the carving of the goddess broken.'

'Broken?' Octa frowned again. He tried to remember what had happened inside the cave, but those memories refused to come to him. 'I... I don't remember.'

Reinald put a hand on Octa's shoulder. 'You rest now. I have men searching the area. If Badulf is out there, then they will find him.'

Octa nodded as he lay back down again. 'Who ambushed us?' He didn't know why he asked that question, but it seemed important to him.

'There are many in this area who are still loyal to Brigantia. They protect her shrine from outsiders, although we never understood why.' Reinald scratched his neck. 'Perhaps they knew about the spear and saw it as their duty to keep it safe.'

Again, Octa nodded and closed his eyes as Reinald left the room.

Octa did not know how long he slept for, but he awoke when he heard the door swing open. He opened his eyes, expecting to see Reinald or Vellocatus, but instead he saw the woman from the tavern in Jutland standing over him. Except it wasn't really her. She seemed taller, cleaner and her eyes shone with a burning intelligence as she stared at him.

He opened his mouth to speak, but couldn't get the words out. His confusion at seeing the wife of the tavern keeper in Jutland here in the Roman fort made it hard for his tongue to function. The woman must have sensed the same because she smiled at him as she offered him a cup.

'Some ale for the warrior who did what no one else could.'

Octa grimaced as he sat up and took the cup from her, his mind still reeling. 'I am no warrior.'

The woman smiled as if she did not believe him. 'If that was true, then Woden would never have sent you on this quest. And you would not have found Gungnir, neither would Brigantia have allowed you to take it from her grasp.'

Octa's heart raced in his chest as he asked the question he was certain he knew the answer to. 'Who are you?'

The woman's smile was answer enough without her having to say a word. *Friga*. Octa felt like he was about to pass out and almost dropped the cup in his hand.

'Take a deep breath and calm your mind, Octa, son of Frithowald. I am not here to harm you, but to warn you.'

'Warn me?' Octa frowned at Friga, certain that it was Woden's wife standing in front of him.

Friga walked around the room and ran her fingers over the

many tools used by Vellocatus to treat his patients. Octa sensed she was disappointed with what she saw. 'Woden wants Gungnir back and yet despite what you promised him, you decided to keep it for yourself.'

Octa thought of the raven he had seen outside the cave and remembered what he had said to the bird. 'I never promised him anything. I never told the old man in the tavern that I would look for the spear.'

Friga smiled at him. 'That is true. But you came back looking for him. You wanted to use the spear for yourself.'

Octa's eyes widened. 'You know?' Again, he thought of the raven outside the cave.

The goddess smiled at him. 'I always knew, which was why I told you just enough to find the spear.'

Octa scowled as he thought of the conversation he had with the tavern owner's wife. 'You told me to join Hengist and Horsa's army. You were the one who told me they were going to Britannia, something no one else knew.' Friga nodded as she walked around the room. 'But you didn't tell me about the sacrifice.'

Friga smiled at him. 'If I made it too easy, then you would not have been worthy of wielding Gungnir. It is a weapon of the gods.'

'I am not worthy of it. That's why I plan to give it to my father.' Friga smiled a smile he did not understand, and he frowned at the way she looked at him. 'You are here to take the spear back to Woden?'

Friga shook her head. 'I am here to make sure that Woden does not get his hands on Gungnir.'

'Why?' Octa frowned and struggled to understand the games the gods were playing with him.

Friga looked at him, her expression serious. 'Because if he has Gungnir, then he will wage a war that will kill us all. So you keep hold of the spear and I'll make sure Woden can't find you. But be warned, son of Frithowald. You have angered Woden and there will be a price to pay. There is always a price to pay when you anger the gods.'

Octa was about to respond when the door opened and Vellocatus walked into the room.

'Who are you talking to?' the Briton asked, and Octa frowned when he realised he was alone in the room. Even the cup of ale he had been holding in his hand was gone.

'I...' Octa wondered if he had been dreaming, but it was too real to be a dream. It felt like he had really been talking to Friga. And as her final words rung in his head, he remembered what the owl in the cave had told him. That the spear will bring death.

'Your leg's healing well, despite what you keep putting it through,' Vellocatus said, unaware of the scowl on Octa's face as he studied Octa's leg.

'Can I walk?'

'You'll need a crutch for a while, but the few days you've been sleeping have helped.'

'Few days?' Octa frowned.

'Yes, you've slept for more than three days. Many of the men are taking bets on whether or not you'll wake up.' Vellocatus smiled at him. 'You've just added a few more coins to my purse. There's a walking stick there. Use it if you need to go anywhere, but I suggest you rest.'

Octa rubbed his head and tried to make sense of what had happened, but he knew he needed to get the spear. He grimaced as he got to his feet, the Briton only stepping back and letting him struggle, but when Octa was steady, he handed him the walking stick. 'Where can I find Reinald?'

'He should be by the main hall,' Vellocatus said.

Octa nodded his thanks and limped out of the building. The bright light blinded him as he left the room and Octa was forced to stand there for a while until his eyes adjusted to the light. The fort was the same as it was before they had set out to find the shrine. Some warriors lay about, enjoying their time away from their duties, while others walked the walls and towers of the fort, their eyes scanning the horizon for any threats. From somewhere in the fort, Octa could hear warriors training while women walked around, some of them carrying buckets of water and others carrying sacks filled with things Octa couldn't see.

'You are awake?' Reinald said with a broad grin on his face as he walked towards him, and Octa wondered if the grin was because of the bet Vellocatus had told him about as he nodded at the old warrior.

'The spear,' Octa said, and the smile fell from Reinald's face.

'This way.' He turned and led Octa towards his quarters. Octa glanced around the fort as he followed Reinald and was surprised at the good condition of the place. It reminded him of Witta's village as warriors walked around in armour, their weapons with them. Men laughed as they told jokes, while over them he could hear a smithy hard at work. They walked past a fenced-off area where a grey-bearded man was training younger warriors. 'The Romans have forgotten about us, so we are forced to recruit from the local population.'

'The Britons fight for you?'

Reinald smiled. 'With us, not for us. Most of us here have British wives. My children were born on this island and will die here, so will I. I've spent more winters here than in the homeland. There is no us or them. Not here. We are all people of this land now and, like us, they fight to defend that land from the Picts.'

Octa frowned and wondered if that was the same vision that

Hengist and Horsa had. To live amongst the Britons and be seen as one of them. But he doubted that. Octa believed that Hengist and Horsa had come to conquer the island.

Octa followed Reinald into his quarters and looked around the sparse room with a raised eyebrow. Apart from the cot bed in one corner and a chest in another, there was little else. Then Octa's eyes fell on the spear wrapped in cloth leaning against the wall. He limped towards it and looked over his shoulder at Reinald, who nodded at him.

Octa let go of his crutch and took the spear. He held his breath as he unwrapped it, almost unable to believe it really was the spear he had found in the cave. But when he saw the spearhead with the two ravens on it, he smiled. In the light of the room, he saw the spear clearly and frowned at the rune marks in the shaft. He ran his fingers along them and read out the spear's name to himself. *Gungnir*. Octa thought about his conversation with Friga and wondered what price he would have to pay for keeping the spear to himself.

'It seems the gods wanted you to find the spear,' Reinald said and Octa frowned at him. 'Many never find the shrine. They wander these lands for a long time until they give up or get killed. Those who learn of its location are usually killed by the cult, but I guess the cult of Brigantia didn't expect such a large group of warriors this time. And the few that make it past the cult, lose their wits and flee. They tell tales of the trees talking to them.'

Octa raised an eyebrow and remembered the voices he had heard in the forest, telling him to leave, but he said nothing of this to Reinald. And then he thought of his conversation with Friga. 'We only found the shrine because of Eadric.'

Reinald shrugged as if that was not important. 'What will

you do now that you have the spear?' he asked, and Octa saw how he kept his distance from the weapon.

Octa stared at the spear again. He lifted it up to feel the weight and wondered how many giants Woden had slain with this spear as he pictured himself using it in battle. But Octa doubted he would ever do that. He was no warrior. 'I go home, back to my father's village, and give him the spear.'

'You'll not return it to Woden?' Octa heard the surprise in the old warrior's voice and shook his head.

'I never came for the spear just to give it back to Woden. I aim to use it to redeem myself.'

'And how will giving it to your father do that?'

'He will see that I am not a coward and, with the spear, he will become the most powerful warlord in the Saxon lands.'

Reinald scratched his beard. 'You really think that Woden will let you use his spear for your own desires? He has sent many men to their deaths to reclaim it.'

Again, Octa thought of Friga's warning and felt the shiver run down his spine. But he had found the spear where others had failed. 'Woden will get his spear back once my father has made himself king.'

'And what about you? You are the one who found the spear.'

Octa shrugged. 'I'm not a warrior and have no need for the spear. All I want is for my father to acknowledge me again and to have my name restored.'

Reinald laughed. 'Not a warrior? There was a dead Jute in the clearing, stabbed in the back and another in the cave. I'm guessing the Britons did not kill them.'

Octa's heart raced as he remembered the two Jutes he had killed. 'I was desperate. They were going to kill me once they got the spear, so I did what I had to.'

'Spoken like a true warrior.' Reinald smiled at him and Octa frowned. 'In battle, we are all desperate and do what we have to to survive.'

Octa looked away from the old warrior and thought back to the battle where his cousin was killed. 'But I ran from my first battle. I was my cousin's shield bearer, and he died because I fled.'

Reinald nodded. 'I pissed my pants during my first battle. I still remember it as if it happened yesterday.'

'But you didn't run.'

Reinald smiled. 'Only because I was pinned in and couldn't. Your first battle is always the most terrifying. It's the fear of the unknown that gets you. The stories they tell you never really prepare you for it. And then after that, you are frightened because you know what is going to happen.'

'How do you control your fear?'

'You learn to use it.' Octa frowned at Reinald, who continued. 'Your fear keeps you alive in battle. It heightens your senses and makes you fight harder. We all claim to want the glory of dying in battle so that Woden can take us to his hall, but the truth is that no one wants to die. Not really. And it's that fear that makes you fight harder than your opponent.'

'But some claim to never know fear,' Octa said, remembering what he had been told by some warriors when he was still a boy.

'Aye, and most of them die young because they are reckless.' Reinald looked at the spear in Octa's hands. 'You did what many before you have failed to do. You found the spear. That alone shows that you are no coward.'

'But I didn't do it alone. Eadric and his men helped and Badulf.' Octa's hands trembled as he held the spear. 'They did most of it. I—'

'It doesn't matter,' Reinald interrupted Octa. 'You were the one we found with the spear.' Reinald sighed. 'You can stay here as long as you need. Recover from your injuries and, when you are ready, you can return to the homeland.' Octa nodded and was about to wrap the spear in the cloth again when Reinald stopped him. 'There's no need for that. The spear belongs to you. No one will take it from you.'

He tightened his grip on the spear, his eyes fixed on the rune carvings on the shaft. He thought of Badulf, killed because of him, and then he remembered Badulf's sister, Brigid. Octa wondered if she would ever find out what had happened to her brother. He remembered Badulf telling him she spoke to the gods of the land. Perhaps they would tell her. All Octa cared about was going home. Back to his father and to his mother.

26

Witta walked towards his cousin's hall, his fists clenched and his head throbbing. He had not sent word of his arrival, but was sure that Frithowald would have heard that he was coming. Frithowald was a great warrior and warlord and would have scouts out all over his lands. That was why he was standing outside of his mead hall, with all his wives at his side and the people of his village gathering around the square. Witta glanced at Berthild, Octa's mother and a woman Witta had coveted once, but she had proved too independent for him. Witta was glad of that though, because she seemed to be only good for breeding cowards.

The entire ride here, all Witta could think of was the old man's words, and his eyes went to his cousin's side and widened when he saw the sword on his waist. He was not sure if that was the same sword because, like him, Frithowald would have many swords. Some were for ceremonies and others were for battle. But to Witta, that looked like the sword he had seen his cousin give to Octa the morning before that battle.

'Cousin,' Frithowald greeted him and the nervousness in his

voice only made Witta suspect Frithowald was hiding his son somewhere. 'We welcome you to my hall. If you had sent word of your arrival, we would have prepared a feast for you.'

Witta stopped a few paces away from his cousin as his warriors spread out behind him. He noticed the arch in Frithowald's eyebrows and knew that his cousin would have been aware of the rest of his warriors outside of the village. His eyes lingered on Octa's mother again, who only glared at him, before he looked at the sword around his cousin's waist. His mouth twitched before he said, 'How goes the hunt for your son?'

Frithowald stiffened, more proof to Witta that the old man had been correct. 'He is no longer my son. I disowned him in front of the gods and you know that.'

Witta nodded. 'Aye, it was beautifully done. All to save your own skin.'

Frithowald glanced at Witta's warriors behind him as his brows furrowed. 'What are you talking about, Witta?'

Witta glanced at Frithowald's sword again, his hand twitching near his own. 'Is that not the sword you gave to him that day?' Frithowald's eyes widened and his hand went to the hilt of the sword around his waist as Witta clenched his fists. 'I thought so.' Witta glared at Frithowald, whose mouth opened but no words came out. 'Where is he, cousin? Where is the coward?'

'I swear on Tiw, I have not seen Octa since that morning.'

'You lie!' Witta's warriors all moved closer, their hands on their weapons as Frithowald's men glanced at him. But Witta knew they would not attack because his men outnumbered them.

Frithowald shook his head. 'No, I swear. I am not lying, cousin. I have not seen Octa since the beginning of the summer.'

Witta's jaw muscles tensed as he glared at his cousin and wondered where he was hiding the coward. 'Then how do you have your sword and your chain-mail vest?'

Frithowald's face paled. 'I woke one morning, and they were in my hall.'

Witta barked out a laugh. 'What? You expect me to believe that? That the gods had returned them to you?'

Frithowald shook his head. 'No, I was certain my son had been here—'

'Your son?' Witta raised an eyebrow at him. 'I thought you had denounced him?'

Frithowald stammered as he struggled to speak. He glanced at his wife, Octa's mother, who placed a hand on his shoulder. Unlike most of the villagers, who sensed what was going to happen, she was calm. She looked at Witta, her eyes filled with fire.

'My son was here, but Frithowald speaks the truth. He never saw him.'

'And you did?'

Berthild nodded. 'But only by chance.' She turned to her husband, whose eyes were wide in shock. Witta realised that this was the first time he had heard of this as well. 'I couldn't sleep and took a walk. I needed some air, and that was when I saw him sneaking out of the hall.'

'Why didn't you tell me?' Frithowald asked.

Berthild sneered at her husband. 'Because you would have hunted him down and turned him over to Witta. I could not let that happen to my son.'

'Your son is a coward!' Witta roared at her, angered that she had let the bastard get away.

Berthild turned to him, her eyes blazing with hatred. 'He is still my son! And I will do all I can to protect him.'

Frithowald looked at his wife, his eyes still wide. 'Berthild? By the gods, woman, you have killed us all.'

'Where is he now?' Witta drew his sword from its scabbard. 'Where are you hiding the coward?'

Berthild turned to him, the smile on her lips angering him even more. 'You will never find my son.'

Before the words even left her mouth, Witta launched himself at her, but Berthild did not flinch. She stood her ground, her shoulders squared and her eyes defiant. Witta cut down with his sword, but before it could take her life, another blade blocked it.

Witta stared at Frithowald in shock as he strained to keep Witta's blade from Berthild's neck. Even Berthild gaped at her husband, who turned to her.

'Run!' Before Witta could react, Frithowald turned his blade and punched him in the face. Witta staggered back as Frithowald turned to a group of warriors standing behind him. 'Protect my wife! Get her out of here!'

'But my lord?' Odalric, one of Frithowald's most trusted men, said, but Frithowald roared at him.

'Now! Protect my wives and children! Get them away!'

Witta saw how he glanced at Berthild, his eyes filled with regret before he turned to face him.

'That was very foolish of you, Frithowald.' Witta tightened the grip on his sword.

Frithowald shrugged. 'No. It was foolish of me to allow you to become so strong.'

Witta smiled. 'Kill them all!' he ordered his warriors.

'Protect the people!' Frithowald ordered the rest of his warriors, but he must have known it was futile. Frithowald launched himself at Witta, almost catching him off guard, but Witta blocked his blow and threw a punch that Frithowald dodged. The two of them had always been closely matched in combat, but Witta had always had more hunger than Frithowald. Behind Frithowald, he saw the group of warriors rounding up Frithowald's wives and children. He knew he could not let them get away, especially not Berthild. Not when she could lead him to Octa.

Witta stabbed his sword at Frithowald, who deflected it with his sword and kicked at Witta's leg. Witta lifted his foot and Frithowald missed, before he turned and slashed at Frithowald's chest. His cousin blocked the blow and stepped back before he attacked. He hacked at Witta, who twisted out of the way and sliced Frithowald's arm open.

Frithowald grimaced in pain and stepped back. He looked around him as his warriors were fighting Witta's men and Witta used the moment and launched at him. Frithowald sensed his attack, turned in time for Witta's sword to miss and punched him in the face. Witta staggered back and smiled at Frithowald as he wiped the blood from his mouth. Over Frithowald's shoulder he saw that some of his men had caught up with Frithowald's wives, but as he watched, Berthild took a sword from one of Frithowald's men and killed one of his warriors. The rest were killed by Frithowald's warriors and Witta felt his anger take hold of him as Berthild got away.

'Is this really worth it?' he asked as one of his warriors threw a torch onto one of the thatch roofs. The flames took hold instantly and grew as they devoured the dry straw. 'Your people killed and your village burnt to the ground?'

Frithowald stepped back, his eyes filled with tears as his people were killed and his village burned. He shook his head. 'No, Witta. This is not what I wanted.' Witta saw him tighten the grip on his sword. 'I never wanted any of this.' He launched himself at Witta and hacked at him with his sword. Witta raised his to block it and his arm shook from the strength in the attack. 'I did what I had to to protect my people.' He chopped down again and, this time, the blow drove Witta to his knees. He looked up at Frithowald and saw the anger in his eyes as Frithowald said, 'I denounced my son! I sent men to hunt him down! And you still attack me?' He hacked at Witta again, who rolled out of the way, but before he could get back to his feet and stab Frithowald's exposed side, his cousin turned and sliced his sword at him. Witta felt the sting as it sliced across his face. He fell onto his back and held his sword in front of him as Frithowald stood over him, his face red. 'I chose you over my son, and this is how you repay me? The other warlords were right about you. It is never enough for you. My only regret is that I had to lose it all before I saw the truth in their words.'

Witta struggled to see clearly because of the cut across his face and he kept his sword in front of him as Frithowald towered over him. His heart raced as he realised he had underestimated his cousin. He had hoped that his cousin would just give in, but Frithowald had always been a fighter. It was just a pity for him that his braver sons had all died and that only the coward had remained. He thought of his own sons. Of Uhtric, brave and strong and destined to be a great warrior, but dead because of Octa. And his youngest boy, who was too soft for the life they had to live. Witta looked up as Frithowald raised his sword.

'Forgive me, cousin, but I need to protect my people and what is left of my family.'

Witta glared at Frithowald. He had listened to the old man and had raced here without making sure he had the upper hand, and he was going to die because of that. But before Frithowald could bring his sword down, a spear skewered his side.

Frithowald grunted as he arched sideways. He turned and

glared at Witta's warrior, who was holding on to the spear. Before the warrior could pull the spear out, Frithowald grabbed its shaft and held on to it as he twisted and stabbed the warrior in the neck. The man's eyes bulged as he choked on Frithowald's sword before Frithowald pulled it out, roaring his anger at the man. Frithowald looked at Witta and dropped to his knees, but he kept his sword in his hands.

'I will kill you before I die, Witta.' He spat blood out of his mouth and Witta believed him, because he knew Frithowald was a man of his word. But then another of Witta's men rushed in and stabbed Frithowald in the back. Again, Frithowald grunted as the sword broke through his chest. He did not look at the blade as it stuck out of his chest. Instead, his dying eyes were fixed on Witta. 'I was a fool to sacrifice my son for you. And I will die knowing that I have failed him. But I curse you, Witta the Bear. On my dying breath, I swear by the gods that your son will be the last of your bloodline. That your daughters will be barren and your seed will run dry. On my dying breath, your line will end with your children and your name will be forgotten.' A breeze blew over them, causing Witta to shiver as Frithowald dropped to the ground and gave his last breath. In his blurred vision, Witta thought he saw the old man standing in the smoke of the burning houses and he knew he had been used by the gods.

* * *

Berthild ran. She had her dress pulled up in her free hand while her right hand held on to the sword she had used to kill one of Witta's men. Behind her, Frithowald's other wives wailed and their children screamed as they fled the violence in the village. She tried to ignore their cries, just like she tried to ignore the fact that Frithowald was going to die because of her.

'No!' she said as she stopped and turned back to the village.

'Lady Berthild, what are you doing?' Odalric asked as he too stopped. 'Lord Frithowald told us to get you to safety.'

Berthild shook her head. 'I will not run while my husband dies.'

'You can't go back there, Lady Berthild. Frithowald would never forgive me if anything happens to you.'

'Frithowald is probably dead by now,' one of his other wives said as she glared at Berthild. 'Dead because of you and your coward son!'

Berthild punched the woman in the face before she knew what she was doing and for a few heartbeats there was only silence as everyone stared at her. 'My son is not a coward. He was not ready for what Frithowald asked of him.' She glared at the other wives, daring them to disagree with her. But they all looked away from the anger in her eyes.

Berthild had her father's spirit in her veins. Her father who had been a great warrior and mighty warlord. And when Octa was born, she had been foretold that he would one day be a great man like her father. That was why she had named her son after her father. That was also why she could not admit that her son was a coward. Berthild took a deep breath and looked at Odalric, who had led them to safety. Over their heads, she could see the dark smoke from the village and knew that Witta had won.

'Take them west, to the lands of the Franks. Frithowald had good friends there and they will honour him by protecting his wives and children.' She looked at the young girls that she had hoped to help raise.

'What about you?' Odalric asked.

Berthild took a deep breath and gripped the sword in her hand. 'I'm going back for my husband. He died because of my son, so it is only right.'

Odalric scowled at her and just when she thought he was going to protest, he nodded and turned to the other warriors. 'Do as she says. I'll go with the lady.'

'Odalric, no—'

Odalric held a hand up to silence her. 'It is my duty to protect you, Lady Berthild. So if you want to go back to the village, then you will have to let me go with you or, as Woden is my witness, I'll knock you out and carry you with us.'

Witta and his army had left by the time Berthild and Odalric returned to the village. Berthild struggled to hold her tears back when she saw what was left of her home.

'Bastards.' The words came out as a growl as Odalric saw the same. 'I should have been here.'

Berthild nodded. 'We both should have been.' She looked at the dead, their eyes vacant as their blood soaked into the ground they had walked on every day. 'We all should have been here.'

'But why did Witta do this? Lord Frithowald had disowned Octa. He sent men to look for him. Even after he woke that morning and saw his sword and chain-mail vest in his hall.'

Berthild shrugged. 'Witta lost his son. I doubt he is thinking clearly now.' Berthild stopped when she saw Frithowald. Or what was left of him. She cried out in despair as she rushed to his body and collapsed beside him. 'Bastards! Fucking bastards!'

Odalric stood there, his eyes filled with tears as he looked at the headless body of his lord. 'They took his head as a trophy.'

Berthild's body trembled as she cried. Her husband was dead because of her. She could have blamed Octa for this, but she knew it was her fault. She was the one who had told Octa to run, and she was the one who told Witta that. Berthild looked up and searched around the corpse of her husband.

'Lady Berthild? What are you looking for?'

'His sword? Where is my husband's sword?'

Odalric looked around, but saw no sign of Frithowald's sword. 'They took it. It will hang on Witta's wall as a trophy. Like Lord Frithowald's head will hang by the gates of his village.'

Berthild nodded and took a deep breath as she looked at the body of her husband. 'Forgive me, my love. This is all my fault.' She thought of Octa and wondered where he was. 'I will find our son and tell him what happened here.'

Odalric raised an eyebrow at her, but said nothing as she got to her feet. 'So where do we go now? To the land of the Franks with the others?'

Berthild shook her head. 'North. To find my son.'

27

'How will we find your son?' Odalric asked in his gruff voice as they ate their morning meal in a tavern. Berthild looked at her dead husband's sworn man, who had refused to leave her side no matter how many times she had told him he could. *Lord Frithowald told me to protect you*, was all he ever said. But Berthild was glad that the gruff warrior was with her. His large frame and broad shoulders, along with his scarred face, scared most people away, which meant no one had bothered them since they left Frithowald's headless corpse in their burnt-down village. They had not been able to bury him, or the many others who had died because of Witta's treachery. Odalric wanted to get away from the village as quickly as possible, worried that Witta's men might return, and Berthild shared that fear.

'The gods will show me the way,' Berthild said, and almost laughed at Odalric's raised eyebrow. Berthild believed it, though. She felt that despite what had happened that Friga was with her and that Thunor protected them. All she had to do was be patient and when the gods decided it was time, then they would show her how to find her son. She wondered where Octa was and, more importantly, if he was making a name for himself. The summer was coming to an end, and it had been many months since she had last seen her boy, dirty and broken outside Frithowald's hall, but she had prayed to the gods every night that he was safe and on a path which would lead him to glory, just like her father. Berthild had dreamt every night of his return as a mighty warrior, but Wyrd had decided that she had to seek him out. She would not argue with her fate, though. Even if it had cost her her husband and her home. Berthild trusted the gods and believed that they would reunite her with her son. And perhaps this way, she could watch him grow into the man her father had been. And the man her husband was before Witta killed him.

'The gods better hurry. It won't be long until Witta's men find us.' Odalric spooned more porridge into his mouth and glanced around the tavern they were in, as if searching for men she doubted were chasing them. They had travelled north for many days, avoiding those she knew were loyal to Witta and staying in roadside inns.

'You really think he would chase us even in the lands of the Angles?' Berthild glanced at her untouched porridge, unable to understand how Odalric could eat the stuff. She wouldn't have fed it to the dogs, yet the tavern owner was charging people for it.

'As long as you live, you'll be a threat to him. Not to mention Frithowald's other wives and their daughters. Witta will have his men scattered everywhere to find us.'

'Witta will be too busy fighting the Thuringians.'

Odalric shook his head. 'They have taken lands in the east and he's done nothing about it. The other warlords all complain, but they are too afraid to move against him. That is what we should be doing. We should go to the other warlords and rally them against Witta.'

Berthild sighed. This was not the first time Odalric had said that. 'No. We need to find my son.' Odalric stared at her and she saw what he wanted to say to her, but couldn't. *Your son is a coward.* She knew what everyone thought of Octa and she understood why. But they didn't know her boy like she did. Even if she wasn't the one who had raised him. She had seen it when he was born, but men would never understand that.

The warrior glanced around him and said, 'I know you believe your son is the answer, but the other warlords will not follow someone who ran from a battle.'

'And you think they will follow a woman?' Berthild raised an eyebrow at Odalric.

'They'll follow the wife of Frithowald. He was one of the strongest warlords.'

'And his head is most likely on a stake outside Witta's hall after Witta killed most of his men and burnt our village to the ground.' Berthild took a deep breath to stop the tears from flowing. Now was not the time to cry. She could do that when she found Octa. 'The gods will deal with Witta. I have no interest in fighting that pig. All I want to do is find my son.'

'So that he can avenge his father?'

'If that is what Octa decides to do, then I'll support it.'

Odalric glared at her, and she saw the vicious warrior she knew he was. 'You don't care about avenging your husband? Frithowald gave you everything.'

Berthild felt her own anger taking hold of her and returned Odalric's glare. 'Frithowald took my son away from me when he was a small boy and let him be raised by others. Then he thrust my son into a position he was not ready for so that he could raise his own stature, and when Octa needed his help, he disowned him to protect his own skin.' Berthild clenched her fists as the image of young Octa, barely eight winters old, being taken away from her flashed in her mind. 'Frithowald's death will haunt me for the rest of my days, but all I care about now is finding my son.' Odalric nodded, but she saw that he still didn't agree with her. 'I told you before, Odalric. You don't have to follow me. You are a free man now and your path is yours to follow.'

Odalric shook his head and said the words she knew he would say. 'Frithowald told me to protect you, Lady Berthild. And that is what I will do until I die. In honour of Lord Frithowald.'

Berthild smiled at the warrior's loyalty to Frithowald. Despite the anger she had felt at the way he had treated their son, Frithowald had always been good to her and his other wives. His warriors as well. 'We will honour his memory by making sure his remaining son grows strong and becomes the warrior I know he can be. The gods will decide if he avenges his father, not us.'

Odalric took another spoonful of his porridge and Berthild thought she detected a grimace on his face. 'Well, how in Woden's name do we find your son? All you said is that you told him to go north. There's a lot of land north.'

Berthild felt annoyed that Odalric refused to say Octa's name, as if saying it would make him a coward, but she had to admit it was a good question. 'The gods will show us the way. It was the gods who told me to send him north.'

Odalric raised an eyebrow. 'The gods told you to send him north? They couldn't tell you to send him to a place where we can find him?'

Berthild understood his frustration; even she understood little of what was happening at the moment. But every night after she had learnt of what had happened in the battle, she had dreamt of a falcon flying north. And when she saw Octa that night, she knew the dream was a message for him. So she had told him to go north. 'You know as well as I do the gods work in strange ways.' Deciding she had had enough of the conversation and tavern, with its stuffy air and noisy patrons, Berthild got to her feet. 'Get the horses ready. It's time we leave.'

Odalric nodded and finished his ale before he left to do that. Berthild glanced around the tavern one more time and frowned when she spotted an old man sitting in the far corner, his one eye fixed on her. Something about the old man sent a shiver down her spine and Berthild felt like she had seen him before, but couldn't work out where. She turned and left, eager to get away from the anger in the old man's face, and was glad to see Odalric ready with their horses.

'Is something wrong?' the warrior asked as he helped her mount her horse.

'No, I'm just eager to find my son,' she said as she made herself comfortable on the horse and waited for Odalric to mount his. When they were both ready, she glanced at the darkening sky and prayed it would not rain as they left the tavern and travelled north.

They travelled for two days over hills and across rivers, passing farmsteads and small villages where people lived through their own daily battles. Odalric spent the entire time looking over his shoulder, still convinced that someone was hunting them, while Berthild could not stop thinking about the old man she had seen in the tavern. Something about him had frightened her and Berthild did not frighten easily. She was the daughter of a warlord and had been raised amongst warriors. But still, that old man had made her want to turn and run and no matter how hard she tried not to, she couldn't help but fear for Octa.

'We should find somewhere to rest,' Odalric said, and Berthild shook her head to clear her mind. 'The sun will set soon.'

She looked at the sky and saw that the warrior was right. And just when she consigned herself to sleeping out in the open for another night, she spotted a small farmstead in the distance. 'There.'

Odalric scowled as he stared at the lonely house surrounded by a fence and a small field to one side. A thin trail of smoke left the house, which showed that someone still lived there, and after glancing at the darkening sky, Odalric shrugged. 'Stay behind me, Lady Berthild. We don't know who lives there.'

Berthild smiled at the warrior as he led the way to the farmstead. When they got there, she saw the fence was badly kept, and that the thatched roof was in need of a repair. The field looked empty, apart from a small patch that had recently been tilled. 'Not many people then,' Berthild said, and Odalric nodded at her.

The warrior dismounted his horse, but Berthild stayed on hers as he walked to the door and knocked on it. After a short while, an elderly man opened the door and scowled at them.

'Who are you?'

Berthild noticed how Odalric tensed his shoulders and knew that the warrior did not like being spoken to like that. Many treated him with respect, but the elderly man seemed not to care.

'We are travellers and seek shelter for the night.'

'No,' said the elderly man, and was about to close the door when a woman's voice shouted at him from inside the farmhouse. The elderly man shrugged and then turned to Odalric again. 'You can tie your horses around the back with the cow. No one will take them.' He glanced over Odalric's shoulder at Berthild. 'Your woman is welcome to wait for you inside.'

'She's not—'

'That's very kind of you,' Berthild interrupted Odalric, and dismounted her horse. She handed her reins to Odalric, who led the horses around the back while she followed the elderly man inside. A woman who was the same age as her mother, had she lived, was standing by a small hearth fire and stirred something in a pot. She smiled at Berthild, revealing that most of her teeth were gone.

'Welcome. Sit.' She pointed to a badly mended bench by the wall of their house. 'We have little to offer. It is only my husband and me.'

'Thank you,' Berthild said as she tried to ignore the stink inside the house. 'We don't require much. Only a place to rest our heads for the night.' Odalric walked in and crinkled his nose at the smell, but he said nothing as he stood by the door and eyed the house. 'Forgive Odalric. He is a warrior and doesn't trust easy.'

The old woman smiled while the elderly man glared at Odalric. 'He's welcome to sleep outside.'

The old woman tutted at her husband and then went back to stirring the pot while Odalric sat down beside Berthild. The bench creaked under his weight and for a moment Berthild worried it might break, but the bench held and soon they were served with what looked like vegetable stew.

Berthild tried a spoonful of the stew and found it was eatable while Odalric wolfed his down, causing her to shake her head. But the old woman only smiled and offered him more. 'It's just the two of you?' she asked as the old woman refilled Odalric's bowl.

'Aye,' the elderly man said. 'The gods took our children a long time ago and seem to enjoy keeping us alive.'

'Two of our children died from illness while our oldest son died in a raid,' the old woman explained, and Berthild found she could only nod. 'But we have neighbours not far from here. They help us when they can. The gods have blessed us with that, at least. Do you have children?' she asked.

'Woman, don't ask that!' the elderly man scolded her.

'It's fine. I have a son, although I don't know where he is.'

The elderly man stared at her for a few heartbeats, his eyebrow raised, as the woman said, 'That's the problem with the young folk. They set off on their adventures and forget about those they left behind.'

Odalric grunted at the woman's words, and Berthild knew what he was thinking. She was glad he kept those thoughts to himself as the elderly man still stared at her. He swallowed the vegetable stew he had just put in his mouth and then pointed his spoon at her.

'Have I seen you before?'

Berthild frowned at him. 'No, I have never been this far north.'

The elderly man continued scowling at her before he turned to his wife. 'Doesn't she look familiar?'

The old woman first shook her head and then her hand went to her mouth when she looked at Berthild again. 'By the gods! The young man. You look just like him.'

Berthild's heart thudded in her chest and she glanced at Odalric who was frowning, his spoon halfway to his mouth. 'What young man?' Berthild asked.

'By Woden, woman. You are right.' The elderly man smiled. 'What are the odds of that?'

'What young man?' Berthild asked again as the old woman sat down beside her husband.

'In summer, a young man tried to steal some bread I baked. I beat him with my broom, but then I felt sorry for the poor boy. He was so thin and frail-looking—'

'Sounds like him,' Odalric said, and then looked away when Berthild glared at him.

The old woman shook her head at the warrior as well before she continued. 'We fed him and he stayed the night. He left the next morning, but only after I made him eat again.'

Berthild's heart was racing at the thought that Octa had stayed in this farmhouse. 'Did he say where he was going?'

The elderly man shook his head. 'Didn't say much. I got the

sense he was running from something, but it wasn't our place to ask, so I didn't.'

'Is he your son? The one you mentioned?' the old woman asked.

Berthild nodded, certain that it was. Once again, she believed the gods were aiding her. It was the only way she could explain finding the same farmhouse that Octa had. 'Yes, he is my son.'

'What happened?' the old woman asked, and the elderly man scowled at her.

Berthild felt Odalric's eyes on her, but she did not want to tell these strangers the truth. 'He made a mistake and had to leave.'

'You mean he was banished?' the elderly man said, staring at her, and all Berthild could do was nod.

The old woman tutted. 'Well, I liked him. He was very polite and even left a gold ring behind when he left.'

'He did?' Berthild's eyes widened.

'You can't have it,' the elderly man said. 'We already used it to buy a new cow after ours stopped giving us milk.'

Berthild smiled at the elderly man. 'I would never ask for it back. And I'm glad that something good came out of his stay.'

The elderly man stared at her for a while before he thumbed towards his wife. 'She thought he was one of the gods and had rewarded us for letting him stay.'

'Well, you all know the stories of Woden's travels,' the old woman defended herself, and Berthild felt a shiver run down her spine as she thought of the old man she had seen in the tavern. Could that have been Woden? But why would the god of war be watching her?

'Lady Berthild?' Odalric asked, and Berthild smiled as she cleared her mind.

'Lady Berthild?' The elderly man scowled at her. 'You are someone important?'

Berthild smiled at the old couple as they stared at her. 'I was. Now I am just a mother in search of her son.'

They sat in silence for a while as they ate their stew, but Berthild could feel that the elderly man wanted to ask questions from the way he kept glancing at her. But he kept quiet and, after the evening meal, Odalric went outside to help the elderly man with something, while Berthild sat on the bench and listened as the old woman told her stories of her children and her neighbours. Berthild sensed she didn't have many people to talk to, so she listened with a smile, even as her mind kept drifting to her son and the old man she had seen in the tavern. Berthild wondered if they were connected and prayed that wasn't so. Especially if the old man might have been Woden, but Berthild could not see that. She couldn't see what Woden would want with Octa, but no matter how hard she tried to forget about the old man, she couldn't get his stern gaze out of her mind.

The old couple gave Berthild and Odalric some old furs to sleep on. They didn't smell very fresh, but it was better than sleeping on the cold ground or the old straw mats that she had slept on over the last few days. Although Berthild couldn't sleep that night as she lay there and stared at the dark roof, wondering if Octa had done the same. She smiled at some point during the night, glad that they were at least on the right path. Octa had been there and the thought of that made her feel closer to her son than she had done in a long time.

The following morning, they ate porridge while the old woman told more stories of the past and the elderly man rolled his eyes as he had heard them hundreds of times. After the meal, Odalric got the horses ready and Berthild thanked the old couple for their hospitality. Like Octa, she gave them one of the gold rings from her fingers, not wanting the old couple to know about the pouch now half full of hack gold and silver they had taken from Frithowald's hall before they had left.

'I hope this helps you,' Berthild said as the elderly man took the ring from her and put it in his pouch without looking at it.

The old woman smiled at her before she said, 'Your son went north from here, towards Jutland. I'll pray to Friga that you find him.'

Berthild smiled back at the old woman. 'Thank you. The gods bless you.'

Odalric helped Berthild mount her horse and, with one final glance at the old couple, they rode north towards the lands of the Jutes.

'At least we know we are on the right track,' Odalric said. 'But it's still going to be hard to find him.'

Berthild rode in silence for a while, not wanting to acknowledge what Odalric had said, even though she knew he was right. Jutland was still a large kingdom, and she had never been there before. Their only hope was to find a large market town and pray to the gods that Octa was there or had been. 'We will find him,' she said, trying to convince herself more than Odalric. 'The gods will help us.'

'And why will the gods do that? He dishonoured Woden and Tiw, and then he fled.'

Berthild bit back her anger at Odalric's words. 'He did not dishonour the gods. And he didn't flee. He came home to face his father, and I told him to leave. I sent him north to make a name for himself before he faced his father because I knew Frithowald would never talk to him otherwise.'

'You really believe that your son could do that? Earn a name for himself?'

Berthild pulled her horse to a stop and turned to face the warrior. 'Why can't you say his name?'

'I...' Odalric's eyes widened as the question caught him by surprise. He took a deep breath to compose himself and, again, she saw the warrior he was. 'Forgive me, my lady, but your son ran from battle and Witta's son died as a result. As far as I'm concerned, everything that has happened since is his fault. The gods are punishing us because of him. So I cannot say his name.'

Berthild nodded, and even though his words angered her, she appreciated his honesty. She also knew there was no point telling him to leave, because Odalric would insist on staying with her and protecting her. Something she also appreciated. 'The gods are not punishing us because of Octa. We don't know why the gods do the things they do, but Octa is no coward. He never should have been made Uhtric's shield bearer. He was not ready for that. And he came home to face his father afterwards.'

'Then why didn't he? Why did he just leave his father's sword and chain-mail vest behind and sneak off in the middle of the night?'

'He must have overheard the conversation we had that night and knew that his father would never forgive him. That was why I sent him north. I swear by the gods that Octa is not what you think he is and when we find him, you will see that for yourself.'

Odalric stared at her for a few heartbeats and then nodded. 'I pray you are right, Lady Berthild. But first, we must find your son.'

Berthild turned her horse north and dug her heels into its sides. She could hear Odalric following her and again wished her husband had never pushed her son to do what he was not ready to do. All so that he could get even closer to Witta. But Frithowald had always been loyal to Witta, something which had constantly angered her. Perhaps when her anger passed, she would be able to mourn the death of her husband, something she still had not been able to do in the many days since his death, because part of her blamed Frithowald for what had happened. The other part blamed herself for not doing more to help her son.

A few days later, they reached a large trading town on the west coast of Jutland. The town looked like all the others she had seen before, but Berthild and Odalric were surprised by how busy it was. The wharves were filled with ships, while warriors crowded the streets and blacksmiths worked hard as they hammered away at red-hot metal. The noises and smells of too many people in a small place made her head hurt, especially after so many days of hearing very little other than the sounds of their horses and the birds flying over their heads.

'Something is happening,' Odalric said as they stopped by the first tavern they saw.

Berthild nodded as she waited for the warrior to help her off her horse. 'A raid, perhaps?'

'Looks like it, but there are families as well. This is more than just a raid.' Odalric glanced at the sky. 'Besides, it's too late to go raiding now. Harvest will be here soon.'

Berthild looked around her and saw that the warrior was right. There were families that looked like they were preparing to leave as well. Before Frithowald had died, they had heard of tribes moving west to escape the Huns from the east. Even the Romans were struggling to contain them. Berthild had often wondered if that was not why the Thuringians were pushing into Saxon lands, or how long until they themselves had to deal with the Huns. 'Where are they going?' she thought out loud.

'Britannia,' someone said from behind her, and Berthild

turned around to see an older woman, her light-coloured hair dishevelled and carrying empty jugs in her hands.

'Britannia?'

'Aye. A large island to the west of here. Used to be part of the Roman Empire, but not any more.'

'Why would they go there?' Odalric asked, and the woman shrugged.

'Perhaps hoping to escape what is to come. Also, word has reached us that the British kings need men to fight their enemies.'

Berthild watched as a mother struggled to deal with her two young children as they fought each other. It was something she never had to deal with, but then, she had never got the chance to be a mother. Frithowald had taken that away from her. As she watched the mother struggle with her children, she heard a falcon cry out above her head. She looked up and saw the falcon circling above her as if it was making sure it had her attention before the bird turned and flew west, across the seas. Berthild watched it until it disappeared in the clouds and smiled, certain that the falcon was a sign from the gods.

'I know where to find Octa.'

'My lady?' Odalric frowned at her.

'We go west, Odalric. We go to this Britannia and there we will find my son.'

* * *

Berthild stared at the camp on the small island as the ship approached it, her heart racing at the thought of seeing Octa again. As much as she tried not to, she couldn't help but scan the warriors to see if one of them was her son.

'You really think he is here?' Odalric asked, his face grim as he glanced at the dark clouds.

'He has to be,' Berthild said. The gods had told her to come to this island on a ship full of warriors and many other people who were hoping to start a new life, so Octa had to be here. Odalric grunted, his face as dark as the clouds above, and Berthild understood why. It hadn't taken them long to find a ship that was destined for Britannia, but the few coins and hack gold they had were not enough to buy them a place on board and neither were the horses, especially not with so many people fighting for a place on the ship. Although Berthild was certain the captain of the ship was using the situation to make himself rich and she had prayed that the gods would punish the bastard for his greed. In the end, Odalric had to give his chain-mail vest and his sword as payment. Something she knew hurt the warrior more than any battle wound ever could. She had not been the one who had told him to do that, and she didn't under-stand why Odalric had done it, but Berthild still felt the guilt of that weigh down on her and had sworn to Odalric that she would repay him as soon as she could. And she prayed Octa could help with that.

'Let's go,' Odalric said as the ship was tied to the makeshift wharf and people disembarked. The journey had been long and Berthild was certain she had lost weight because of the lack of proper food while they had travelled along the coast of the continent. Even Odalric seemed thinner, but the man still looked like a warrior as he walked towards the centre of the camp, his broad shoulders tensed and his hand on his seax knife, the only weapon he had left. 'So where do we find him?'

Berthild wrapped her cloak around her shoulders and shiv-ered as the air seemed colder here. She studied the large camp and saw men building a wooden wall around the island, while somewhere else warriors were training. Tents were dotted everywhere, and she wondered where they would sleep, something she had not thought about before. She had hoped there would be a village where they could get accommodation, but the sight of the camp made her realise that was not going to happen. 'We find whoever is leading this army and ask them about my son.'

'You really think they would know who he is?'

Berthild shrugged. 'Frithowald knew the names of all of his warriors.'

'Lord Frithowald also grew up with most of them and saw the others become men. We also assume that your son gave them his real name.'

Berthild glanced at the warrior. 'Why would Octa hide his name?'

Odalric grunted and walked ahead without responding, which annoyed Berthild. She prayed they found Octa soon, and that he had already earned a good reputation, even if it was just to show to Odalric that he was not a coward. She crinkled her nose and did her best to ignore the stink of so many warriors cramped on to a small island.

'How many do you think there are?' she asked Odalric, who raised his eyebrows and scrutinised the other warriors, and somehow looked unimpressed. Something only experienced warriors seemed to do.

'There are five ships, along with the one we arrived on. At least half of those were fighting men, more than enough to start a war.'

Odalric's words sent a shiver down her spine as they walked towards the two large tents they saw in the centre of the camp, while many of the nearby warriors scowled at them. But she knew that a war would be a good place for Octa to make a name for himself. *It is also a good place to die.* The thought came to her and her hand went to her neck where her spear pendant would normally be. She remembered she had given it to Octa and prayed that it had kept him safe.

Two warriors stopped them as they approached the large tents and Berthild sensed Odalric was eager to fight the men. She put a hand on his shoulder and glanced at him before she turned to the warriors. 'We seek the man who leads this army.'

'Why?' one of the warriors asked, his eyes studying her figure.

Odalric saw the same and stepped forward. 'Look at my lady like that again and I'll rip your eyes out.'

'I'd like to see you try,' the warrior said as his companion stepped towards Odalric. But her husband's warrior did not back down as he glared at the two Jutes.

Berthild sighed and wondered why men always had to fight to solve their problems. 'I am looking for my son, Octa.'

'Octa the Saxon?' one of the men said, and Berthild's heart skipped a beat before she nodded. The two warriors glanced at each other and Berthild wondered about the look they shared before one of them went into one of the tents. A short while later, the warrior came out, followed by a man who was clearly the leader of this army. Berthild had to admit he was handsome with his broad shoulders and strong face, but it was the cleverness in his eyes that caught her attention.

The man stopped in front of them and glanced at Odalric as if he was a prize bull, before he turned his attention to her. 'You are Octa's mother?'

Berthild nodded, feeling an unease in the pit of her stomach at the way the man looked at her.

'My name is Hengist. My brother and I lead these men. We knew Octa well and liked him. He saved my son's life.'

'Knew?' Odalric asked the question Berthild couldn't as she struggled to breathe.

Hengist nodded, his face showing his remorse. 'Octa fell in an ambush to the north.'

Berthild felt like she had been kicked in the chest as she stared at the leader of the Jutes. 'No,' she said as she shook her head. 'Octa can't be dead.' The lump in her throat made it hard for her to speak, but she refused to believe that her son had died in some ambush. Berthild had been told that Octa would be destined for great things. The gods had never let her down before, so she knew they would not have allowed him to die. 'Octa is not dead,' she said again.

'I wish it was true,' Hengist said. 'I liked Octa, which was why I sent him north with some of my best men.'

'Why?' Odalric asked, his brows creased.

'We had heard of an important shrine to the north and I sent men to find out more about it. But they were ambushed and only three of the twelve men I sent made it back alive.'

Berthild shook her head. 'Octa is not dead,' she said again. She looked around her. 'I want to speak to these survivors!'

'That is not possible—' Hengist started saying, but Berthild cut him off.

'By Friga, you do not tell me what is not possible!'

'Lady Berthild,' Odalric said, and she noticed how Hengist raised an eyebrow at her, but she didn't care about that. All she cared about was finding her son. 'You need to rest. It's been a long journey.'

Hengist nodded. 'Your man is right. I'll find you a clean tent and perhaps we can talk about this later. I will summon my men who were with your son and they can tell you what happened.'

Berthild glared at the Jute, annoyed by his compassion and certain he was lying to her. She took a step towards him. 'I will find my son.' Without another word, she turned and walked away, with Odalric on her heels. Her head spun from the news, but she refused to believe that Octa was dead. The gods would not bring her here if that was true, she was certain of it. But as she looked around at all the warriors glancing at her, she realised she was lost. Her husband was dead and her home gone. People she had called friends were either dead or had fled. All she had that had kept her going was the thought of seeing her son again.

'What do we do now?' Odalric asked her, and Berthild looked up to the skies.

'I don't know.'

29

Winter was hard. It wasn't the cold or the snow that had made it unbearable for Octa. Neither was it the frustration of being stuck in Corstopitum with Reinald and his small force of Saxon foederati. It was the wind. The blasted wind that never ceased and cut through everything he wore. Octa had been given a fur cloak by the wife of one of Reinald's sons, but it never seemed to be warm enough for him. Unlike those who had spent almost a lifetime on this wall.

Throughout the winter months, the Saxon foederati and the local Britons patrolled the wall and the surrounding lands, and once Reinald had to send out a scouting party after reports of an attack on a small village north of the wall. The warriors trained every day in the few hours of daylight they had. All the while, Octa sat in front of the hearth fire in the main hall of the fort and shivered as his wounds healed. Not even the flames could warm him up.

The winter solstice and Yule had been a strange time for Octa as well. It was the first winter he had spent without Uhtric by his side, and Octa had found it hard to feel the same joy as those in the fort. His guilt had eaten away at him, especially when he was asked to help them find the right tree for the Yule log, something he and Uhtric had loved doing. But then he would look at Gungnir and his resolve would return. He would honour his cousin's death by making amends for it. That had been his promise to the gods as the Saxons lit the Yule log. Octa swore in front of the flames that he would be the warrior his cousin would have been. He could not explain why and often wondered if it was the spear, but Octa had felt different ever since he had woken up in the fort after he had found Gungnir. But the familiar fear that had been his constant companion did not seem so strong any more. Although Friga's words haunted him most nights, even as the nightmares of the battle against the Thuringians lessened. But as time went by, nothing happened to make Octa believe that Woden was punishing him.

Once the Yule month was over and the days were lengthening, Octa had joined the Saxon foederati and the Britons in their training sessions. His wounds had all healed during the winter months, but his body had become weak. And Octa knew that if he wanted to keep his promise to Uhtric, then he needed to train like he used to.

Octa had been amazed at how light the spear felt in his hand during the first of the training sessions. Its balance was better than any spear he had ever trained with in the past, and with each passing day, he had become more convinced that it belonged to Woden. That and the raven watching him over the winter months. But the raven was not the only bird that seemed to watch him. Once in a while, he would spot a white owl in the trees near the fort and he would remember how the owl had also warned him about Woden, before it attacked him. The scars on his arm were a constant reminder of that day and Octa often wondered if he needed to fear the cult that was supposed to protect the shrine. He also wondered what had happened to Badulf. They had never found his body, or his horse, despite the many patrols Reinald had sent out, so Octa often wondered if the Briton was still alive.

As winter gave way to spring, Octa felt his strength returning with the warmth of the spring sun. The old Saxons treated him as if he was one of them and they would often tell him tales of when they had first come to Britannia. A few even told him of how they had seen the Romans cut stone and build some of the towns, something Octa still found hard to believe. It reminded Octa of the stories Witta and his father would tell him, which only made him miss his homeland even more and made him more eager to return and give the spear to his father. Octa had also learned some words of the language the Britons spoke. It had not been easy and had left him frustrated when he had first started, but over the winter and spring, he had learned enough words to talk to the Britons.

'Are you sure you want to give that spear to your father?' Reinald asked Octa one day as they sparred. 'You use it like it was made for you.'

Octa lowered his shield and looked at the spear. In the morning sun, the ravens of Woden were more visible, while the runes on the shaft seemed more hidden. He had had the same thoughts since he started training with the spear. He knew he shouldn't have done, but Octa had been curious about how it would feel. 'My father is a mighty warlord. With the spear, he could make himself a king if he wanted to.'

'And you will be his heir?' Reinald raised an eyebrow at him.

Octa shrugged. That was what he had hoped for, but first he

had to pray that the spear would redeem him in his father's eyes. Before Octa could say anything, a horn blew from the wall.

Reinald looked towards it and shielded his eyes with his hand as he tried to work out what was happening. Around Octa, the other warriors had also stopped their training.

'A raid?' one warrior asked.

'It's too early for a raid, but with the Jutes in the south beating them back, the Picts have become unpredictable.' Reinald glanced at Octa as if he knew more about it, but he only knew as much as they did. News had reached them that the brothers fought with the spear of Woden and Octa guessed that meant that Eadric had made it back to the island where the Jutes where camped. Octa had thought little of the man who had tried to kill him, but only because Octa doubted he could get his revenge for that. Eadric was too good a warrior for Octa to defeat. Even with Gungnir.

Since word had been spread about the spear, the Jutes' numbers had slowly increased as more ships came from the east to join them. Many had been unhappy about that, and there were rumours that the other kings were plotting against King Vortigern because of his alliance with the Jutes. People were nervous, even more so in the north by the wall. The Picts' raids had been unsuccessful in the south because of Hengist and Horsa, which meant that they had increased their attacks on the towns and villages in the north. Places where the Jutes weren't.

The fort gates opened and one of the scouts Reinald had sent out came racing in on his horse. The young Briton pulled the animal to a stop in front of the old Saxon, who barely flinched, and said, 'A large force of Picts are marching towards the gap in the wall.'

Reinald scowled at that. 'Where are they headed?'

'Cair Hebrauc?' someone suggested, and the others nodded.

'Plenty of farmsteads and villages between the wall and Cair Hebrauc,' Reinald said, as if he agreed with the man.

'They've not risked attacking Cair Hebrauc for a long time. It's a well-fortified city,' one man said, and Reinald glanced at Octa again, who remembered the city and what had happened when he was there with Eadric and the Jutes.

'Aye, but the success of the Jutes in the south has made them desperate.' Reinald turned to his men. 'Get ready. We march before midday. If the gods are with us, then we will meet the Picts by the wall.'

Octa watched as the old Saxon warriors ran with the urgency of young men and was about to go back to his room when Reinald put a hand on his shoulder.

'Where are you going?'

Octa glanced at the warriors as they got their armour and weapons ready. 'I am no warrior,' he said.

Reinald smiled at him, something that Octa had not expected. 'You killed men to get your hands on that spear. And now when there is fighting to be done, you run away?'

'I...' Octa hesitated and then lowered his voice. 'I'm afraid.' Although he wasn't sure if he was afraid of fighting or Woden's wrath. The old Saxons in the fort believed that the gods of his people had power here and if Friga could show herself to him, then Octa was sure that Woden could make sure he fell in battle.

'So am I. I'm an old man. I'm not as fast as I used to be or as strong. But it is my duty to protect these people and Tiw demands that I do that.' Reinald's voice softened. 'Just stand strong and keep your shield in front of you. You are a skilled warrior and you fight with the spear of Woden.'

Octa glanced at Gungnir and felt his cheeks burn with shame. If men as old as his father, some even older, were preparing to fight a large force of Picts, he knew he couldn't hide away. So he took a deep breath and nodded at Reinald. 'I'll fight.'

Reinald smiled at him again. 'Good.' He turned to one of his men. 'Find Octa some armour!' The warrior nodded and ran off, while Octa watched the other warriors. Their faces were as hard as stone as they prepared armour and weapons. Even the young Britons, local men recruited to help the Saxons, seemed grim as they put old Roman armour on and collected Roman spears and shields.

Octa's hand went to the spear pendant he wore around his neck. *Thunor, watch over me*, he prayed as the warrior returned with armour for him. The armour was the same as the Saxon foederati and British warriors wore, with the small metal plates stitched onto a thick padded tunic. Octa stayed silent as the warrior helped him put on the armour, his limbs trembling at the thought of standing in a shield wall again. No matter how hard he tried, he could not get his cousin's face out of his mind. When the warrior was done, he looked at Octa and smiled.

'Just listen to Reinald and you'll be fine. The man is one of the best warriors I have ever known.' The warrior gripped his shoulder and Octa nodded at the man as he felt a sudden urge to piss himself. He looked at the spear in his hand, seeing how the marks of Woden glinted in the sunlight, and tried to find the resolve he had felt before. But it was easier to be strong when ale flowed in your veins and all you had in front of you were friends and a burning log. With a deep breath, he mounted Warda, who had been brought to him by one of the boys that lived in the fort. The same mare that had brought him here all the way from the south of Britannia, and Octa patted her neck as he found comfort in her presence.

Reinald gave the order for them to leave when everyone was

ready and they rode in silence until they reached the point in
the wall where a large portion had been taken away. Huge
blocks of stone littered the ground around the hole in the wall,
stones too heavy for people to carry away, and in Octa's mind it
almost looked like Thunor had punched a hole through the wall
with his mighty hammer.

'Local people started taking the stones as soon as the
Romans left,' Reinald explained as Octa stared at the wall. 'They
use it to build houses for themselves or boundary walls for their
land. But the fools never stopped to think about why the wall
was built in the first place and they complain to us that the Picts
are raiding their lands.'

'The people here got too used to living in peace when the
Romans were here that they forgot how dangerous things can
be,' another of the Saxons said with a shake of his head.

'Were the Romans really that good?' Octa asked as he
glanced around at the men wearing old Roman armour.

Reinald shrugged. 'They were once. Most of the continent
and the lands around it was once under their heel. But even they
got too relaxed and too greedy. Powerful men started fighting
each other for the right to rule instead of defending the borders
and now their empire is crumbling down around them.'

'Everything comes to an end. Even the gods eventually die,'
one of the Saxons said, and the others nodded. Octa's hand went
to the spear pendant he wore around his neck as he remembered the old man he had met in Jutland, Woden, and now Octa
was about to fight with his spear.

'That is why they are not real,' one of the Britons said, and
the Saxons only shook their heads at him. 'God, the Almighty, is
real and eternal.'

Octa frowned at the man, but before he could say anything,
Reinald said, 'Ignore him. The Christians have been saying that

to us since we arrived on the island, yet more and more of them join us when we hold our feasts for the gods.'

'They're coming!' They all looked up at a scout racing towards them on his horse. 'They're coming!'

'How many?' Reinald asked as the scout pulled his horse in front of the old warrior.

'More than we have. It looks like they are planning a large raid.'

Reinald scowled as he looked around him, and then his eyes stopped on the gap in the wall. He seemed to chew on the inside of his cheek as he thought of something, all the while the others waited for him to speak. Octa felt his fear creeping up his spine at the thought of facing that many Picts. The battle against them from the previous summer was still fresh in his mind and he couldn't help but glance around and wonder if any of these men would throw him in the middle of the Picts.

'Archers, on the wall on either side of the gap, the rest of us will form up here.' Reinald pointed to a spot in front of the wall. 'We meet them at the point where they have to pass through the gap. That way, their numbers won't help them.'

The Saxons all nodded and Octa watched as a group of Britons split into two and started scaling the wall on either side of the gap. Reinald turned to Octa and smiled at him. Even in his old age, Octa could see the excitement of the coming fight in his eyes. Something Octa wished he could feel instead of the icy fingers of fear gripping his stomach.

The Saxons dismounted from their horses and took their shields from their backs. Octa did the same, but couldn't help but glance over his shoulder along the path they had come from. All he had to do was jump on his horse and race away. No one here would stop him. Then he could find a ship and return to his father's village. He could tell him of the few battles he had fought, so that his father would think he had redeemed himself. Octa was sure that once he had the spear of Woden in his hands, then his father would forget about what had happened before. And Witta would be powerless as the other warlords would flock to his father and fight for him. And all he needed to do was jump on his horse and run away. Octa wrapped his fingers around the shaft of Woden's spear and the thoughts of running disappeared.

He looked at the Saxons, all of them older than his father, yet they were all preparing to fight. Even Britons stood amongst them. Men of different faiths, all standing together to fight for a common cause. To protect their homes and families. Octa looked at the spear, seeing the symbol of Woden glint in the sunlight, and remembered the oath he had made by the Yule fire. He would not run. He had fought the Picts before and he had survived. More than that, he had killed men to get his hands on the spear. He would not dishonour Woden by fleeing with his spear. Perhaps that way Woden would not punish him.

Reinald smiled at Octa when he walked towards him. 'Stand by me and do what I say,' the old warrior said to Octa, who could barely hear him as his heart beat hard enough to drown out most of the surrounding noise. He tightened his grip on the spear and fought to keep hold of the resolve he had felt moments ago. 'Keep your shield up and your eyes open.' Reinald raised his voice so that everyone could hear him. 'We will stand as strong as the wall built by the Romans. Our shields will not break and our spears will not blunt. The Picts will crash into us as if we are made of stone and they will die by our blades. We will feed the ravens with the blood of the men from the north. We will show them that though we might be old men, we still fight with the strength of our youth. The gods are with us! Tiw guides our blades while Thunor keeps us safe.' Reinald raised his spear in the air. 'To the gods!'

The Saxons and the Britons all echoed Reinald's cry and to Octa it sounded like thunder as their voices bounced off the wall. He looked at the spear in his hand. *Woden, give me the courage to kill my enemy with your spear.*

30

Octa gripped his shield in front of him. The oval Roman shield felt strange in his hands compared to the round shield he was used to and he found he had to tilt his head to see around it. Gungnir, though, felt like it belonged in his hand and Octa could already see himself killing his enemies with it. But the rest of his body did not feel the same. His legs trembled and felt like they might give way at any moment, while his sweaty palms made it hard for him to keep hold of his shield. And then there was his stomach, which seemed eager to expel his morning meal. All Octa could do was pray to the gods that he would stand his ground and not run from his enemies.

They heard the Picts before they saw them. From the singing they could hear, it seemed that the Picts were not aware of the Saxons waiting for them, and Reinald smiled at that.

'The shock of seeing us will slow them down and make them hesitate.' The old warrior glanced at the archers on the wall before turning his attention to Octa. 'Stay strong, brother. You fight with Woden's spear.' Octa nodded, but the resolve he had felt before had left him and he wished he had run when he had the chance to. 'You are a Saxon. You were born a warrior and have the blood of warriors running through your veins. Forget the past and focus on what is in front of you.'

Octa closed his eyes and thought of the battle against the Thuringians, of the huge warrior that killed his cousin. Octa could have saved him that day, but he had run instead. He then thought of the skirmish against the Picts. Of how he had fought for his life after he had been thrown amongst the enemies. And of the Jutes he had killed in the cave to get the spear. But then he remembered the owl and her warning, as well as Friga's words, and he felt his limbs go cold.

'Ready!' Reinald's voice made Octa open his eyes, and he gasped when he saw the Picts glaring at them from the other side of the wall. The icy fingers of his fear gripped Octa again, and he noticed how the point of the spear trembled in his hand.

The leader of the Picts stepped forward, a large man with no hair, and glanced at the top of the wall. 'Step away, Saxon, and let us through. Your men don't need to die for the Britons.'

Reinald smiled. 'My men and I will die protecting the people of this island, if that is what Wyrd has decided for us. But I will say the same to you. Turn your men around and return to your homes.'

The Pict hawked and spat. 'I have more men than you and you tell me to turn around.'

Reinald, still smiling, said, 'You might have more men, but we have a large wall.'

The Pict glanced at the wall again. 'Walls don't fight. They just stand there.'

'That's all this wall needs to do.' Reinald raised his spear. 'Archers! Fire!'

The Pict raised his shield above his head, but many of his men were too slow. Octa flinched at the snapping sound of arrows being loosed and would have run from the screams of the Picts as the arrows struck if it had not been for the man behind him. The warrior gripped his shoulder and kept him in place, while Reinald whispered to him.

'Stand strong, Octa. Today you make your father proud.'

'Charge!' the Pictish leader roared, and stormed towards the gap in the wall.

Those of his men not cowering from the arrows followed him. More of the Picts were killed by arrows as Reinald ordered his shield wall to take a step forward, forcing the Picts to fight on uneven ground. Three volleys of arrows rained down on the Picts before they stopped and the Picts, emboldened by this, roared as they all charged at the Saxon shield wall. But they were forced to condense as they charged through the gap of the wall and that was when Reinald shouted, 'Javelins!'

Octa watched as the warriors of Corstopitum launched the small throwing spears they were carrying into the condensed Picts, many of whom were all still holding their shields above them. The Picts cried out as the javelins struck them and Octa gasped as many of them collapsed, only to be trampled on by their own people, while their leader swatted a javelin to the side with his shield and roared for them to charge at the Saxons.

'Again!' Reinald ordered, and the Saxon feoderati threw another volley at the oncoming Picts. Octa wished he had been given the throwing spears as well, but knew that with his hands trembling like they were, he would have missed his mark.

'Kill them all!' the Pictish leader roared as soon as the second volley of javelins struck his men, but the Picts struggled to get over the bodies of their dead and the large stones on the ground.

'Shield wall!' Reinald ordered, and Octa locked his shield in with those on either side of him, just as he had been taught to do by Witta. 'Hold your ground, Octa,' Reinald said, his voice just carrying over the battle cry of the Picts. 'Use your fear. Feed on it and use it against your enemy. You fight with Woden's spear. It never misses its mark.'

Octa glanced at the wavering point of his spear and remembered the stories he had been told as a child. He tightened his grip on the shaft as he fought the urge to run, before he took a deep breath to calm his nerves. His fear crept up his spine, and he tried to feed on it as Reinald had said, even if he didn't understand what the warrior meant by that. But Octa did not want to let Reinald down, so he forced himself to keep his eyes open and face the Picts.

'Hold your ground,' Reinald said to him. 'Think of those you love and fight for them.'

Octa thought of his mother, his father and his cousin as the Picts came close enough for him to make out the colours of their eyes and see the missing teeth in their mouths. He remembered the promise he had made to his mother and tightened his grip on Gungnir, determined not to let his mother down.

Octa closed his eyes when one of the Picts was only a few steps away from him and stabbed forward with the spear of Woden. He felt his arm judder as the spear struck something and fought to keep his arm straight. Reinald roared beside him and when Octa opened his eyes, he saw the Pictish warrior gaping at him as his spear was stuck in the man's chest.

'For the gods!' Reinald shouted, and the Saxons of Corstopitum surged forward.

Octa felt a surge as his battle lust took hold of him. It was something he had heard of but had never felt before. He felt strong and invincible, as if the gods were fighting with him. It was intoxicating, and Octa screamed to the gods as he punched forward with his shield and pulled the spear out of the Pict's chest. The Saxons charged at the Picts as they struggled to get firm footing over their dead and the large stones on the ground.

Reinald stabbed forward with his spear and pierced the neck of one Pict before he was forced to duck behind his own shield. Everything Octa had been taught since he was a child came to him now. The many days of lessons with Witta and his best warriors meant he moved without thinking, like the spear was guiding him. He raised his shield to block the axe of one Pict and stabbed the man in the side with his spear, before punching him back with his shield. Warriors screamed as they fought and died, their blood drenching the soil under their feet. Picts cried out in their tongue, their words unrecognisable for Octa, while the Saxons called out to the gods. Even the Britons were shouting Tiw's and Woden's names as they slaughtered those who threatened their homes and Octa revelled in it all as he twisted out of the way of a spear and punched down at the Pict's leg with his shield. The man's piercing shriek tore through the sounds of battle as his leg snapped before Octa stabbed him in the neck with his spear. But as quickly as his battle lust came to him, it fled when another spear went unnoticed and grazed the armour he was wearing. The blow forced Octa back half a step and for a moment his fear threatened to take hold of him when he remembered he could die here. And Octa was not ready to die yet.

He glanced over his shoulder, looking for a way out, and did not see the spear coming for his face. Octa only knew of it when Reinald blocked it with his shield and another of the Saxons cut the Pict down. But this had left the Saxon warrior exposed and the leader of the Picts took his chance and cleaved his head off with his sword. Octa gasped as the Saxon's blood washed over him and, for a moment, he was back in the battle against the Thuringians and staring at the large warrior who was about to kill Uhtric. Octa had been too afraid to face that warrior, just like he was too afraid to face the Pictish leader. And just like on that day, there was no one to help him as Reinald was busy fighting another warrior.

The Pictish leader sneered at Octa as he raised his sword, and all Octa wanted to do was turn and run, just like he had that day. But his legs refused to obey him and Octa couldn't understand why. He wanted to close his eyes, not wanting to see his death coming, but like his legs, his eyes refused to obey him as well.

'Fight, Octa!' Reinald's voice broke through the fog of his fear and Octa remembered he had been here before as his eyes went to the Pict's exposed stomach. Octa was not ready to die yet. Not until he had redeemed himself. In his mind, he saw the Thuringian who had killed Uhtric again, the large warrior standing over them with his two-handed axe in his hands, and Octa roared as he did what he should have done that day. He stabbed forward with Woden's spear, the weapon that never missed, and with all the noise of violence around him, he heard the Pict grunt as the spear found a gap in the man's armour.

The Pict's eyes bulged as he stared at the spear in his stomach and then at Octa, who glared at him. 'This is for Uhtric,' he said through gritted teeth, before he took a step forward and pushed the spear in deeper. The Pict dropped his sword and grabbed the shaft of the spear with both his hands before he screamed something at Octa. But Octa didn't try to make sense of the words that came out of the man's mouth as he pushed the spear in even deeper. 'I am the son of Frithowald and I will no longer be afraid.' Octa let go of the spear and before the Pict could react, he pulled his seax knife from its scabbard and stabbed the Pict in the throat. 'Woden!' he roared to the skies as the Pict died. Octa left the knife in the

Pict's throat and pulled Woden's spear free, its shaft with the runes soaked in the man's blood. *Accept this offering and allow me to use your spear to do what I must*, Octa prayed to the war god because, as he stared at the body of the Pict, he knew there was something he had to do first before he could go home.

The Picts cried out in dismay when they saw their leader was dead and, without an order being given, they turned and fled. Those who weren't fast enough were cut down, while Octa stood where he was, his eyes on the spear and wondering if it was the spear that had fought the battle or him.

'The spear is just a weapon,' Reinald said as if he had read Octa's mind.

'But this isn't just a spear,' Octa said, his mind going over the battle again.

Reinald, his face covered in blood, smiled. 'Aye, but that doesn't matter. The spear does not move on its own. It was your hand that guided it, just like it was you who overcame your fear.'

Octa looked at the Saxon warrior who had died because of him. 'Not soon enough, though.'

Reinald's smile disappeared as he looked at the man and the others he had lost against the Picts. 'He died with honour and the gods will reward him for that. Just like the others who died to protect those who live by the wall.'

'You really believe our gods are here?' Octa couldn't help but ask.

Reinald nodded. 'Our gods are wherever we are. How else can they bless us when we fight and die so far from the homeland?' Reinald looked at Octa. 'Learn from his death and the death of your cousin, Octa. Use it to make yourself a better warrior.' Reinald looked at the spear in Octa's hand. 'The stories never tell us that the spear fought the battles on its own, but always that it is wielded by Woden. Woden used the spear to win his victories and now you will use it to win yours.'

Octa nodded as his battle lust left him and his legs trembled. 'I need to sit down.'

Reinald smiled. 'Aye, that is normal. You rest, Octa, son of Frithowald. We'll do what needs to be done here and then we'll head back to the fort.'

Octa frowned at Reinald. 'How do you know my father's name?'

'You shouted it when you killed the Pict.'

Octa nodded and guessed he must have done as he sat down and watched the Saxons go through the dead and injured. Those of their own they took to one side where their wounds were treated, while the Picts were killed. The archers came down from the wall and walked amongst the dead to collect what arrows could be used again, and looting the dead Picts. Some warriors stood by the wall and kept an eye out in case the Picts returned, but Octa could not see why they would. Their leader was dead, and the Saxons had the upper hand.

'What do we do with him?' One of the Saxons pointed to the dead Pictish leader.

Reinald looked at the man. 'Cut his head off and put it on a stake over there.' He pointed to a spot on the north side of the wall. 'Maybe it will discourage other Picts from raiding these lands.'

'The gods know that won't happen. They're like fleas on a dog. As soon as you think you got rid of them, they come back.'

'Aye.' Reinald glanced at Octa, who wondered what the man was thinking. He looked at the spear again, amazed at how light it had felt during the battle. He barely noticed it in his hand, and the blade was still as sharp as it was when he took it from the cave. A flutter of wings made Octa look up, but instead of the raven he expected, he saw the white owl. Octa scowled at the bird, wondering why it kept watching him.

'Strange seeing them out in the day, especially near people,' Reinald said as he, too, stared at the owl.

One of the Britons said something which Octa couldn't hear and he noticed how many of them rubbed the iron of their weapons. 'What did he say?'

'He said it was Brigantia watching you.'

All Octa could do was nod at that, because he didn't know what to say. What he did know, though, was that he needed to go south. With a clarity he had never felt before, Octa knew he needed to kill the man who had left him for dead in the cave. The spear demanded it.

31

It didn't take them long to deal with the dead. A cart had been brought from the fort and the Saxon dead were placed on it, while the Picts had their heads cut off and placed on their own spears on the north side of the wall. A warning to other bands of raiders who wanted to use this gap in the wall to attack the local people. It was something they had also done in the lands of the Saxons, but there the heads were taken as trophies and were displayed so that others could see that you were a great warrior. By the time they were done dealing with the dead, the sun was sitting low in the sky and Octa, like many of the others, was eager to get away from this place. No one wanted to be there when the spirits of the dead started roaming around.

The men were grim as they returned to the fort, and Octa could understand why. They had lost friends and family members, men they had shared ale and food with. Men they had stood alongside for many winters. And although Octa understood the pain these men felt, he was glad he had survived and, more importantly to himself, he had shown that he was not a coward. Octa had stood in a shield wall and he had not run.

Even when he wanted to. He had faced his enemies and his fear and he had defeated them both. Again, he glanced at the spear and wondered if Woden's weapon had given him that courage or if it had always been there.

When they reached the fort, the injured were taken to the building where Octa had been treated while the dead were put in another building.

'They'll be cleaned and dressed properly. Tomorrow we will bury them.' Reinald watched as the dead were taken from the cart and carried away. He turned to Octa. 'Come, let's celebrate our victory and honour the dead.'

Octa went back to his room and, for a long while, just stood there and stared at nothing. Eventually, he removed his armour and his tunic, and looked at the blood on both before dropping them on the floor. He checked his body for wounds and found only a few minor cuts on his arms which were not protected by armour. Octa looked around his room and found the bucket with water he had been searching for. He picked up a stool and sat down in front of the bucket. For a few heartbeats, he stared at his reflection in the water. His face, covered in blood and dirt, looked the same as it did before, even though he felt different. The constant fear that had gripped him before was gone. His hands no longer trembled, and even his legs felt sturdier than they had before. Glancing over his shoulder at Gungnir, he wondered what magic the weapon possessed to cause this change in him. Or was it as Reinald had said? The spear was only a weapon. Nothing but wood and iron.

Octa did not know the answer to that as he rinsed his face and then cleaned the blood off his arms. The water in the bucket turned red as he cleaned himself and when he was done he took his tunic from the floor and wet it before he cleaned the blood off the spear. The spearhead gleamed in the dim light of his room and Octa couldn't help but rub his thumb over the symbol of Woden. He was convinced the spear had helped him find his courage during the battle, but he still couldn't understand the calm he had felt. After the battle, he had been exhausted, his legs could barely hold his weight, but as he sat there and watched the Saxons clear the dead and help the wounded, the calm had come. It was as if he suddenly understood his path, even if much of it was still covered in fog.

Octa looked up when the door to his room opened and saw one of the British women, Diseta, that helped around the fort standing there, her eyes on his naked torso.

'Reinald told me to bring you new clothes,' she said in the British tongue, and Octa nodded as Diseta stood there, her eyes still fixed on him and not moving. Octa felt something stir in his loins, a feeling he had not felt for a long time. He had always been confident around women. Back in the homeland, he could have anyone he wanted because he was the son of a warlord, but since the battle where Uhtric had died, his fear and shame had suppressed those feelings. For a moment he thought of Heilwig and wondered what had become of her. But as he stared at Diseta, with a seductive smile on her lips, Octa forgot about the woman he had once thought would be his and before he knew what he was doing, he stood naked in front of Diseta, who did not move. Not even when he stepped towards her. She looked up at him, her eyes filled with lust, and before she could say another word, Octa wrapped his arms around her and kissed her.

A while later, they both lay on the bed, their naked bodies pressed together and stinking of sweat and sex. Octa stared at the roof of his room as Diseta lay there, her arms still wrapped around him.

'What are you thinking of?' Diseta said in the British tongue, and Octa glanced at her to see that she was staring at him.

'Nothing,' he lied as he also responded in the British tongue, and saw from the smile on her face that she didn't believe him.

Diseta sat up and wrapped her arm around her breasts, her sudden shyness making him smile. 'I need to go. I'm supposed to be helping to prepare for the feast tonight.'

Octa nodded. 'Soon, I go.' He wasn't sure why he said that, but he knew it was time for him to move on. He had hidden from his wyrd long enough, and it was time to face those who had tried to kill him.

Diseta nodded. 'Does Reinald know?' Octa shook his head, feeling the kick in his chest that the woman did not seem to care that he was leaving. But then, she wasn't his woman and apart from her bringing him new clothes and helping him learn the British tongue while he had been here, this had been the first time they had slept together. 'You should tell him before you tell anyone else. He likes you.'

'Reinald good man. Good leader,' Octa said, and meant it. He had been surprised at how even the Britons in and around Corstopitum respected the old Saxon. At how, during the skirmish against the Picts, they had all followed his commands without thought. Octa knew he could learn a lot from the old man, but he had already stayed in the fort longer than he should have done.

'He hoped you would stay. Believes you can do good things here.' Diseta got up and collected her dress, which she put on. She looked at the bucket of water and grimaced, before she turned towards Octa. 'I'll have someone bring you clean water.' She left before Octa could say anything and Octa just lay where he was, his eyes fixed on the roof of his room.

Noise woke Octa a while later and he had not realised that

he had fallen asleep. He looked up to see one of the boys who ran around the fort putting a bucket of fresh water on the floor. The boy smiled at him before he left again and Octa frowned, wondering what time it was. He got up from the bed and went to the bucket. After rinsing his face and cleaning himself again, he got dressed in the clothes Diseta had brought him before and left his room. He made his way to the main hall, and already could hear the Saxons sing songs of the homeland. Octa stood outside the hall and closed his eyes as he let the songs carry him back to the lands of the Saxons. He thought of his father and his mother and wondered how they were and if they missed him. Octa doubted his father did. He had disowned Octa after all, but all that would change when Octa delivered the spear of Woden to him.

'I'll be home soon,' Octa said as he gripped the spear pendant his mother had given him. He was about to go into the hall when he heard a noise behind him. At first, he thought it was one of the children as they were always running around and playing games, sometimes with the dogs in tow, but then he heard footsteps rushing towards him. Octa turned in time to see the ugly snarl of his attacker before the man stabbed at him with a knife.

'For Brigantia!'

Octa's heart skipped a beat in his chest and for half a heartbeat he thought he was going to die, but then his instinct kicked in and he twisted out of the way of the knife before punching the Briton in the face. Something came over him, something unfamiliar to him, but it warmed his limbs as it coursed through him and Octa used it as he grabbed the Briton by the neck before he could fall to the ground and pushed him against the wall of the hall.

'Why kill me?' he asked the man, who only spat in his face.

Octa, struggling to control his anger at almost being assassinated when he had finally overcome his fear, punched the man in the stomach with his free hand and asked him again. 'Why kill me?'

The songs and music inside the hall continued as the people were oblivious to what was happening outside. The Briton glared at Octa.

'You defiled her statue. You killed my brothers.'

Octa frowned and then ripped the man's tunic open and, in the dying daylight, he saw the mark of the cult of Brigantia. The spearhead inked on his skin. He struggled to make sense of it. 'Why now?' he asked. He had broken the statue the summer before and no one had attacked him for it. 'Why now?' He repeated the question, but the man only laughed.

'You Saxon scum! You will die for what you did to our mother.'

Octa knew he should kill the man. His hand even went to the seax knife in his belt, but he couldn't. He could not kill someone in cold blood, so instead he punched the man again, whose head struck the stone wall behind him, and when Octa let go of him the man collapsed on the ground. Octa heard a flap of wings and saw the owl land on the roof of the hall.

Octa glared at the bird. 'What do you want from me?'

'Octa?' one of the Saxons said as he stepped out of the hall. He looked at the man on the ground and frowned when he saw the knife lying next to him. Octa watched as the owl flew away and then turned to the Saxon.

'He tried to kill me.'

'He still lives?'

Octa nodded. 'I think so.'

The Saxon scowled at the man. 'Who is he?'

Octa shrugged. 'A Briton, but I have never seen him before.'

Octa didn't want to tell the Saxon that the man was from the cult of Brigantia, but he was sure they would figure it out.

The old Saxon leaned down and looked at the man. 'I know him. He is from a village not far from here.' The Saxon sighed. 'Go inside. Reinald is waiting for you. I'll deal with this man.'

Octa nodded and walked into the hall. He had been to many feasts before, but never one after a battle, and he was surprised at how lively it was. Hiding his trembling hands behind him, Octa made his way to Reinald, who was sitting at the far end of the hall. There was no raised seat like in Witta's hall, even though Reinald was in command while the leader of the Saxon foederati in Corstopitum was away. But he had told Octa before that he preferred to sit at the same level as everyone else. He was not a warlord and not the son of one either.

The Saxons sang the songs they had been taught as young men in the homeland, while the Britons clapped along. Octa frowned at the laughter and the smiles he saw on the faces of everyone. He would have thought they'd be upset. That they'd be mourning the loss of their friends. He said as much to Reinald when he sat down beside him.

Reinald smiled. 'We do not mourn their deaths. We celebrate that they died with honour and that they have joined Woden's army.' Reinald drank from his cup. 'And besides, they would not want us to cry for them. They'd want us to drink and to sing in their honour. And that is what we do.'

Octa nodded as he took a cup of ale and, before he drank from it, he wondered if Witta had celebrated the death of his son, like these warriors celebrated their friends.

32

A few days later, the Saxon foederati were all there to say farewell to Octa as he prepared to leave. The few belongings he had were packed in a sack and tied to the back of his mare. It wasn't much. A spare tunic and enough food for him and Warda for the trip south so that Octa did not have to risk going into towns. He wore the armour he had fought the Picts in and had a round shield on his back. It had belonged to one of the Jutes that had travelled to the north with him. And then there was Gungnir. The spear that would earn his redemption.

'Are you sure you don't want to stay?' Reinald asked him again, as he had many times since Octa had told him that he was leaving. 'The young warriors could do with a leader like you, and a warrior to show them how to fight.' Octa was surprised to see tears in the eyes of some of the older Saxons. He had not realised they would be upset to see him leave.

Octa shook his head. 'I am no leader. And there are better men to show them how to fight.'

'But they don't carry the spear of Woden.' Reinald glanced at the spear and smiled. But Octa could not return his smile. Not while the memory of him being attacked a few days before was still fresh in his mind. He did not know what the Saxon warrior had done to the man, and he decided he didn't want to. But Octa was certain that there would be many more attempts on his life. The Britons believed they fought for the honour of their goddess.

'You can always come with me to the south,' Octa countered. And this time Reinald shook his head.

'My life is here now. My wife is buried here and so are two of my children.' The old Saxon sighed and looked around the fort. 'This is where I will die.' Octa nodded and the two men embraced before Reinald handed Octa a seax knife. Octa stared at the knife, its hilt made of horn and with two snarling wolves carved on it. He frowned at Reinald, not sure why the old warrior was giving it to him. 'I wanted to give it to my son, but never got the chance to.' Octa was about to say something, but Reinald stopped him. 'Take care, Octa, son of Frithowald. I will pray to the gods that you find the redemption you seek.'

'So will I,' Octa said as he put the seax knife in the sack with his belongings and mounted his horse. He fixed his cloak, so it protected him against the unusual chill in the morning. In the corner of his eye, he spotted Diseta and smiled at her. She returned her smile and then walked away as he turned to face the other Saxons. Men far braver than he could ever be. Men who gave their lives to protect a people they did not belong to. But yet, they lived amongst the Britons, and not only that, but the Britons had also accepted them. Married them and bore their children. Many of the Britons spoke some of the Saxon tongue and even worshipped the Saxon gods. Octa wondered if that was what the future of Britannia was. 'Farewell,' Octa said to the Saxons. 'May the gods be with you.'

'And you, Octa,' Reinald said as Octa tapped his mare's sides and Warda trotted towards the gates.

As Octa passed under the gates, something made him look up and he wasn't surprised to see the white owl sitting there, its large eyes following him as he left the fort. Octa rubbed the spear pendant around his neck and prayed that he would not be ambushed on his way south. Apart from the attack a few days ago, no one had come after him, something which Octa had found odd.

The sky was grey and the wind strong, but Octa doubted it would rain. He couldn't smell it in the air and felt that the wind was too strong for it to rain as he used the old Roman road Reinald had told him to use as he travelled south. While he was in the lands of the Brigantes, he avoided any settlements he saw, still concerned that there were others who wanted to kill him. During the day, he kept glancing over his shoulder, but didn't see anyone chasing after him and neither was he ambushed at any point on the road. At night, he would leave the road and find a spot where he could not be seen and would sleep wrapped up in his cloak, as he did not want to risk making any fires.

When he entered the lands of the Corieltauvi, Octa felt just as tense as he had in the lands of the Brigantes. He gripped the spear as tightly as he could and kept his eyes open for any sign of trouble, not sure if followers of Brigantia were in these lands as well. He also remembered the skirmish against the Corieltauvi, which made him want to avoid them even more. But as he rode the many days south, just like in the north, there was no sign of trouble. Most people he came across paid him no more attention other than to glance at him and then move out of his way. A few even greeted him and asked where he rode from and Octa wondered if it was because of the old Roman armour Reinald had given him.

Perhaps the people thought he was one of the Saxon foederati the Romans had left behind. Tired of sleeping in the open, he even attempted to sleep in a tavern he came across along the road.

Octa used his limited British to book a room and a place for Warda in the stables, but the sleep he had hoped for never came. His dreams were plagued with images of a burning hall which reminded him of his father's mead hall. The following day, he was on the road again and soon found himself in the kingdom of the Cantiaci. Octa doubted he could relax even as he neared his destination. The last time he had been here, the king of the Cantiaci had been unhappy with King Vortigern's decision to employ the Jutes, and even while he was in the north with the Saxon foederati, he had heard stories of skirmishes between the Jutes and the locals near the island of Ruym. But he had also heard of how Hengist and Horsa's Jutes had been successful in keeping the river free from raiders and how trade in Londinium had increased.

When Octa reached the large river near the large fortified city that he believed was Londinium, he followed its course out to sea, like Reinald had explained, and not long after he saw the island of Ruym. His hands trembled and Warda must have sensed his unease because she shook her head and pawed the turf when he stopped to look at the camp Hengist and Horsa had built. A wooden wall had been erected around the camp, which made it hard for Octa to see the tents inside, and he could see warriors patrolling the wall, their armour and spears glinting in the sunlight. What surprised him, though, was the wooden bridge that had been built between the mainland and the island. Octa guessed the brothers had it built so that they could leave the island whenever they wanted and did not have to wait for the tides. He then frowned when he saw six ships instead of the three Hengist and Horsa had arrived on and wondered if more warlords had joined them.

'Do you think they would welcome me with open arms?' he asked Warda, who shook her head as if she understood his question. Perhaps she did, but Octa already knew the answer. Hengist and Horsa thought he was dead, that he was certain of because he knew that Eadric had made it back to the island. That was the only way they would tell people that they had what they believed was Gungnir. But would they be pleased that he was still alive, or would they be angry? Octa knew that depended on what Eadric had told them, just like he knew that Eadric would not be pleased to see him alive. 'We'll have to do our best to avoid him until we can reach the brothers,' Octa said to Warda as he prayed to the gods that they were on the island and not in Cair Urnahc. And once he spoke to the brothers, he would kill Eadric.

Octa tightened his grip on the spear and took a deep breath as he tried to find the strength to ride towards the camp. Even after everything he had been through to get the spear, and even though he now had the spear, Octa found it difficult to even think of facing Hengist and Horsa. And Eadric.

A raven flew overhead, its cry startling Octa. The image of the burning hall flashed in his mind again, and he wondered if that was a message from Woden. He glanced up at the raven as it flew towards the camp and knew that he could put it off no longer. He patted Warda's neck.

'Let's go. It's time to face our wyrd.'

Warda whined as Octa tapped her sides with his heels and he sensed even she did not want to go back to the camp. Something Reinald had said to him when they buried those who had died in the fight against the Picts came to him and Octa straightened his back as he rode towards the camp. *You can face your fear or run from it. Running might seem to be an easier choice, but once you take that first step, then you'll never stop running. But if you face your fear and overcome it, then you never need to run again.*

Octa's heart raced as he approached the bridge and the two warriors guarding it glared at him. He expected them to challenge him, but they only stared at him as he rode past them, the clatter of Warda's hooves on the wood almost in time with the sounds of the waves breaking on the beach. Perhaps the warriors thought he was a messenger, or that he was part of the army. He did not recognise them, so he guessed they did not know who he was either.

As he crossed the bridge and made it to the island, he turned Warda towards where the brothers had their tents before and was disappointed to see that the tents were gone. He worried that they were in Cair Urnahc and wondered if Eadric would be with them.

'What are you looking for, friend?' he heard someone say, and turned to see a warrior about his age staring at him.

Octa cleared his throat. 'I'm looking for Hengist and Horsa.'

'Why?'

Octa watched the man for a few heartbeats and when he felt certain that the man did not know who he was, he said, 'I have a message from the north.'

The warrior nodded. 'Follow that path.' He pointed to a path that led to the centre of the island. 'You'll soon come across a village. The brothers are in the main hall.'

Octa nodded and wondered when the brothers had moved into the village. And what had happened to those who lived there. He still remembered the night when men from that village had attacked them. Octa was about to set off towards the village when he heard.

'Octa? Is that you?'

Octa pulled on Warda's reins and she protested at the sudden movement as Octa stared around the camp, certain he had imagined his mother's voice. And then he heard her again.

'Octa! My son!'

Octa scowled as he scanned the camp, and then his heart skipped a beat when he saw her running towards him. He jumped off his horse, his hands trembling as he struggled to believe what he was seeing. Before he could say anything, his mother wrapped her arms around him and squeezed so hard that he could hardly breathe.

'My son, I knew you weren't dead,' his mother cried in his ears. Octa hugged his mother, not sure if what was happening was real or a dream.

'Mother?' Octa pulled her off him and gaped at her. Her face was thinner and her dress patched up. She wore none of the jewellery that she used to, but her hair was still neatly combed and she still had that fire in her eyes. 'What, in Woden's name, are you doing here?'

His mother didn't answer, though. Instead, fresh tears erupted from her eyes and she hugged him again.

'She came here looking for you,' another voice he had not expected to hear said.

Octa's heart skipped when he saw Odalric standing there, a fresh scar on his cheek and thinner than before, but still the same warrior Octa knew. Odalric wasn't wearing his armour and the only weapon he had on him was his seax knife, but he still looked dangerous as he glared at Octa.

'Why?' Octa pulled his mother away from him again and, when he looked at her, he remembered what Friga had said to him. *You have angered Woden and there will be a price to pay.* With a shiver, Octa finally understood the dreams he had been having. 'Mother? What happened?'

Berthild took a deep breath and straightened her back. In a blink of an eye, she became the woman he had always known her to be.

'Witta came. He believed your father had helped you to escape his men.'

Octa's heart was racing as he stared at his mother. His legs felt like they wanted to give way and it took all his strength not to collapse. With a trembling voice, he asked, 'What happened? Where is Father?'

'Your father is dead,' Odalric said, his voice strained. 'Witta marched his men to our village. He killed those who couldn't escape and burnt the village to the ground.' As Odalric said the words, the image of the burning hall came to Octa again. He looked at the spear, still in his hand, and knew it was because he had refused to take the spear back to Woden. Friga had warned him, but he had been too blind to understand what she was saying. He believed Woden would come for him. Never had he thought his family could be in danger. 'But not before he killed your father and took his head.' Odalric clenched his fists as he glared at Octa.

'Odalric,' Berthild said, but the warrior paid her no attention.

'And all because of you. Because you are nothing but a coward.'

Octa thought he could hear Woden laughing as Odalric's words slapped him in the face. He turned to his mother, his eyes wide. 'Is it true? Father is dead?'

His mother nodded. 'Witta destroyed everything. Your father fought him so that we could all escape—'

'Almost beat him as well,' Odalric interrupted her, and Octa glared at him.

'Why are you here? You are his sworn man. You should have fought by his side!'

Odalric stepped towards Octa until they were nose to nose and returned his glare. 'You don't get to talk to me about fighting by another's side.' Octa tightened his grip around the spear as his blood pumped in his ears and he fought the urge to attack Odalric.

'Enough.' His mother pulled them apart and Octa was aware of the other people in the camp gathering around them. 'Your father ordered Odalric to take me to safety. The only reason I made it to this place was because of him.' She turned to Odalric. 'And you will forget the anger you have towards my son. The gods know this isn't ideal, but this is our wyrd and we need to stand together if we want to make the most of it.'

Octa and Odalric glared at each other for a few more heart-beats before Octa nodded and looked at Gungnir. He had wanted to give it to his father and now he was dead, and Octa knew it was because of him. The words Brigantia had spoken to him in the cave came to him then, and Octa knew he should have listened to the goddess. *You have much to lose, Octa, son of Frithowald.*

'Why do you keep looking at the spear?' Odalric asked him, and Octa smiled a sad smile.

'There is much I have to tell you, but first there is something I must do.' Without another word, Octa turned and walked towards the village. His anger pumped through his veins, a feeling Octa was not used to, and he fed on it as he walked towards the centre of Hengist and Horsa's camp.

'Where are you going?' his mother asked him as she and Odalric followed him.

Octa glared at the raven that flew over him, his blood still pumping in his ears. 'I have a man to kill.'

33

Octa kept his eyes fixed to the front as he walked through the village, his mother and Odalric behind him, and his heart beating hard as he remembered being left for dead in the cave of Brigantia. He did not know where he was going. Octa had never been in this village before, but he guessed if he went to the centre of the village, then he would find Hengist and Horsa, and gods willing that bastard Eadric.

The warriors he walked past all frowned at them, and Octa was certain they were wondering who he was. But no one stopped him as he approached the large building in the centre of the village, which he hoped was the hall where he had been told Hengist and Horsa were. A group of warriors walked out of the hall and Octa's heart raced when he saw Eadric in the centre of them all as they laughed at something. But then that laughter died when Rembert saw Octa standing there. His face paled and he gripped Eadric's shoulder, who looked annoyed until he saw what Rembert was pointing at. Like Rembert, Eadric's face paled, and for a few heartbeats the two Jutes just stared at Octa.

'That was the warrior who told us you died,' his mother said behind him.

'He should know,' Octa said as he tightened his grip on Gungnir. 'He left me to die.'

His mother gasped as Eadric composed himself. He said something to one of the warriors, who ran back inside the hall, before he made his way towards Octa.

'You should have stayed dead.' Eadric glared at Octa, who stopped in front of him and returned his glare.

'The gods decided it wasn't my time.' Octa noticed how Eadric frowned at the spear.

'Why would the gods care about a coward like you?'

Octa only smiled in response. The icy fingers of fear that would have crippled him before were not there. Instead, the heat of his anger warmed his body and heightened his senses. Again, Eadric glanced at the plain-looking spear in Octa's hand. He raised an eyebrow as he saw the ravens on the spearhead and the spear's name on the shaft.

'You expect me to believe that is the spear of Woden?'

Octa glared at Eadric. 'I don't care what you think. You killed Badulf and tried to kill me.'

'And?'

Before Octa could respond, Eadric turned to the men behind him.

'Grab this bastard and make him disappear before Hengist and Horsa see him.'

'No!' Berthild screamed as she made to step in front of him, but then Odalric grabbed her hand and pulled her back. Octa would have been mad, but he knew the warrior was only protecting his mother.

Octa turned to face the men coming towards him, their eyes filled with violence, and knew he had been foolish to just walk into the village like that. But he had been fuelled by his anger, just as he still was. So instead of backing away, he took the shield from his back and pointed Woden's spear at the warriors, who only laughed at him.

One of the warriors rushed at Octa, who dodged out of the way, but before another could do the same, Hengist's voice echoed above their heads.

'Enough!'

They all turned towards the hall as Hengist and Horsa walked out, with Hengist carrying the spear Eadric had taken from the cave. But then both brothers looked surprised to see Octa and Hengist raised an eyebrow at Eadric as he walked past the man towards Octa, whose heart was still racing. Octa's mother and Odalric stood behind him as he lowered the spear, but he still kept an eye on Eadric and the warriors around him. All Octa heard were the whispers as everyone gathered around them and tried to understand what was happening.

'Octa the Saxon. The gods must by enjoying themselves,' Hengist said as he glared at Eadric, who looked uncomfortable. 'We were told you were killed in an ambush by the protectors of Brigantia.'

Octa glanced at the spear Hengist had in his hand, the golden-rimmed blade glinting in the sun. It was a spear worthy of the gods, but Octa knew it was not the real spear. It was a decoy to fool those who did not listen to the gods. 'I guess you were also told that is the spear of Woden in your hands?'

Hengist looked at the spear in his hand, and the one Octa was holding. 'We were. Eadric told us how he got it from a cave near the wall built by the Romans. Did he lie to us?'

'Eadric, explain yourself,' Horsa said, his face an ugly grimace.

'I thought he was dead,' he said, somehow with confidence as if that was true, as he scowled at Octa.

Octa glared at Horsa, no longer feeling the same fear he had felt for the man before, and spoke. 'He did not lie about where he found the spear.'

'What did he lie about?' Hengist asked.

'I wasn't killed in an ambush by the Britons—'

'That we can see,' Horsa said, and some warriors laughed, but Eadric's face was turning red and Octa wondered if the older warrior was going to attack him.

'Eadric tried to kill me in the cave after he found that spear.'

'Eadric should have done a better job of that.' Horsa scowled at the warrior, who shrugged.

'Octa is harder to kill than I thought.' Eadric hawked and spat.

'Because Octa is the son of a powerful warlord,' his mother said, and Octa wished she had kept quiet. 'It will take more than a common warrior to kill him.'

Eadric glared at Berthild and Odalric took a step forward, his hand on his seax knife as Hengist laughed.

'So you said before.' Hengist looked at Octa. 'We should have guessed, seeing how good you are with horses. No low-born Saxon would be taught to ride a horse before he could walk.'

'Aye,' his brother said. 'But this son of a warlord must have fallen far considering the state we found him in. Makes you wonder what he did?'

'Or didn't do?' Hengist scrutinised Octa as if he was seeing him for the first time. But Octa did not care. The past was behind him. All that mattered was in front of him.

'Octa is a coward, that much I can tell you.' Eadric hawked and spat after he said the words.

Octa tightened the grip on the spear as he took a step towards Eadric. 'I killed two of your men. I stood in a Saxon shield wall and fought against the Picts. I killed their leader with this very spear. The real Gungnir.' He heard his mother gasp behind him, but he kept his eyes on Eadric.

Eadric's nostrils flared as he stared at Octa. 'You are still a coward.'

Octa took another step towards the older warrior, his heart pounding in his chest as his anger kept his fear at bay.

'Well, the gods know that this is all very entertaining, but we have a problem far larger than Octa's reputation,' Hengist said, which caused many of the warriors to frown at him, including his brother.

'What are you talking about?'

Hengist looked at the spear in his hand. 'We were told that this is Gungnir. We have sent word back to Jutland that we fight with Woden's spear and that they should join us. And yet, Octa tells us that the spear he has is the real spear of Woden.'

'It's obvious that the spear you have is the real spear,' Eadric said. 'Octa's spear is just a plain spear, one he took from the old Saxons by the wall. Yours looks like it belongs to a god.'

Hengist nodded and looked at his spear again as he ran his finger along its edge. 'And that is why I wonder if this is the real spear. Woden is known for his trickery.'

'So how do we know the truth?' Horsa asked.

'Does it really matter?' Eadric added.

Hengist scowled as he looked at the spear in Octa's hand. 'How did you find that spear?'

Octa hesitated, but then told them how he had found the spear. He left out the part where he spoke to an owl because he didn't want them to think he had lost his wits.

'So it was hidden inside the statue?' Horsa glanced at his brother.

'Horse shit!' Eadric said. 'I searched that statue and saw nothing to show there was a spear hidden inside. The coward is lying to you!'

'You see the problem?' Hengist asked his brother as he ignored Eadric's outburst.

Horsa nodded. 'So how do we know which spear is the real spear?'

For a while Hengist glanced at Octa and Eadric, his brows furrowed as he thought about it, and then he smiled. 'We let Woden decide.'

Octa's heart skipped a beat and for a moment he thought of Friga and Brigantia. Both gods had warned him not to trust Woden, but the war god had already killed Octa's father. He was certain of that as he prayed that Woden would stay out of this.

Horsa returned his brother's smile. 'We let them fight it out?'

Hengist nodded. 'Octa against Eadric. His spear against this spear.' He threw the spear to Eadric, who caught it and smiled at Octa. 'If Eadric wins, then the spear he brought us is the real Gungnir. If Octa wins, then his spear is. Neither man will wear armour and will be armed with only the spears and shields.'

Octa's heart raced in anticipation as Horsa asked, 'A fight to first blood?'

Hengist shook his head. 'To the death.'

Berthild gasped. 'No.'

Hengist looked at her, his eyes showing some sympathy. 'Forgive me, Lady Berthild. But Octa admitted he killed two of my men. That alone would normally get him hanged.'

'But—'Berthild started, but Octa raised his hand to stop her. It was time he faced his wyrd.

'It's fine, Mother. If it is my wyrd to die today, then I will not fight it.' His heart still raced in his chest and his legs felt like they might give way at any moment, but Octa was tired of letting his fear control him. He had done much already to show that he was no coward. It was time others saw the same. And besides, Octa got what he had come for. A chance to kill Eadric. He glanced at the spear in his hands, certain that Woden would not let him lose. Because the war god's honour was on the line as much as Octa's.

'And what about Eadric?' one warrior asked.

'You really expect that coward to beat Eadric?' another said, and Hengist looked at Eadric.

'Well, if what Octa says is true, then it means that Eadric lied to us. Not just about the spear, but also about Octa's death.'

'Octa is a coward. He does not deserve to live,' Eadric said, his brows creased.

'That may be, but I still asked that he not be harmed. I told you to bring him back alive. We even rewarded you with a ship and men to row it.'

'Eadric is right, though,' Horsa said. 'Octa is a coward.'

'Octa saved my son's life. I owe him a debt.' Hengist glared at Eadric. 'What Eadric thinks of Octa does not matter. My word is law.'

Eadric nodded and then looked at Octa. 'The gods will decide which of us speaks the truth.' He smiled and Octa sensed he believed it had nothing to do with the gods. And perhaps it didn't. Perhaps it would all come down to who was the best fighter. 'You should have stayed in the north,' the older warrior said as he took his tunic off.

Octa turned and faced his mother. He wiped the tears from her eyes and smiled at her. 'You have nothing to fear, Mother. The gods are with me.'

Odalric hawked and spat. 'They won't win this fight for you.

You have to do that yourself.' He started untying Octa's armour and glanced at Eadric behind Octa. 'He is an experienced warrior, and no doubt has fought many of these battles. Remember your lessons and—'

'I know,' Octa interrupted him. 'Keep my shield up and eyes open.'

Odalric nodded as Berthild took a deep breath and looked at Octa. 'You are the son of Frithowald and the grandson of Octa the Ferocious. They were both mighty warriors and their blood runs in your veins. Forget what happened before and kill that bastard.'

Octa nodded at his mother and took strength from the fire in her eyes. She had believed in him even when he was broken. When it felt like even the gods had abandoned him. Octa removed his tunic and saw how his mother smiled when she saw her spear pendant around his neck.

Octa took the shield that Odalric handed to him before he turned to Hengist and Horsa. 'If I defeat Eadric, do I have your word that you will not take this spear from me?'

Horsa laughed, as did many of the other warriors, but Hengist stared at him. 'Why would we do that?'

Octa squared his shoulders and glanced at the scar the owl had left on his arm. 'Woden had asked me to find the spear, not you. And I am the one who found it. By the law of our gods, the spear is mine.'

'I don't care if Woden handed you the spear himself—' Horsa started but then Hengist cut him off.

'No, Octa is right.' He glanced at Octa's mother. 'I have a feeling that Octa has already paid the price for finding what he claims is the spear of Woden.' Hengist looked at Octa and nodded. 'You have our word. If you defeat Eadric, then we will not take the spear from you.'

Octa nodded, relieved by that, but the relief was short-lived as he turned to face Eadric.

The Jutes cheered while Eadric stood in the centre of the square, a grin on his face as he loosened his muscles.

Octa took a deep breath to calm his nerves and closed his eyes for a heartbeat. 'I am a Saxon warrior and I'm not running any more. My fear will no longer control me.' Octa opened his eyes and glanced at the spear in his hand. Despite what Odalric had said, he knew this was in the hands of the gods.

'This time, I'll make sure I kill you.' Eadric lifted his shield in front of him and readied his spear. The older warrior's muscles tensed as he prepared to attack, all the while sneering at Octa.

Octa felt naked without his armour and tunic, but he did not feel the fear he would have done in the past as his heart beat hard in his chest. 'I have the blood of warriors in my veins.'

The surrounding warriors all fell silent as Octa and Eadric circled each other. The spear wavered in Octa's hand, no matter how hard he tried to keep it steady, like Eadric's was. Octa had had many sparring sessions, against Uhtric and against Eadric. Against Uhtric, he had won his fair share, but he had never won a sparring session against the older Jute. Although, those fights were not to the death. Not like this one. Octa took a deep breath and pushed those thoughts out of his mind. He was done being afraid.

As he and Eadric circled each other, his eyes fell on his mother, who nodded at him. She had believed in him, even when Octa doubted himself. Octa took a deep breath and glanced at the sky. *Woden, do not let your spear fail me now*, he prayed. *I will spill Eadric's blood in your honour if you let me use your spear.*

Eadric roared and charged at Octa, whose heart skipped as Eadric's spear came for his head. He lifted his shield and felt the spear strike it. The force of the blow sent Octa a few steps back and with a jolt Octa realised Eadric had been holding back when they had their training sessions in the past.

34

The Jutes cheered, the sounds of their voices deafening as Eadric attacked again. He swung his spear as if it was a sword and Octa was forced to duck under it while fighting to keep his balance. Eadric's attack was fast and vicious and Octa struggled to keep up, let alone find a moment to launch his own attack.

'Fight back!' Odalric roared at him, and Octa cursed his father's warrior as he blocked another spear jab from Eadric.

'Listen to him, Octa,' Eadric said. 'Fight me or you will never win this.'

Octa gritted his teeth and took a step back, his breathing already heavy, even though the fight had only just begun. He lifted his shield in front of him and scrutinised Eadric as he tried to find a weakness in the older warrior. Eadric's movements were as natural as breathing. His attacks came with a force Octa struggled to deal with, but the way he moved never faltered. He never left any part of his torso exposed as he kept Octa ducking behind his shield.

Eadric smiled as he must have sensed the doubt in Octa's mind before he charged again and stabbed high with his spear.

As Octa lifted his shield to block the attack, Eadric stepped in and struck him in the stomach with the rim of his shield. Octa grunted as he bent over and the air was knocked out of him, and as he struggled to stay on his feet, Eadric kicked him in the face, sending him sprawling to the ground.

'Get up!' Odalric shouted while Octa's mother stood there in solemn silence, her hands clasped in front of her. 'You fight for your honour. For the honour of your father!'

Octa glared at his father's warrior, but then heard the warriors cheer and turned in time for Eadric's spear to miss him as the Jute tried to stab him while he was distracted by Odalric. Octa kicked at Eadric's leg and the Jute dropped to one knee and, still on his knees, Octa stabbed at Eadric with his spear, putting as much force into the strike as he could. Eadric rolled out of the way, but there was a collective gasp from the Jutes as Octa's spear nicked Eadric's shoulder. Octa had drawn first blood. A minor victory for him, but Octa knew it meant nothing. Eadric glanced at his shoulder, his mouth twitching as they both got to their feet.

'Not bad. But this fight is to the death!' He attacked again and Octa, feeling more confident, twisted out of the way and swung his spear at the Jute who got his shield up in time to block the blow. Eadric kicked at Octa, who blocked it with his shield, but the kick still sent him staggering backwards and this gave Eadric time to set himself. He jabbed at Octa with his spear, the attack almost too fast for Octa to see, and forced him to twist out of the way because he could not get his shield up in time to block the spear. Eadric's spear cut across Octa's chest, but Octa had no time to think about it as Eadric followed up by punching at him with the rim of his shield. Octa's movement made it impossible for him to block the blow with his own shield, and all he could do was swing his spear at Eadric's head. The shaft struck before Eadric's shield could, which softened the Jute's blow, but again the wind was knocked out of Octa as he fell to the ground.

'Kill him, now!' Odalric screamed and Octa looked up to see Eadric was dazed from the blow to his head, but Octa was still struggling to get his wind back. Even if he wanted to, Octa couldn't attack. He tightened his grip on the spear and forced himself to get to his feet as Eadric shook his head to clear it.

'That was your chance to kill me,' Eadric said as he shook his head again. 'You won't get another chance like that again.'

Octa tried to ignore him, just like he was trying to ignore the cut on his chest, which was difficult because it stung, as he still struggled to breathe. Eadric looked like the blow had barely affected him as the Jutes cheered him on. Behind him, Hengist and Horsa both watched the fight with expressionless faces.

Octa glanced at the spear and wondered for a moment if it was the real spear of Woden, but then he remembered how easy it had been to use the spear when he had fought against the Picts. Reinald's words came to him, telling him that a weapon was just a weapon and it depended on who used it. Octa clenched his jaw. He refused to lose to Eadric. He refused to disgrace his family more than he had already. Octa looked at his mother, her face unreadable, but she nodded at him and he nodded back.

'The fight is not over yet,' Octa said as he lifted his shield in front of him. Out of the corner of his eye, he spotted a white bird flying overhead and wondered if that was Brigantia's owl before he charged at Eadric. The Jute raised his shield to block Octa's spear, before stabbing at Octa with his own. Octa ducked under Eadric's spear and shoulder barged the older warrior. Eadric staggered back, but recovered quickly enough to twist out of the way of Octa's spear thrust and roared as he swung his spear at

Octa. The shaft of Eadric's spear struck Octa in his side and Octa arched to the side as the shaft of the spear broke in two. Octa cried out and dropped his shield, but kept hold of the spear as the pain bent him double. His vision blurred and, for a moment, Octa wondered if he had broken a rib as he dropped to one knee.

There was a stunned silence from the Jutes as the spear they had thought belonged to Woden broke, but Eadric did not seem to care about that as he stabbed the broken shaft at Octa. Octa, having no shield, tried to twist out of the way, but couldn't because of the pain in his side, and the broken shaft caught his left shoulder. He cried out as the broken shaft bit into his muscle, the pain burning into him and the confidence he had felt only moments ago left as his blood ran down his arm.

Octa struggled to his feet and staggered backwards as he tried to keep his distance from Eadric, who was stalking him around the square, the broken shaft still in his hand and its tip dripping with Octa's blood. The Jutes all cheered for Eadric again, their voices drawing out the sounds of the nearby waves and the seabirds flying above them. Hengist and Horsa both scowled. But Octa was not paying attention to any of them as he held his spear in front of him as if it was a shield. His left arm was numb and his ribs ached as he thought of Uhtric and Badulf, of his father, who was killed because of him. The past was not important, but it was all Octa could think about as Eadric sneered at him.

'You really thought that Woden would choose you to wield his spear? That the god of war would let a coward fight with Gungnir?' Eadric asked. Octa couldn't help but glance at Woden's spear in his hand and even he started to feel the same doubt. He spotted the white owl siting in a tree above the tent, its head tilted as it watched him, and remembered Brigantia's words. *The spear will not be your redemption, Octa, son of Frithowald. It will be your death.* Octa shook his head, refusing to believe that as Eadric said, 'The spear you have is not Woden's.'

Octa looked at the broken spear in Eadric's hand. 'And yours is?'

Eadric didn't bother looking at the broken shaft in his hand as he shrugged. 'It doesn't matter. All that matters is that you die today.'

Octa stumbled backwards, desperate to stay out of Eadric's reach. His heart was racing in his chest as he glanced at the broken shaft in Eadric's hand and a thought came to him, as if Woden had put it there himself. 'Even if you kill me, Hengist will only kill you afterwards.'

Eadric stopped and tilted his head. 'Rubbish. If I win, then it shows that the spear I brought back is Gungnir.'

Octa grimaced at the pain in his side. 'But you broke the spear. So how can it belong to Woden?'

This time Eadric did look at the broken spear shaft in his hand and that was the moment Octa had been hoping for. He screamed as he summoned the last of his strength and charged at the Jute. Eadric looked up just as Octa stabbed the spear at him and tried to bring his shield up to block the attack, but he was too slow to stop Gungnir from piercing his chest. Eadric grunted, his eyes wide as he stared at Octa, who bared his teeth at the man who had left him for dead in the shrine of Brigantia.

'I am a warrior. I am not a coward,' Octa said as he pushed the spear in deeper. Eadric dropped the broken shaft and his shield as the Jutes fell silent, all of them gaping at Eadric as the blood flowed fast from the wound in his chest.

Octa held on to the spear, his eyes never leaving Eadric. The past was not important, but as Octa thought of all those he had failed, he screamed and, with one final shove, drove the spear straight through Eadric, who grunted again as the spear ripped out of his back. Eadric dropped to the ground, dragging Octa to his knees as he was too exhausted to stay on his feet. No one moved for what felt like a long time and as Octa, sitting on his knees, looked around at the Jutes, he gasped when he saw the old man with the broad-brimmed hat standing there and smiling at him. Octa stared at the old man, unable to believe that he was in Britannia as a raven cried out from the clouds above. He glanced up at the sky and when he looked down again, the old man was gone.

Before Octa could make sense of what he had seen, Odalric pulled him to his feet. Octa kept his hand on the spear, and Odalric looked at him.

'Let me.' Odalric hesitated for a heartbeat. 'You fought well, Octa.'

Octa frowned at his father's man and then turned as his mother embraced him, not caring about his blood dirtying her dress. 'I knew you could do it,' she said to him, but Octa was barely paying any attention to her as he searched for the old man, wanting to make sure he had really seen him.

'Octa,' Odalric said before he pulled the spear out of Eadric's corpse and handed it to Octa, who turned and saw Hengist and Horsa approaching, along with a handful of warriors behind them. Octa tensed and knew that if there was going to be another fight, then he would die. He did not have the strength to fight again. But then Odalric surprised him by stepping forward and standing by his side, his seax knife in his hand and his teeth bared.

Hengist smiled at the Saxon warrior. 'You can tell your man to stand down. You won the fight and I am here to congratulate you. And by Woden, what a fight that was. I really believed Eadric was going to kill you.'

Odalric glanced at Octa, who nodded but said nothing as he stared at the brothers.

'So that really is Gungnir?' Horsa asked.

Octa hesitated. 'It is.'

'Then give it to us.' Horsa held a hand out and Octa tensed. But then Hengist shook his head.

'No, brother. I promised Octa he could keep the spear. If we take it from him now then we would have to face Woden's wrath.'

Horsa glanced at his brother, and then he pulled his hand back before he nodded. 'So now what? People come here because they think we have the spear of Woden.'

'People will still come either way. Whether we have the spear or not. The lands here are fertile and the people can't defend themselves. There are many in Jutland and the lands of the Saxons who haven't got land to farm. And there are many more who were chased away from their lands by the tribes coming from the east. Britannia offers them land where they can build homes for their families and grow food to feed them.'

'But the Christians will never accept our gods and our way of life,' Horsa said, and Octa thought of what he had seen in the north. How many Christians had already abandoned their god in favour of the gods of the Saxons who protected them?

'The Christian god's grip is not as strong as you think,' he said to the brothers, who frowned at him, as he remembered the cult of Brigantia. 'And there are many who still hold on to the gods of their ancestors.'

Hengist smiled. 'See? The gods want us to take this land for ourselves.'

Horsa nodded and then turned to Octa. 'Eadric was a great warrior. But he died in disgrace. His armour and weapons are yours.' He glanced at the spear in Octa's hand. 'I pray that that spear brings you more fortune than it did for him.' He turned and walked away before Octa could say anything.

Hengist gripped his shoulder. 'And I pray you stay and fight with us. With you by our side, we can accomplish much in Britannia. Perhaps even make it our new home.'

Octa nodded and, as Hengist walked away, he turned to his mother and Odalric.

'Is that really Gungnir?' Odalric asked and Octa nodded as he looked at the spear.

'It is. It is why I came to Britannia. I was going to give it to Father and ask for his forgiveness.'

'The spear is yours to keep now,' his mother said, and Octa stared at her.

'The village is truly gone?'

His mother nodded. 'There is nothing there for us any more.'

'But Witta needs to pay for what he did.' Octa tightened his grip on the spear and then frowned when his mother shook her head.

'Witta is too strong and you have no army. No, it's time we forget about the past and focus on the future.' Octa smiled at his mother's words, which were similar to Reinald's, as his mother looked around them at the Jutes, many of them glaring at Octa, but they kept their distance from him. 'And I believe that our future is here.'

'And besides, the Jute was right,' Odalric said. 'There are many in search of a new home and a new life. Many Saxons who have been forced from their lands by the Thuringians because Witta has been too focused on finding you to fight them. And the other warlords are too busy arguing amongst each other about what to do. We can send word back to the continent, tell the people to come here. You can lead them and help them find a new home.'

Octa heard a raven cry out from the clouds again. He closed his eyes and thought of everything that had happened to him since the battle against the Thuringians. He had come far since then, but as he opened his eyes and looked at Woden's spear, he knew there were more dangers ahead. Just like he knew his mother and Odalric were right. Britannia was his home now and, with the spear of Woden, he would forge his own path and be greater than his father ever was. He would be more than a warlord.

EPILOGUE

The two enormous wolves raised their heads, their lips curled back to reveal long fangs as growls escaped from their throats. But then they recognised her and the growling stopped. One wolf bounded towards her and she ran her fingers through its thick fur as it circled around her.

Woden, god of war and mischief, did not turn around to see who approached him. He didn't need to, just like he didn't need his two wolves to warn him of her arrival. He recognised the sounds of her footsteps, which were assured and yet graceful, and knew why his wife had come to speak to him.

'I thought I'd find you here, husband, staring at the flames of your hearth fire again.'

Woden kept his one eye on the dancing flames. 'The fire is the truest representation of who we gods are. It has the power to destroy life, but in its wake, there is always rebirth. The flames take life, but they also give life.'

Friga smiled. 'And people fear the flames as they fear you.'

Woden grunted as the one wolf joined the other by his feet. Above his head, his two ravens sat on the beams which supported the roof of his giant hall, their heads tilted as they watched and listened. But Woden knew they spoke only to him, so he didn't care that they were listening in on this conversation. Friga stood beside him, her back straight and with an aura that could even intimidate him about her. Of all the gods, she was the only one he feared, because she was the mother. And without a mother, there would be no father. Without Friga, there would be no Woden.

'The boy has the spear,' Friga said, and Woden only nodded. He knew this already. Friga glanced at him, a small, playful smile on her lips. 'He kept it for himself. He wants to use it to earn his redemption.' Again, Woden only nodded and the smile fell from Friga's mouth. 'Just like you knew he would.'

Woden turned his one eye to her. 'Just like I wanted him to. Nothing the son of Frithowald does is new to me, just like it is not new to you.'

Friga nodded, the smile back on her lips. 'And with Gungnir, he will spread your name and influence to a new land while the lands we have controlled for so long fall to another.'

Woden curled his lip and the two wolves did the same as they sensed their master's anger. 'An impostor from another land.'

'He is not the impostor,' Friga said, the smile gone from her face. 'The people elevated his son, not him. You know this.'

Woden grunted. 'It doesn't matter. His name spreads through our lands and the lands of others like a fire, destroying all that was before. Erasing our names and deeds as if we never existed.'

'But there will be a rebirth,' Friga said, using his own words.

And that was what frightened Woden. He could not see the world that came after the flames died out and, because of this, he did not know his place in it. He glanced at Friga again. 'I know it was you. It took me a long time to understand that, but it was you.'

Friga didn't deny it, which he appreciated because he knew she liked to play her games with him. Men were not the only ones fooled by women. Gods suffered the same. 'Yes, I took Gungnir from you.' She looked at the fire. 'I had a dream where rivers ran red with blood and everything burnt. I knew if you had Gungnir you would wage a war that would kill us all. Without your spear, you could not do that, so I did what I had to.'

Woden grunted. 'And then you gave it to Brigantia. You used your magic to hide it from my sight and make me believe another was responsible. For too long, I thought the Roman people were responsible.'

Friga nodded. 'I did use the Roman people to deliver Gungnir to her. I saw what was coming and knew she needed it if she was going to stop the spread of his name in her lands.'

'She still failed.' Friga nodded again, but stayed silent. 'As you knew she would, but she helped you hide Gungnir from me.' Woden turned and faced Friga for the first time. 'War is still coming. Your dream will still come true. All you did was to prolong the inevitable. There are gods from other lands who threaten us. And not just the one from the desert lands.'

'The gods from the north?'

Woden nodded. 'They do not heed my words. They think I'm a fool. A warmonger.'

Friga smiled, and he knew she thought he was both of those things. And perhaps he was. But he was also Woden. He had sacrificed much to gain the knowledge he had, and he knew he would have to sacrifice more if he was going to stop the fire that was coming.

'What you did to the son of Frithowald was cruel and unnecessary.'

Woden glanced at Friga. 'Cruel and unnecessary?'

'You did not have to cast that spell on him.'

'If I hadn't cast the spell on him, then he would have fought well and earned a good reputation. Instead, he ran from the battle and was desperate enough to search for my spear. I needed him to be afraid.'

'A brave warrior would also have looked for your spear. Many have done before.'

'And they all died or gave up. Desperate men fight harder. They never give up, even when it looks like everything is against them, because for them, the alternative is much worse.'

'You didn't need to kill his father,' Friga said, and he only grunted. 'So you sent this young warrior to find your spear, knowing he was going to keep it for himself? Why?'

Woden stared at the flames of the hearth fire again and nodded, pleased that he had outsmarted Friga, his wife, who could see what was to come. 'It's all part of my plan.'

Friga scowled at him. 'The British gods fear him, especially now that he has Gungnir.'

Woden smiled. 'So they should.'

* * *

MORE FROM DONOVAN COOK

The first in another action-packed historical adventure series from Donovan Cook, *Odin's Betrayal*, is available to order now here:

www.mybook.to/OdinsBetrayalBackAd

HISTORICAL NOTE

The fifth century must have been a dark time for the people of Britannia. Whether you were a Christian or a pagan, you must have believed the gods had abandoned you.

In AD 406, the Roman army in Britannia revolted and after rotating through a few candidates for who they believed should be the new emperor of the Western Roman Empire, they eventually settled on Constantine III who in AD 407 crossed to Gaul with most of the Roman army which were based in Britannia.

Up until this point, most of Britain had been part of the Roman Empire for almost four centuries, and many of those who lived in the island's south had got used to the peace brought by the Roman military. But by the early fifth century, the Roman Empire was not only fighting for her own survival, by having to fend off regular incursions by the Goths, Vandals and the Huns, but also had to deal with revolts by their own military. Constantine III was a victim of another revolt and was executed in AD 411.

This left the people of Britannia with a problem. They did not have much of a military force left to defend themselves and it wasn't long after the last of the Roman armies left that the first raids by the Picts (from modern Scotland) and the Scots (from modern Ireland – I agree it makes no sense, but this was a long time ago and a lot has happened since) must have started. On top of that, Saxon pirates came from across the English Channel and, along with the Picts and the Scots, devastated the island and its inhabitants. In AD 429, Germanus of Auxerre arrived in Britain and expelled the pirates and raiders, but the peace brought by the man who would later be sainted did not last long. The Picts and the Scots soon started raiding again, and as before, the kings of Britannia sent a letter of appeal to the Roman authorities in Gaul, asking them for help. But this letter went unanswered and the people of Britannia were on their own.

The historical sources tell us that in AD 446 the high king of the Britons invited two brothers from Jutland to come to Britannia and to fight the Picts and the Scots. This was not a new idea amongst the Britons. The Romans did this all the time and there were still Germanic warriors on the island who had been brought over by the Romans as mercenaries (foederati) and had been left behind when the Romans departed. In fact, there were probably still some Roman legionaries on the island as well, but we would have to imagine that they would have been old men by this point.

Gildas, a sixth-century religious conservative, was the first to tell us about this in *De Excidio et Conquestu Britanniae* (*The Ruin of Britain*), which is more of a scathing letter to the British kings about their failings as rulers than an accurate historical text. Gildas was not a historian and his letter lacked any factual information. He didn't say who the king was that invited the Saxons as he referred to them, and neither did he give us a date of their arrival. Only that it happened during the third consulship of

Aetius. It was the Venerable Bede, in *Ecclesiastical History of the English People* written in the eighth century, who gave us the name of the British king, King Vortigern, and the names of the two brothers, Hengist and Horsa. He also gave us the year of AD 449 for their arrival, most likely based on what Gildas had written some two hundred years before him. In fact, Gildas wrote his account of the events almost a hundred years after the supposed arrival of Hengist and Horsa with their three ships.

The problem is that archaeological data suggests that there was a large population of Anglo-Saxons in the south of England at least ten years before the date given by Bede. This archaeological evidence mainly comes from gravesites and the goods from those, but it made historians question the reliability of Gildas and Bede, as well as other historical texts which talk about this time, especially as most of them seemed to be based on what Gildas wrote.

There are also many other questions about what is arguably one of the most important time periods in English history. The true name of the king that invited the Anglo-Saxons is still a mystery as it was suggested that Vortigern was a title and not a name as it means 'high ruler'. The names of the brothers have also been questioned, as there are no other records of them anywhere else. As is the idea that they came with only three ships and yet somehow, over time, took over a large part of the island.

So while we might not know the truth about much of what happened, what we do know is that the arrival of the Anglo-Saxons in Britain changed the course of Britain's history.

ACKNOWLEDGEMENTS

I'll be honest, this year has been very different for me. I signed a new contract with my publishers and embarked on a new series which is a time period I've not done before. And I've enjoyed the challenge of learning about a part of history that I didn't know that much, and trying to make sense of a mythology we know very little about. Meeting new characters and seeing how their journeys unfold, which is, for me, one of the greatest joys of being a writer. The biggest change though, has been the birth of my daughter and learning how to juggle parenting and working. Something I'm far from mastering, if I ever do. My writing schedule is now based on her nap times and when she is awake it's all about containing the chaos that she and our dog unleash. I am of course overexaggerating a bit, but it has been an interesting experience so far.

In this new series, I wanted to do something different for myself and explore a part of English history that is not that well known. It has been a challenge as there is little information about both the events and the mythology, and what information is out there doesn't really match up with the archaeological evidence. This, though, is my take on the story of the first Anglo-Saxon kingdom in Britain, the way I think it could have happened, and I hope you all enjoy not only this novel, but the series as well.

As always, I'd like to thank my editor, Caroline, for her guidance and encouragement, as well as her patience and support as

I adapt to a new way of living. To Ross, for using his magic touch to bring the best out of my novels, and to Susan, for using her laser vision to fine-tune my novels even more.

To my wife, Anna, as ever for her support and understanding. Writing a novel isn't always easy, especially when you don't always know where the story is going. I thank her for her patience and putting up with me being a bit difficult as I struggled with this novel. And to Joey, our French bulldog, for the long walks and being willing to listen to me work through the plot (in exchange for a treat of course). To our little girl, Elizabeth, for always finding ways to distract me from my work.

To my author friends, MJ Porter, JC Duncan and many others for making this journey feel less lonely.

And to my readers. None of this would be possible without your support and kind words.

Happy reading and thank you.

ABOUT THE AUTHOR

Donovan Cook is the author of the well-received Ormstunga Saga series which combines fast-paced narrative with meticulously researched history of the Viking world, and is inspired by his interest in Norse Mythology. He was born in South Africa and currently lives in Lancashire, UK.

Sign up to Donovan Cook's mailing list here for news, competitions and updates on future books.

Visit Donovan's website: www.donovancook.net

Follow Donovan on social media:

 facebook.com/DonovanCookAuthor

 x.com/DonovanCook20

 bookbub.com/authors/donovan-cook

ALSO BY DONOVAN COOK

Charlemagne's Cross Series

Odin's Betrayal

Loki's Deceit

Thor's Revenge

Valhalla's Fury

The First Kingdom Series

Woden's Spear

WARRIOR CHRONICLES

WELCOME TO THE CLAN ✕

THE HOME OF
BESTSELLING HISTORICAL
ADVENTURE FICTION!

WARNING:
MAY CONTAIN VIKINGS!

SIGN UP TO OUR
NEWSLETTER

BIT.LY/WARRIORCHRONICLES

Boldw⦿⦿d

Boldwood Books is an award-winning fiction
publishing company seeking out the best
stories from around the world.

Find out more at www.boldwoodbooks.com

Join our reader community for brilliant books,
competitions and offers!

Follow us
@BoldwoodBooks
@TheBoldBookClub

**Sign up to our weekly
deals newsletter**

https://bit.ly/BoldwoodBNewsletter